THE DEBTOR'S GAME

THE Debtor's Game

Isabelle Mongeau

ЯENEGADE

First published in the United States in 2026 by Ballantine Books
an imprint of Random House
a division of Penguin Random House LLC

First published in Great Britain in 2026 by Renegade Books
an imprint of Quercus
Part of John Murray Group

1

Copyright © 2026 Isabelle Mongeau

The moral right of ISABELLE MONGEAU to be identified as
the author of this work has been asserted in accordance with
the Copyright, Designs and Patents Act 1988.

Internal illustrations by natalypain/Shutterstock
and globe_design_studio/Shutterstock
Map illustration by Francesca Baerald
Book design by Elizabeth Rendfleisch

All rights reserved. No part of this publication may be
reproduced or transmitted in any form or by any means,
electronic or mechanical, including photocopy, recording,
or any information storage and retrieval system,
without permission in writing from the publisher.

This book is a work of fiction. Names, characters,
businesses, organizations, places and events are
either the product of zthe author's imagination or
used fictitiously. Any resemblance to actual persons,
living or dead, events orlocales is entirely coincidental.

A CIP catalogue record for this book is available
from the British Library

HB ISBN 978-1-40875-058-2
TPB ISBN 978-1-40875-059-9
EBOOK ISBN 978-1-40875-060-5

Typeset in Sabon LT Pro

Printed and bound in Great Britain by Clays Ltd, Elcograf S.p.A.

Papers used by Quercus are from well-managed forests and
other responsible sources.

Quercus
Carmelite House
50 Victoria Embankment
London EC4Y 0DZ

John Murray Group
Part of Hodder & Stoughton Limited
An Hachette UK company

The authorised representative in the EEA is Hachette Ireland,
8 Castlecourt Centre, Dublin 15, D15 XTP3, Ireland (email: info@hbgi.ie)

*To the women who have folded me into their hearts—
it is everything*

If you owe the bank a hundred thousand dollars, the bank owns you. If you owe the bank a hundred million dollars, you own the bank – American Proverb

—DAVID GRAEBER,
DEBT: THE FIRST 5,000 YEARS, 2011

PART ONE

House of Illusion

Matter and Mind
Blood and Bone
The Many Senses
The Severed Soul

Live one

Wed another
Bear greater power still—
'tis duty to steer the mouse's will

—"HOUSES AND MOUSES,"
HIGH FAE NURSERY RHYME

Chapter One

I CANNOT BE LATE THIS MORNING, LEST SOMEONE DISCOVERS I'M smuggling a feast fit for a king. And I am no king.

My mistress rarely rises before noon, but the other faerie servants have already scattered about the palace of Versara, polishing it to perfection for the coming coronation. If I'm found for a thief and not among them, my hand will be forfeit. I'd like to keep all my limbs.

I tighten my grip on the pack slung over my shoulder, passing the subterranean pantries of dried meats and canned goods, closets of cleaning supplies, washing rooms, the icehouses, storage filled with spare furniture and linens and silver. The underground tunnels allow us to move beneath the sprawling labyrinthian palace without disturbing the High Fae above. It is the Nest, the common room for faeries, that is always the most difficult to navigate.

Already, I feel my genius fluttering awake, humming in the back of my skull. While my eyes and ears take in light and shouts and laughter spilling outward from the end of the tunnel, my genius detects the magic of others and helps me perform my own.

Stepping into the Nest, I am hit hard by the hundreds of faerie geniuses, sweet and cool as fresh soil between the toes, that crowd the ever-present plane of magic. Hordes of inked faeries cluster around long tables lined with stinking pots of cabbage stew. Only in the Nest can Base servants come in from the farms, Scarps from washrooms and kitchens, and Crests from High Fae chambers to sit and share a meal. It's the one place in Versara I have found my shoulders dropping, stomach aching with laughter—and the rotten leftovers we're allowed to eat. I keep my head down and cross the room, avoiding—

"Avery!"

Shit.

A gentle tattooed hand grasps my shoulder. Reluctantly, I look at the tall, leanly muscled Scarp faerie. Black ring tattoos mark him fingertip to neck, whereas mine start at my wrists and reach my shoulders. Whispers in the Nest claim that a single gold coin tipped from a High Fae could clear away an entire debt ring, no matter how thick with interest it is. I wouldn't know; our salaries only come in coppers, and the interest for our debts builds every month. Yet even several gold coins couldn't make up the difference between Jeremee's and my balances. While I have twenty rings, he bears over thirty. He could be indebted for a century more than me. Focusing on his angular face, I take in the dark auburn hair, straight nose, and warm moss-green eyes, his lips tugging into a half smile, and ignore a pull in my chest.

"Hey, Jeremee," I say, forcing a casual tone.

"What's in the pack?"

"King Gregor's corpse, what else?"

He coughs, flushing to the points of his ears. "You shouldn't joke like that."

"You shouldn't ask like that, Jae."

He surveys the room, worrying his lower lip. "Well? Lead the way."

I groan, then motion for him to follow. "Fine, let's go."

We reach the far end of the room, then head down a passageway, the scent of boiled food fading to damp stone and earth. Soon the only sound is that of our footsteps, mine clipped and his an awkward clop.

"I'm buying you new shoes at the next Full Moon Festival, I don't care," I mutter.

"Save your money."

"Yours are two sizes too small! You'll deform yourself."

He shrugs, smiling. "It's okay. Glenn thinks I'm as beautiful as a fox."

"Is that so?"

"And what do you think?"

We touch gazes for a moment before looking ahead once more. It's a game we play, as if jests about being under each other can chase away the reality of being beneath the High Fae. A game of teasing words and tracking stares through the thick of the festival throng, of leaving with the same sex but never the opposite. Last month, he split from the crowd with Glenn, and I kept company with a cup of cider. Two moons before that, I found fun in a blushing brunette, though maybe the real fun was tempting her away from him.

"That you have a loud gait for an accomplice." My pace slows, the stones beneath my feet drifting farther apart in the dirt like lily pads across a pond.

"This is bold," Jeremee says. "Stealing in broad daylight."

"You sound like my mother." The grip of a familiar grief tightens my throat.

"Why, because I want you alive?"

"You want me to do less."

"Hey," he says, halting. This far down into the tunnels, away from storage and bunkrooms, the darkness hides the burn in my eyes. "I want you to do less on your own."

"I can't be late." I move around him.

Running those long, tattooed fingers through his hair, he says nothing. I stride down the tunnel, and behind me he sighs, as if resigning himself to my shadow.

We reach a split in the passageway, the right side veering to a different wing of Versara. The tunnel entrance to my left is framed by twisted tree roots, leading into darker, danker depths.

"You're not coming," I say.

"Fucking planes," Jae mutters, leaning against the wall. "Why not?"

"Not risking you or Benji."

He looks away, crossing his arms over his chest. That always shuts him up. No matter how much Jeremee and I care for each other, we care for his little brother more. His birth and infant tattooing were the first I'd ever witnessed. The Healer delivered him, staying only long enough to ensure that the teller marked both Benji and their mother for services rendered. At the time, I didn't think it could get worse than the enchanted quill tapping newborn flesh with indentured ink. But everyone must pay to be born, one ring to each House, and mothers must pay even when a Healer leaves before the afterbirth can properly expel. Days later, Jeremee held his wailing brother as my mother and I lowered his mother into the ground.

Jeremee still bears her delivery and funerary debt. Though Benji started work as soon as he could carry a bucket, his six rings still had years to thicken with interest.

"I'll be right back," I say, the sentence catching in my throat.

"Five minutes and then I'm coming after you," he grumbles. "Scream if you need me."

"You could always wait in the kitchens."

"No." My best friend glares at me. I smile back.

"Listen for the scream," I say.

He groans. "Don't jest about—"

I duck under the roots and into the tunnel, leaving him behind.

The passage is uneven and small, buttressed by crumbling brick for the vendors who truck goods into the hill upon which the palace perches.

A candle smacks me in the forehead. Swearing, I bat it away, drops of wax and wick bobbing through the air. Someone, some time ago, stole a handful of enchanted candles and sent them across the dark like petals down a stream.

As a little girl, I would squeal when my mother pointed out the lights floating several feet above my head, daring me to catch them. Maybe she was trying to distract me during the frequent moves between the palace and the Peri, the surrounding faerie village, where we'd stay with my father until they fought again. Maybe she was trying to distract herself.

Dipping under the next candle, I spot a bony figure leaning against the wall, the light casting an orange hue on the dozens of tattoos scrawled from his toes to his scalp. The faerie has four limbs of debt, rendering him unemployable to most. An Unluckie. Even the whites of the faerie's eyes are spiderwebbed black with the magical ink.

A giant, old bloodstain marks our meeting spot on the brick wall, roots curling through the cracks. The Unluckie straightens to his full height.

"Found the spot," he says, gesturing to the blood. "Who do you think died here?"

"No one," I answer, swinging off the pack. His black-rimmed blue eyes follow the food.

"You actually brought it," he marvels.

"Bread, meats, and grapes, enough to feed a family of five."

"I didn't think you'd come."

The crack of wonder in his voice pierces my chest. When I began stealing and distributing food two years ago, I could only find those in need through whispered word of mouth. That's how I met my first Unluckie and realized when the High Fae said Unluckies were dangerous, they meant hungry. While each House decides what their servants can eat, Amyrian law bans any handouts to the Unluckies. It felt wrong that there was so much wasted food in the Illusion kitchens and wasted life outside them.

"Be sure everyone eats a bit of everything. Only grapes, and you won't fill up. Bread, and you'll burn out fast, and just meat and your head will ache from dehydration." I open the pack so he can peer inside.

"Sorry, it's just . . ." He laughs. "I just didn't think I'd be able to get here from—"

"Don't say it." I hand over the contraband. "No names, either. It's better this way."

"And there's nothing you want for it?"

"Only your silence and secrecy. If I lose my head or hands, the food stops."

"Right."

"So, for next week, send along only someone you trust with your life. If you have any doubts, come again yourself."

The Unluckie stares into the bag, a fissure of fear splitting his gaunt face. I pinch off a grape and pop it into my mouth, the sweet juice bursting on my tongue. The Unluckie gasps, the forbidden fae food now touchable. Consumable. He reaches in, grabs a grape, and crunches on it, crooked teeth showing through a smile.

He swallows, glancing at the bloodstain on the brick. "I heard it's from the Dark Rebellion," the Unluckie whispers, as if members from the House of Death might appear after seven hundred years of banishment.

I take another grape. "It's from a birth. The mother had only the roots to clutch as she bore the child."

"And how do you know that?"

"It was my mother."

She was quiet and hardy, my mother, sneaking me food in the Illusion kitchens each day. When she died, it was only fitting that I start a network of nourishment in her honor.

"Did you not receive the First Five?" the faerie asks, eyes dropping to my arms.

"It's only four tattoos if there's no Healer," I say.

In the end, we all must go to the creditor, Healer or not, for unregistered children are slain. Debt or death, and when nature did not claim my breath that day, the Houses had to claim my skin. How painful it must have been for my mother: to hand over her untouched newborn to a life of service.

"Didn't know it was possible to survive without a Healer," the faerie remarks. Though many mothers don't survive even if there is one.

"She lived until two years ago," I say, staring at the bloodstain again.

In polite respect, the faerie offers, "May she wander well."

"May she wander well."

AS I EMERGE from the Peri tunnel, Jeremee lunges for a hug. His hair sticks up, so I know he's been running anxious hands through it.

"I gotta go," I say, squirming. "I'm going to be late."

"Lady Kassandra doesn't get up until the afternoon and you know it." He buries his face in the crook of my neck.

"Yes, but I'm supposed to be up there now!"

He pulls back, hands heavy on my shoulders, scanning my face. "Did everything go okay? What was the Unluckie like?"

"He was normal. Polite and in shock as they usually are."

"Right," Jeremee says. "Of course."

Laughter filters toward us, a set of footsteps growing close.

I stiffen in Jae's grasp, panic rising. The only servants down in the Nest at this time are Scarps like Jeremee or Bases on break from the fields. My system only works because the Night Crest servants are now asleep, and the other Day Crest servants think I'm on my twelve-hour shift. No one in the kitchens knows that Lady Kassandra sleeps so much and eats so little. According to them, I've already served her breakfast at the normal hour and on a silver tray. Not in a jute sack to an Unluckie.

"We need to leave," I say.

"We can go back into the Peri tunnel, but we may be spotted."

"Let's just put our heads down as we pass them. They might not recognize me," I try.

"Of course they will," Jae whispers. "You've lasted under Lady Kassandra longer than a year."

"It's only been two!"

"Still more than most."

The voices round the corner, coming down the corridor.

"Sorry" is all Jeremee manages to say before pressing me to the wall, his body bracketing mine. Stones push into my back. Jae lowers his head, blocking the light. I'm tall for a faerie, but he's taller, his lithe body curled around mine. I could tell him to back off and he would, but the laughter of males fills my ears, and though they are faerie does not mean they are friend. Long ago, the redheaded cook accused my mother of slipping me apple slices. When the halfling guards punished my mother even after I purged the apple in absolution, the cook almost looked guilty. She still took her reward: five copper coins in exchange for each fingernail they splintered. My mother became more cautious in the following years.

I think of the wonder in the Unluckie's voice, those inked eyes. He will be punished more severely than that if caught.

I shiver. Jeremee rubs the goosebumps budding across my arms.

"Stop fidgeting," he murmurs, but his hand pauses on my biceps. "Am I making you uncomfortable?"

"Of course not. It isn't every day I get to pretend I'm one of your lovers."

I meant it as a jest. But he stills, and his eyes find mine. Heat rolls off his skin, his breath on the side of my face. My heart thumps. I cannot look away first; to do so is to admit more than I'd like.

The faeries spot us. Jae goes even more rigid. Planes, he frets more than a grandmother might.

I yank him closer by the shirt, and he lets out a puff of surprise. His hard chest pushes me against the wall, and he cradles the back of my skull before it can hit the stone. Fingers twining into my waves, he glances down at my lips, his own a breath away. His heart hammers in my palm, his throat bobbing, and I want to scrape nails along his clavicle. Bring forth a blush to his flesh that's building under mine. But we are just playing a role.

The snickering males pass by, one whistling. Jae's attention is rapt, as if I had slipped a hand between his legs to hold him there instead.

When their voices fade, he steps away, slipping hands in his pockets. Cool, empty air rushes my skin.

"Sorry." I shiver again, then slip past him without another word, taking the passage to the Nest once more. He follows, silent. Only after I've reached the threshold of the Illusion kitchens does he speak.

"Careful," he says. "Please."

"Always," I answer, forcing a smile.

"I didn't mean to—"

"It's okay," I cut in. It would hurt to know exactly what he *didn't mean*: to touch me, to react to me? Had he hated it? The truth is, my feelings started to shift after my mother's death. But no matter how much not having him pains me, I cannot lose him, either. I'm a faerie, after all. I know how to settle for scraps.

"Okay," he says. "Well, I'll see you at dinner later."

I brush his hand goodbye and then enter the Illusion kitchens. Built for scale and efficiency, six-foot-tall hearths flank the space, firing up pies, stews, stocks, vegetables, preparing feasts for the Illusion nobles at court and the parties they throw. Piles of potatoes, onions, turnips, and cabbage line long wooden tables.

I stare at the spot on the third table where my mother and I prepped meals for most of our lives. Her gentle hands would wrap around mine, position my fingers on the handle of a knife, mimic the methodical, rhythmic chopping that would forever remind me of her.

I thought we would spend the rest of our lives as Scarps—cooking, laundering clothes, repairing shoes. Before, my mother thought she'd always remain a Base in the fields with her family, until a late-blooming ability with fire graduated her to the kitchens as an adult. Two years ago, death came for her, and shortly after that, my mistress came for me, propelling me from Scarp duties in the kitchens to a coveted Day Crest position, a personal servant to the High Fae. A cruel irony, as if we can only ascend to a new layer of wealth after shedding loved ones.

"Coming in!" I shout into the noise of lunch preparation. "Lady Kassandra requests croissants and grapes for her late-morning snack!"

"How does that little thing eat so much?" a cook grumbles, glancing at the table of pastries and fruit.

"You know how the High Fae are," I say. "Insatiable."

Lies and truths fall out of my mouth faster than rotting teeth, and one day, someone will catch on.

Just not today.

The noon bell rings out as I exit the kitchens.

I am already late.

Chapter Two

THE SUN-DRENCHED CREAM WALLS BURN MY EYES WITH THEIR brilliance. In the parlor, plush round chairs and rose settees are artfully arranged on a soft white rug. High Fae love white décor for its clean look; faeries hate maintaining it.

Lady Kassandra stretches out on a settee, delicate fingers twirling her long silver hair. Though we are both in our late two hundreds, her skin is smooth and unmarred by any debt rings. The sight of so much untouched flesh is still a shock each shift, but this is the kingdom of Amyria. You either owe or you own.

The servants' door clicks closed, and those pale eyes cut to me like blades. The plane of magic pitches with a tug from her genius, stronger than any faerie's. The hairs on my forearms rise with the static, like a storm fomenting on the horizon.

Shit.

My own genius scratches the back of my skull, desperate to escape notice. Lady Kassandra tilts her feline face back to her tutor, a curly-haired male standing several feet away, arms full of parchment paper.

"I can't possibly take any more notes," she tells him. "My hand will cramp, and I need it for later."

"L-Lady Kassandra, it's imperative you understand the Head and Heart rule," the tutor says, his name still unknown to me. He's only been around a few months.

Her unflinching look could split the plane itself. "*The Head and Heart must never share a body, only a bed. One must lead, and the other must wed.*"

"Y-yes, but what that implies is—"

"As Heart of Illusion, I am to be bred like some country cow while my brother, the Heir of Illusion, will inherit the House. So, unless you're here to tell me that our future king should *not* put a babe in my belly, I don't care. And my brother and father don't care either, until that happens."

The tutor drops his papers. "Lady Kassandra, it's very complex—"

"You may leave," she sighs. "Send in the next one."

He rushes out the main entrance and into the front hall that only High Fae and halfling guards can use. I approach with the pastries and fruit and a pot of coffee that warms the silver tray.

"Hold it," she commands, examining a split end.

"My lady?"

"Hold the tray until I tell you to put it down."

My hands singe with the heat of the coffee. A chestnut side table with scalloped edges and ornate legs is tucked at the end of her settee, only a few feet away. Practically within my reach, but even if I had permission, I'd hesitate to put the hot tray on the delicate wood.

Her cool face remains expressionless like a statue in the Illusion courtyards. A gentle, comforting breeze filters in through the propped door, and I wonder if winter has gasped its last frigid breath.

A moment later, a brown-skinned High Fae arrives, his black hair closely cropped and his tawny eyes glimmering behind spectacles. Warm magic floods the plane, coating the chill of Illusion.

"Kass, what did you say this time?" Lord Eli Seccler asks.

She draws herself to a sitting position, tucking slender legs beneath her.

"Only that I'll listen to his droning when it includes something interesting and delightful, like my brother is dead or I don't have to marry Max."

Lord Eli stops short. Though stocky and broad, he surpasses faeries in size and magical ability like any other High Fae. Like a wolf to a dog. So, even as his shoulders soften with pity, he still has teeth and claws. And she still has me holding the burning tray, my palms screaming, and I bite my lip to remain quiet.

"Prince Maxian may make a kind husband," he offers, sitting next to her. "He seeks to be a fairer ruler than his father—"

"Who was a boorish war general, so I should hope so," she says. "May he wander well, of course."

"Yes, may he wander well." He pauses. "Are you still having trouble sleeping? I could prescribe a night tonic."

"I'm assuming it can't mix with wine."

"That would not be wise."

"Then no thank you."

Lord Eli gives her a look before his attention shifts to me, hovering over her shoulder. "Have you eaten yet?"

Please eat, I think, hands itching with pain. Has the coffee grown hotter? Is the pot enchanted?

Kass frowns. "Not hungry."

"Why don't you try?"

Thank fuck. My gaze slides to the scalloped chestnut table in front of the pair, my arms trembling. My mistress adjusts her robe.

"Eli, have you seen my new side table?"

The head of House Healing leans forward. "Very nice."

"Notice the details?"

"It's very intricate, yes."

"Avery, put the tray on it."

Lord Eli raises his brows. I blink, watching her face that gives nothing away.

"What?" She bares white teeth. "Have you decided to be deaf today, or merely just dumb?"

"My lady," I say in a strained voice. "Will it not mark the wood?"

"Do you enjoy disobeying me?"

She will punish me regardless, so I place the tray on the table, but it slips straight through to the floor with a giant crash, the contents scattering like roaches.

I leap back, mind spinning to catch up. There, then not—the table flickers in and out of sight before solidifying again, shadow and all. I could almost believe I imagined the entire incident if not for the shattered breakfast cutting through the table's legs as if it were made of mist.

"Stunning!" Lord Eli exclaims, bending low to examine the scene. "A perfect Illusion."

"That would be the case if I could make you feel as if the grain were real when you touched it," she replies.

"Very few Illusion fae can do that."

"Pity. Well, what are you waiting for, Avery? Clean it up."

I kneel to place the croissants and muffins back on the tray, reaching through the mirage-table. I shiver at the feel of the magic, cold as snow.

My cheeks burn as the pair watch me pick up scraps of wasted food that faeries and Unluckies would kill over. After turning the pot upright, I pull out my rag to soak up the hot liquid, my hands red and tingling from holding the burning silver. Gritting my teeth, I work the rag, scalding my skin once more.

"Is that not hot?" Lord Eli asks. "You could use your genius to call to the water in the coffee to move it." His voice softens. "Unless . . . you suffer from being a Molder?"

I focus on the muddied rag in front of me. "No, my lord. My genius is intact."

"And nature still grants most of your requests?"

"It has not denied me in years."

A point of pride among my kind—but I am not among my kind. Like the way bugs and plants can emit signals to one another, so can a faerie genius send out a call along the plane of magic to the elements. An appeal to water or dirt or even fire, and nature fulfills or denies the request. Only the High Fae can wield the elements and other creatures without their consent. Only faeries fall victim to Moldhood, when nature rejects their appeals over and over until the genius atrophies with disuse. Becoming a Molder is to become magically mute, and like with everything else, the High Fae cannot be silenced.

"Then why do you not use magic to complete your tasks?" Lord Eli asks.

Over the arm of the settee rises Kassandra's pleased face, chin propped on her palm.

"Tell Lord Eli why you must do your chores by hand," she commands.

She wants me to say it.

I swallow. "It's that—"

"Look at him while he's speaking to you."

I lean back on my heels to take in the befuddled High Fae standing over me and the other grinning like a cat with her favorite rat.

"Because my magic smells, my lord."

Kassandra bursts into giggles.

"It *reeks*!" She claps. "It's the most disgusting thing you've ever smelled. Must be the human blood mixed in there."

Eli shakes his head. "The likelihood of human blood after their extinction is so low—"

"Then I swear she was birthed from her mother's ass!"

I clutch the rag, longing to slap her across the face with it.

"Kass," Eli cuts in, frowning, as if to spare me. "Maybe we should start our lesson now. To practice your water play."

"Did you not just see my Illusion?"

"Your father and brother requested root magic for your display at the coronation."

"Planes, they want me weak, playing in the dirt like the faeries."

Forgotten, I smack the rag onto the pile of waste, then pick up the tray as the two argue.

"Just because your genius can perform more than root magic does not mean your genius should forget it," Eli answers, helping her to her feet. "You must walk before you can run."

"But why walk when you excel at running?"

He sighs. "Where's the water pitcher?"

"Briar set it on the dining room table before her shift ended. Avery!"

I jolt, nerves fraying at the mischievous flicker in her eye. Still, I head from the parlor to the adjacent sky-blue dining area, which similarly soars with gilded ceilings and glitters with ornate flourishes of marble mantels. On the massive oak table rests a glass pitcher filled to the brim. Approaching, I notice that the water does not ripple with my tread. My genius pushes out onto the plane, requesting the water to move. The scent of earth permeates the air.

Nothing, not even the densely packed feeling of a refusal. There is no feeling at all. Setting down the tray, I wave a hand through the Illusion, cold like mist. Great.

The Night Crest, Briar, did not leave the pitcher out, and based on Kassandra's expression, it was at her behest. All so that I would need to either return to the parlor to admit defeat or waste time chasing down a real water carafe from the kitchens. Everything that is extra work for us is a game to her.

I search a forgotten servants' cart in the corner of the room for a vase or water sack, but the cart only holds napkins, silverware, and wipes.

A knock inside the wall.

Straining, I feel the pulse of another faerie's genius on the other side, earthy and sharp. Finding the seam, I open the servants' door cut from the wallpapered paneling.

"Went to clean the fireplaces and noticed the water was missing for her lessons," Jeremee whispers on the other side, pressing a heavy carafe into my hands. It's identical to the Illusion, no doubt what inspired my lady's trick. For once, I'm grateful he's here, as selfish as it may be.

"Thanks," I whisper back. "Now go, before she sees you."

His green eyes widen. "What happened to your hands?"

The water magnifies my irritated palms cupping the glass.

"Nothing," I say, bumping the door with my hip. "Talk later."

He grabs the door before it slams. "I haven't started on the fireboxes and grates in the dining room yet. She has a guest this evening, so it must be done today, but I can only clear them during her lessons in the parlor."

"Right, of course." I move back.

True enough, Jeremee steps inside carrying bags and brass fireplace tools. While my cotton uniform dress may be worn and repaired, it's still a stark white to his gray tunic. Unlike Crests, Scarps do not need to dress up like window treatments. A Scarp must carefully time their duties to remain invisible to High Fae. Leaving him to his task, I reenter the parlor, closing the door behind me so that he will not be spotted.

"Perfect," Eli calls, gesturing for me to enter. Beside him, Kassandra squints at the water in my hands.

"Where'd you get that?" she demands.

Her fury is a flame I can't help stoking. It's the only control I have.

I lower my head. "From the table, my lady. Like you said."

"You insolent little—"

"Shall we try butterflies first?" Eli clears his throat. "Please?"

The head of a House, begging for reprieve. So we're not the only ones who find each other's company torturous. Why she pointed a painted fingernail at me in that lineup two years ago, I will never know. On either side, Scarps had quaked as the mistress stomped about, having already hired and fired all other backup Crests, at least the ones who hadn't ended themselves or run away. Untrained at service and manners, the Scarps were still the next best thing compared to Bases, and, freshly grieving my mother, I hadn't cared when Kassandra picked me. I care now.

She huffs. "Butterflies? Fine, let's go with bloody butterflies."

The water sloshes from the carafe in my hands. As I peer over the lip, a butterfly formed of water smacks me in the face. I jerk away, spluttering, nostrils burning.

"My mistake," she says.

Outstretching the carafe does nothing. A dove splashes me next, then a bee, a blue jay, a spider, and although they are small, my nose and mouth fill. I gasp for air but inhale only water controlled by root magic. A giant raven floods my face, and for once, I wish it were an Illusion because maybe then I could breathe. My vision blurs.

"Kassandra—" Eli's voice hardens.

"I'm trying!" she whines. "Like you said, I need to work on my water play."

"But the faerie—"

My lady shrieks, the water splattering to the ground. I cough viciously, weak with relief, air filling my lungs.

"What is that!" she cries.

Wiping my eyes with my sleeve, I take in my mistress pointing at something behind me. I whirl around.

Jeremee stands on the threshold, bag of ash in hand, arms and face dirty, an angry glint in his gaze. My heart turns to ice. He doesn't move, as if he wants the High Fae to truly see him. As if he violates the rules for a good reason.

I need to bring her attention back to me.

Pivoting to my lady, I let the carafe slip through my fingers. Water arcs through the air, splashing her. She screams again, jumping back. Meeting her bedraggled appearance and gaping stare, I keep my expression flat and try not to show any hint of satisfaction.

"My mistake," I say.

The plane of magic yanks in her direction, the air pressurizing like a killing freeze. I fall to my hands and knees, and Jeremee stumbles, gripping the frame for a hold. I grab the pitcher, my genius calling to the puddles seeping into the oak. The water rises and coils into the glass once more. The stench of swamp pollutes the plane.

The High Fae may be stronger than any faerie, but that doesn't mean we're weak. Especially not my genius. For years, my mother begged me to hide its strength. Back then, I didn't want to, but now—I can't. In the days after her death, my magic putrefied to something sour and persistent.

Any other High Fae would kill me for the display of power, and for disobedience. But not Kassandra. No, something deep and delicious flickers in her gaze instead. Like the cat that plays with its food but finds the rat's hide tougher than expected.

Lord Eli frowns, glancing between us.

As if remembering herself, Kassandra covers her mouth, flushing again. "Ugh, I don't care why you're here, just *get out*!"

"Yes, my lady," Jeremee says.

"And drag her out by the hair if you have to. She reeks!"

I stand, pitcher in hand like a weapon, and curtsy. "My lady."

"Disgusting faerie."

My indiscretion now eclipses Jeremee's. I will be the one remembered and punished. As we scurry away, I almost laugh.

The only thing my mistress and I agree on is how much we hate each other.

Chapter Three

Later that afternoon before dinner service, I join the line for the creditor's counter, a niche carved into the bedrock wall of the Nest. Kassandra needs more time alone; when I stuck my head into her chambers an hour ago, I had to dodge a silver-backed hairbrush she hurled at me. Jae should be back from his extra Scarp work soon, and normally I wait for him to collect our paydays together, but in case Kassandra leverages a complaint against me—

Someone throws arms around my waist, and blond curls brush against my nose. "Got you!"

"You did." I smile. "How's it going, Benji?"

"I got to scoop horse shite today." The young faerie pulls away, cheeks shining.

I laugh. "Don't let your brother hear you say that."

"Hey, you think I'm gonna get this one off today?" He points to the first of his six debt rings. Such a rarity to have so little.

"Do you know which House it belongs to?" I ask.

"It's my birth debt, so Healing."

"It could! My first Reign ring disappeared last year, and you have fewer tattoos."

The boy counts the three on his small wrist. "The birth ring to House of Healing for delivering me. Then the additional Healing ring for general care. This one is for Reign, for ruling over us and fixing things like the roads and wells." He points to the three debt rings on the other wrist. "This one is House Illusion for the arts and the parties. And this is to House of Death, for protecting our borderlands and . . ." He looks up, puffing out his cheeks.

"What is it?"

"I heard that the Death faeries have to fight white scorpions, and that the giant sand turtles can swallow us whole."

Suppressing a smile, I say, "Well, those creatures remain in the Amyrian Desert, and besides, it's like you said. House of Death protects us from them."

Benji nods, gaze dropping to his final debt ring. "And this one's . . . from my mom and dad."

My arm wraps around his shoulder and he grasps it, attention shifting to the bands of black along my limb.

"You have a lot from your mom and dad. Like Jeremee has," the child says, voice small.

I squeeze him closer. "That was his choice, and he wouldn't have done it if he wasn't okay with it."

Only to stay in accordance with the law did Jeremee let Benji inherit one debt ring from their parents, whereas most siblings divide them evenly. For only children like me, there isn't a choice. Regardless of the rings, it's a surreal feeling to earn a salary larger than my parents' combined now that I'm a Day Crest.

"What if Jeremee never gets his rings off because of me," Benji mumbles.

"Hey." I spin him in my arms so he's facing me again. "It's not because of you."

"But what if he can never work it off?"

"Have you heard about the laundry Scarp named Nova?"

He shakes his head.

"Well, Nova cleaned clothes better than anyone else. He was fast, too. They get tipped for going above their quota, and he turned in more garments than required every single day. By the time he reached five hundred, he had worked off all his rings."

"Really? So you think I can get off my birth ring today?"

"Maybe," a voice says behind us. "Just don't focus on that too much."

Jeremee loops an arm around my shoulder, then tugs Benji from my side to his. Though he beams down at his sibling, I catch the weariness in his eyes. How can I blame him?

Nova left the palace inkless but marked in other ways. He had no wife or children; his hands shook constantly, fingers gone numb long ago; and a nasty cough always rattled his chest. An older laundress once told me he traveled west to Remiti, the Healing capital, to live in the constant sun. She also told me he was a great tale spinner.

We all shuffle closer to the front, Benji moving ahead of us.

"Let him hope," I murmur to Jae.

"They'll crush it."

"Better them than you."

"I should be the one to let him down easily. It'll happen either way."

I know. Planes, believe me, I know, I want to cry. I remember the gut-wrenching years of hope and defeat as the interest compounded on debt I was born into, that my parents were born into, that their parents were born into. We cannot control where the tattoos will appear or how many. All we can do is work until we earn our way out. Or take on more rings so that others do not.

"How was prepping the coronation hall?" I ask.

Jeremee shrugs. "The room hasn't been touched in centuries, so while we weren't the first cleaning crew, it still needed to be scrubbed down, windows washed, chandeliers dusted."

The corners of his mouth pull tight. Turning my head into him, I whisper, "What's wrong?"

He leans down, and for the second time today, we look like secretive lovers. His breath tickles my ear as he cups a hand over it. "The grout was pink, and no matter how hard I scrubbed, I couldn't get the color out. Thought it was some strange fae fashion, but an older guard told me something else." Jeremee grimaces. "It was blood that had soaked into the floors during the Dark Rebellion."

"Halfling prick," I breathe. In front of us, Benji giggles, and we gesture him along.

"How many stones are in this room?" Jae asks.

"It must be hundreds," the child says.

"Then you better get counting. Practice your numbers and I'll get you a chocolate at the next Full Moon Festival."

The boy gasps before getting started.

"The guard was jesting," I whisper, though not quite convincingly. Even with only one fae parent, some halflings can live as long as the High Fae themselves, almost a thousand years, so it's possible the guard could have been telling the truth. Halflings tend to hold prestigious positions over faeries—guards, tellers, accountants, and so on.

Jeremee leans forward. "Says he survived the palace massacres as a child."

"That was seven hundred years ago. Times are different now."

"There hasn't been a new king in seven hundred years, either."

"House of Death isn't invited to the coronation. There can't be a second Dark Rebellion."

"What if the Houses are shifting?"

"Who cares? Debt or death, those are our options. Does it matter who the creditor is?" Jeremee shakes his head, pulling away, but I grasp his ringed forearm, drawing him back. "Nothing is going to happen," I say, glancing at Benji still loudly counting the stones. Jae follows my gaze.

"And if it does?"

Pulling his pointed ear down to my lips, I whisper the treasonous thought I should snip into submission. "Then let them eliminate each other. It'll be easier for our kind."

I squeeze his shoulder, his dark auburn hair grazing my knuckles. His gaze locks with mine. "Don't you understand, Avery? The High Fae will not kill one another first. They will kill one another last."

I flinch.

"I'm up!" Benji proclaims, and we break apart and watch as the young faerie steps up to the teller. He's barely tall enough to see over the stone ledge serving as a counter. A wrinkled halfling sits in the niche, quill in hand, only one ring on each wrist, a stack of empty parchment next to his elbow. Like all halflings, his mother was a faerie, his father a fae. If the parentage were reversed, the halfling would've been killed after known conception, and the High Fae female severely punished and wed off immediately to another noble House to live in the countryside, far from high society.

He waves the quill. "Hand."

Benji grips the counter edge. The teller clucks his tongue, grabbing the young faerie's wrist to jerk him closer. Jeremee stiffens but remains where he is, and so do I. It's illegal to harm a teller; the sentence is death.

The halfling pricks Benji's finger. The quill touches the parchment, and numbers and symbols scroll across the page.

"I spent extra hours in the stables this week," the child says. "Maybe I can get one of my rings removed?"

"Not this week."

"Next week?"

"No."

Benji hums. "But it'll happen. You have less than me and you're old."

I bite my lip to stifle a laugh.

The teller raises his fluffy gray eyebrows. "You need to learn to manage that mouth."

Jae winces next to me.

"This is why faeries accrue so much," the halfling mutters, putting down the paper. "You earned ten copper coins this week. Three go toward your room and board here at the palace, two toward maintaining public resources, one toward your birth debt, one toward military protection, and one toward the free entertainments and yearly celebrations. That leaves you with two copper coins. Would you like to pocket them or use them to pay down your debt?"

"That doesn't make sense," Benji says.

My heart sinks.

"I'll repeat myself. You earned ten copper coins this week . . ."

Jeremee bends down, whispering something in his ear. The child straightens. "I'd like to pay toward my debt, please."

"See, this is why you have so few rings," he says.

Jeremee blows out a breath. Benji seems to accept this, skipping to the side as the teller wipes down the quill and shouts, "Next!"

I step up, prick my finger, hold my breath as the parchment zings with writing. It will be bad this time, I know. The longer hours, the hand-done chores—these are not true defenses against the complaints that High Fae like Kassandra can sling our way. I wanted to do this without Benji or Jeremee around, but sometimes we can't hide the horrors of our world.

"You earned fifty copper coins this week," the teller says. After room and board and taxes to all the Houses, and my significant interest, I'm left with ten copper coins.

"No complaint against me?"

"No complaints."

Hmm. Maybe Kassandra's threats were empty. So I pay five toward my debts and pocket the remaining five to spend at the next festival for Jeremee's shoes.

"Congratulations," the teller grunts. "You've made a significant enough dent in one of your debts. Enough to thin it."

"Oh?" I straighten. This can't be true. Is it time? He gestures, and I outstretch my arm. Another prick and I watch in awe as the first ring on my right arm tingles with the feeling of a hundred tiny needles.

"Benji," I say. "Come look."

He rushes over, small hands clasping my forearm. We watch my wrist as the first tattooed ring shrinks, thinning in half. I've paid down enough interest in the ring to make a visible difference.

"Oh my planes!" He bounces next to me, and I pass two copper coins into his pocket. Jeremee gives a nod of thanks, mouth tight, before stepping up to the counter. Benji slips his fingers into mine, and tears prick my eyes. Perhaps I should resent that this child has not endured as many dues as we have. Many older faeries feel this way, but why should those who come after me suffer because I have?

"It seems there's a complaint against you," the teller tells Jae.

My stomach plummets.

"What House?" Jeremee demands.

"Illusion."

"Wait." I join Jeremee at the counter, dropping Benji's hand. "What's this complaint?"

"Damage of property. Which means he needs to pay the value of the damaged property. Three hundred silver coins."

The world spins. "But . . ."

"Jae-jae?" Benji starts. "What's happening?"

A roaring in my ears drowns out everything else. I had splashed water on her silk robe and slippers. I sullied her clothes and slung insults. All to distract her from the violation of a Scarp daring to be seen aboveground, daring to interrupt her slapping my face with beautiful fucking butterflies.

"There's been a mistake," I say. "This complaint is meant for me."

The teller shakes his head. "It's labeled for him."

Another Illusion, another cruel trick. Kassandra letting me think I've been spared only to punish us both. This would set Jeremee back almost a century. He's already saving his brother, paying off three generations of lives lived.

"Let me pay," I demand.

Jeremee starts. "Avery—"

"I deserve the debt."

The teller sighs. "You know the laws. You cannot pay off another's debts until you have fully paid off your own."

"There must be some way—"

"Can you afford to free yourself? Looking at your accounts, the answer is no. No, you cannot pay for him, either."

We stand in numbed silence. That could take centuries, and by the time I would get to his, he might be entirely consumed, even the whites of his eyes black with ink.

"Avery." A small hand weaves through mine. "I'm sure it'll be okay, right?"

I can't meet Benji's eyes.

It's not okay. It's very much not okay, I want to cry.

Instead, I can only watch in horror as the teller gestures for Jeremee's ringed hand. Reluctantly, he slides it across the counter. A prick from the quill.

I blink away the tears, staring down at the small space beneath his chin. If that amount pushed him to a new level, then a ring would sear along the empty skin there.

A palace vendor once told me of an Unluckie's corpse found on the edge of the Peri, picked over by vultures. Even the bones were carved with the debt that marred the flesh in life.

"You could declare the Desert Walk," I offer weakly.

Jeremee shakes his head, mouth set.

Of course he will not abandon Benji here, with no family. Even for the sliver of a chance at freedom. Very few survive crossing the Amyrian Desert, but those who do join the House of Death in banishment with their balance wiped clean.

"Why is Avvie crying?" Benji asks, voice shaking.

Avvie, what he used to call me when he couldn't pronounce my name. A baby's babble. Benji needs his big brother, and his big brother needs him. The palace pays more than the market, the farms, the building projects in the cities beyond Versara. It is not the torture of the mines. It's our safest bet, even if it isn't safe.

Jeremee cries out, doubling over, then collapses. Benji screams, and I pull him away.

"It'll be okay, it'll be okay," I rush to say, holding the child to my chest so he doesn't see.

Jeremee scrabbles at his ankle, pushing up his trousers. Three thick black tattoos curve around his calf.

He is only a limb away from becoming an Unluckie. The line behind us shifts uneasily, whispers growing, sympathy and fear alike in the onlookers' voices.

"Next!" the teller shouts over the noise.

I grab Jeremee's arm and haul him to his feet. He leans against me, breathing through the last of the pain, tears streaking down all three of our faces now. I slip my remaining three copper coins into his pocket.

"It won't make a difference," he rasps.

"I'm going to pay this off, every single coin."

"Me too," Benji sniffs.

"No," Jeremee snaps. "No. *Please.*"

"Bee, keep your money," I say. "And, Jae, I swear to you that I will."

"How?"

An idea comes. "The night shifts. They pay more."

He shakes his head. "Because they're dangerous. I can't let you."

"Becoming an Unluckie is dangerous. Think of it as repayment."

Jeremee raises my chin with an inked finger, his eyes overflowing. "You will *never* be indebted to me."

My throat pinches with pain. I force out my next words. "But you are indebted to them, so we'll fight it together."

We reach Jeremee's room, a four-cot space he shares with other male faeries. I lower my friend to his cot, and Benji climbs onto his brother's lap. The siblings cling to each other, weeping.

"I will hurt them!" Benji wails.

"Shh!" Jeremee clutches him tighter. "Shh, do not say that. Never say that."

Kneeling before the pair, I clasp on to Jae's arm.

"I will fix this," I say.

I speak my wish into existence, send my hopes along the plane like dead leaves floating down a stream. Jeremee and I lock gazes over his brother's shoulder. He shakes his head, swallowing, and I know what he holds back for the sake of the child between us.

You can't.

But I will, I think. *I have to.*

Even if it takes all my energy, all my time, my days, my body, my life—I will pay it all. I will free this family of mine.

Chapter Four

"If requested, you must do it straightaway," Briar, the Night Crest, says that evening. She zips up the spiral stone steps, bedding in hand. I follow closely behind.

"Of course," I say.

"No matter the ask," she answers.

"I understand."

"Do you?" She stops, facing me. The lines deepen around her mouth as she frowns.

I shrug. "I've been harmed in most ways."

"They enjoy finding different ones." To my surprise, Briar's brown eyes soften, and she turns, climbing again. Over her shoulder, she quips: "The coin is good, but the price is high."

I stumble, my hand bracing against the cool stone. Could she get any more ominous? Yet the thought of Jeremee, all four limbs chained down in dues, is even more menacing. It was almost too easy, submitting the paperwork to the teller today. It was almost too fast, the way House Illusion accepted a new body for the same night.

At the top of the steps, we veer down the passageway that surrounds the Illusion House, and then Briar stops before a servant's room. "You can still visit the Nest, but once you take the blood oath of silence, you cannot speak of what you do and see up here at night. You can swear the blood oath now, or after we settle you."

"After is fine."

"This is your room." She waves fingers over the lock, showing me the sleight of hand. The door creaks open, revealing a room so narrow I could stretch out my arms and almost touch both sides. But that's not what snatches my breath. It's the tiny window on the back wall, a bright square of light breaking up the stone.

Drifting forward, I breathe, "I have a window."

"You do."

"I haven't . . ." My voice fails. While Base faeries work in the fields and Crests work upstairs, some Scarps go their entire lives without seeing the sun, especially those who launder, sew, and cobble. The first time I felt the sun sink into my skin for hours on end was as a Day Crest when chaperoning Kassandra on walks through the Illusion courtyards. Growing up, I would gaze at the stars on the occasional nights in the Peri when my parents were too busy making up to care about my whereabouts. Now I can look at the blazing sky without perimeters.

Pressing palms to the stone, I peer through the open space, just large enough for my head. A cool late-afternoon breeze caresses my cheeks.

A lawn of cropped, pear-stained grass stretches away from the base of the House Illusion building to the inner wall that holds the state rooms—the coronation hall, the Great Gallery, the public kitchens, and more. Halflings march along the tops of the battlements. Some hold whips, the official weapon for the descendants of the House of Reign. Others sling bows and arrows over their shoulders for the members of the House of Illusion, and a very few clutch the long staffs of the House of Healing.

Although I cannot see beyond the inner wall and its parapets, I know from my mother's stories and my grandmother's history that the palace farms make up the land between the inner wall and the outer wall. Beyond that is the Peri, the faerie villages of Versara. To the north is the Reign stronghold of Cont, to the west the Healing city of Remiti, and to the south the Illusion fort of Fraulus. On the horizon is the purple smudge of the mountains and the tans of the Amyrian Desert. And somewhere even farther beyond that, the mythical House of Death.

"Where are the state gardens?" I ask, surveying the barren turf before me.

"You're looking at them."

I jerk back into the dimness, gaping at Briar. "But it's just half-dead grass! Where are the fruit trees? The herbs?"

"In my lifetime, I've only ever seen faeries watering and cutting the lawn. Pulling out anything else that grows." Her austere expression does not falter.

That doesn't make sense. In a valley kingdom surrounded by rough mountains and desert, surely every inch of land must be purposeful.

"Then what's the point?" I exclaim.

"Perhaps that there is none." She shifts, glancing at the door, then back at me. "Were you born into a palace family?"

I take the cue to switch subjects. "My mother was an Illusion Base, but my father was a fighter in the Peri. My mother and I moved between the palace and Peri until she became a Scarp in the kitchens and felt secure enough to stay in one place."

It's not the entire truth, but it's an easier one. Even now, I still struggle to understand if she was running toward something, or away.

"You've been to the Peri?" Briar stretches out the sheets, and my mouth drops open—a superior making my bed? Tucking the corners under the cot, she asks: "What's it like out there?"

The memories stumble back. "Sometimes there wasn't enough food. There was thievery and fights everywhere. But once you were done with your tasks for the day, you could go home. You would just . . . be."

"It sounds . . ."

Nice. It sounds nice.

It had been. When my father wasn't around.

"Strange," I supply.

"Strange," she echoes, then straightens, falling into formality.

"Are you ready to take the blood oath to Illusion and the Morella family?"

I nod.

"I must warn you that while night service is always challenging, the Morella family has a rotating door of attendants. More so than the other families in Illusion and even the other Houses."

"You believe I should decline the blood oath and continue as a Day Crest."

"No one will judge your decision."

But I will, I think. *I will judge myself.*

Jeremee and Benji will collect debt rings as the interest builds, never able to pay enough at once to touch the principal loans. For them, the blood oath, the danger of night, is more than worth it. Kassandra already terrorizes me. May as well make more money off it.

"I will swear the blood oath to the Morella family to perform my duties as an Illusion Night Crest," I say.

"And indulge their desires?"

"And indulge their desires."

Briar nods, pulling an item from her pocket. A silver feather quill.

I glance at the door. "Where's the teller?"

"It is unlike a normal ring. There is no debt attached to it, just the oath. As your supervisor, I will ink it, though it's a unique process. More painful."

Holding out my hand, I declare I'm ready. Briar grasps my elbow, pushes up my sleeve to the shoulder. A searing cut across my upper arm. I cry out, jerking away, but Briar holds tight and drags the sharp nib across the flesh.

"Why are you doing this?" I gasp.

Her mouth opens but only a grunt ekes out. She took a blood oath of silence herself.

"I'm sorry," she grits. "It requires a certain amount of blood."

I see it now. As the red nib rips skin, crimson sucks up the shaft of the feather, dyeing the barbs and vane from the inside out.

"Must you stain all of it?" I pant. She cannot answer but meets my gaze, as if to say *Yes*.

For the next few minutes, my new supervisor carves a ring deep into my upper arm. It's not the normal sting of a knife; it burns and wriggles, as if burrowing into me, worming up my shoulder and neck before settling behind my ear. Blood dribbles down my fingertips and spatters on the ground. The room sways, but she holds me up.

Dark spots blot my vision.

Then I am sitting on my cot, sweaty forehead plastered against the cool stone as someone wipes a cold rag down my arm. Blinking, I look at Briar, a healing kit resting on the cot. When did she retrieve it? She smears salve on the injury and I hiss, flashing my incisors. A natural sign of aggression I rarely give in to—one my father always did.

"I know," she mutters. "I know."

After wrapping the injury, Briar lowers me onto the mattress. I don't protest. The room wavers, my head pounding.

"As we've both taken the blood oath and are sworn to secrecy, I can explain more when you're ready. For now, you must rest. We cannot call on a Healer because any magic done to the wound may interfere with the contract. You can request a Healer once the skin has scarred to help with any residual pain, but not before then. We have a few hours until evening service. I will come check on you before then, and you can begin your first shift."

I nod, a heavy fatigue settling over me like snow. For a moment, I feel a brisk brush of hair from my forehead.

"Welcome to the night service, Avery," she says.

A stubborn hope blooms. No one in my family has ever been a Night Crest before—and no one has paid off their debts. Maybe this life cycle, things will be different. Maybe I can save not just Jeremee and Benji but my descendants, too. My future children. Maybe it can all begin and end with me.

I do not hear the door shut as sleep pulls me under.

Chapter Five

Only an hour into service, and I am going to dump this wine on Kassandra. I pour her a glass, hand trembling, my shoulder sore. Sweat trickles down my neck. Briar and I had prepped the dining room for company, laid the table for two, and brought up dozens of platters of vibrant fruits and vegetables and sliced boar and jam and pastries. This, at least, is another benefit of the night shift. More High Fae food to thieve for Unluckies.

Kassandra glowers at her untouched meal, sneaking looks at the main door. What has she even eaten today, if at all? We both know her breakfast ended in disaster, so shouldn't she be ravenous? Especially with how much energy she's wielding.

She siphons the plane in small strips, the energy resembling the wriggle of a heat wave. She layers it across her shoulder blade, her wrist, her spine, storing power for some larger Illusion that, once complete, will release the magic to the plane once more. If faeries can only send appeals along the plane, like a fallen branch down a river, then High Fae can build dams. We can follow the current of energy; they can redirect it. Perhaps this is the true power of the High Fae: They save while we simply survive.

I top off her wineglass with an easy, medium-bodied red from the vineyards outside Remiti.

"Avery," Kassandra says. "Imagine my surprise seeing your application to Night Crest service. I can't imagine why."

The glitter in her mercury gaze tells me she knows exactly the reason why. My vision blurs. *Because you are a spoiled child who wanted revenge. Because you have saddled Jeremee with an impossible burden. And because no matter how much I abhor you, I still must serve you.*

"Thank you for approving the switch, mistress," I manage to say past the knot of anger.

Her nostrils flare. A delicate finger traces the rim of her wineglass. Briar returns the boar to the warming station set up against the wall.

I head to the serving table to grab another bottle. *Is night service always like this? Wasteful and empty and depressing?* No wonder Kassandra naps throughout the day and struggles in her lessons. More wine must run through her veins than blood.

I pop the cork from the new bottle.

The plane yanks in the direction opposite Kassandra's. I waver, the blood oath burning. Briar finds my elbow and squeezes.

The dining room doors fly open, slamming against the walls. A silver-haired, towering High Fae male strolls into the room. A tight whirlwind of energy buzzes along the plane.

My mistress sighs. "You're late."

"You missed me." His coal-black eyes seem to suck up all the candlelight. The resemblance is striking, and yet his sharp features make Kassandra look warm. A wolf, if I have ever seen one.

"I'm hungry," she says. "Sit down so I can eat."

The click of a tongue. "From the reports, you've been eating plenty."

My ears prick up, throat tightening. My lies to the cooks are leaving evidence behind. But surely she can't believe this male. Kassandra is small for a High Fae, physically frailer than both Briar and me. Yet no retort comes.

"Lord Dominik," Briar says.

The wine decanter almost slips from my grasp. Lord Dominik Morella—the heir of House Illusion. Fierce strategist, enigmatic entertainer, and Kassandra's older brother. In all my years as a

Day Crest, I have never collided with his notorious presence, only the rumors of violence and chaos he leaves behind.

"What can I serve you tonight?" Briar asks. "We have wild boar, mashed potatoes, apples, some lovely fresh bread—"

"All of it."

My supervisor begins piling up his plate. Kassandra's wineglass is once again empty. I contemplate cutting off her supply, but fae can handle more drink than faeries. A bottle for them is like a cup for me. So, I move toward her.

His stare blisters my skin, the air thinning. Both siblings are siphoning from the plane now, draining all the energy in the room.

"I'm parched," he announces. "I'd like a taste of that wine."

My cue. As I pivot to him, the hairs on my arms prickle with the slide of power in his direction, as if the floor itself is tilting. I must focus to stay on two feet. He may be the strongest High Fae I've encountered yet.

"I would like my glass filled first," Kassandra says.

I pause.

Her brother laughs. "So this is a special plaything of yours?"

"I can't possibly keep up with your multitude of delusions."

"You refuse every halfling lady-in-waiting."

"They're incompetent and boring."

"They're proper company."

"I'm impeccably thirsty. Avery?"

I choose her.

"And insolent. Faerie, come here." The plane jerks toward Dominik's end of the table, and I stumble.

"He is not your master."

My eyes flick between the siblings as they glare at each other. The plane pulls taut like a string. Briar hovers on the other side of the table, throat bobbing.

For a moment, I wonder if the plane of magic can snap. I thought I was a rat to Kassandra's feline, but I was wrong. In the presence of Dominik, my genius seems like nothing more than an insect.

The coin is good, but the price is high, Briar had said.

Finally, Dominik waves a hand, the plane sagging. "You will have the first pour, Kass."

Across the table, Briar lets out a breath. Keeping my eyes downcast, I approach Kassandra. I don't make it far.

Illusion magic surges in a rush of wind.

I am jerked and spun around by invisible hands, the decanter slipping from my grasp. My back slams into a wall, the breath pushed out of my lungs, my legs tangling. Only when a very strong, very real arm wraps around my waist do I understand. I am not against a wall; I am in Dominik's lap.

Kassandra gapes at me—at us—from across the table. The decanter floats toward her, tipping to one side. Her glass fills.

"Did I not say you'd have the first pour?" the heir says. "Now drink."

She glares.

A cool chuckle behind me, icy fingers twining through my hair. He inhales, and I swallow bile. Briar hovers a yard away, gripping a platter of pastries, face neutral.

"Are you afraid, little faerie?" he whispers.

Kassandra stands, her chair scraping in the silence. Dominik laughs again, a cruel, dead sound.

"Sit, Kass."

But she does not sit. She grips the table's edge, expression frozen. The air chafes in and out of my lungs.

"Is it scared or turned on?" he asks.

"Dominik," my mistress warns.

"I think both."

The metallic smell of fear leaks from my pores. He plays with my hair, exposing my neck, his thumb rubbing over a tendon.

"You're disgusting," she seethes. "Touching one of them."

"I sense jealousy," he sings. "But of me or her?"

"Dom!"

A mouth descends onto my throat. I cry out in shock, but a

phantom hand holds me still. Slowly, he licks up my neck, incisors scraping against my throbbing pulse.

Kassandra leaps forward.

"Sit," Dominik murmurs against my skin. A force shoves her back, the chair rocking. For a moment, no one moves. Not even Briar. Then my mistress takes a swig of wine. Tears threaten to spill from my eyes. I squeeze them shut, breathing.

"Good," the heir says. "Now, tell me of your lessons with Eli."

"They're fine."

"Elaborate."

Something bites my ear.

I jerk, eyes flying open, but it's not his mouth that did it.

The side of my face drips with sticky wine as every liquid in the room—water, alcohol, broth, cream—flies out of cups and bowls and hovers above the table. They burst outward into tiny snowflakes of white, crimson, brown, and blue. A dazzling display of colorful crystals glimmers across the entire room.

The snowflakes float back down into their respective dishware, the liquid in Dominik's cup rising with each bloody drop. In a moment, the entire room falls back in order.

It was the most impressive display of root magic I have seen from Kassandra. My mistress dabs her napkin against her flushed cheek. "Elaborate enough for you?"

"No," Dominik rumbles at my back.

"Did you not just see—"

"I *saw* that every snowflake was the same. You did not create a storm where each crystal is unique, as in nature. You came up with a simple design and then repeated it."

"It was as powerful as one of my Illusions."

"Then you clearly misunderstand our House magic," he snaps. "An Illusion is the truth in another light. Our task is to change the light. This is why you cannot capture the king's attention."

Get up! I think, and yet I cannot move, the phantom hands holding me still.

She leans back in her chair. "He's not the king yet."

"Nor you the queen. You had one job as Heart of Illusion. *One*. The coronation is in two days, and you have yet to convince the male who will fuck anything to fuck you."

For a moment, I am weightless. Airborne.

Then I crash into the hard floor. My ears ring, vision spinning. Someone shrieks. My blood oath feels like it's burrowing deeper into my skin—a venomous parasite that will eat me from the inside out. I hear it then. The sound of choking.

Lifting my head, I stare in horror.

Dominik—the Heir of Illusion—thrashes in the air as something unseen strangles him. Energy swirls around Kassandra like a snowstorm, her trembling arm raised. His body slams against the far wall, legs kicking, neck straining. His hand grips the invisible force around his neck.

"You forget yourself," he spits.

Then Dominik rips at the energy around him, prying the translucent grip from his throat. Kassandra cries out, grabbing her head. She collapses to the ground just as Dominik lands on two feet.

Briar yanks me up and away.

"Wait—"

"This is between the High Fae," she whispers. "We are forbidden to interfere."

As Dominik strides to his crumpled sibling, he swallows up all the energy in the room. The air fills with the sound of chimes, wind ripping at the curtains. Dishware rattles across the table before crashing against the tile.

The heir flips Kassandra onto her stomach, her cheek against the floor. Tears and snot slide down her face, fear sparking in her eyes.

Abuse is a well-known play to me, one I was forced as a child to watch my parents enact. No, I refuse now, as an adult, even if the actors are High Fae this time.

"Wait!" Wrestling from Briar's grip, I lunge forward. The heir whips his head around like a snake about to strike. "Please, let me . . . get the dessert."

Dominik blinks. "I have dessert in my hands right now."

My stomach sours. "Well, I could—"

My head jerks to the side, my body dropping. I didn't see the smack coming; it was done with an unseen hand. Blinking, cheek stinging, I stare at the silver-haired fae sprawled across the floor from me. A tear drips off her nose.

"Please," she whispers. "Dom—"

Kassandra screams as both arms jerk behind her back, Dominik bending over her.

"You will master root magic like every other fae female and leave the Illusions to me."

Another screech of pain as he contorts her arms, the sockets popping. Kassandra's arms can't take it anymore. I can't take it anymore, refusing to watch. I crawl to her.

Another blinding slap, my head smacking against the floor. Stars burst behind my eyes.

Briar grabs my shoulders, hauling me up. Kassandra closes her eyes and my heart sinks. She has given up.

My genius reaches for the plane in a last attempt to stop this scene, but the plane is stretched too thin and tight by fae geniuses.

"Remember your place tomorrow," he says.

Then the Heir of Illusion snaps my mistress's arms in half, the bones breaking.

Kassandra wails. Dominik drops her to the ground, wiping his hands on his robe. She whimpers, sliding into unconsciousness. It's a mercy.

Before we can reach her, he is in front of us.

"No Healers," he says.

I gasp. "My lord—"

"You will be next if you do not be quiet!"

I clamp shut. Dominik smooths down his hair, adjusts his tunic.

"She heals quickly on her own, but dismiss the Day Crests

anyway. Lock the door, as usual," he says. "If you try to speak of what you have seen tonight, you will have to face the consequences of the blood oath."

It takes everything in me, and Briar gripping my shoulders, not to lunge for his face and scratch out his eyes. Dominik steps beyond us, toward the front hall. Without looking back, he tosses something over his shoulder.

Two coins ping against the tile, rolling toward us.

"See you at the coronation, little faerie."

The doors slam shut.

A coin circles at my feet, metal clinking until it falls flat. A silver medallion. More money than I have ever beheld in my entire life. The sight of it makes my skin slither.

Briar was right. The coin is good, but the price is high.

Chapter Six

BRIAR AND I TAKE SHIFTS BY THE BEDSIDE, WHERE KASSANDRA moans and writhes as muscles and tendons and bones contort and sew together beneath pale skin. There is no time to stash the extra food from the dinner. Briar sends it down to the kitchens to be tossed.

Because faeries rarely can afford Healers, we are taught a myriad of herbal remedies, salves, and tinctures. I use the techniques my mother did to tend my father after a bad fight in the pits, the same ones she needed after their own fights when my hands wouldn't stop shaking. They don't shake now.

When my mistress cries out in agony, I mix a ginger-turmeric remedy to slip into her mouth alongside water. When her eyes flutter open, I give her chamomile tea. While she rests, I dab lavender oil across her forehead with a damp cloth. With my magic, I keep her pillow cool.

It is not enough.

Dawn breaks. When the new Day Crest knocks on the door, I dismiss them. The faerie passes a silver tray into my hands. Toast and grapes and coffee and cream. A simple breakfast—one that I delighted in stealing when my mistress turned down her meals. Now I know why Kassandra so often refuses to eat.

As I take the tray into the room, I stare at the reclined figure. Her pale face peeks above the duvet, a yellowing bruise on her cheek, lips chapped, silver hair falling to her shoulders. Neither of us says a word.

I set the tray on the serving table to the left of her bed and mix another tincture. "This will help with the pain."

"Go away."

"After you take this medicine." With downcast eyes, she opens her mouth. Just slightly. When I lean forward, Kassandra winces. I pull back. "I'll need to be near your face to give this to you. When you're ready."

My voice comes out soft and deep, a tone I've never used with her before. She has heard my fear, pain, forced respect, and apathy. Until last night, I did not think this High Fae, the Heart of Illusion, ever needed anything from a faerie other than obedience. Kassandra licks her wounds in a canopy bed while I must tend to mine in a cot. Yet despite her privilege, I would not want to trade places.

Silver hair swishes as she gives a curt nod. Leaning over her, I catch the faintest tug of magic. The smallest trickle of the plane that wraps around her pinky.

"How are you doing that?" I ask before I can stop myself. "You're still siphoning power? Even while healing?"

She shrugs. I tip the vial into her mouth, and she swallows.

"You tried to stop him," she croaks.

"I am sorry for failing."

"I . . . I leveled a complaint, though."

I wince. *I know,* I want to say, but understand she's asking something else. Why help her?

"No one deserves that," I reply.

She watches me for a few moments, frowning. Then the sheets rustle as she sinks lower into the bed, face once again hidden. In a moment come the soft sounds of her sleeping. I do not feel relieved.

I have seen many shades of my mistress, from taunting to dismissive to downright cruel. This numb, silent shell of a creature may be the most disturbing of them all.

. . .

WIND RIPS AT my clothes, stings my skin; I am in a tempest. I lurch from sleep, gasping, fumbling for a candle in the dark—but it is daytime. The plane whips around, the room spinning and swirling. Someone is screaming.

Kassandra. I stumble toward the bed, her body thrashing, kicking. Phantom nails rake across the sheets, shredding the fabric. The linen canopy rips on one side.

"My lady!" I yank the rest of the sheets off her twisting body, tears and spittle running down her anguished face. Do I wake her? Will that worsen this pain?

She wails louder.

"Kassandra!" I scream.

Her eyes fly open. She surges forward over the mattress, and I catch her, her body slamming us onto the ground. She shivers on top of me, gasping, then scrambles off and bares her canines.

I don't move, my heart seizing. Her pupils dilate, her teeth glinting. She is a predator once more. Then recognition dawns, and her face loses its tension.

"Leave," she seethes, rubbing her thin, bruised arms.

"My lady—"

"Get out!" Her voice cracks.

"Yes, my lady."

I brush off my skirts, climb to my feet, and exit to the parlor.

A disheveled faerie catches my eye.

I jump at the reflection in the glass hung on the wall. My chestnut hair tangles in matted waves past my shoulders, brown eyes hollow. A tight set to my jaw. That isn't all.

It's as if someone dipped a paintbrush into a storm cloud and smudged purple and black across my collarbone. The bruises streak under the simple scoop of my plain cotton dress. If I were to lift the garment up, I know what I would find underneath; the aching in my body tells me. This was only from a few invisible slaps. Nothing compared to—

The mattress creaks with her weight once more, the sound of broken sobs filling the space.

This will not do. None of this will do.

Just because I'm blood sworn to keep these secrets in doesn't mean I can't act out.

It is time to make a plan.

I KNOCK ON Briar's door. After a few moments, my superior answers in a cotton nightdress, dark hair in a loose bun. I hold up a bag of stale bread rolls offered to the faeries this morning. Sometimes we get scraps right before they fully turn to supplement the gruel they give us. Sometimes I'd rather have just the pasty porridge. Before I left the kitchens, I warmed the rock-hard bread with butter.

"Here."

She rubs her face. "What time is it?"

"Late morning."

"So we have a day until we need to start prepping her for the coronation. Her arms should only need a few more hours to fully mend."

I grimace. "How often does this happen?"

Briar steps back, opening her door for me to enter. Inside looks exactly like my new room, skinny but with a small window and cot. As we settle on the mattress, I take out a roll and hand it to her.

She sniffs. "How'd you convince the cooks to part with fae butter?"

"Told them a guest of Kassandra has a dog."

She smirks, biting into the roll. I tear at mine with my teeth, chewing. After a few moments, Briar says, "There were several years when I would intervene and he would break my arms, too."

Cringing, I say, "I am sorry."

She shrugs. "As faeries heal slower than fae, I couldn't be there to tend to her, and Dominik refused to allow any day servant in.

She was left alone, and I was left broken for weeks. Then I spent some time begging the guards for help, but forgot whose orders they must follow in the House. We can only speak of it now because we are both blood sworn."

My stomach tightens. "This is a nightmare."

"My point is—redirect. I've found this is the best way to reduce harm overall."

"How can you say this?"

"I've been doing this for a long time, Avery." Her eyes go misty. "When Kassandra was a baby, she had the loudest howl I ever heard. She could scream for hours upon hours upon days. Back then, I changed the soiled sheets and her clothes, bathed her, and did other nightly duties. But no matter what I did, she would just wail. She wouldn't stop because . . . well, she was hungry." Briar frowns and continues, "It's custom for High Fae lords and ladies to only be fed by their mothers. I've heard in the countryside they allow wet nurses and goat's milk, but not here. When I slipped Kassie sheep's milk, she immediately spit it up. I thought it had something to do with being a High Fae babe. Something different that their genius needed. She was hungry, and I felt helpless."

"And the late Lady of Illusion?" I ask.

Briar shakes her head. "She would rarely nurse. She only visited when Kassie was too weak to cry. It was torture—for Kassandra, and for me. My whole body would ache. I couldn't stand it anymore. And then one day, it happened. My breasts produced milk."

I gasp. "How?"

Briar looks down at her empty hands. "I always wanted a child. I still do. But Kassandra found me just as much as I found her. I can't explain it other than that. Sometimes, I wonder if she's so frail because of me—my faerie milk. Other times, I feel like keeping her alive has been my greatest challenge and accomplishment." She clears her throat, dropping her voice. "Do not make an enemy of any of the Morellas. They are strange, unfeeling fae.

They are not like the royal bloodline; they fought, fucked, and fabricated their way into the Upper Court."

My mouth dries out, my palms slick with sweat.

"I know," I tell her. "I know."

But I did not understand. Not until now, when two of them despise me.

"Briar, what if there's a way we can save Kassandra?" I finally ask. "More than just redirecting."

A TOWERING, LITHE male lingers by my door. The image of Dominik flickers back to me, vicious and lethal. I stop short in the dark hallway, my genius flickering to awareness.

"Avery?" Jeremee asks.

I sag against the wall in relief. In a moment, he's in front of me.

"I heard the servants were dismissed for the day. Did something happen?"

Images of the night tumble through my mind. "I—"

It's as if glass marbles roll up my esophagus, blocking the sentence until it dies in the back of my throat. I swallow and try again. "It—"

I gag.

Jeremee steps back. "The fucking blood oath."

My eyes sting as I wait for the magic to subside, a hint of metallic blood in the air. With all the secrets I keep these days, lying has become easier than breathing. Yet this blood oath makes me bear the truth in sullen silence.

"Are those bruises?" There it is again, that angry glint in his gaze I've seen twice this week, but rarely before. The blood oath means I cannot tell him anything, and a newfound fear grips me. A deadly force lives inside me—and it is not my own.

"Please," I manage.

He swears again, rubbing his jaw with a rough hand. We stare at each other. Finally, I slip the coin into his palm. When he holds it up to the dim light, the silver shimmers.

"Avery, no."

"Yes."

"I can't take it."

"I can't give it to Benji; there are no tips in the stables. The teller will assume he stole it. But *you*—you've been a servant in the palace for years. Someone could've easily offered silver for your silence."

"Like someone did for yours."

Something sharpens in me, a frustration I've never felt toward my best friend.

"Just let me help, okay?" I snap.

His jaw sets. "Like how you've let me help these past few years?"

"That's different."

"*How?* Planes, it's as if you want to be caught." I step back, and he takes a breath, his voice softening. "She didn't die because you failed in some way, Avery. It just happened."

My eyes burn. "Take the coin. Please."

"Okay." He slips the coin into his pocket, then gestures to my chamber door. "You were looking to rest?"

I was, but now adrenaline sparks in my veins. I don't want to slip inside to a privacy I've never known. To hear the ringing silence in my head, feel the supernatural baubles form in my throat. To be haunted by the overwhelming power of the High Fae, the sound of Kassandra's bones breaking.

"The silver stallions in the stables," I say instead. "Are the rumors true?"

"Their coats do seem to glow."

"Are any available for tomorrow? I need one for Kassandra during the coronation."

He eyes me, brow furrowing. "All of the silver stallions are off with the halflings on guard duty."

"Then a silver mare will do."

"I've only heard of the stallions."

"How do you think they make them?" I smirk. "Don't you know where little faeries come from?"

Jeremee flushes. "I know how breeding works."

"Breeding!" I exclaim, a hand to my chest. For a moment, the heaviness lifts, laughing with him an addictive, dangerous high after so many lows. "I pray to the planes for the females you bed."

"Why's that?"

"They must love the mounting."

His eyes flash. "They do."

A familiar vision sparks, one I have never acted on. His long, tattooed fingers sliding through my hair, tugging me into him, his lush mouth descending onto mine. Those hands spinning me around, pinning me to the wall, pulling down his trousers, pulling up my skirts. Something snags in my belly at the image, the gateway into a moment of distraction that could build to other moments in shadowy corners and stone corridors.

The dark hallway is quiet, except for the sound of our breathing. He leans against the opposite wall. I cross my legs, pressing my thighs together. His gaze dips down my body, then back up again.

"You're thinking of us right now," he states. "Together."

"Have you abandoned all manners?"

"Do you want me to?"

How much closer can we crawl, on hands and knees, to the line without crossing it? Who will be the first to break the rules so that we can form new ones?

"Seems you already have," I answer. "What are you thinking, Jae?"

He quirks a brow. "I'm wondering if you've ever been taken from behind before."

Desire coils low and hot. I can hardly breathe. This is the closest we've ever gotten.

"I don't like to share," I say. "Only steal."

"Especially my prospects from the festival. Tell me, are you truly satisfied afterward? Is it ever enough?"

What are we doing? I think. *Why now?*

I want to be with Jeremee, the invitation to my bed a second from escaping my lips. But he'll see my battered body. He will feel the shake in my hands. When he wraps long arms around me, will I think of Dominik?

Are you afraid, little faerie? The feel of those icy fingers. A flood of last night's memories. My best friend stepping closer, eyes heavy-lidded, and my bruised chest heaves.

Am I still the day faerie from yesterday? Am I something less, and the male in Jeremee can sense it, ready to pounce on a thing that will lie down?

Is it scared or turned on?

I grip my door handle, and the heady air dries up.

Jeremee stops, blinking, as if the spell has been broken. "Avery, I'm . . . confused."

Me too, I want to cry. We are pulling in two different directions—him spiraling into an Unluckie, and me soaring into an elusive Night Crest.

When we are together, I want it to be a beginning, not a goodbye.

I clear my throat. "The silver mare."

The heat dies in his eyes, in my chest. He looks down the hall toward the light of the stairs, the sounds of the Nest below. "What about it?"

"Once the lady approves, I can share the plans."

"Is it safe for Benji?"

"Absolutely. I promise."

"Okay, then." He scratches the back of his head. "I guess I should get going . . ."

"I'll see you tomorrow," I say.

He nods and turns away, descending into the Nest. He doesn't look back.

The only other time we have come close to crossing the line had been after my mother died. I had reached for him, tear streaked and in mourning attire, but he had gently refused and guided me to bed, tucking me under the covers, and left.

We've never talked about it since. He was a safe harbor after her death, when I needed him the most. Sometimes I wonder how much grief plays a role in our game, for him and for me. He lost his own mother shortly after Benji's birth ten years ago. Grief spoiled my magic, my personality, and shrank my world. What has it done to him?

Unlocking my empty room, I undress, fingers grazing tender flesh in the shadows. I want to peel off my skin, layer by layer, to find the depth that Dominik has not touched, to escape the sound of bones snapping.

As long as the Illusion heir torments Kassandra, she will torment us, levying violation after violation, setting back any financial progress. But the opposite could be true: If I could ensure her safety and happiness, perhaps that would trickle down to us. Perhaps she would even consider revoking the complaint against Jeremee, if such a thing is possible. Tomorrow, Briar, Jeremee, Benji, and I will help her excel in the one area that might release her from Dominik's grip and into the cushy embrace of royalty, bringing us with her.

Her prospect to the king.

We'll pull together a great performance, flicker enough light and shadows for it to seem real. This is the House of Illusion, after all.

All Kassandra has to do is step into her role, play this game just once. All I have to do is convince her. It shouldn't be too hard.

Chapter Seven

"Are you moonstruck?" Kassandra snaps later that afternoon. "There's no way I'm doing that."

I wipe sweaty palms on my skirts. The coronation is tomorrow, and this is my only chance to get her to agree. Kassandra is propped up in bed, arms resting on the plethora of pillows. Her arms are almost healed, and her complexion has started to return.

She gestures at Briar, who stands at her bedside. "Well, what do you think?" she asks.

"Truly, mistress?"

"Truly, Briar."

My brows shoot up. Briar practically raised Kassandra, but it is startling all the same to see such intimacy between High Fae and faerie.

Briar gives a slow nod. "It would be quite the entrance."

"So you're both moonstruck."

"My lady, if I may speak plainly," I say.

"Ugh! I can't think straight with your thoughts pressing against the plane. Your anxiety tastes like iron."

"I—" I stop. *What did she just say? My emotions . . . leave a residue on the plane?*

"Mistress, what do you know of the crown prince currently?" Briar asks. "You grew up together, but surely, he must be the same male."

"He thinks himself an intellectual, but I suppose there are worse males. And worse-looking."

"What else?" I ask.

Kassandra picks at a piece of lint on the blanket. "They always thought me annoying. Always tripping after Maxian and Dominik and Eli when we were children. I'm sure he still views me as a sister."

"Force him not to."

"And how would this plot help with that?"

"The seamstresses have been working on something special for a few months now," Briar answers.

"For planes' sake, I'll think about it," Kassandra mutters. "First, I need something modest for tonight, unless you fools think it wise to visit my father in lingerie."

"I pressed your conservative navy dress," Briar says, lips twitching with a smile.

"Good. I'd rather not shock his weak heart and hasten my brother to head of House."

Once we finish readying Kassandra, Briar and I follow her into the palace halls to her father's room. Upper members of House Illusion swirl around the four-poster bed in the center of the musty chamber: A blue male scribbles on parchment while a blond male paces. In bed lies the Head of Illusion, his breaths scraping in and out of his open mouth.

I try not to stare from my spot in the corner, but the sight of a High Fae decaying from time is one I have only ever seen in this room. Until adolescence, I didn't know that High Fae could even pass away, with some in the Nest claiming their masters to be well over a thousand years old. Although faeries birth more children and in a shorter time, most of us die in our six hundreds, from a weak heart, a drooping left side, or diseases like the one that took my mother. But time, like death, seems to track down everyone in the end.

Kassandra kneels by the side of the Head of Illusion, reaching out to clasp the papery hand from the blankets. "Papa," she starts.

"Dom," the male rasps.

"No, Papa, it's me."

"My Heart?"

"Yes." Her shoulders sag in relief. "Tomorrow, I will be the one to present the Illusion gift to Maxian. Lord Tomas, your advisor, has already approved."

The sky-blue male looks up from his parchment. "That's right, my lord. It is a grand gesture that could solidify a union between Illusion and Reign."

"We are not yet partnered?"

"The contracts take time, my lord."

"Where is my child?"

"I'm here," she says, stroking his arm.

He glowers at her hand.

"My son," he blurts. "I want my son."

Something shifts, a pang in my ribs.

"I'll send a guard to gather him." Kassandra sighs. Leaning forward, she presses a kiss to her father's forehead.

When we exit his chambers, striding down the hall, she does not look back at me, following with my head down. "Tell me again of this idea. It's a mare, you said?"

Briar and I exchange a look. "Yes, my lady. And that's not all."

And together, we begin to shape the plan.

THE NIGHT AIR is cool on my skin the following evening, the ground damp beneath my feet. A bullfrog bellows. If I close my eyes, I could pretend we are playing in the woods around the Peri, and not skirting the neglected, unused lawns of the state gardens, on our way to the coronation. Halfling guards march the procession of faeries toward the inner wall.

The servants had been given orders to enter through the back entrances of the coronation room, like moving, expensive décor: The more of us, the wealthier the fae look. For the hundreds of

High Fae gathering at Versara this evening, there will be a thousand attendants to serve them.

I add these grounds to my incomplete mental map of the palace, drawn for me by my mother. Over chopping onions and stirring stews, she described what she knew of the labyrinth—buildings inside buildings, separated by mazes, each inner layer a different House. First, the state rooms, then Illusion, Healing, and finally, the Reign residence. Still, details of the ruling House, the center of this sprawling chateau, remain unsketched, unknown to most, even other nobles.

Above the crowd, I spot the familiar crop of auburn hair. "Jae!" I call. He turns, his face lighting up. "Briar, this is my friend Jeremee," I say when I reach him.

"Nice to meet you." She nods. He nods back, then bends forward so that only I can hear.

"I should apologize," he says.

I make a face. "For what?"

"For not inviting you down to the Nest last night."

For leaving you in that dark hallway, alone.

"We're not conjoined. We can have separate dinners."

"Do you want that? To stop eating dinner together?"

"You think because I'm a Night Crest now, you can be rid of me?" I laugh.

He gives me a small smile. "I don't want to be rid of you."

Our knuckles brush against each other's and I think of our moment in the hall, the question he voiced, the one in his eyes, as if we always need to find each other in a crowd to excuse the press of our bodies.

"We'll talk tomorrow?" I wonder. "About . . ."

To my horror, I blush. He laughs this time, nodding, moss-green eyes sparkling. "Never thought you'd react like that because of *me,* but I'm not complaining. I might even like it."

I give him a shove as he laughs again. "You were talking big earlier."

"Just trying to keep up with you. Always just trying to keep up with you."

Hiding my grinning face, I think about what tomorrow might bring, and it's like the painful flutter of an adolescent crush, for maybe he truly does want us to have each other.

But I do not simply want to have Jeremee; I want to keep him, and for him to keep me, no matter the shape or stamp of it. To bring each other a cup of tea at the end of a shift and sit side by side, divulging the most innocuous details of our days. I fantasize not only about love but also about freedom. I don't know if I'll ever truly be satisfied until I have both. Then again, when have I ever been satisfied with being or doing or wanting less?

You must try to hide yourself, my mother would beg. *Or else they'll sense your power.*

Why shouldn't they? I'd snap as an angry adolescent. Only when she fell ill did I understand that it was too late to repair our frayed relationship. All I could do was hold her frail frame and beg an unraveled mind to forgive me.

"Jeremee!" a blond faerie calls, weaving through the crowd of servants from behind.

"Hi." Jeremee grins at the sight of his roommate.

The blond faerie, shorter and wider than Jeremee, reaches us, cheeks flushed. He slings an arm around Jae's torso, hand grazing his ribs.

"Glenn," I say.

"Haven't seen much of you lately, Avery."

"Night Crest now."

His face twitches in sympathy. "What's that like?"

I open my mouth, but Jeremee cuts me off. "She swore an oath."

"Still a Scarp?" I tease instead.

"Still bad at it, too." Glenn snorts. "Spilled shoe polish all over a lord's linen tunic yesterday. Added about twenty more years of service."

I wince, attention cutting to Jeremee. His face gives nothing away, his eyes straight ahead while mine fall to his trouser leg. Does he resent what I have done? Could I blame him if he did?

"I'm sorry to hear that," I tell Glenn.

He shrugs, then nudges Jae. "More time with this one."

My friend groans. "Your socks stink."

"Not as much as your morning breath."

I choke out a laugh, and Glenn beams.

"You two are the worst," Jeremee mumbles.

We share a giggle, and while I should envy any faerie who's been with Jae, I know Glenn gives him things that I cannot. Glenn has a good heart even if he can't hold his cider, and he includes and indulges Benji even more than we do. When we're all together, it doesn't feel like competing. It feels like love compounding.

"Avery, we must go," Briar shouts from a few yards away, the inner wall looming ahead. She stands at the mouth of a wide servants' entrance cut into the stone, a stream of faeries flowing in, directed by guards.

"But you love us," Glenn says to Jeremee.

Jeremee slings an arm around Glenn's shoulders, a grin on his face, and suddenly I fear I might not like what Jae has to say tomorrow. But I need his honesty, even if it hurts, and he needs mine. If I can stand up to a High Fae even after getting smacked down, then I can do this.

"Avery!" Briar calls again.

"I should join her," I say, stepping away. A hand reaches out, tugging me close. Jae embraces us both, Glenn laughing, and I feel crushed with care.

"Good luck out there," Jeremee whispers into my hair, kissing the top of my head. He squeezes me tighter to stop his trembling.

"Don't get yourself killed," Glenn quips, and I elbow him in the stomach. "Hey!"

"Don't spill the sparkling wine," I say. "Apparently, that stuff's good."

I untangle myself from them. It's going to be a long event, and tonight, Kassandra and I will need to impress the most privileged in the land.

I steel my nerves as I reach Briar.

"Your family?" she asks.

"I'd like to think so." We move under the stone arch of the inner wall and toward the back entrance of the coronation hall. Bright lights and sounds spill toward us.

"Good." She nods. "Good."

"Do you have a partner?" I ask, knowing she doesn't have a child.

"No, I'm waiting."

"For them to find you?" I smile.

My supervisor pulls up her sleeves to reveal her tattooed forearms.

"No, for another century of work to pay off," she says. "I just keep telling myself it'll be worth it. To eliminate their debt before it can ever touch their skin."

"Whose debt?"

"Any child of mine."

We near the threshold, and the plane of magic washes over us, undulating in hundreds of directions with High Fae geniuses pulsing and wrestling for control. My stomach twists. Faeries peel off from the group, staggering back outside. Some grab their heads; others drop to their knees and heave. Briar and I grip each other and enter.

The throne room shimmers with a kaleidoscopic cacophony of High Fae, lanky and large, sage-skinned and magenta or coiled-haired, dressed in gowns and tunics of silk, gossamer, and satin. Some tug white fur around their shoulders. Though the fashion styles are wide-ranging from all over Amyria, the one thing the High Fae have in common is their skin remaining untouched by debt. How much wealth and power amalgamates in this room alone? Yet faeries must deny ourselves children to provide for our families.

Two colonnades run along the space lengthwise, propping up a soaring ceiling, painted with a pastoral scene. Craning my neck, I take in the mural of an enormous tree on the far side of the room, its branches spreading out like thousands of arms, its leaves brilliant gold. The thick trunk descends to a raised dais, where hundreds of roots are woven together, forming an immense but simple seat. The throne.

Floating in the air above the crowd is a sea of candles and crystals refracting the light. Briar and I lean against a shadowed column in the back of the room, my skin still hot with nausea, and she rubs her temple to help her genius adjust.

"You'll get used to it," a faerie says nearby, his gaze trained on the floating candles and crystals. "Been here for a few hours. They know how to taper their geniuses. They just don't want to."

"As with anything else," I mumble.

"We should get to our spot," Briar says. As I kick off the column to join her, the other faerie doesn't follow.

"Where are you stationed?" I ask him.

"Right here." The faerie keeps his head tilted back against the column, attention above. "About three thousand candles light the space. Only about thirty of us control them."

Briar gapes as I search the space and spot faeries and halflings tucked in shadows and alcoves, some sweating, others swaying. The faerie before us looks haggard, sweat pouring down his temples.

"Aren't they enchanted?" my supervisor asks. "How else do they float?"

"It's the prestige of a crafted flame. Burn too quickly, and it'll rain wax. Burn too low and it'll be too dark."

I marvel at the concentration and aptitude, like the control of a dancer on the most minuscule level. "Do you need water?" I ask.

"No."

"Do you want to be by the open windows? Get some fresh air?" Briar wonders.

His brown eyes slide to us. "In Remiti, we do not make windows so large, and the High Fae especially do not purchase this much glass."

"Isn't it quite hot there?" I reply. "Why not?"

He squints. "Windows can be shattered."

A candle smacks the floor by our feet, hot wax splattering against the tile, startling me.

The faerie stares at the candles once more. "I must focus."

Another comes to clean up the mess as Briar tugs me away. We run along the right-side wall, long tapestries draped between the expansive windows, depicting scenes of the Three Planes.

The first tapestry depicts the High Fae with their pale, translucent wings—their truest, most original form—in the celestial plane. The next tapestry shows the earthly plane full of fire and overgrown plants and naked, beastly humans who crawl through mud. The last tapestry centers one descending High Fae, Lucan the Wanderer, wingless but carrying an orb of celestial energy to plant and grow into Lucan's Tree, which spawned the plane of magic.

Briar and I join the servants in the shadows, carrying trays of water and food and sparkling wine, or cloths to mop up mess. I pick up crumpled napkins, discarded feathers and fans from the growing number of High Fae who traipse around the room. Snatches of tongues and tones I've never heard before brush over my ears, and my eyes take in styles of shoes I never could've imagined—tall heels that could take out an eye, loafers that curl upward at the tip. Sometimes I forget how isolated the faeries of the palace of Versara are, even if we live in the heart of our country.

"The columns are square. So austere!" one fae hisses.

"You know the old saying, yes?" another answers. "*There are no curves in Versara but for its females.*"

An eruption of laughter.

"What do you think Prince Maxian's testament will be?"

"I heard his father split the earth itself—"

"From the first kissing king? Perhaps it'll simply be a love bite!"

"Maybe he hasn't married yet because he wants to marry us all."

More laughter.

The harp melody changes and a blare of trumpets echoes from a balcony above the space. Illusion halflings play the start of the procession, and the crowd parts for the arrivals of the head, heir, advisor, and heart of each House. I join the rest of the faeries behind the fae, craning my neck for a glimpse. I spot Kassandra in her dove-gray silk gown, silver hair braided with pearls and tiny pink flowers. Her cream gloves reach up to her elbows. She lifts her chin and places a petite hand in the large palm of the lord next to her.

Lord Dominik.

The heir is dressed in a black tunic trimmed with silver thread, and his sharp features could almost be considered handsome. Still, his vicious dark eyes cut across the room. Kassandra beams up at her brother, cheeks bright with rouge I applied. My stomach lurches. The sky-blue advisor—Lord Tomas—enters behind them, a sage-skinned spouse on his arm.

"Let's go," Briar says.

We follow a parallel path on the outskirts of the crowd, and I snag a tray of sparkling wine. Dominik and Kassandra reach the dais, and he turns, kissing her knuckles. When the heir straightens, his eyes find me. Swallowing, I keep my face plain and neutral like Briar's. I must fail because he smirks, then mouths two words: *Little faerie.*

I recoil.

Dominik strides up onto the dais to the far left of the throne. Part of the new king's Upper Court, the heir represents the Head of Illusion for tonight.

Kassandra glides toward us next to the dais, lips pressed together. "We're going to need more wine than just a tray."

I nod. "I will make sure you're well supplied tonight. Anything you need."

She frowns. "I miss when you were a combative day servant. Not this dribbling Night Crest."

I clench my jaw. *I was never a combative day servant. I just didn't go out of my way to—*

"There you are." Kassandra smirks. "I can taste your vexation, remember?"

Maybe it's the loud throng of bodies or the high expectations for tonight, but it's as if my mistress goads me into playing with her once more.

"Something to wash it down, then?" I hand her a glass. Her eyes spark with mirth as she wraps gloved fingers around the stem.

"I quite like the bitterness." She pauses, tilts her head.

"What is it, my lady?" Briar asks.

"Brace yourself," she says. "Death is here."

Just then, the plane of magic *stops*.

It is like running downhill, legs pumping faster and faster and faster—until I run straight into a stone wall. Briar staggers and I reach forward, legs wobbling. We're not the only ones.

A clang of metal and shattering glass as several faeries fall to the ground. We would be reprimanded any other time, but even the High Fae wave fans, sway, cough. On the dais, Dominik and Eli remain standing, arms clasped behind their backs, undisturbed. Kassandra rolls her eyes, exhaling.

"Go," she waves. "Lean against that pillar over there before you embarrass me."

"Mistress," Briar breathes. "I'm so sorry—"

"It is Death," she says. "Few can stomach the halfling."

The tray tips to one side in my grasp, the glasses sliding. An invisible hand levels it.

I gape at Kassandra, but she turns away in dismissal.

Briar and I stagger into the shadows, reaching for a pillar. I place the tray on the ground, then flop down next to it, panting.

The plane stills further, a muffled, cold thing, like a stone slab sliding over a sarcophagus.

Cool crystal presses against my arm. I glance down as Briar offers sparkling wine. I grin, lowering my voice. "You can't be serious."

"It'll dull your senses. Might be easier if we can't sense the plane at all." An endearing half smile melts years off her face.

We clink and sip. The wine fizzes on my tongue, crisp and light. Sharp like biting into an apple, but with a soft aftertaste. As I drain the glass, I realize she was right—my hold on the plane slips away, and so does the disorientation.

The music strikes up again, warbling this time, trumpets wavering. A ripple goes through the crowd as High Fae step back. Leaning against the column, I haul myself to my feet. Briar comes up next, swaying.

A masked figure stalks through the hall, towering a head above most other fae. A black cloak whips and snaps behind him, its hood pulled over his face.

The only member of the House of Death not banished to the borderlands.

The king's executioner.

He takes his place on the far right of the dais, leaving an empty space next to the throne. My heart stutters. I'm not sure what I suspected under that hood—a skull? A monster? But not a male whose face is wrapped in black cloth save for a slit of olive skin and amber eyes that survey the room. From this view, I spot an enormous sword slung low on one hip.

Briar hiccups next to me. Those amber eyes slice to us. My blood chills under my skin and Briar gives a clumsy curtsy, grabbing the tray from me.

"Look busy," she urges, face red.

"You took my tray!"

"It was mine first."

That gaze slides to the rest of the room until finally, something shifts.

A deep vibration arises from the earth. My eyes flick to the windows, but the night is clear and starry beyond. The candles wobble, some extinguishing. The chandeliers clink and the tiles beneath me tremble until I feel a reverberating energy deep in my bones, skin tingling.

Everyone drops to their knees, High Fae included.

This is Reign magic. Royal power.

Footsteps. I keep my head down, staring at the ground before me. My teeth chatter with the energy.

The footsteps grow closer. Two sets.

Sneaking a glance, I watch the king's advisor, Hector Vandorne, step up the dais, red robe billowing behind him, gray hair pinned back behind large ears. Of mixed noble heritage, he comes from the House of Reign and the House of Healing. Reign may be the oldest and most powerful House, but it's also the smallest. To have a fae with pure Reign blood is an anomaly. It is said there is only one left.

My body shakes as Crown Prince Maxian Vandorne, son of the Sun King, passes right in front of me.

The entire room quakes as the prince climbs the steps and turns, facing the crowd. Impossibly tall and broad-shouldered, the Reign fae has tan skin, honey-brown hair, and a set of piercing violet eyes unlike any color I have ever seen before. They catch the candlelight, glimmering with gold. He wears a robe of the same shade.

I suppose there are worse males. And worse-looking, Kassandra had said. Perhaps she views him like a sibling the way he does her. Or perhaps it is the dirt in me, the faerie, that feels stunned by his terrifying radiance. Whatever the case, Kassandra was misleading.

Prince Maxian Vandorne—Maxian the Mountain—is utterly, brilliantly beautiful.

The ground stops quaking. The plane's energy dies down to a hum.

No one lets out a breath.

"You may rise," he thunders, yet his voice is rich and deep and somehow gentle.

The denizens stand, preening under his attention. Perhaps it's not that Prince Maxian fucks anyone, as Dominik said. Perhaps it's that everyone wants to fuck him.

My mistress turns to me. "Get more sparkling wine. In the time it takes for Hector to give his speech, even the children will have gray hair."

Nodding, I back away as Hector steps forward, and the coronation begins.

Chapter Eight

KASSANDRA IS RIGHT. HECTOR SPEAKS FOR OVER AN HOUR IN A gruff monotone voice that has the High Fae nodding to stay awake. He starts at the beginning, with Lucan the Wanderer.

Lucan, a High Fae of the celestial plane, took pity on the brutish beasts of the earthly plane who devoured and destroyed one another. He brought a piece of the celestial plane with him as he descended, losing his wings, and planted celestial seeds into the earth, spawning a new plane: one of magic.

Lucan's Tree spread magic through the air with its sap and seeds and roots. He and his descendants used their geniuses to access magic, and to guide the beasts and humans into the light. Children of the humans and fae became the faeries, those with little genius. The humans, diseased and distrusting as they were, began dying off. Even the mighty fae could not help the unclean.

As the centuries rolled over, the High Fae fine-tuned their magic until each House could control different areas of the body and soul while faeries merely plateaued in power. It was only logical, then, for the High Fae to govern themselves and the faeries. It was benevolent, truly. So, the Houses divided up the valley of Amyria and governance for the good of all, establishing the system of debt and labor.

House of Death disagreed, and so began the Dark Rebellion. And the rise of General Gregor Vandorne and his Lynx of the

Lowlands, Iros Morella—Kassandra and Dominik's father. Together, they raised armies to defeat even Death itself, banishing the House to the desert as repentance.

"The four Houses perceive the genius differently," Hector says, nodding to Lord Eli. "For House of Healing, it is like a muscle; Illusion, another sense; and for Death, our essence. But the House of Reign never mixed with the humans, and so their geniuses remained pure. In this light, we understand it to be the most important element in all of Amyria: inheritance."

I place a drink in Kassandra's gloved hand, and she knocks it back faster than I can blink.

"Tonight, Prince Maxian Cornelius Vandorne will prove the power of purity. Tonight, the only living descendant of the Sun King, Gregor the General in life and Gregor the Great in death—may he wander well—"

"May he wander well," the crowd echoes.

"—will claim the title of king of Amyria and display his testament. Just as his father did, and his father before him. He will once again prove that the Houses stand longer when they stand together, and guided under one, they can prosper on the same land. So, with great pleasure, I call up the son of the Sun King, the Mountain—Prince Maxian Cornelius Vandorne."

The male rises from the throne. With every step, energy ripples outward, the High Fae swaying. He drops to his knee before his uncle, facing the crowd.

Hector waves his hand. Between one blink and the next, a lacquered box appears in the advisor's grasp. The crowd inhales, murmuring. It is as if Hector pulled the box from the plane itself. He lifts the top and retrieves a golden crown, speckled with rubies and sapphires and diamonds.

"Do you, Maxian Cornelius Vandorne the First, vow to protect and serve the realm until your last breath?"

"I do."

"Do you, Maxian Cornelius Vandorne the First, vow to improve the lives of all under your protection until your last breath?"

"I do."

Protection? I raise a brow.

Hector turns to the other males on the platform. "Will the representative of the House of Illusion please step forward?"

Dominik does, then drops to his knee. Hector repeats the oath of fealty to Eli, representing the House of Healing, and the king's executioner, representing the House of Death. Then he turns to the crowd.

"Do you, noble High Fae of the realm, accept and swear fealty to Maxian Cornelius Vandorne the First, and the House of Reign, should he ascend to the throne?"

A collective "We do."

"We do," I mutter.

"Then"—Hector beams, weathered face crinkling—"as we are all in agreement, I declare Maxian Cornelius Vandorne the First as the head of House Reign and king of Amyria."

He places the golden crown on Maxian's brow.

As the new king rises, he gestures for everyone to do the same. He gives a small smile, almost self-conscious, but mostly endearing. Dominik sweeps up to him, bowing. The king nods in approval and the Heir of Illusion faces the crowd.

Kassandra stiffens as his gaze lies upon her, then slips to me. He raises his fist in celebration or in warning; I am unsure.

"Houses Illusion, Healing, and Death propose an additional title that shall be used in reference to your new status and life as king, and that shall be called upon until your death, when granted a new title."

The king smiles fully now. "And what is this title befitting the life of my reign?"

"We propose 'Maxian the Magnificent'!"

No one moves. Then the king nods, face gleaming in the candlelight. "I accept the title."

The High Fae erupt into cheers and shouts, glasses raised, wine spilling. Someone jostles me from behind, but I plant my feet firmly on the marble. Dominik claps the king's forearm and raises up his fist. The crowd yells in delight.

"Time for the Housewarming gifts!" the Illusion heir shouts. "And more wine!"

The High Fae around us sparkle with laughter. Kassandra turns to me.

"Time to perform," she says.

"Time to impress," I say, ignoring the bubble of nerves.

As the king lounges on the throne, a goblet of wine in hand, the executioner drifts to the bottom of the dais. A pair of servants emerge from the opposite side of the hall carrying a black chest. They lay it before the executioner, who lifts the top. Dominik hovers closer. From my spot up front, I can hear him suck in a breath.

"Three black opals from the House of Death!" he announces.

The shuffling of noble feet, some clapping.

As the chest of gems is placed at the king's feet, he picks one up, holding it to the light. The midnight-black stone catches the light—laden with specks of crimson and orange and sky blue and mint green. The rarest stone in all of Amyria.

Delegates from the House of Healing present their gift next, a range of the finest spices and herbs from the Healing gardens. In the chaos of the crowd, Briar and Kassandra leave to prepare her gift. I haul a giant bucket of water from the servants' entrance.

I watch the back of the room, waiting, hoping, praying to the planes that this works. Dominik expects her to conjure little songbirds, but pretty performances and twinkling tears don't garner favors.

"And the gift from the House of Illusion," Dominik bellows, scanning the room for his sister.

That's my cue.

I heave the bucket in front of the dais. It slops down before the set of stairs, liquid teeming over the edge and splattering onto the tiles. My heart pounds, but I meet the stare of the Heir of Illusion. His lupine grin strains as he bends down so that we are eye to eye.

"What are you doing?" he grits out.

"Presenting a gift for the king."

"Is this some sort of ruse?"

"No." I smile. "It's an Illusion."

"When I get my hands on you—"

"Dom," a voice calls.

Dominik pulls back. The violet focus of the new king falls on me. I curtsy, tugging up my beige skirts.

"Y-Your Magnificence," I stammer.

The sound of fabric shifting. My heart drums louder as the thud of boots crosses the dais.

"You're fucking dead," Dominik hisses, retreating.

"You may stand," the king declares. Again that voice, deep and soft like distant thunder. I straighten and keep my gaze fixed on his boots. A faerie had shined them to gleaming perfection. The king speaks again. "You bring water?"

"Your Magnificence, I . . ."

They are running late. To ensure she doesn't look the fool and I'm not smitten where I stand, I have to think of something. I think of my mother.

Calloused hands peeling potatoes. A calm, melodic voice, telling of the twists and turns of the palace map. Rubbing small feet, sore from hours of running buckets of water in a sweating kitchen. Taking a breath, I cup the sound of my mother's voice in my memory. I draw on that calmness, that alluring lowness, the lilt of her sentences.

"You may look up," the king murmurs.

When I do, I can't breathe at the curiosity curving his brows. He is not angry at a bucket of water; he wants to know why I've placed it here.

He thinks himself an intellectual, Kassandra said. Perhaps he is one.

"As you know, the House of Illusion entertains," I start. Over the king's shoulder, I see Dominik stiffen. "But it is so much more than that. Its females are so much more than that."

Dominik steps forward. "My king, she—"

The king waves a hand. "Is this not one of yours? Let us see what you have taught her."

The Illusion heir glowers. I force myself to look at the tanned face and square jaw of royalty. While his attractiveness should twist my nerves, it does something else. He may be the most powerful creature in this room, but right now I have his attention. He is young to adulthood, like myself. He is a striking stranger who sits across from me in a tavern whose attention I want to capture and keep.

"The House of Illusion does more than entertain. And so can its females, when given the chance," I say. "What is an Illusion? The wise Lord Dominik once said that it is truth in another light. All the Illusion fae do is change the light."

"I see." The king scratches his jaw. "And how does this relate to a bucket of water?"

A small chuckle ripples through the crowd, and I realize the room has gone silent. My nerves rack up, but I focus on that beautiful face. A friend. I am in a tavern, telling a handsome friend a story.

"Tonight, the water will change shape. It will appear as many things, but it is always water. You may see a female in one light. Pretty, delicate . . ." I wet my lips, taking the risk. "Fuckable."

A laugh from the king as he runs a large hand through his bronze locks.

"But a female is many things," I rush on. "As are males. And just like a male, she can perform. She can please. And she can push."

The doors to the entrance hall swing open. A gasp from the crowd. Before retreating from the dais, I speak one last time: "Your gift, from the House of Illusion, Your Magnificence."

But the king's gaze has already caught onto the figure at the back of the room. As I turn, my jaw goes slack. I knew it was coming, and still—I almost fall to my knees at the sight. Kassandra can be cruel, vindictive, spoiled, and jealous. There is a part of me that is twisted and mangled and ashamed of myself because she has said I should be.

Yet she is magnetic. As the doors part, Kassandra enters the throne room atop a pregnant silver mare. The animal nudges forward, flipping her silver mane, and so does Kassandra.

All my lady wears is a constellation of diamonds and pearls that drape across her skin and over her nipples and pool between her thighs. Lingerie made of gems, swirling and streaking along her toned stomach, perfectly curated to her measurements, meant for her wedding night, which has yet to happen. Her lips are a smudge of blood red, as are her sharpened daggerlike nails.

I detest my mistress, but not even I can deny the truth.

She is the most stunning fae in the room.

The loud male swallow behind me indicates I'm not the only one who thinks so.

The crowd parts as the silver mare enters the space. Her sides bulge with a growing foal, though one that will not come for many months. It makes the horse appear larger, more powerful. A mountain of a creature. And the fae atop her like some celestial being.

I back up with the group of nobles who crane their necks. If they could tear their gazes away from Kassandra for a moment, they would see Jeremee, walking along the aisle of people, the horse's reins in his tattooed hands, hovering just at the wings of this performance. And if they were to look beyond Kassandra, which no one is doing but me, they would see Benji with a rake, pushing manure into a contraption.

With Jeremee's help, Kassandra guides the silver mare to the king and Dominik, their mouths agape. It stops about a yard away, stamping at the ground with a hoof. King Maxian blinks as if in a stupor.

Kassandra slides off the mare, Jeremee helping her down. She flashes him a smile, and he blushes. My stomach lurches. To anyone else, he's another Crest; to Kassandra, he's a part of the plan. The king shifts, his jaw sets, a small bulge of muscle on one side.

Kassandra sweeps toward King Maxian and curtsies. He offers a large hand, and she slips hers into his palm. He kisses her knuckles, eyes dipping to her mouth.

"Lady Kassandra."

"Your Magnificence," she hums.

I almost choke at how different her voice sounds. Husky and deep. Intimate in a way that I shouldn't be hearing. But that's the point.

"The Healers say she will have a colt," Kassandra announces, gesturing to the mare.

The water rises out of the bucket, swirling and forming into a shape four feet tall. A foal made of water. The king tears his gaze from Kassandra's breasts to observe the advanced root magic, which shifts and molds into a detailed rendering of the animal. The water horse whinnies, and the crowd gasps at the sound. Even the mare huffs in response.

Kassandra does not just draw upon her root magic. No, she layers her Illusions on top of it. When the water colt tosses his head, the mane swishes.

She continues, "When she gives birth in four months, that silver colt shall be yours. It will be the first silver stallion that the House of Illusion gifts away, and we gladly gift it to you."

The king's eyes spark. "Oh? Well now, count me a lucky male."

A soft chuckle through the crowd. I catch the small step Dominik takes forward. Kassandra levels her brother with a glance.

"Yes," she says, flicking her hand.

The colt springs to life, galloping up and down the throne room, false hooves clacking against real tiles. The High Fae gasp and stumble back as the water creature flies past them.

Kassandra twirls a pointed finger in the air.

From the back of the gallery, the horse breaks into a full sprint. Galloping and galloping, he rushes past the mare, which whinnies, and Jeremee places a hand on her muzzle. The water colt speeds toward the dais.

The king shifts, a hand going to his side. It's then that I spot the weapon of the House of Reign on his belt. The Golden Whip.

Please don't react, I think. *Not yet.*

"Do not fear," Kassandra coos as the colt rushes up from behind.

He flies toward the king, and she holds up a hand. The Illusion halts, then crystallizes into an ice sculpture.

"Would you like to pet him?" she asks.

As he reaches forward, the horse shatters, and thousands of shards pool on the ground at his feet. Kassandra stiffens, the king raising a brow. Behind them, Dominik tuts.

"Cute," he says. "Now, let us continue with our night."

Kassandra purses her lips, gaze narrowing. "Cover your eyes, brother." She looks to the king. "Do you prefer diamonds or pearls?"

"What?" both males say.

My heart thuds. *What the planes is she up to?*

"Diamonds or pearls, Your Magnificence?" My mistress gestures to the glittering gems skimming her body.

The king pauses. "Diamonds."

An interesting choice. Diamonds are the lesser jewel—there are so many of them—but then again, they are the hardest gemstone in Amyria.

"I knew you were a male of practicality," Kassandra says.

Diamonds begin plucking off her lingerie, the spider silk stringing them together falling away from her body like strands of hair.

"For fuck's sake . . ." Dominik glances away.

I gawk as a year of work is deconstructed. The jewels float off her body, the pearls scattering across the floor. For several moments, the diamonds just hover in the air like raindrops captured in time. Kassandra breathes, sweat beading her upper lip. The diamonds swirl in the air.

"An unbreakable reign deserves an unbreakable weapon."

The gemstones glow, twist, form a giant lump that spins and spins as it elongates. A shape emerges, the bottom half sculpting into a hilt. A sparkling dagger.

Kassandra has forged a dagger out of diamonds.

"For you, Your Magnificence," she says, swaying.

She floats the weapon toward the king. He watches it, puzzled, but reaches forward. His hand grips the handle, plucking the object from the air itself.

The crowd gasps.

I blink, and blink again. Kassandra's Illusion is so powerful it seems real. It seems . . . material. Maybe it is—but that would be an impossible feat.

No one seems to breathe.

Then the king holds up the knife. "A diamond dagger!" he announces, and the room erupts into enthusiastic applause.

Kassandra tips backward, a shimmer around her as energy returns to the plane. Jeremee catches her, naked and shaking, eyes rolling into the back of her head. The nobles around us surge closer to the dais for a better look, whispering:

"—have you ever seen—"

"But a female?"

Briar throws a cloak over the fae as I reach her side. Her head lolls back.

"That was . . ." Jeremee glances down at her limp body. "I didn't know they could do that."

"I don't think Illusion can," I say.

Briar shakes her head. "I'll grab some water."

Locating the smelling salts, I pull them out of my pocket. They were in case the water foal trick fatigued her, but that wasn't the grand Illusion for which she stored the plane on her skin. She had come up with her own grand plan. A public display of female power. Respect blooms inside me.

I hold the salt under her nose. My mistress gasps. Her face is pale, sweaty. Eyes bloodshot. In a moment, Briar is back with a goblet of water, tipping the liquid into Kassandra's mouth. Jeremee props her on her feet.

"On the horse," I say.

He lifts her shuddering frame up onto the mare's back, sidesaddle. She leans against the horse's neck, wrapping an arm around the creature, clutching the cloak to her figure. Jeremee wraps the reins around her wrist.

"Did we do it?" she groans. "Are they dazzled?"

I glance up at the dais as the males of the inner circle examine the diamond dagger. I turn back to Kassandra.

"You did," I say, smiling.

My mistress smiles back.

It doesn't last long.

Not as her brother strides forward, slicking his hair back. His beady black eyes find us. He wanted a performance. She gave him one.

"A powerful trick." The king beams, dropping onto his throne. "Maybe even more powerful than you, Dom."

The High Fae chortle, some sneaking glances at Lord Dominik.

The air rushes around us with the icy feel of an Illusion. Dread sinks into my stomach as the sound of Dominik's voice hisses in our ears, low and biting. *What the fuck have you done?*

Kassandra flinches.

"High Fae of the realm," Dominik calls to the room, face flushed. After they quiet, he bows to the king. "For your patience during my sister's Illusion performance and as a gesture of goodwill between our two Houses, I would like to grant you one last gift."

"Two gifts from Illusion!" Maxian says. "I truly am lucky, aren't I?"

The High Fae laugh uneasily. Dominik stalks off the dais, unbridled rage glinting in his eye. Jeremee tenses beside me, and Kassandra struggles to sit up.

Dominik's going to hurt her, I think with sudden clarity. Right here, in front of everyone, he will hurt her.

"You," Dominik snarls. Kassandra stifles a sob.

Dimly aware of Jae hissing my name, I step in front of her, drawing to my full height. I may only have root magic, but my genius is not drained. Dominik bares his canines.

I bare mine back.

"No one comes between us," the male seethes. "No one."

Instead, the Heir of Illusion grabs me, yanking me into his chest. Another hand clamps down on my startled cry. Dominik reeks of wine and sweat and something stronger. He's not just angry; he's drunk and unraveling.

A frozen whisper in my ear. "Now, you're going to behave—"

I bite his palm and the fae grunts.

"You just made it so much worse," he says. Then he lets go. I sway for a moment.

"Avvie?" a small voice asks behind us.

Benji.

I forgot he was there, and that was the point of his role tonight. I glance back to see Benji and Jae looking at me with expressions of undiluted terror. Before I can tell them it'll be okay, Dominik shoves me toward the dais. I tumble toward the ground, but invisible hands right me on my feet, squeezing my arms.

"Lord Dominik?" the king asks, sitting forward.

Before me are the most powerful males in the realm. King Maxian Vandorne, his advisor, the executioner, and the Head of Healing. Their gazes all fall onto me, and my body trembles with the power flooding the plane. If it weren't for Dominik's invisible hands, I would not stay upright.

"Our most loyal night servant." Dominik gestures. "You may have her."

My stomach bottoms out.

If I go to Reign, what will happen to Jeremee and Benji? I can't slip coins in their pockets if I no longer live in the Nest. I've never even met another faerie from the center of Versara. No, it's too soon. Jae and I are talking tomorrow.

Please don't let me go, I think. *Please.*

"She is yours," Dominik tells the king.

"Wait!" Kassandra cries from behind us.

Surprise murmurs through the crowd.

The king's attention slips over my shoulder, his forehead shiny, the crown crooked.

He's drunk, I understand. *They're all drunk.* The service has been going on for hours, and they're bored. Bored fae break things for fun.

"Lady Kassandra?" the king asks.

A shuffling of feet, then a pause.

I understand even as a faerie: *Illusion looks divided.*

"She . . ." Kassandra clears her throat. "She does my hair the way I like."

Dominik pinches the bridge of his nose.

The king's attention swivels back to me, a grin tugging at his lips. Every part of me screams to drop to my knees, to look away. A primal instinct, bowing to the stronger predator. Yet I plead with the king, unmasking my fear and desperation and hope, purging my potent genius onto the plane around us.

He cocks his head, nostrils flaring.

"We can share her, if you'd like," he says. "A gesture of goodwill, as your brother calls it."

"Your Magnificence, do not feel for my sister over this servant. Kassandra gets attached easily—"

Lie, lie, lie.

The king holds up a hand to stop Dominik. "I will share the faerie, since I love my dagger so much," he says. "Two moon cycles with me, then one with you."

"Thank you," Kassandra whispers. "Thank you."

This must be an Illusion, a nightmare, another world.

The phantom hands let go. I sink to my knees, head bowed before the king, who still lounges on his throne.

"Your Magnificence," I whisper.

"Besides, Max," Dominik mutters, so that only the Upper Court and I can hear. "You did say you enjoyed the faerie's mouth. Now you can enjoy it almost every night."

A sob escapes me.

Movement to the right of the throne. The king's executioner says in a gravelly voice, "I wouldn't do that, boy—"

Something brown splatters against Dominik's silver tunic. He shrieks, and a rank smell cascades over me.

Horse manure.

The executioner flashes forward and lifts up a small faerie boy with golden curls. I catch a glimpse of Benji's round face, streaked with tears.

The court explodes into chaos.

Chapter Nine

Shouts puncture the air, and the stink of dung fills the halls. The High Fae jostle one another to get a better look at the Heir of Illusion covered in horse shit. Pure terror grips me, and Jae cries out Benji's name, but the mare rears, and he pulls the reins. Dominik throws himself toward Benji in the hands of the executioner.

"You fucking disgusting faerie!" he screams. "I will *kill*—"

"Silence!" King Maxian thunders. The ground trembles. The chandeliers swing above, and glass explodes. The room halts, and a rockslide of power tumbles through my body, freezing my muscles.

I drop to my knees and curl forward. Groans escape those who fall around me.

Get up, I tell my legs. *Get up!*

But my muscles are held by the will of another.

Crashes echo through the coronation hall as the crowd drops to the marble tiles, necks craning to look up at the throne. My breath becomes stifled, as if my lungs are petrifying to stone.

Thousands of candles undulate, hot wax sprinkling onto the crowd, and King Maxian waves his fingers, pulling the lights up again. He draws to his full height, no strain in his calm face.

"Now," he says. "I have allowed you all to drink and swear and even squabble at my coronation."

My gaze stays glued to him, eyes burning. I itch to blink but cannot.

"I will not tolerate the mockery this night has turned into. I am your king, so let me make that clear. This is my testament tonight. Remember this feeling."

My nose presses against the ground. A collective whine fills the space as others are pressed forward, I can only assume.

The crunch of boots over ice shards.

"Executioner, bring me the boy."

My genius thrashes, reaching out for the plane of magic, searching for water or a plant or dirt I can call to, can ask aid from, but it slams into that rock wall of power. It can only claw at the inside of my skull like a caged animal, spitting and scratching and raking nails against the hold of Reign.

My vision blurs and stings with tears, as I cannot blink.

"You have few tattoos," the king observes. "Yet you are a stable boy?"

Silence.

"You may speak."

"Y-yes, Your Magnificence," Benji stammers. My heart splinters.

"Why do you have so little debt? Surely you inherited some. Go on, speak."

"M-my brother."

I cringe.

"Is he alive?"

"Yes, Your Magnificence."

"Point to him. Yes—you must."

More movement. Tears drip onto the marble.

"Blink," the king commands.

I do. The exhale of breath around me, the tiniest relief. My vision clears, throat straining with a trapped scream at the horror before me. Jeremee was right.

The grout is pink.

"I want everyone's attention!"

My head snaps up, as do the heads of everyone else in the room in unison.

The executioner stands before the king, a gloved hand on the nape of Jeremee's and Benji's necks. Two of the most powerful males of the realm holding on to my boys.

My family, my mind weeps. *My family.*

The king waves at the crowd. "Blink again. I want everyone to see."

My cheeks dampen.

"You have so many debt rings, and yet your brother has so few?" the king says to Jeremee.

"I took on all of our parents' save one, Your Magnificence."

"Why?"

"I wanted to protect my brother."

The royal's face twitches. "You should've given him more. It would've taught him respect and courtesy for the fae."

Jeremee and Benji don't move. With my eyes still trained on the dais, I cannot find Kassandra or Briar or Glenn. No one is stepping in to help. No one can.

"Hector," the king calls, and his advisor rises from his spot near the front. "What would my father have done?"

"Whipped them, and if they survived, sent them to the mines to work until death."

"But I am not my father," King Maxian says. "So I will be swift. The punishment will be dealt tonight, then no more."

Something glints in the candlelight, movement like a snake uncoiling from the king's side. Benji starts to sob.

"Please," Jeremee chokes out. "He's only a child, a baby, truly. Please."

Realization hits me. My genius twists inside my mind, desperate to get out, to stop this. *Planes, no. No, please.*

The Golden Whip.

After a hot, dry summer full of dead crops, my grandmother took the punishment for her field, according to my mother. She died after three lashes. How many can a child endure?

A shriek swells in my chest.

Jeremee drops to his knees of his own volition. "Please, he's just a boy. Our parents are dead. The responsibility rests on my shoulders—"

The king tilts his head, listening.

"I beg you, punish me instead. I will take what he owes. I will give anything."

The royal holds up his hand. "I have heard your points and agree you will receive the punishment. Your brother will know he is the reason for your suffering, and that will be his burden."

Relief and terror seize me at once, like the heat and cold of a fever.

No, I think. No, I will. I will because Jeremee has given so much already. Jeremee has nothing left to give. He cannot keep giving.

"However," the king says, "I'm not the one who was humiliated. Dominik?"

The silver-haired lord staggers to his feet several bodies ahead of me, brushing dirt off his clothes.

The king gestures. "You shall have to settle for the older of the two. What shall be the appropriate punishment for your debasement tonight?"

I do not see Dominik's face, but I wonder if he has the gall to smile.

"Death," he says.

No. Spittle sprays from my gritted teeth, a guttural growl ripping out. Tears blur my vision.

The king watches his friend, expression darkening. Finally, he speaks. "I'm a male of my word. A quick death it shall be. We will not offer the drawn-out suffering of the whip or the mines or the Walk."

No!

Jeremee hangs his head. The king's executioner steps away from Benji. The boy wails but, through the king's power or his own fear, remains frozen in place. The cloaked figure strides before Jeremee.

"Blink," the king whispers, and the room does. Only this time the anger leaves his face, leaving behind a grim expression. The king's executioner does not reach for his sword. He places a hand on Jeremee's forehead.

Blood fills my mouth, my tongue cut, my forehead pulsing with strain. The protest does nothing. Jeremee twists his neck, scanning the crowd. Our eyes meet and it is agony.

I'm here, I try to scream. *I'm here. I love you. I—*

Jeremee parts his lips, but it is too late. In a blink I cannot take, my best friend is rendered red mist.

He becomes nothing.

Nothing.

Not even a singular shoe remains.

No body to bury. No cold hand to hold.

Just one touch to the forehead and his entire existence is . . . *Just. Gone.*

Benji drops to the ground, wailing. No one moves, not even the king, as the child writhes and screams, his pain echoing in the otherwise silent, cavernous hall.

Then the first of the black rings sear his thin arms. His screams pitch higher.

I cling to consciousness. I try. I try.

But tattoos strangle the sensitive skin, and Benji is shrieking like the day he suffered the mistake of being born. Only now the whole of his small body is marred with debt, and he is not the same child as the moment before.

Benji is an Unluckie.

I can fight it no longer. Darkness takes me under.

PART TWO

House of Reign

*Before the beginning, after the end.
Magic never gives, only lends.*

—UNESSE PROVERB

Chapter Ten

Days pass. I beg to see Benji. The child refuses to speak, skin raw from new tattoos, and so Glenn and the other roommates sequester him. And because Kassandra does not call, I remain leaden on my cot, drowned at the bottom of a swamp. Through the muck and dark, I float. I sink.

Someone leaves water by my bedside. I reach for it only when the itch of thirst becomes unbearable. Someone speaks muffled words to my waterlogged senses. I nibble on stale bread left behind. I throw it up.

My knees are still pressed to that floor. I am still watching.

Doing nothing as my life disintegrates into nothing.

Every inhale is for Benji, each exhale for Jeremee.

Only for them.

I must keep breathing for when my little brother is ready to see me.

A splash of water. My body jolts awake, my knuckles grazing stones. My soaked clothes stick to my skin. Briar places the empty bucket on the ground.

"I guess you'll have to change now."

I shiver. "Why'd you—"

"You smell."

"Well, I—" Coughing, I try again. "What I need is—"

"Let's start with a glass of water and a bath. New clothes. Then we can talk."

"I don't want to talk."

"You want to rot, I know. But your mistress is awake and I thought you might want to show your face before starting your night service at Reign."

I look up. "Awake?"

"She's been sleeping, restoring her genius, but now she's up. We don't want her to know you've been resting."

"Resting?" I seethe. "My friend is dead."

Briar puts her hands on her hips. Circles under her eyes, frown lines round her mouth. She's been covering for me in all aspects.

"You can take your grief with you," Briar says, softer now.

I am so tired of grieving. I grieved my mother when lumps formed beneath her armpits and she couldn't lift her head. It was slow and deep, the careful erosion of the faerie I knew into a sallow, frail creature who soiled the bed. Each piece that the sickness took from her also took from me, as I changed and washed her, fed and held her for that last, rattling breath. She was my creator, and I her keeper. I will despise and cherish those last few months together.

Jeremee is the reason I survived losing her. Only she could've gotten me through the loss of him. Now they are both gone.

"I want my mom," I sob. "I need my mom."

"Oh, honey." Briar melts onto the cot beside me, but she doesn't reach out, and for this I am also grateful.

Balling up my hands, I press fists into my thighs. "She said to look at the floor. Always look at the floor, don't walk too quickly or too slowly, and never show my full genius in front of them, and I hated her for saying it and so I didn't—I didn't listen." I hiccup. "I wouldn't listen. And now, because of me, Jeremee—he's—"

Briar lets me cry. I hadn't known I had any tears left, and it hurts so much, this ceaseless anguish, the despair at the infinite cruelty of the High Fae.

When my cheeks ache and the tears dry, Briar takes a breath.

"I do not know what faith you follow," she says carefully. "But I will mourn with you in any manner."

I blink, glancing at her. "You did not convert to the High Fae faith of the Three Planes?"

Briar looks to the closed door, then back at me. "Just because it is illegal to be Unesse does not mean it is wrong."

The ancient faerie faith, one only murmured in storage spaces and bunkrooms by the older generations. My mother never ascribed to one or another, and for once, I wish the High Fae are right about the Three Planes. Perhaps my mother is helping Jeremee find his path in the celestial realm.

I sniff, adjusting on the cot. "Tell me more."

"Everything pulses with energy, no matter how small, and therefore everything has a genius, a soul. Magic is a call and response between two energies, and we are all one connected system of nerves across existence that began with the Tree. Of life, of magic—they are the same."

"And . . . the High Fae?" I wonder.

"What about them?"

"Did they not bring magic down from the celestial plane? Are Lucan's Tree and the Tree of Life one and the same?"

"I believe so," she answers. "The difference is that the High Fae think they own it, but under Unesse, they do not."

"Then who does?"

She chuckles. "No one. You can't own something that was never yours. In fact, there's no ownership in Unesse, only stewardship."

"What do you mean?"

"There's a saying in Unesse," she whispers. "*Before the beginning, after the end. Magic never gives, only lends.* They borrow life and magic just like the rest of us."

She will not say *our masters,* but I do not need her to. Still, it sounds like a nursery rhyme to comfort faerie children for the little control we have over our lives. Looking down at my sullied dress I wore for the coronation, I think that maybe I am no different.

"Come on," Briar says, standing. "Let's get you cleaned up."

But I don't want to scrub away the sweat and tears I shed that day. It's all I have left of him. I want to seethe and choke on my rage until it boils me from the inside out. I want to wrestle and fight and scream and rip down the sky. I want to burn.

My clothes feel warm. My hand touches my tunic. Dry.

The smell of soil, of spring rain lingers in the air. Root magic, faerie magic. *My magic.*

At some point, I had evaporated the water.

"I've never done that before," I say.

"Still doesn't count as a bath," Briar replies. She holds out her hand.

Begrudgingly, I take it.

CHOKING DOWN FAERIE food was challenging when, as a child in the kitchens, I saw where it came from. The sawdust in the flour, maggots in the meat, cockroaches in the coffee grounds. Now it's near impossible. The turnip mash sticks to the back of my throat.

You must eat, I tell myself. *You cannot be there for Benji if you do not.*

Settled on a bench in the Nest, hair damp, I glower at the bowl in front of me. I swallow, each bite a battle.

I see the child before he sees me.

Ringed in black from head to toe, Benji's pallid skin is hardly visible save for his face. His expression is drawn, eyes purple with fatigue, mouth pinched in a frown, shoulders slumped. A cohort of male faeries surrounds him—Jeremee's roommates, who encase and protect the boy. One of them bends down, a shimmer of blond. *Glenn.* They glance my way. Benji shrugs Glenn off, marching in my direction.

I stand, aching to run to him, to sweep the child into my arms and drop kisses on his face. But the glint of fury in his gaze keeps me rooted to the spot.

"Benji," I breathe when he's in earshot.

The boy stops, the table between us. His bottom lip quivers. Tears slide down my cheeks that I can't bring myself to wipe away.

My voice cracks. "Benji."

His eyes glisten as he wipes his nose with the back of his hand.

"I hate you," he spits. I flinch. Behind Benji, so does Glenn. "You and your ideas got my brother killed."

"I am so, so sorry—"

"I *hate* you, Avery. I hate you and I will never, ever forgive you."

He wipes his face again, then glares at me with a might that shakes his small frame, so fragile now, so weighed down in dues.

This is better, I think. *I'd rather he hate me than the king. It is safer this way.*

"I hope the king hurts you," he says. "I wish for it, and I hope the plane delivers."

I suck in a breath.

"Benji," Glenn says behind him.

"I never want to talk to you ever again."

"Wait—"

My shin knocks into the wooden bench, bruising, as I maneuver around the table. It's too late. Benji slips through the crowd, and I feel a gentle hand on my arm.

"Let him go for now," Glenn says.

"I . . ." My throat feels tight. "I don't know what to say."

"Me either."

He drops his hand, his eyes red, face puffy from crying, hair mussed. An image comes to mind, the gentle graze of his thumb against Jeremee's ribs. The way they look at each other. Looked.

"You loved Jae," I say.

"Of course I did."

"You really loved him."

Glenn glances around the crowded space. "I don't know what you mean."

"I would never report," I say, low.

His eyes fill, and he glances away. This time, my hand finds his shoulder. We stand apart, wordless, as the room bustles around us. Faeries rush by with clothing, halflings with their creditor's papers, the general mirth and convivial nature of the Nest restored for most. The death of a palace faerie is not uncommon.

Even if Jeremee were still alive, he and Glenn could never officially pledge to each other, never receive the one-time, one-ring debt forgiveness bestowed to married faeries of opposite sex. They could never have been together in public, never have told anyone except those they trusted to keep a secret. But it's no matter. A loss is a loss is a loss.

"I am sorry," I rasp. "It is all so unfair."

"I was happy to love him in secret until I no longer had the breath to tell him," he says. My chest cracks just a little more, but then Glenn clears his throat. "Benji cannot carry all that guilt and anger and sorrow, so he's taking it out on others."

I rummage in my apron and offer up two copper coins. "Say this is from you. Spending money, so he can put his entire salary toward the debts."

"He loved you as well." Glenn cradles the money as if it's something precious. "I wish you safety, Avery."

He runs a trembling hand through blond hair, trying to grant luck and outweigh Benji's wish. An old faerie tradition, but from what faith I do not know. The plane now has two requests it could fulfill: to harm or harbor me.

To Glenn, I can't voice the lurking thoughts. That I agree with Benji. I want to take the punishment, all of it. Enough pain, and maybe it will tip the scales, bring Jeremee back. I wish for it.

"See you," he attempts, giving me a final hug before disappearing into the crowd again.

"See you," I say to no one.

But I don't see how to put back together my family.

Maybe Briar was right. You can't own something that was never yours.

Chapter Eleven

That evening, the muggy air coats my clammy skin. I scratch at my hairline, then lift my waves to cool my neck.

"Will you stop fidgeting?" Kassandra hisses ahead, never looking back at me. Her dusty-rose gown cuts into a V down her back and flutters away from her waist.

"Apologies," I mutter. We stroll in the cloisters surrounding the Illusion courtyards, the evening light dipping every leaf and stem in scarlet.

To our left, the hedge heights rise and fall like rolling hills. Even now, I still have yet to grasp the shape of the Illusion grounds, a winding labyrinth that twists on precarious whims. Only from the movements of the sun that stream through her windows have I been able to gather that Kassandra's apartments occupy the southern wall, her parents' apartments on the eastern side, above us at this moment.

I barely spoke a word to Kassandra when I appeared for service early in the evening. I could hardly look at her without thinking of Jae, of him catching her in his arms after she formed the diamond dagger. That she and the king's executioner were the last to touch him. Stemming the grief and rage and hatred in order to function felt like choking down more faerie food.

If Kassandra hadn't saddled him with more debt, I never would have become her Night Crest. Wouldn't have suggested the scheme in the first place. If she had just stopped at the water foal, the plan would have gone perfectly.

Yes, Jeremee's death is my fault. It is also hers.

Dread grips me now at where we are headed. An invitation to Kassandra from the king had popped into the air early into my shift, asking her to accompany him tonight for a stroll through the Illusion courtyards.

To distract myself, I ask, "How did the king make that note appear?"

"Ah, finally decided to talk to me tonight?" Kassandra says, and I feel a flash of loathing. "The note was laced," she explains. "Moved through the plane like Hector did with the crown box at the coronation." I try to ignore the rise of memories. Kassandra goes on. "There's an old fae nursery rhyme, 'Houses and Mouses,' to help children remember the abilities of each House in addition to root magic. 'Matter and Mind / Blood and Bone / The Many Senses / The Severed Soul / Live one / Wed another'—" She stops. "You get the point. 'The Many Senses' refers to Illusion's ability to manipulate the senses into perceiving what isn't there. 'Blood and Bone' is Healing's power to stimulate blood flow and mend bones. 'Severed Soul' is Death."

"And 'Matter and Mind' is Reign," I say.

"What does control look like, exactly? Is it the rock that directs where a river flows? Or is it the river that erodes the rock over time, carving its path? Control takes many forms, and Reign decided to name itself. Matter and Mind."

"And lacing is the control of matter?" I ask.

"It's Reign magic that works in tandem with the plane. The king broke down the very matter of the parchment so he could weave its essence into the plane on the smallest level. He can then zip the letter through the plane to a desired location and separate out its essence into earthly matter once more. Hector laced the box and crown from a safe location to his hands last week."

"He remade it," I say.

"More like re-formed it. The Vandornes seem to be the only fae who can do it."

I bite my lip. "Could you use the plane to lace an Illusion to someone? Not a physical letter but perhaps the appearance of one? Or an auditory message like what . . . when Lord . . ."

What the fuck have you done? her brother had seethed right before he did the unthinkable.

Kassandra quirks a brow. "Since when do you think before you speak?"

"Since there is much to think about."

We fall silent, passing an Illusion guard in silver armor, a bow slung over his shoulder. The arched cloister meets another, and based on the setting sun, we've reached the northern side. The temperature drops in the shade. Halfway down the corridor, Kassandra stops in front of a break in the stone, an entryway that leads into a hedge. She strides forward, the air wavering, and melts into the plant.

A mirage. Great.

I bite the inside of my cheek, trying to discern the edges of the Illusion, lest I scratch an eye on a real branch. The plant in front of me smells fresh, earthy. It appears detailed. Yet when the wind blows, a cluster of leaves remains stagnant while the surrounding ones tremble. It's a small, discreet opening. I reach forward, and my hand disappears behind a curtain of cool haze.

I step through the Illusion. Twinkling lights greet me, small glowing orbs that float through a courtyard. Rosebushes encompass the space, complete with stone benches and an empty birdbath in its center, the pedestal dripping with vines.

Kassandra perches on a bench, eyes closed, the fading sunset drenching her in tangerine, her silver hair licked by fire. A second-story stone balcony peeks above the enclosed hedges.

"My lady," I start. "If you'd like some more privacy, we could choose another courtyard?"

"This is perfect."

My boots crunch over gravel, finding a shaded spot in the corner. The courtyard cools in the elongating shadows. Still, a bird chirps, and the plane hums a lovely, low presence. Fresh air expands my lungs.

Jae would have loved this place.

My genius twitches to life. I haven't felt it in days, too weighed down by grief.

Go away, I tell it, anger rising at the memory of helpless scratching. *You're useless.*

The genius spasms. As if I am the one who failed it and not the other way around. As faeries, we're told that this part of us is simply another tool, like hands for scrubbing and legs for bowing. Yet sometimes, mine acts as a separate entity inside me, with its own needs and wants.

Go. Away.

"Are you arguing with the ants?"

I snap back to the dusky courtyard. My mistress still lounges on the stone bench, not looking my way.

She waves a hand. "Your ire is like peppercorn under the nose."

"*How?* How can you sense my emotions?"

Kassandra tenses. I suck in a breath, shocked at my own bluntness. But shock soon fades to apathy. I have spoken out of turn; I will be punished.

Instead, my mistress tilts her head. "Do you remember when I picked you? When all the faeries lined up, the parlor stank. I couldn't figure it out because the smell was being picked up by my genius first, not my nose. It was a magical marker of some kind. I had never sensed such a thing before. It was . . . fascinating."

That day, every breath had been torture, so heavily I missed my mother, who had passed only weeks before. I hated being in that gilded room, watching Kassandra survey our lineup, a Healer tending blisters from her shoes. Not when my mother refused a Healer despite my begging.

I will not put you in such debt, she had rasped toward the end. Even when I brought one anyway, she tried to bite off the

Healer's finger. Debt or death. She had been determined to die without treatment to spare me a century of repayment. So as Kassandra stomped around her parlor that day with bandages for a blister, the other Scarps had trembled with fear, but I trembled with hate. With fury. For we already cannot afford to live, and still, they ensure that we cannot afford to fucking die.

"There you are," Kassandra says now. "Stinking of that feeling again."

"Is this a facet of Illusion magic?" I manage through clenched teeth. "To sense the emotions of others?"

"No." She shakes her head, and I fall quiet. "You have another question," she states.

Her permission takes me by surprise. "Faeries understand that most High Fae can smell fear because sometimes . . . well, sometimes, we can smell our own. If it's strong enough."

"Metallic and sharp, like blood." My mistress smooths out her skirt, her face hidden behind curls I styled. "Yours is the only full spectrum of emotions I've been able to perceive."

The silence that follows is deep and unsettled.

Finally, I ask, "Is this why you picked me, my lady?"

"I picked the rot in you," she says. "I picked you, for I do not like feeling as if it only exists in me."

Silence again. We have crossed so many lines in this conversation, I do not know where we stand anymore.

"What is the rot in you, my lady?"

My mistress does not move, as if to do so would break the spell. She breathes and says so quietly I almost miss it, "That I look at other females."

The words slice through the swamp of grief I've been drowning in. So we are both rotten in more ways than one. A faerie servant who can't manage her pride and the Heart of Illusion who cannot beat for High Fae lords.

She has trusted me with a dangerous secret. One that, if revealed in the wrong light, could get us both punished. It's harmless, cute even, when adolescents are simply practicing with one another for their husbands one day. It's fine when males are allowed to leer, to cheer on and grope afterward. Yet a lady married to another does not create an heir, does not continue a legacy of wealth. A female faerie married to another does not produce a worker. A debt system only works if the owed and the owned both multiply.

I would not out another, even a High Fae. To do so is to risk their life. But Kassandra is about to meet the king for an evening tryst and tonight I am feeling curious and reckless.

Cocking my head, I ask my mistress: "Is that all?"

"What do you mean, is that all? It's illegal!" She looks over her shoulder, profile rimmed in red light.

"It's illegal to touch another female," I say. "The law says nothing about looking."

Her throat bobs. "Have you . . . do you look, too?"

I hate her. I hate that my service to her cost me everything. Yet I want to heat her blood. The closest I can get to spilling it—taking control from them as they have taken from me.

"I'm looking right now," I murmur.

"Stop." Her eyes flick over my thin cotton dress as a breeze picks up. Its coolness pebbles my nipples against the fabric. She looks forward again, crossing her legs on the bench.

"Avery."

My heart thunders. "Yes?"

Then her body goes rigid, hand abandoning the loose thread of her skirt I will need to repair.

"The king is here." She clears her throat. "He has company."

The intimacy of the moment vanishes like the last of the sun's rays. The garden falls into soft shadows. A rumble of air, then a figure materializes in front of Kassandra.

The king steps forward from nothing, an inverse of Jeremee's death.

My mistress perks up at the arrival of my best friend's murderer, extending a hand to be kissed. Once again, we are the player and the played, my safety like a pawn in those delicate fingers.

The king wears a loose white tunic and brown riding pants, casual but of quality. The luxurious leisure feels stark against the memories of kneeling on marble lined with pink grout, the glint of the Golden Whip, the crook of the crown.

The royal grins. "Kass."

"Max," my mistress breathes, a sultry façade that grates against me, as if we had not just been . . . *looking* at each other. The pink flush of her cheeks and sparkle in her eye paint her as the perfect blushing bride. I ate from her palm like a bird, and once again, it is hard to tell what is an Illusion in this place. The thick floral aroma of the garden is sweet and heady and nauseating, like strong perfume sprayed in a confined space.

"Hope you don't mind the presence of Death," the king is saying.

"How else would we feel alive?" Kassandra asks.

Maxian barks a laugh. The air behind him darkens. Smoke with no source pours onto the gravel, wisping across grass. The plane petrifies. The king's executioner emerges from the black cloud.

My vision swims, my legs weakening.

"What's that smell?" the king announces. "It's like a bloodbath out here."

A bloodbath. My fear saturating the plane, bloody as the gentle mist my friend became.

My knees sink into damp soil, my fingernails digging into grass. Someone clutches my elbow to keep me from collapsing entirely. A phantom hand, firm but assuring.

A familiar, cold voice says, "She's unused to lacing, you see. A weak thing."

"Faeries always fold to great power," Maxian says. "It's simply their nature."

A new emotion rises from the depths of the swamp, like a shoal, like anger. I lean into that sensation, like trekking onto a desolate island where the sand burns the arches of my feet. It is grounding, painful. I breathe again, and this time my head steadies, my vision coming back into focus.

When I glance up, the king stares down at me, his golden skin seeming to glow in the evening light. Draped on his arm, small fingers trailing along his muscles, is Kassandra, her face impassive once more. They are like a marriage portrait, striking and grand and distant, and I feel like a thief caught with a blade in hand before I could cut the canvas.

Something must shift in my face, because the king quirks a brow.

"She's back," he mutters, then waves a hand. A goblet of water appears, and he holds it out to me, lips twitching into a smile. "Here you are, faerie."

My hand itches to smack the glass from his grip, shatter it across the ground. How dare he? How dare he bestow charity upon me as easily as he sent my friend to death and a child to impossible debt? As if I could forget his malice in the face of a smiling offer.

"Avery," Kassandra quips, voice tight and high. "The king is gracious enough to overlook your blunder and even seeks to aid you. Do not insult him with your slowness."

I lean back onto my feet and stand. Head down, brushing dirt off my palms, I mumble, "My apologies, Your Magnificence. It was the grandness of your power that overwhelmed me."

"I can understand that," the king acknowledges, like a benevolent handler.

The goblet of water floats before me, but not on some precarious phantom wind like Illusion magic. My ears roar with Reign power as one side of the goblet is blurred, as if stitched into the plane itself. He is, in a way, lacing again.

I take the crystal, surprised to find it heavy, the real thing, and take the expected sip. Cool liquid calms me. The king nods in approval, and Kassandra tugs him toward the bench once more.

"That wasn't necessary, Max, but it is appreciated," she coos as they sit side by side. Across the garden opposite me, the king's executioner watches the scene.

"You seem surprised," Maxian says.

"More so impressed. Even as king, you have kept your kindness."

"My mother wouldn't have allowed me to be any other way."

"May she wander well."

"May she wander well," he echoes. "How is your father?"

"Aging."

"As we all are. Though I can't complain in your case. You've grown into a magnificent female."

"As magnificent as you?"

"You tease, but I see you're already flushed."

I wrinkle my nose. Glancing away, my eyes catch the amber ones of Death, glowing like coals in a dark hearth. I push my repulsion back like bile.

Kassandra clears her throat. "Some privacy, perhaps."

A laugh. "Then why are we stationed beneath your brother's balcony?"

The stone balcony that overlooks this courtyard.

"He's out," she snips. "Would you rather sit beneath my father's, where we can feel his stale breath?"

"What of yours?"

"You know a lady cannot do that."

"Ah, yes, and you are the finest of them all. Even with that mouth of yours."

Wincing, I glance at Dominik's glass balcony doors, which remain dark. *You did say you enjoyed the faerie's mouth. Now you can enjoy it almost every night.*

Does the king truly dole out the same lines to fae females and faeries? Has three hundred years of flirting left the males of the Upper Court lazy even in their vileness?

"Careful now," Kassandra tuts. "Talk like that won't give our onlookers time to leave."

"I see," Maxian growls.

He grips her waist and hauls her sideways onto his lap. Her slipper flings off a foot, and she squeals in delight. I head for the hedge where the Illusion still shimmers. My fingers graze the mirage, the image of the leaves rippling like a reflection on a pond.

I'm not sure what makes me look back. Perhaps it's the sudden change in Kàssandra's demeanor, my genius fumbling to feel if she has fallen under Reign magic. Yet the plane hums pleasantly, consistently, around us. The king slides his hands through her silvery hair, his broad back to me as he cradles the fae in his arms. Kàssandra's head tilts, and Maxian claims her mouth.

Our eyes meet, her gaze glittering in the dark. She watches me as he kisses her. Indeed, she is flushed, but I know it wasn't his doing. Like any king, he is merely taking credit for another's work.

An unseen force shoves my shoulder, and I fall through the Illusion.

Chapter Twelve

I CRASH ONTO THE STONE FLOOR OF THE CLOISTER.

"What are you doing, Crest?" An Illusion guard peers down at me, a debt ring on each arm.

"Waiting on my mistress," I say, climbing to my feet.

"I do not see her anymore." He surveys my dirty clothes. "What has happened?"

"She's with the king in the courtyards. Do you not feel his power?"

It's a dangerous game, baiting a halfling guard. They can be understanding of those below them or eager to please those above. Yet the guard's eyes go glassy, head leaning to one side as if listening.

"They sent me away," I say.

He coughs, stepping back. "I understand."

"Do you serve Lord Dominik directly?"

"As heir, he commands all of the guards. 'Tis tradition in the Illusion House."

"Let your superiors know that the king courts Lady Kassandra."

The guard's face flames, but he nods, marching off. Leaning against a column, I stare out at the darkened gardens, now silver-lined in the moonlight.

A shadow flickers to my left.

I jerk back, hissing.

"It is only me," a voice says. A hooded figure emerges from an arch, passing in front of the moon. Death looms before me, shadows skittering away from his robes like spiders.

"Only you?" A terrified laugh catches in my throat.

As I grow accustomed to Death, like eyes in darkness, another feeling rises above the fear, one more powerful, one meant for the fae. I stumble upon the shores of my anger once more, a small island of reprieve in my muddled grief.

"Are you well?" he asks. "You look tired."

"Fuck you."

"No, thank you."

I spit on the toe of his boot. He glances down.

"Mm," he grunts. "Brave or stupid, spitting on Death."

"I just see a dog who sits when Master commands it."

That gaze narrows like a panther's. Have I struck a chord? "Stupid, then," he amends.

"I'm a gift to the king. It would be *stupid* to do anything to me. Besides, my mistress would know, too."

"There are many ways to harm without leaving a mark."

I only exhale when he looks away, willing my legs not to shake.

"I assume you knew the faerie who died," he says. "The younger brother sought to protect you."

I hate you, Avery. I hate you and I will never, ever forgive you. I hope the king hurts you.

Tears burn my eyes.

"You didn't hesitate," I rasp. Humiliation should drag me down, but it would first have to pry me from grief's iron grip. "You didn't hesitate at all."

That raised hand, our gazes locking. We never shared a goodbye, any goodbye. I never got the chance to tell him what he truly meant to me. I never will.

"It's not my job to hesitate," the executioner says.

"A dog, like I said."

The air around us drops. It is a funerary silence, filled with buzzing insects and bellowing bullfrogs, swishing grass. The executioner could reach out and dissolve me into mist. He could use his shadows to strangle me or unsheathe his sword and cut in places others will not see.

Instead, he says, "Your friend is in a safer place now."

"How can you know that?"

He says nothing for a moment, then, "Your soul is weary."

"Are you offering to eat it?"

"You can always declare the Desert Walk. Either you perish in the sands and join your friend once more, or complete the Walk, reach the House of Death, and be absolved of your balances."

"Death or banishment; either way I will be free," I mutter. It is tempting, so tempting, like finding a plot of land to rest on after years of walking. But although my legs feel like giving out and my heart like giving up, I cannot.

"I must protect the younger brother," I say.

"Then that is your reason to keep going." Before I can press the executioner further, he turns. "Something has upset the king."

The ground trembles. In the corridors above me, the pound of feet, guards shouting.

"What's happening?" I ask, but he has already disappeared, the last wisp of smoke fading from the air.

I push off the wall and sprint through the Illusion hedge.

Kassandra sits on the stone bench alone, her nose pink, lips smudged with color. By the time I reach her, Death is already by her side.

"Is everything okay, my lady?" he asks. "Where is the king?"

"He left," she says. "He returned to his chambers."

"Thank you, my lady." Then he is gone once more.

Kassandra stands, wiping her mouth with the back of her hand, her eyes empty. *What has happened?* Despite myself, I reach into my skirt pocket for a handkerchief and offer it to her. She dabs her face with it, then meets my gaze.

Her brows pull together. "Stop looking at me like that."

Like what?

"Let's go." She moves beyond me, and I follow, hands clasped together, head down. As she marches out of the gardens, she balls up the cloth, then snaps it open again and again. As we head down the eastern cloister to her apartments in the southern building, she spins around.

"If I tell you what happened, will it stop the press of your puzzlement? Or do I have to retire myself tonight to get a reprieve from your maddening emotions?"

We fall into a brief silence, only punctuated by the occasional rumble of the earth.

"The least you can do is talk back," she huffs.

"So you'd rather I be disrespectful?"

She glares at me, an icy fire once again sparking in her eyes. "He asked how I forged the diamond dagger. He wanted me to replicate the Illusion."

"And did you?"

"I couldn't."

"I'm sorry, my lady," I say.

"I could not replicate the Illusion because it was not an Illusion."

Somewhere, an owl calls. "If it wasn't an Illusion, then what was it?"

"I don't know. I meant it to be real. A real . . . creation. But House Illusion is not capable of such a thing. No fae is, save for Reign." She wraps her arms tighter around herself.

The owl calls again. *Who who who.*

"That is why the king left?" I ask.

"He's lending the dagger to House of Healing to see if Eli can test it, see if I left some type of magical residue on it so they can trace the true source of its power." My mistress turns away, pacing down the corridor once more. "Perhaps my magical marker will reek, too."

Her words should sting, but they don't. Now I see that they come from a place more complicated than cruelty. They come from grief. They come from unspent energy and anxiety and rage because she is strong in a way that females are forbidden to be, and that makes her dangerous.

In two days, I will begin to serve the king. Perhaps I can glean the answers, arm Kassandra with them to help tip the scales of power in our favor. How would Kassandra reward such an act of service? Paying off the debt of a young faerie boy should be nothing to her. But I need leverage to ask this. High Fae only know how to speak in games and deals.

It's worth a try. There is so little left I can lose. Besides, now I know what rules the Heart of Illusion, and it is no male. And I know, for certain, her interest in me is of a different nature.

Chapter Thirteen

My knees against tile, my genius scratching to get out. The veins in my neck stretch, bulging; I cannot move. I cannot do anything. Not as Jeremee becomes nothing, not as a child screams in pain.

I lurch awake, gasping with fear, heavy and hollow.

I study memories of Jae like river stones: his auburn hair, his long slender hands, the timbre of his voice, his embrace. Joking and dancing and laughing with him at the Full Moon Festivals. I sharpen these images lest the current of time smooths over the details and takes all I have left of him.

I shift, feeling the damp sheets. Soaked, actually. I'll need to bathe before tonight's service. Yet as I sit up, the smell hits me, the putrid, unnatural stink lingering beside the sweat and piss of my night terrors. But it's more than that. It's a marshy odor of salt and corpses. I rip the sheets away from the bed.

It smells of swamp. My magical marker has never been so strong, as if in neglecting my genius, I am letting it fester. I need to air it out.

That night, Kassandra dismisses me, my pungent presence giving her a headache. My last night in Illusion for two moons, and I sit in my room alone with a bucket. My genius reaches out to the water in the bucket, whispering its request.

The water rises, dripping and lopsided, before taking shape. I think of the lessons Eli demanded of Kassandra, the little birds and bats and butterflies. My genius morphs the water into tighter creatures that begin to resemble moths. They fill the air, multiplying, and flit around the room.

It's not enough.

It hurts, keeping it all in, and I don't have the strength to be small anymore. So I do what I do when I can no longer follow my mother's instructions. I follow my father's.

Teeth clenched, I press into a push-up so deep my nose touches the cold stone. Up and down, up and down, up and down. A burn builds in the muscles in my arms, my back, my core. The moths circle me in a torrent, raindrops splattering my back and limbs. My genius feeds the root magic, unfolding and flourishing. I do not stop when sweat gathers on my brow. Not when breath comes quick and tendons quiver. Not when my jaw aches and salty tears drip to the stone, mingling with droplets of water. Faster and faster the creatures whirl. Harder and harder I push up and down until my name is forgotten and dawn cracks across the solitary bedroom window. Only then do I and the creatures collapse.

Gasping, I lie prone on the wet floor, clothes soaked. When my pulse finally calms and air comes more easily, I gather myself.

The Illusion kitchens are quiet, save for the occasional line cook moving between storage and ice rooms and the long counters. In the moments they move out, I dart in, snagging what pieces I can. Apples, a hunk of cheese, bread, a handful of broccoli. Little by little, I fill a sack until it's bulging, then bring it to the bloodstain in the tunnels.

I'll miss whatever Unluckie visits tomorrow, but that doesn't mean they have to miss out on meals. Next week, I'll have to figure out what to do, but that's a problem for later. I just need to get through hour by hour, day by day.

My palm presses the bloodstained brick framed by roots.

"I miss you, Mama," I say. "Take care of Jeremee for me."

When I leave, my hand is wet not with blood but with the tears I scrub away.

. . .

THE FOLLOWING EVENING, a Reign Crest faerie comes to my room to collect me, giving me a gold tunic uniform that is smooth and slippery to the touch. *Silk.* I've only handled the material a few times when dressing Kassandra. But this silk is my own now, and I should feel elated to don the same material as the High Fae. A mark of my status as the most noteworthy of faeries—a Reign Crest. The best of the least. It feels like a cruel joke.

"Are you all right?" the faerie in front of me asks. She introduces herself as Lila. With mahogany eyes, coiled hair, and deep bronze skin, she appears like a celestial being in her golden uniform. The shirt is cropped at her taut midriff, the loose pants cinched at the ankle. It doesn't surprise me that the other faerie I'll be working alongside is exceptionally beautiful.

"Just wondering how to clean this," I say. "Such a delicate fabric for a servant."

"Oh!" She smiles. "Lemon juice in warm water, and dab the stains. The night shift for the House of Reign is different work. The day servants take care of most of the cleaning. We serve and entertain." My stomach clenches, and she gestures to the uniform. "Come on, let's get you changed and give the oath so we can be on our way."

My arm burns at the memory of Briar dragging the silver feather across skin.

"Won't that bloody the clothes? Not sure how to scrub out a large stain like that," I say, mouth dry.

Lila's eyes widen. "Large stain?"

"For the oath?"

"Planes above, no!" She searches my face. "Each House has a different form of the blood oath. House of Reign requires just a few pinpricks."

So House Illusion chose for the bond to be that brutal.

I spot a figure hovering outside my bedroom. Briar peers inside, her face tight.

"I wanted to say goodbye," she says. My heart deflates. Another consequence of the separation, another way for Dominik to punish us all.

"I'm sorry to leave you," I say.

"You will return."

I face Lila. "May I?"

Lila nods, and I pass her the uniform, then meet Briar in the hallway and throw my arms around her. She squeaks in surprise, her strong arms wrapping around my waist.

"You'll be okay," she murmurs. "I'll see you when the moon is full again."

I squeeze her tighter. "Will you be okay?"

"What do you take me for, a doe?" A hearty laugh. Briar pulls something from her apron. A letter. "For the king, from Kassandra."

"Will she see me?"

Briar shakes her head.

Despite myself, I feel a twinge of disappointment. Not that Kassandra and I would say goodbye, not that she would even care if I am gone, but she has become a constant in my life. She is a scar that I'm used to seeing every morning in the looking glass.

Briar drops her voice. "If only you could tell me what happened between the mistress and the king. Kassandra has been in a terrible mood ever since."

I try, but with Lila so close, my mouth fills with pebbles. I think of the "Houses and Mouses" nursery rhyme and joke, "The silver cat met the mountain two nights ago."

Nothing. No choking, no unseen marbles clogging my throat.

Briar's eyes widen. "What were you picturing just then?"

"A cat climbing a mountain."

"Nonsensical," Briar whispers. "As long as our minds imagine our analogies, it will not detect the truth." She shakes her head. "I always knew you were a clever one. It's no wonder Kass keeps you around."

We grin at each other, at the new possibilities unfurling before us. Yet my superior looks behind me, expression taut. The smile drops from my lips, and I glance to see Lila waiting patiently in my bedroom.

Perhaps we have not discovered something new. Perhaps we have discovered something dangerous.

The older faerie squeezes my shoulder. "If you need anything, you know where to find me."

"Same to you."

She gives a small smile before departing. I return to Lila, who is examining a thread on my uniform. She hands over my clothes, patting my arm.

"It's nice to see," she says. "Friendship, in a place like this."

Once Lila slips out of my bedroom, I quickly change. The gold silk coats my skin like chocolate melting on the tongue. For a moment, I wonder if this is how the High Fae feel. Yet once the clothes settle around each one of my curves, I remember for whom I am on display.

I open the door. Lila's face brightens.

"You look lovely!" she exclaims. She breezes in, surveying the space. "Could you lock the door? The oath can't be witnessed by another."

Goosebumps pinch my skin. Another secret behind a closed door.

I lock the door before I can second-guess myself and hold out my arm. From a pocket in her pants, Lila pulls out a glinting gold signet ring, its surface blank.

"Remain where you are," Lila says. "It'll only be a moment." She crouches before me. "Do you swear the blood oath to the Vandorne family to serve them during the night?"

"I swear the blood oath to the Vandorne family to serve them during the night," I say.

"And indulge their desires?"

"And indulge their desires."

Lila reaches for the hem of my pant leg, tugging it up. I stiffen.

"What are you—"

"It's a quick recovery," she says.

She presses the face of the signet ring against my exposed knee. A prick of pain tunnels deep into my kneecap, like a needle piercing the bone to the back of my knee, anchoring into the tendons. Then a pulling sensation forward, a tug.

My leg gives out and I fall on that knee, gasping. Lila has moved back, now face-to-face with me. Sweat beads across my brow as I meet her eye.

"Just a prick?" I seethe.

She grimaces. "At least there's little blood?"

She presses the signet ring against the other knee, and once again, I feel a burrowing, a latching on, and a yanking forward. Unlike the Illusion oath, I keep my consciousness. Still, I pant on my knees.

Lila stands.

"What the planes are you doing?" I wheeze, though I know she can't reply. Instead, she just holds out the ring for me to see. In the center of the oval are now two vertical, parallel lines, engraved deep into the gold.

"That's it?"

"No, I'm sorry." Lila circles behind me. "Please stay as you are."

I force myself to breathe, and still I'm unprepared when she touches the ring to my bare shoulder blade. The pricking sensation fastens to my bone. This time, however, it doesn't exit. It remains attached to my back, weighing me down. When she brushes against the other shoulder blade, the pain evens.

Lila steps away and helps me to my feet.

"Congratulations," she says. "Welcome to the House of Reign."

In her other palm rests the gold ring. On either side of the parallel lines, the surface is engraved with wings, intricately webbed and dotted with two circles each, resembling eyes.

"Moth wings!" Lila says.

"What?" I squint down at the ring.

"When each faerie takes the oath, wings appear on the ring. The wings are your essence reflected as an animal."

I make a face. "But a moth?"

"They're nocturnal, unlike butterflies. Fitting, don't you think?"

As much as I may begrudge it, the moth does feel right for the flitting, anxious genius that sparks in the back of my mind.

"What animal is yours?" I ask.

She pulls another ring from her pocket and slips it onto her slender finger. The engraving catches the light, a thin and feathered wing. "Hummingbird."

"That suits you." I smile, and she returns it.

"Now, we're going to be using these rings to boost our own magic and use the plane to transmit ourselves elsewhere."

"Are you speaking of lacing? Faeries can't lace."

"With these, we can." She wiggles her finger. "They're enchanted."

"But—how?"

"Normally, I'd guide you through the process, but for the first time, I think it would be easier to take you myself. May I?" Lila touches my forearm after I give a nod. She beams. "Hold on!"

Reign magic tumbles up my arms, through my torso and legs. Then I am being flattened, stretched, my lungs screaming, joints popping. The darkness becomes weightless, intangible, howling.

Wind brushes through my hair, warmth on my face. Lila giggles.

The fear drops away to something else. It's like flying.

It's . . . exciting.

Lightness bubbles up in my chest like a sunburst. As the palace and its gardens blur by us, sounds and sensations warping, I laugh for the first time since Jae's murder.

The rushing comes to a stop, my body snapping into shape once more, slamming together. We stumble into a dark hallway. Lila catches me before I can fall. Her skin feels warm and a little damp, but she stands strong. I right myself, hands patting my body.

"Am I okay?" I gasp.

"Do you feel okay?"

"Everything's where it should be. I don't feel like I've . . . died?"

Lila laughs. "You haven't! You've merely been reassembled."

"How? How can the rings do that?"

Lila shrugs, grinning. "They're imbued with Reign magic."

Holding up my hand, I gawk at the object. Such a small band, and yet it grants so much power.

My mind spins with the possibilities; if the ring can borrow abilities from the most powerful House in Amyria, what else can it do? And why can't faeries just wear jewelry to level the playing field?

The same reason we must take a blood oath before we wear them. The same reason we remain weighed down in debt while the High Fae stay unmarked. Somewhere between the dawn of the fae and now, someone has invented equity. And only the disadvantaged do not know about it.

"I know," Lila says suddenly, softly.

"Apologies," I manage, vision blurring.

"Never apologize for feeling."

It's nice to see. Friendship, in a place like this.

I stare at her for a moment, perhaps seeing her for the first time. "How lonely it must be to carry this knowledge around, unable to share it with anyone."

Lila smooths down imaginary wrinkles from her gold pants. She raises her chin, dazzling me with a smile, the corners of her eyes glistening.

"Now there's you," she says. "But we both don't want to be late." She beckons me down the hall, coming upon a bronze door. "Oh—something else. I do not know what it was like in Illusion, but when we're in the rooms, never say anything you don't want them to hear. Because they will hear it."

I nod, swallowing. "Understood."

"Even in the servants' halls we need to be careful. Now, are we ready?"

I'm not, but I force a smile. "Let's do this."

She grabs the handle and swings it open.

Chapter Fourteen

WE WALK INTO A SMALL PRIVATE LIBRARY, A CONTRAST TO the grandeur I had expected. Leather chairs cluster around twin stone fireplaces that flank the room. A round table stands in the center, a cloth draped over its top. Rows and rows of books are crammed into shelves that run along the walls. I manage my basic letters and have always been jealous when Kassandra gets lost for hours in dense, scratched-up novels.

"Tonight, we'll just need to set the table for two." Lila crosses the room to the bookshelf on the opposite wall and takes out plates from cabinets built above the shelves.

"Who's dining tonight?"

"The king and the advisor. You'll feel them coming."

I retrieve silverware, crystal cups, and napkins, stunned at their weight and richness of details. The plates are not glass, nor the napkins cotton as they are in the House of Illusion.

"What is this material?" I ask, centering a plate.

"Porcelain. It's made of a white clay that can be found in the Amyrian Desert."

I pause. The kingdom of Amyria occupies an expansive valley between two mountain ranges, and the desert skirts around it all. My gaze drops to the plates.

"Who collects the clay?" I ask. "And makes the plates?"

Lila doesn't look up from the serving tray she is setting up by the servants' entrance, placing a water pitcher and wine bottle down. "I can ask the king."

"No—I mean, I was only curious."

Lila shrugs. "He speaks to the faeries."

"But . . . he's the king."

"He was like that even as a prince. An older faerie once told me it's because his mother was like that. Always asking us our names and opinions." Lila pauses. "But sometimes, when he's between fae females and feeling bored, he flirts. He is a male in power, after all."

Dread curls in my stomach. "I understand."

"It is more a curiosity to him than a true desire, I think. He usually finds a new fae quickly after that."

A creeping, sickly sensation worms through my veins. It would be easy for the king to overcome me, and the only thing stopping him is a flimsy conscience and attention span.

I need to learn how to fight in every way possible. The thought pops into my mind before I can stop it, my hands still on the dishware. My muscles, though sore from working out last night, are already honed from many years of physical labor. But it's more than that. The fae males have the physical and magical advantages. *What do I have?*

Two blood oaths and riddles to get around them. A rotting genius looking for a challenge. If I've learned anything from my short stint as a Night Crest in Illusion, it is that even the most tightly wound secrets unspool in the dark. Information, and a way to carry it to the light, is power. I will free Benji. But perhaps I can work to free more than just him.

For the first time, I regret not asking the names of the faeries I have fed. I regret not learning my former roommates' names. There was so little I asked my mother when she was still here, and now I feel the disrespect of that sharply. She said to keep my head down and my genius in check—but she also butchered her julienning so that I might have more scraps to eat. After her death, I felt that stealing fae food could somehow continue her legacy. I focused so much on the thrill of the thieving, I forgot why my mother broke rules in the first place: to give. To give an advantage to me, her child, in any way she could.

Jeremee said to do less alone, and for the thousandth time, he was right.

I need a network. A network of peers.

A bookcase swings forward, and King Maxian steps through the concealed door, quickly shutting it behind him. An expansive muscled chest peeks out from beneath the undone laces of his tunic. His tousled dark-honey hair seems damp. He seems . . . relaxed, more so than he did with Kassandra.

I compose myself, falling beside Lila as she backs from the table.

"The table is ready whenever you are, Your Magnificence."

"Thank you, Lila. And you as well, Avery."

My name on the king's lips jars me.

"Would you like to begin with wine this evening? Or a specialty drink?" she asks.

"I would love a Lila specialty. Have you named it yet?"

"I'm thinking of calling it Lavender's Breath."

"Brilliant." The king smiles. Then he pulls out his own chair and sits down.

How is this the same male who allowed the order that—

I stop the thought before it unravels me. Lila turns to the serving table, opposite the wall from which the king entered. I follow her to the cutting board, the bowls of sliced lemons and limes, lavender flowers, a carafe of bubbling water.

"Your mouth is open," she whispers, and I close it. She hands me the water pitcher. "Serve this while I make his drink, please."

"What exactly is it?"

"Liquor mixed with lemon, lavender, and sparkling water."

"Where did you learn this?"

"I invented it." She turns to me. "Your mouth is open again."

I close it once more.

Approaching the table, I catch the king's scent of soap and

vanilla and male. Of all my expectations, I never thought he'd wear body oil. As I pour him a glass, I feel those eyes slide to me once more.

"You were shocked by my interaction with Lila," he says, his voice warm and smooth like honeyed tea. Nodding, I circle the table to fill the other glass. He clears his throat. "You may answer."

"I'm still learning the rules of decorum for House Reign, my king," I say. "The House of Illusion is a great teacher."

"But a strict one."

I bow my head, heart pounding in my ears. If I confirm, he may find it disloyal. If I disagree, I am opposing the king of this land. It's a verbal trap; one I refuse to step into. So I remain quiet as I pull the letter from my pocket and hand it to him.

"From my lady."

The king raises his hand, and despite myself, I wince. He looks at me once more, lips twitching. "I'm going to lace a letter opener from my private office to here. No harm will come to you."

He waits for my nod, then waves his fingers. A golden letter opener appears in his palm. He slits the envelope and scans the parchment before slipping it into his own pocket. The opener disappears, and he tilts his head. "You agree that the House of Illusion is strict despite their . . . alluring nature?"

"I—" My face heats. "I-I'm unsure."

"You may answer truthfully. In my House, you can make your choices within reason, but you must own them."

Lila places a cloudy pale drink beside his hand. He brings it to his lips and sips, attention never leaving me.

You must own them. My knees had hit the floor so forcibly that night.

King Maxian leans back in his chair. "Tell me your thoughts."

Lila moves around the table, giving a small nod. Yet her optimism may only reflect years of building their precarious nighttime intimacy, like Briar with Kassandra.

Do not insult him with your slowness, Kassandra said. But she also said, *He thinks himself an intellectual.* Perhaps I need to pose it as a question that only he can answer.

"You say in the House of Reign that we must own our choices. Yet the chief ability of Reign fae is control over others and our world. I feel I may be missing how those two are not contradictory."

The king's eyes brighten. He leans forward, and despite my best efforts, my body shivers with the rush of power, a thrumming in my very core.

"You find it ironic," he muses.

"I find it interesting, my king."

"Control is the most dangerous power to possess. It must only be used as a last resort—an ugly necessity." He swallows his drink, staring at the table. "I was worried about a brawl breaking out on my very first day as king. Not only could that have harmed everyone in the room, but it would have shaken the confidence of the most powerful families in Amyria. That can't happen." He examines his glass, finger tapping on the table. "Uncertain nobles are scheming ones. That leads to fae and faeries dying." He glances up. "Do you know of the Dark Rebellion?"

The grout was pink.

It was blood that had soaked into the floors during the Dark Rebellion.

"House of Death lost faith in Reign. Felt we had become too soft—and so they staged an uprising. The royal palace was a bloodbath for months," he says.

A bloodbath. It smells like a bloodbath. It smells like fear.

"Until one day, all that remained were corpses and rubble and a few members of each House. It's why the palace was rebuilt as a labyrinth. It's why all the Houses have their own area of the maze, except for Death," he says.

"Death accepted their banishment to the borderlands," I respond.

"And why only one halfling representative is allowed in court." King Maxian grimaces. "On coronation day, I became . . .

alarmed. That history was top of mind. Training is one thing. Doing it is something else. You are still learning the decorum of Reign, and I am still learning to be king. We have both taken important oaths."

Why would he show such vulnerability? Why would he think I care when he killed my best friend? Lila prepares another drink, humming. Surely this is an Illusion. This can't be real.

"Speaking of Death . . ." Maxian finishes his drink and stands. In a moment, he transforms from that handsome stranger in a tavern to the towering figure of power and might. A cloud of black smoke explodes next to me, the plane stilling.

I dart over to Lila. "What can I help with?"

"Serve them while I grab the first course from the Mouth."

"The Mouth?"

"The king's private kitchens," she says, and passes me a brown drink with an orange peel. It smells strongly of the liquor that's stored in barrels in subterranean levels of the palace.

Maxian shakes hands with Hector Vandorne, the king's advisor. The cloaked figure of the executioner stands off to the side, arms clasped behind his back. The king gives him a nod, and with another puff of smoke, the executioner is gone. Maxian and Hector exchange pleasantries as they settle into their seats. I bring the brown liquor over to Hector, who nods as I place the drink down. Wrapping thick fingers around the glass, he drains it instantly.

"Your Magnificence, I have some concerns," he says, voice gruff.

The king gestures. "Please."

"It's regarding the coronation."

I force my legs to move as the servants' door opens. Lila carries a tray of greens topped with apples, crumbling cheese, pine nuts, and a dressing. The leaves look fresh, sweet. I keep my eyes on the dishes as I place a bowl before the king.

"Should we not speak in private, Your Magnificence?" the advisor is saying. "The gifted faerie . . ."

I pause, but the males do not look at me.

"She has taken the blood oath to Reign," Maxian says.

"Of course, Your Magnificence. It's just that, is she not still also sworn to Illusion? If asked a specific question, which oath would win out?"

The king scratches his chin. "Interesting. I suppose the oaths would yank her in opposite directions and eventually destroy the body to keep fealty to both Houses."

My mouth dries. Hector grunts, picking up his fork. Shaking, I return to the side of the room where Lila waits.

"At the coronation, Dominik was out of control," Hector says between bites.

"It was a disgrace and an embarrassment."

The entire room shivers and several volumes of books plummet to the ground. A dark cloud appears and the executioner steps out of it. He opens his hands as a vase falls from a top shelf, catching it in his gloves.

"I felt a disturbance in the plane."

"Everything's okay, Executioner," the king says, his eyes trained on his advisor across the table. "My temper. You may return to your post."

The executioner floats the vase up to the shelf again on a shadow. Then he's gone. Maxian lets out a breath, picking up his fork. The two men eat in silence for a moment. Finally, Hector speaks.

"I see your magic is still maturing."

"It has shown no signs of slowing down," the king mutters.

My pulse picks up. It took three decades for my magic to fully mature along with my body. Now that I am in my late two hundreds, my magic only grows in precision, not power. The king must be in his early to mid three hundreds, and his is still maturing?

"They named you the Mountain for a reason," Hector adds. "The Mountain will keep Dominik in line."

"I think we'll switch to wine now, Lila."

"Of course, Your Magnificence." Lila turns to me, lowering

her voice. "Are you okay to serve while I gather the main course?" I nod, and she slips out.

Reaching for the bottle of wine—a dry white from the southern city of Fraulus—I listen as the king speaks again.

"What did Eli say of the dagger?"

"It's real. It's made of natural diamonds, and we traced it to her."

"How? How is that possible?"

I wipe a cloth against the sweating wine, bringing it to the table.

"She must have distant Reign blood. An ancestor several generations back," Hector says.

"Would it impact the health of future children?"

The males share a look. Hector sighs. "You should've married before ascending the throne. I felt the instability in the air at the coronation, and we're lucky that faerie died to be the main talk among the nobles."

The wine wobbles in my grasp, and it takes everything in me to remain upright. I leash my emotions before they spool out onto the plane and ruin the meal.

"My betrothed died, if you recall," the king says tightly.

"You were both eight. It was a tragedy, but it is also history."

The servants' door swings open. Lila enters, carrying two heaping, steaming bowls of stew that smell of rabbit, carrots, and onions.

"Have you heard the nursery rhyme about Daisy?" the king asks.

Daisy. The name strikes me.

A memory bubbles up from the depths of my mind, Jeremee and I and other faerie children grasping sweaty hands, running around in a circle in the common room, chanting the familiar rhyme: *Daisy, Daisy—in the springtime you grow, in the summer you glow. Daisy, Daisy—winter is here, beware the snow! Daisy, Daisy—why did you go? Poor, poor Daisy—don't you know flowers freeze in the snow?*

Daisy was a real fae child who had died. A deep horror washes over me.

"I'm seeing Lady Kassandra again soon," the king says. "It would be the first royal marriage in a millennium that isn't between two Reign fae. It is not a decision I take lightly."

"If you fear the dilution of Reign blood, you could always wed Rose Tunes."

"We are second cousins. Again, would that not risk the health of a child more?"

"Your parents were first cousins, and they created the most powerful fae in our history."

Another pause.

"You have no heir, Your Magnificence, no wife to give you a legitimate one, but you know it's not just about legacy." Hector drops his spoon in the bowl, splattering the cloth. "When you graduated to your father's spot on the Council of Keepers, you left your heir seat empty. There is no pregnant Heart to fill in, either. Illusion and Death still have all three votes, while we only have two."

"Healing has just a head and an advisor like us, and when the old Lynx of the Lowlands finally dies, then Illusion will also only have two votes. No House has an heir seat anyhow, except for Death. That is why I did not wed before. It's time to see what the other Houses are willing to give to breed their blood into the royal line."

The Council of Keepers . . . is real. I've only heard the rumors that one may exist, a voting body between all four Houses, but when and how and where it's held, no one but the Keepers knows. Not even the Hearts.

"There are worse brothers-in-law than your oldest friend," Hector is saying.

Dominik. The hairs on the back of my neck rise.

"What I find odd, Uncle, is that you do not promote a union between your two bloodlines. What is your hesitation with a Healing wife?"

"You already have their loyalty, and I can influence their vote. They are traditional and immovable in their morals."

"So you agree. Dominik is an uninhibited heir, and may be a worse head," Maxian says, then waves. "More wine." I approach, legs shaky, and pour for the king as he continues. "Illusion is having a moment of prosperity and ambition, much to his influence. But bringing him within arm's reach of the royal Reign family may only encourage the sharpening of his claws."

"But don't you see," Hector says. "Drawing the wolf closer means its hide is within range of your whip."

"Who would fill his place if anything were to happen?"

"Who cares? It's time to see if Illusion is more than just smoke and silver."

I retreat, returning the wine to its ice bucket and joining Lila against the wall with my shaking hands clenched behind my back.

Silence, for a moment. Then Maxian says, "I will marry soon. Secure an heir for the future of Amyria and the Reign fae."

"When?"

"Before excitement sours to unrest."

My blood roars in my ears, and I press my lips together. Realization dawns like a swift stomach illness.

Jeremee had been right.

The Houses are shifting, and every faerie should fear it.

Hector wipes his mouth, tossing his napkin down. "Stew was pleasant. The rabbit was very tender." The advisor laughs. "I could not taste the fear this time."

The king smiles. "We improved the cages."

For the rest of the evening, the fae finish plate after plate, their appetite unending, leaving no scraps behind to steal.

Chapter Fifteen

WHEN THE DINNER FINALLY ENDS AND THE MALES DEPART, Lila and I push the cart of dirty dishes down the servants' hallway. We reach the Mouth, warm light leaking out onto the dark stones. The door swings outward, revealing a blond male with only four debt rings on each arm. He is my height, and we both tower half a foot over Lila. Behind him, the clamor of the kitchens washes over us, smells of butter and onion filling the air.

"How was dinner?" His crooked half smile snatches my breath, so strongly does the expression remind me of Jeremee.

"Oh, you know." Lila shrugs. "The same as always."

"Self-important and full of the advisor's open-mouthed chewing?"

"Shh!"

They laugh until his attention finds me.

"Oh, hello," he says.

"This is Carter, the king's personal valet," Lila chimes in. "Carter, this is Avery."

"Night Crest for Illusion," I start. "And, well—Reign, too."

"Ah, so you were the one . . . *gifted* at the coronation. My condolences."

"Well, I'm grateful she's here," Lila says. "We'll have to show her that being in the Pith isn't so bad."

"The Pith?" I ask.

"What we call House Reign. Something the older faeries used to call it, and now it's tradition."

"How tolerable it is being in the Pith depends entirely on what the king had for dessert," Carter says. "I'm heading to his chambers now to prep the nightly routine."

Lila grimaces. "He chose the custard."

Carter groans, knocking his head back against the open door, then shouts, "Fern, my love!"

From the clatter of the Mouth comes a boisterous voice. "I've got a knife in my hand, little shit!"

"Chef Fern!" he corrects, sapphire eyes flashing with mirth. "Why do you continue making these dairy desserts?"

"To torture you, of course!" A wave of laughter from the Mouth.

"You know he picks them every time," Carter says, facing us. "Even at the cost of the bathing chamber and the nose of his personal valet."

Lila covers her mouth. Something in my mind shifts another degree, just as it did with the smell of the king, that no matter how powerful and beautiful, he still has a body. And all bodies bleed.

"Well, I should get going," he says.

"Do you want to come in for a snack?" Lila asks me. "There should be leftover custard."

I look between them. "Is that . . . allowed? We can eat their food?"

"Food is food, of course. Well, we have to wait until they're done, but Fern always keeps extra of everything so that there's leftovers."

This is how I could start a network of my own. This is the answer, and yet I cannot stomach it now, when it's right before me. The more I learn about other practices in the palace, the less my upbringing makes sense. How small was my world before? How small is my perspective still?

Suddenly, it is all too much. Lila's eager face and Carter's grin, the slippery gold silk on my skin, the heat of the ovens on my neck, the aroma of tomorrow's bread that will never be broken and shared with my oldest friend.

"I think I'll just wash the dishes and head back home," I reply, my voice faltering on the last word.

"We have someone to wash them," she says. "But I can help lace you back?"

I step back. "It's okay. Thank you, though."

"Are you sure? Lacing can be complicated. You have to perfectly picture where you want to go, a path to get there."

"I understand."

"Are you feeling all right?" the male asks. "You look like you're going to be sick."

"This is just how I look."

If they are taken aback, they say nothing.

"Thank you again for training me today," I say to Lila. "Sorry, I just—I need . . . sleep."

"Of course." Her wide mahogany eyes roam over my face, and my throat thickens because it is so *nice*. She seems nice, and Carter seems fun and even Chef Fern makes others laugh, and it is all so bright and loud and joyful and smothering like gorging on a feast after starving, and I cannot breathe, I cannot think, it hurts unbelievably so.

"I'll see you tomorrow night," Lila says as I turn.

"Nice meeting you," Carter adds.

"You too." I hurry away, wondering if I have ruined this, too, like a reeking creature whose touch spreads rot across everything good.

My genius collides with the golden ring, and the metal warms and warms and warms, a tingling back up my arm, across my chest, like insects buzzing in my bones, rattling my teeth, and it hurts, this confluence of my root energy and Reign, but it is a good hurt, a powerful one, like the bellyache after all that sickness, a magical fever that vibrates everywhere until the two energies connect with the plane of magic.

I disintegrate into nothing.

I sigh into it, spooling out into the blankness of being as my consciousness zips along the plane, picturing, as Lila said, home. The smell and taste, the feel, the aching for what never was.

I sprawl out onto stone, limbs snapping back into place, mouth tasting blood, ears ringing. Cracking my eyes open, I am not greeted with my empty chamber.

Several familiar male faeries stare down at me, all with tattoos up to their shoulders. The hairs on the nape of my neck rise.

"What the fuck are you doing here?" one of them sneers.

"How'd you do that?"

I scramble to my feet, adjusting my Reign clothes, surveying the bunkroom.

Jeremee's room.

My heart plummets as the males cringe back, and through their torsos, I spot Glenn. He stands straight, shirt rumpled, arm blocking the bunk behind him. His blue eyes widen.

"Avery," he breathes.

A whimper behind him in the lower bunk, like a little animal's. My chest cracks open as he shifts, and there is the small, waxen face of Benji, poking above the covers. The child watches me with empty eyes, drawing up a too-long sleeve to wipe his nose, the neck of the tunic too wide for such a small body because it was never meant to be worn by a child. Because it is one of Jeremee's tunics. Tears burn my world.

Standing between us, Glenn watches, attention on the boy despite the muscle clenching in his jaw.

"What can I do for you, Bee?" he asks softly, the whole room hushed now.

The child does not blink. He does not shrug or cry or scream, and suddenly I wish he would. Instead, he rolls over, his back to us. My heart sinks, and I feel the weight of many gazes on me once more. Glenn steps forward.

"How did you get in?"

"I—" My mouth fills with pebbles. The oath. Slipping the ring inside my pocket, I try again. "I wasn't trying to—"

"But you did," a roommate says.

"It was an accident."

"Is this some sort of forbidden magic?"

"Get out," another growls.

Keeping my eyes on Glenn, I swallow. "Please, I didn't mean—I will leave. I promise. I didn't intend to—"

"There are a lot of things you did not intend to happen," he says. "But they happened anyway."

Tears roll down my cheeks and when I turn, I notice the coiled body language of those around me, the poses of creatures ready to pounce. I need to get out. I need to get out before their anger spirals deeper. Yet I remain in the circle of the males, no one moving.

A male points a tattooed finger. "Don't think I've ever heard of a double-sworn faerie before, have any of you? No, it's odd. Odd, unless you're a spy for the fae. A spy disguised as a Crest."

A murmur goes through the males.

"Don't be ridiculous," Glenn snaps. His hand clamps around my elbow as he forces his roommates to part. But they must know, they have to, that I did not do this on purpose, that I am grieving just as much as they are, that fighting among ourselves isn't helping anyone but the High Fae. So as Glenn opens the door, I look back at the males who obscure the silent child in an adult's tunic.

I start. "I am so, so sorry that—"

Something wet smacks into my face.

"Hey!" Glenn shouts. "Enough of that."

Someone spit on me. Someone I used to eat meals with, laugh with as we were all brought together by my friend's magnetism. But he is gone, and so is that shared connection.

The door slams shut.

The ripping of fabric, and a cloth is pressed into my hands. I wipe my face with the scrap of Glenn's shirt.

"Thanks," I murmur, eyes stinging.

He leans against the door, arms crossed, as we stand in a hallway. He gestures to the band of Reign silk around my breasts, the pants that start above my hips, the exposed stomach.

"You don't have sleeves to . . ."

"It's quite ridiculous, I know," I say, forcing a smile.

He does not return it. "What was that? You appeared out of the air like . . . well, like a fae."

I shake my head, pointing to my throat. "It was a mistake," I finally say.

He sighs. "Aren't you supposed to be in Reign?"

"I haven't gotten—"

The sentence is choked out by magic.

I don't have a room there yet.

"I will be paid in a few days," I say. "I'm setting aside money for Benji and you."

"He's suffered enough," he says. "I'm sure Jeremee would appreciate any help for his brother."

"What are you truly saying?"

He sighs, running a hand through his hair, blinking bloodshot eyes. "Benji does not want to see you, so you will not see him."

"It may take time."

"What if he never changes his mind? Will you accept that?"

I can't lose another person, especially not him. The child I love like my own, a part of Jeremee that's still here. My family. My family. My mother and Jeremee and now Benji.

"We will let the boy decide," I finally say.

"We will." He nods. "But in the meantime, I understand if you don't want to share your coin with someone who won't see you."

"You think me so shallow that I would buy my way into the child's life and if he refuses, would refuse him, too?"

Glenn just watches me with a drawn expression. "I don't know what to believe."

Pain, like love, seems to always plummet to a new depth I did not know existed until I hit it.

"You know me. We know each other," I say desperately.

"Do we? Besides Jeremee, what else do we have in common?"

Not this. Anything but this.

"Benji. We have Benji in common now."

Glenn nods, eyes shining. "I promise I will deliver whatever you can pocket for him. To help the boy out, but only for his sake."

"Thank you."

"Avery, you were . . ." He presses the heels of his hands into his eyes. "You were always going to be the one that Jeremee married."

A hiccup escapes my lips, and I cover my mouth.

"I couldn't pledge to him, you know this," he says, voice shaking. "But I would've been happy when you took my place."

"I hoped we'd reach a time when anyone could pledge to another."

"Perhaps we will, even if he won't."

Tears stream down my cheeks at the thought, at infinite time stretching on like an endless river, some of us following the flow of the current while others slip under, forgotten.

"Jeremee didn't like to choose," I say.

Glenn lets out a hoarse laugh. "He didn't."

"But perhaps he would've chosen you instead, if he could. If it were allowed."

"I don't know." His voice breaks. "You should hate me."

"I don't. Do you hate me?"

"No. You understand what it was like to be loved by him. And how large a hole his absence has left behind."

The scrap of Glenn's shirt is damp in my hand, and I clear my throat, my body weary, my heart heavy. "When I'm paid, we can meet in private for Benji's coin so as to not upset the others."

He nods, looking away. "I am sorry, Avery."

Before I can say I am sorry, too, the door closes and I am left alone in the corridor. With the absence of light, of company, of possibilities, I do not know where to go, what to feel, or even which faith to follow. All I want is to curl up in a ball and call out for my mother.

Instead, I make my way through the chattering and chaos of the Nest, swiping up a small plate of food. Climbing the stairs, I reach the servants' hall outside Kassandra's apartments. The mistress whose fate I am tied to. Who leveled a complaint against Jeremee, which Benji now carries. Who used me to arouse herself for the king. My loathing for her returns.

I could go back to the Pith, but there is nowhere to sleep, no one I feel like explaining myself to, not even Lila and her kindness. Staring down at my plate of chicken and bread and beans, I feel ill. It is too much of what I do not want. But it is not all for me.

I wrap up the pumpernickel roll in the cloth napkin and leave it outside Briar's door. I knock but do not wait for an answer. When I reach my room, I strip off the silk and work out until I am covered in sweat, my muscles aching, then sit on the scratchy blankets of the cot and eat in silence. Eat to keep up the strength of a body I would like to retire from, just to feel free of the weight of grief. I finish the meal in this newfound loneliness disguised as privacy.

Brushing away the crumbs, I throw on a loose tunic and slip on the golden moth ring once more. Every constant in my life has been stripped away, everything and everyone but the vital organ with which I was born—my genius. It is mine, not just a tool for service, and it's stronger than most. So is the desire to disappear.

So I lace.

I lace back to the Pith, the sparks of laughter filling my ears.

I lace to the hallways outside the Nest.

I do it again, reveling in the transmutation, the act of dissolving only to be violently remade, shoulders slamming stone, knees scraping, body shivering and mind numb. Again and again, I become nothing, then something.

I lace back to my room, sweaty, exhausted, buzzed. When I close my eyes to the pink light of dawn, I welcome the fatigue and become nothing once more.

THE NEXT MORNING, Lila collects me and laces us to the Pith, my genius still spent.

"You'll get used to it," she says. "Soon, you may be able to lace a few times a day."

"I thought my genius was done maturing," I reply.

She shrugs. "Maybe it needed more of a challenge than just cleaning."

A week passes while the fog of loss remains. It turns out the king has many duties that take him away from the palace. As a smaller House, yet the most powerful, Reign requires less work compared to Illusion. The Pith feels almost overstaffed. There are messenger faeries, packers, dishers, moppers, food runners. It's as if any duty a Scarp may perform in Illusion has several designated roles in Reign. In the downtime, Lila offers me new soaps for my skin, and even a little pot of cream for after the bath.

"It'll soften calluses," she explains.

"A servant with soft hands?" I almost laugh.

"I suppose the royal family doesn't view us like servants. More like . . ."

"Pets?"

Lila grimaces. "They still pamper their pets?"

I take the soaps. Lila redirects me to Fern to help nurture my wavy hair, for hers is coiled.

"We have different soaps for different hair." The cook rummages through a box of extra items. She hands me a rosemary-scented bar. "Give it a try."

Perhaps an old part of me would deem this unnecessary, but the new me is so very tired in my bones. I still bathe in the shared Illusion washrooms, but when I rub the soaps into my skin and hair, I sigh. It feels luxurious and refreshing, and I want to cry. I remember to tuck the soaps away in my room to cherish them.

I rarely sleep that week, between my workouts and my attempts at lacing foods to the tunnels in the blue hours of the night, when the Day Crests have yet to rise. Fern and Lila have already explained that I can eat any food left out, but still, it feels like a trick. Like a halfling guard is waiting around the corner to catch me and shove spikes under my nails.

The first time had been a bowl of strawberries sitting on the center table, like overplump teardrops of summer. I waited until I was sure no one was around, then snatched a handful and laced. Stretched thin, gasping, it has become a thrill that I have managed. My knee scratched against stone as my body re-formed outside my room. Sticky red juice dripped from my hands, the strawberries gone.

Every night I have tried to lace food back to Illusion, to the Nest and the tunnels beneath. Every night I have failed. The food always disintegrates. I could keep stealing from Illusion, but it would be much more difficult without the cover of being Kassandra's current Night Crest.

As my first week draws to a close, I find the creditor's counter, the Nest a loud, dirty bustle that I both miss and want to escape. I don't see Benji in line. We haven't spoken since I laced into his room, and missing him is a constant ache. Offering my hand, the teller pricks my finger, and I pay my remaining balance to my debt.

"Congratulations," he says. "You've paid enough to disappear your thinned ring, and another."

"What?" I blink.

He takes my hand, pricking it again. My arms tingle, and I gawk down at the sight.

Nine on my left arm, nine on my right. Over a month ago, I had twenty from wrist to shoulder.

But I didn't work harder for it. In fact, I worked less. I just happen to be closer to the center of power. Is this how nobles and highly esteemed halflings feel?

What a load of bullshit.

Staring down at my arms, I finally understand that greater effort does not inherently mean greater impact. In fact, those with the longest hours, the hardest work, the greatest pains would be the Unluckies. The poorest of us all.

Rage chases me up the stairs to my room. My fists tighten and tingle with a fury that I try to rub out on my old cotton skirts.

A burning smell singes my nose.

I stop on the stairs, halfway between above and below, and gasp.

My skirts smolder with shadowy handprints seared into the cotton. I yank at the fabric, warm to the touch. Turning my pulsing palms upward, I see that they are red and mottled, as if I've been burned. Yet it doesn't hurt. It's as if *I* am doing the burning.

Checking in with my genius, I find the organ thrumming and active, almost satisfied.

A late-blooming ability with fire. Just . . . just like my mother.

What is going on?

My genius only hums in response.

Chapter Sixteen

THE KING LOUNGES IN A LEATHER CHAIR, STARING AT THE SIMmering fireplace after a meal he took alone in the library. Nearing the end of my second week of his service, I still scarcely see him beyond the occasional meal; he's constantly been away at meetings with other Houses, sectors, industry rulers. Lila and I clear and clean the space. Having something to focus on, even if it is a High Fae, helps distract from the grief, along with my continued nightly physical and genius routines. I've now started trying to coax out the heat in my veins, but it doesn't always respond. Though now I know the fire is there. It's almost as if the more I allow my genius to breathe, the stronger it becomes.

Carter hands him letter after letter. The king opens each one and tosses it onto the table. Another, and another. Finally, he sighs. "Do you have blank parchment, Carter?"

"I could retrieve it from your room, Your Magnificence."

"Please do. I am resting my genius for some new exercises tomorrow."

Carter nods, then heads out of the library from the servants' entrance.

"I've given more thoughts to your proposal, Lila," the king says. I glance between the two, and the king explains, "Lila writes out her thoughts on laws we are considering passing in Amyria. I'd like a faerie's perspective on them, especially a clever one."

"Thank you, my king," Lila says.

"We'll talk more about it, but first, I'd like something sweet from the kitchens."

"Did you want to speak to Chef Fern?" she asks, and I see the out she gives me to collect myself.

"Why don't you go ahead, Lila," the king says, and my pulse picks up.

She gives my arm a reassuring squeeze on her way out. In the quiet moments of shining silver and setting tables, she and I have begun to talk these past two weeks. Small things, like how tangerine is her favorite color, how I prefer the trousers of Reign to the skirts of Illusion, and she prefers dresses to anything else. How Hector's grunting while eating is off-putting. It is simple and slow, but like a small creek, friendship begins to flow.

The servants' door clicks closed, and I am alone with the king.

He leans back in his seat. "I seek to change many things, but it is difficult knowing what to prioritize or even where to start. It feels like trudging up a muddy slope."

I hesitate, then say, "It must be overwhelming."

The king glowers at the fireplace. "My grandfather founded most of the laws in this land, and my father strengthened them. I understand we need accountability, but perhaps the pendulum has swung too far."

Blood roars in my ears. I balance on the eye of a needle: One side is a backslide into the safety of invisibility; the other is a leap toward the danger of ingratiating myself. Two opposing destinies. One heartbeat to decide. *Impact over effort,* I think.

I take the risk.

"We do need accountability," I say. "And it sounds as though you have a vision."

"What does it mean when the vision for my legacy is to break down theirs? Who does that make me?"

Something in me stirs. "May I answer, Your Magnificence?"

He gestures, glancing up at me once more in earnest. "Of course."

I take a breath. "It makes you a king posed for peace and prosperity. It makes you . . . an intellect," I finish, thinking of Kassandra's words. "That could be your legacy."

His eyes focus on me, and my pulse skitters. He clears his throat, voice deepening.

"I suppose that may be true." The king shifts, loosening the laces at the top of his tunic. His hands have small nicks and scrapes. They are not the smooth ceramic of Dominik's.

"You're staring," he murmurs. His tousled hair rests against his thick neck, and I wonder if it's soft the way Kassandra's is, or coarse.

"Your hands, my king."

He turns wide palms up. "I've been practicing a new technique. One for Lady Kassandra."

"Oh?"

"Yes," he says. "I will forge her a diamond dagger."

My heart sinks, as I mull over how that will be received. But I already know; she'll be unimpressed by the lack of creativity.

"You think this is a poor idea," King Maxian observes.

"No," I rush to say. "No, I was just imagining how yours may differ from hers."

"How long have you served Lady Kassandra?"

"Two years, my king."

"Have you spent most days at her side?"

"Every day."

He rubs eyes bleary from hours of reading. "I'm seeing her again for another walk in the courtyards. So I have time to decide if she would like the diamond dagger."

"That's delightful." I smile, and this one is real. If they are getting closer to a betrothal, then Kassandra may be free of Dominik, and I can erase my and Benji's debt faster. If Maxian and Kassandra marry, I may maintain the salary of a Reign Crest, may even experience another pay raise in serving the king and queen. I could be like Lila, with her three rings on each wrist, or even Carter, with only four on his arms altogether.

"I hope so," the royal says, but I catch the hint of anxiety: a dry swallow, the creeping flush to his cheeks. "The last I saw her two weeks ago, I was denying that the diamond dagger was a creation. I couldn't understand how it wasn't an Illusion—but now we know she must have some very distant Reign magic she drew upon because I'm forming diamond daggers as well. Except I'm not quite sure how I should go about speaking with her again."

"Well, I'm sure . . ." I stop.

A ghost of a smile on his face. "You may say what you think."

"If you'd like Lady Kassandra to warm up to you once more, then apologizing would be a good start."

The king blinks up at me, shocked. Then he laughs, deep and gentle.

"I will start there," he says. "What else do you think? What is the trick to making her happy? I remember her laughing often when we were children, but in the decades since, that has faded away."

The cracking of her bones, her constant frown, the merciless bullying . . . The closest I came to seeing Kassandra happy had been in the garden, when she revealed her rot to me. It had only been to arouse herself for the king, and yet, as she'd kissed him, her eyes turned molten in the fading light.

"My lady is more intelligent than some realize," I say.

"She was always the best during our childhood games. But how does this impact her happiness now?"

I weigh my words carefully. "I believe she longs for the respect that comes with being considered a worthy opponent."

"You understand more than you let on." He looks up at me again, and my breath seizes in my chest at those violet eyes, so striking even among the fae.

"A-apologies, my king," I stammer, my face warming.

"Don't apologize. I asked for your thoughts," he says. "If we're going to spend this much time together, now and in the future, I want to be surrounded by clever creatures. Something my mother taught me: The king should never be the smartest in the room. Do you have any questions for me?"

It's the way he looks at me, grinning and expectant, as if he wishes to explain himself to me, bestow wisdom.

"Any question?" I ask.

"Yes, anything."

"When we lace, do we die?"

"No," he exclaims, barking a laugh. "No, we do not. We are simply remade."

"Is that not a death of some kind?"

Maxian cocks his head. "You're a peculiar faerie."

"It's not the first time I have been accused as such," I say, and he chuckles. "I have another question, my king."

"Go on."

"One day, when I have earned your trust, may I . . . submit a proposal like Lila does?"

He leans forward in his chair, weaving fingers together. "Do you have a proposal in mind?"

My heart begins to hammer.

"The food the palace throws out at the end of each feast, ball, or even dinner," I blurt. "There is so much of it. What if it were given to the Unluckies?"

"What are Unluckies?" he asks.

There's an uptick in vibration in the plane, but whose magic it is, I am unsure. I swallow, aghast that he doesn't know. "Faeries with four limbs of debt."

"Ah. We call them the Unskilled."

Unskilled? All labor is skilled. I smother the retort.

The plane rumbles, and he looks to me. "Giving out free food to the Unskilled is illegal."

"Apologies, my king." I blush for effect, and in the heat of the room, the pump of blood in my ears, it is not hard. "I suppose I do not know much about ruling. I do not understand what the High Fae do."

Yet he continues to frown. "Well, it's because the Unskilled cannot become skilled like you if we gift them everything. Besides, those faeries need . . . gentler food than fae food. Easier on their bodies."

My heart pounds in my ears, the strange logic applied to justify inequality so at odds with what is practical. The High Fae do this in almost everything—value silly ceremony over common sense. Females can only wear skirts, High Fae must rest yet by nature need less sleep, some faeries can't process fae food. Deprivation untangles these rules—faeries clothe a baby in whatever garment they have on hand and take shifts sleeping because all must work, and the king's own kitchen staff eat the leftovers of what they've prepared because that is what's there.

"There's more on your mind," the king observes.

I fix my face. "Apologies, my—"

He waves his hand. "Tell me your thoughts. Please."

"What is 'gentler food'?"

"Well, it's . . . it's easier to . . ." The king stops, giving a sheepish smile. "I'm sorry, but I have no idea. It's what I've always been told."

"Like a legacy."

He watches me. "Careful. We are getting into radical territory."

Recklessness grips me. If Lila offers proposals in writing, then perhaps he can handle a small dose of truth. "Because . . . the Unskilled do not deserve food?"

"Now . . ." He shifts, uncomfortable. "When you put it like that, it sounds cruel."

"Are not all legacies radical during their time? Otherwise, why else would they be remembered?"

A brief pause, and I wonder if his violet eyes will be the last thing I see.

Finally, he declares, "I like you." Then he's picking his quill up once more, twirling it. "Reign governs the harvesting of the crops. I don't even think I would need council approval, if there's as much waste as you say."

I curtsy. "The kitchens keep track of the inventory and food waste, so you could always gather a report from them. Like I said, I know very little about ruling, so I do not know if I could think up the right solution."

An intellectual needs a puzzle.

"Ah, but you do know much," he answers. "You know about Lady Kassandra."

"She likes the color lavender on a male," I say. "And it will bring out your eyes, my king."

A lopsided smile grows on his face. "Thank you, Avery."

The plane hums around us and I am unsure what he is feeling. I only know that it is not bad, that it keeps me alive, and relief washes through me. The servants' door opens behind us. Carter waltzes in with a satchel of parchment and a plate of something that smells of cinnamon.

"Apple pie, my king," he says. "Apologies for the delay, we ran out of custard and Lila needed an extra hand." Carter gives me a look. A laugh bubbles in my chest, but I push it away.

"I suppose that will do," the king says. "Oh, and, Carter? Be sure that my lavender tunic is cleaned and pressed for tomorrow."

"Yes, Your Magnificence."

I suppress a smile.

The king reaches for his fork. "Carter, if I ask you a question, would you answer it honestly?"

The valet straightens. "Of course."

"Is there much fae food waste in the kitchens?"

The valet cuts his eyes to me, then back to the king. "Well . . . some, yes."

"Why not prepare less food if so much is being thrown out?" Maxian asks as Lila reenters the room with a carafe of sweet wine.

"If the cooks prepared less food, then there would be fewer options to choose from," Carter says.

"Mm," the king muses, digging into the apple pie, dismissing the conversation. Carter and Lila steal glances my way, and I keep my expression blank. A new feeling pumps through me, deep and delicious, breaking up the mucky waters of my grieving mind.

Influence. A no-name faerie servant. An unassuming moth flitting about, blending in with the dust and the night, small enough to slip under the crown and whisper in pointed ears.

Why offer up a sack of food to one faerie when I can garner new laws for all? One is navigating the current, the other is redirecting the flow of the river. Why not start at the source? A beautiful monarch whose fancy is as flighty as a butterfly.

Chapter Seventeen

Banging on my door wakes me from a fitful sleep the next day. Groaning, I roll over. Dusky light filters through my window, indicating the late afternoon. Who needs me at this hour?

"Avery!" Briar shouts from the other side.

"What?" I mumble.

"Wake up!"

I drag a shawl across my shoulders and stumble to the door. Briar gathers her hair into a bun, stray pieces falling out.

"Get dressed."

"My shift doesn't start for another few hours," I grumble. "And I don't return to Illusion for at least another moon."

"Change of plans." She rubs her eyes. "The Upper Court is indulging in games in the state gardens this afternoon, and we're required to be there."

"Why not the Day Crests? I can't miss my shift—"

"The king will be there, but dress as if you are an Illusion Crest still. The lady's orders."

I'm still an Illusion Crest, I think glumly, but do as I'm told.

THE SPRING SUN is high and warm, the breeze soft and soil-scented. I shade my eyes and follow Kassandra, clad in a flowy white sundress, a lacy white parasol propped against a shoulder. *You'll look like a bride,* Briar had said, to which Kassandra snapped, *I look boring.*

My lady then turned sharp eyes on me for the first time in half a month and tutted, *Your genius smells different.* Before I could respond, she declared she was ready for her picnic.

We approach the lawn where several figures mill under a white tent pitched off to the side.

Kassandra groans, glancing at us over her shoulder. "I hate this game."

I scan the flat lawn. "What game, my lady?"

"Prize of the Pith."

Only when we reach the edge of the lawn do I understand. Red, black, gold, and silver squares wind around the entire grassy area, forming a giant square that spirals inward.

"They painted the plant to make the board," Kassandra says.

We reach the tent and the cluster of fae in its shade: Death, Eli, and the king, clad in lavender. My blood sings at the sight of the royal in that color, for while small, it's my doing. Kassandra slows, Briar and I stopping short. The males take her in.

"My king," she says, curtsying. "Lord Eli."

"Lady Kassandra." The Head of Healing nods, smoothing down his embroidered red waistcoat.

"You look lovely today." King Maxian kisses her hand.

"You as well. That color suits you."

He grins, eyes flicking over her shoulder to me. He winks, then draws Kassandra closer, taking the parasol from her grasp and leading her to a long table lined with emerald wine bottles and two-bite cakes. They order sparkling wine from the faerie behind the table.

Lila emerges from the shade at the far side of the tent. Her golden silk uniform flutters in the spring breeze, and she curtsies to Lord Eli as she passes him. "My lord."

"Lila." His gaze roams over her. "How are you faring?"

"Better now that the weather is warming. Thank you for the tip about mushrooms."

He nods. "Did you try fish as well?"

She makes a face, and he laughs. They exchange a few more words before she joins Briar and me by a corner tent pole.

"What was that about?" I ask.

"Oh, Lord Eli suggested foods to improve my mood in the wintertime."

Yet Eli still looks at Lila with not appetite but rather something akin to awe, like a creature spotting sunlight after a storm. I store the observation away to ask her about it later.

"Do you know this game?" Briar asks Lila, who shakes her head.

I drop my voice. "Is it not odd that we're here?"

"Apparently, each High Fae was allowed to bring two of their . . . favorites." Lila winces. "Carter and I will be moved by the king, you and Briar by Kassandra. The two faeries by the food and drink are Healing Crests."

My gaze cuts to Kassandra, laughing at something the king says. Eli converses with Death brooding in the opposite corner.

"Oh, here come Carter and . . ." Lila stops, brows knitting.

I turn to see what has caught her attention, and my stomach bottoms out. Carter leads Lord Dominik toward us in a white-and-gold tunic, smiling like a wolf.

"Dom!" the king shouts. Next to him, Kassandra grips the stem of her glass and finishes her drink.

"Friends," the Heir of Illusion drones, striding under the shade of the tent, as I and the other faeries back away to make room. My stare drops to his boots, their shiny pointed toes pompous in the growing midafternoon light.

Briar catches my eye, and I understand our mistake. The siblings match in their white, and in the state gardens, with the flowing liquor and the little cakes, it looks as if they are getting married.

The three males clap one another on the back, smiling, laughing. Kassandra stands apart, inching around the crew. She darts over to us while Carter joins the king's side. The groups form—the females and the males—despite the varying statuses.

"I look ridiculous," Kassandra seethes, swatting at her skirt as it balloons in the wind. "Like one of those overfrosted cakes on the table."

Lila gapes. "No, you are a vision, my lady."

"Ugh, I don't seek flattery, but I always welcome it, so thank you."

"Would you like me to fetch you another wine?" Briar asks.

"Or two."

Briar nods, taking the empty glass from Kassandra, and departs. My mistress narrows her attention on me. "What did you say to the king?"

My tongue depresses with the weighty oath.

"For fuck's sake, Avery, if I wanted to interact with an entire casing of sausages today, I wouldn't have skipped breakfast," she snaps. Lila coughs, covering her mouth. Kassandra studies her for a moment. "You're Maxian's Lila, right?"

Maxian's Lila. As if Lila's a beloved pet.

"Yes, Lady Kassandra."

"He speaks highly of you during luncheons. He says you're the only thing that has kept him sane all these years."

Lila's blush deepens, and I close my mouth, trying to suppress the shock at my mistress's soft words and kind tone. It is not the smooth, light voice of a well-bred female or the surly retorts of a demanding superior. It's something else. It's her true voice.

"Thank you for relaying these words," Lila says.

"I have a favor to ask. Will you help keep *me* sane by keeping my dunce of an attendant in line? Perhaps some of your positive qualities could rub off on her, though miracles are rare these days."

My mouth drops open again. "Mistress, I—"

She whirls on me. "He and I were supposed to have a date—by

ourselves—tonight. Yet here we are instead, playing a childhood game with Eli and *my brother*. And the king wore my favorite color on him. Don't give me that look—just because they're slobbery dogs doesn't mean I can't occasionally admire the coat!"

"I didn't say anything!" I protest. A lie.

Lila goes to apologize for me, but I shake my head. It's not like that, not with Kassandra. To become a simpering fool would only anger her further. She wants a fight but can't have it with the males around her, so the best target is a faerie who will not submit easily. The plane swirls in her direction, my skin prickling.

"Avery," Kassandra warns.

"Act like it's still a date," I whisper.

The eddy of the plane slows, and my body sags with relief.

"Act like it's a date," I repeat. "Dominik may be repulsed by the flirtation, but he'll be appeased that you're pursuing the king. That way, he may not push so much anymore. He may even leave you alone."

Briar returns, handing her a glass. Throwing her head back, Kassandra downs the entire drink, then wipes her mouth with her hand.

"Fine, but I'm winning." She hesitates, eyeing me up and down, and a phantom hand squeezes my biceps. My heart jolts, but I don't move as she remarks: "What are you, made of rocks now?"

"I've been exercising while at Reign, my lady."

She wrinkles her nose. "Keep that to yourself."

Without another word, Kassandra stomps away.

In her wake, Lila shifts. "Is it always like this?"

"Yes," Briar and I reply.

"But . . . she values your opinion."

"She called me a dunce," I say.

"She's still following your advice." Lila nods.

Kassandra rejoins the males, reaching for the king, who takes her hand once more, cupping her palm as it grazes his cheek. Dominik makes a face. The king glances up, surveying the tent.

"High Fae and faeries! The game will begin when Lord Dominik's attendants arrive."

The Illusion heir glares at his sister from across their circle. Even by the king's side, Kassandra stiffens. The king glances between the siblings, angling his shoulders to face Dominik directly.

"Is everything all right, brother?" he asks.

"I knew they would be late," Dominik snorts.

"They're children, are they not?"

Briar sucks in a breath. I follow her gaze to the servants' entrance, which spits out two Unluckies, one tall and the other petite, ringed head to toe in debt. My mind registers his curls, his growing limbs, the wide and wild expression.

Benji.

My heart plummets, mouth drying out.

"Get over here!" Dominik yells, and I recoil.

The other faerie breaks into a jog, and Benji struggles to keep up, little chest heaving, face growing shiny already. "Benji!" I lurch forward, but Briar clutches my arm.

"Not here," she says.

He glances my way, fear in his eyes, and Dominik grabs his shoulder, smirking. Cold sweat rolls down my back. It's as if my night terrors have come to life.

Maxian quirks a brow. "The boy from the coronation?"

"You said I am to play on behalf of House of Death, as my sister is playing for Illusion and the executioner will be the game master. As there are no Death faeries here, I chose the Illusion Bases that are closest to death."

The king gestures to Dominik. "You seem to be feeling generous today."

"Perhaps we give the boy a chance at redemption."

"Pawns, to your places!" the king commands.

We line up at the start of the labyrinth, the widest part of the path at the bottom corner of the board. To my left are Lila and Carter. Briar stands on my right, and beyond her are the Healing faeries, then Benji and the other Unluckie.

"A quick overview of the rules," Death states, gruff voice scraping the air. He stands on the edge of the lawn with dice in hand. The High Fae linger beneath the tent for shade.

"His Magnificence will go first. All parties are forbidden to speak or touch one another for the duration of their turn. I will roll the dice, then reveal the number only to the king, who will move his faeries that many spaces. The High Fae can split the number between both faeries, but no two pawns of opposing teams can occupy the same square simultaneously.

"If the faerie lands on gold, they will move four more squares. If they land on silver, the High Fae will either swap them with another pawn or reverse another House's next number in the round, so their pawn moves backward. If the faerie lands on red, they are immune from a silver-square attack. Land on black, and the pawn must return to the starting line. Whichever High Fae can get their faerie of the same House to the center of the Pith first wins."

The king clasps his hands. "Thank you, Death. Now, after each round, High Fae and their faeries can strategize together for two minutes. Whichever pawn wins will keep the Prize of the Pith. Spend it, save it, give it away." He pauses, considering. "It is one gold coin."

A glint of gold appears in the center of the labyrinth, floating in the air. A collective gasp. One gold coin is worth one hundred silvers, one thousand coppers—what I make in a year as an Illusion Crest. Paid all at once toward debt . . . How many rings would that shave off? What lies at the center of the Pith is not just a coin. It is a once-in-a-century chance at freedom.

Sweat drips down my spine as the faeries shift eagerly. On the other side of the Healing attendants, Benji jerks his chin up.

If I cannot help Benji win, then I shall win and give it to him. The realization descends like a heavy blanket. The fleeting vision of my unmarred skin dies out.

"Are you ready to lose?" the king asks the other High Fae as he swaggers from the shade of the tent and toward Death.

"If history is any indicator, I will win." Kassandra smirks.

"Much has changed since then, Kass."

"Aye, but the crown did not come with a brain."

The king barks a laugh. When I glimpse my mistress, she is baring her teeth, and because she is a lady, the males perceive it as a smile and not a threat.

The executioner tosses the dice into the air, which disappear in the light of the sun, then land in his hand. Death reveals the result to the king, who nods.

The plane cascades with a sharp, jerking energy. To my left, Carter grunts. The valet teeters forward like a wooden toy. *Reign magic,* I realize with horror. The High Fae are using their magic to move us. We cannot even move ourselves.

Carter crosses two spaces, landing on a red square. Lila steps forward just one to a silver square, and the two switch places. She lands on the third spot, while he returns to the first.

Eli takes his turn and moves his pawn forward five spaces to the only gold square on this leg of the route, advancing another four spaces to the corner square, the first turn of the labyrinth. The king and Dominik swear, and Kassandra is silent.

Death rolls for Kassandra next. Briar passes Carter and Lila, stepping to the sixth spot, a red square. She is protected from silver-square attacks.

An unseen hand grabs my wrist, and I lock eyes with Kassandra, who raises a brow. I am yanked beyond Carter, Lila, and Briar, and the force lets go of my wrist.

My shoes glitter with gold paint. The males under the tent groan.

Grinning, Kassandra advances me the additional four spaces, until I occupy the same square as the Healing servant.

"We have our first match-up," Death announces. "As two faeries cannot occupy the same space, they must fight for it. The fights can include root magic, but the High Fae will decide. First to draw blood will win the spot. The losing faerie will be disqualified."

The Healing faerie swallows. My hands dampen with sweat. Kassandra's pale eyes pierce into me, cold and distant, and I do not keep the hate from mine.

How dare she? How dare she set me up like this? She chose to split her number this way—protecting Briar and setting me up for a fight and elimination.

"Lady Kassandra," the executioner says. "Will this fight include magic?"

"No."

I glare at her. The faeries whisper. The High Fae whip in her direction, mouths agape.

I think of the phantom hand, feeling my arm. *What are you, made of rocks now?*

The executioner simply nods. "Then it will be a fight of the fists."

My mind goes blank. If anyone protests or cuts in, I do not hear or see it. I only register the male in front of me widening his stance. We are similar in height, but his tattooed arms are as lean and muscular as mine from physical labor. He may outlast me, so I must end it quickly.

"I will give the signal in three," Death says over the murmuring High Fae.

They are betting.

They are betting on us.

White-hot anger flashes through my mind, and I remember standing outside a fighting pit long ago, watching my father pin down another faerie, pummeling him over and over, sweat and spittle and blood flying in every direction as coins changed hands and new bets were made.

"Three. Two—"

The executioner whistles.

I lunge, tackling the faerie, my back slamming on the grass as he twists to land on top of me. The air knocks from my lungs, his knee crunching my side. He winds up for a punch, but I surge forward, smashing my skull into his nose.

The faerie jerks back, swearing, but there's no blood yet. I throw an elbow against the nose with a crunch. He flops onto the ground, blood gushing from his nostrils.

"Fuck," he spits.

"Sorry," I say, offering a hand as I climb to my feet.

He knocks it away. "Don't bother."

He walks off the lawn, eliminated.

My dress stains with pigment, and I wipe the sweat from my forehead. From the tent, there's a quick shout, a laugh. Death announces my victory. The next turn commences, and I scan the board.

Benji cries out from the starting line.

He lands on the fourth square, a black one. My heart wrenches. He returns to the beginning, blinking, face blotchy with the onset of tears.

"The round is finished," Death declares. "You may speak to your faeries now."

The High Fae scatter like pearls off a snapped string. Only Dominik stays behind, grabbing another drink, a smirk on his face.

He will not let Benji win. He just wants to torture the boy. Fury awakens my genius, tingeing the air.

Kassandra whispers with Briar before making her way to me. When she reaches my side, I clench my fists.

"When plans changed, I asked Briar to tell me everything about herself and anything she knew of you," my mistress says. "She told me she's quick with water and your father was a fighter in the pits. Then you showed up, your genius and body different, and I knew how I wanted to place my bets."

I grit my teeth, then ask, "What's different about my genius?"

She looks across the field. "It's . . . fresher. As if you've been letting it out more. Now, do you want to win or just ask self-absorbed questions?"

I exhale. "I want Benji to win."

"Dominik will only tease him."

"I know," I mutter. "What's in it for the High Fae? If we get to keep the coin, what do you get?"

Kassandra frowns. "We take side bets each round with the biggest bet being the winner."

"How? I see no exchange of coin."

My mistress shifts. "It's complicated."

"One minute left!" the executioner shouts.

"I'm still blood sworn to you," I say. "I cannot tell a soul."

She looks away. "We buy and sell faerie debts."

"*What?*"

"Sometimes we trade debt. Other times, it's a one-way purchase."

"What are you saying?" I hiss. "Why jest with me like this?"

"I'm not jesting."

"But why own debt willingly?"

"Because then I become the creditor, and the creditor makes the coin. Say I buy one hundred Healing rings—birth debts—across different faeries. The House of Healing receives a full payment for those balances up front. But all future payments faeries make toward that debt and its interest go to me now. It's the interest that is key. It's about who owns whom, and for how long."

Nausea rolls through me. *They trade our debts like cards.*

"And what have you bet on?" I seethe.

"Just that you would win the first round. I haven't made the big bet yet. The winner obtains one hundred thousand rings of Reign debt across the most consistent-paying faeries."

I gasp. "You—"

"Don't step out of the square."

"Time's up!" the executioner shouts. "High Fae, back to the tent."

"I'll see you next round," she says, nodding. "You will win this. I will make sure."

"Don't you mean 'we'?" I cry.

Kassandra returns to the tent without responding. Panic builds in my throat, the urge to scream so strong I ache.

How are they able to purchase thousands of faeries' payments in one afternoon? I would never see that kind of money even after many lifetimes of working.

King Maxian takes his turn. Lila lands on the silver square behind me.

"The next time Illusion rolls their dice, they will reverse their steps!" Maxian calls out.

I glance at Lila. "I'm normally not violent."

"You had to be," she says. Her skin seems to glow in the sun, while mine has begun to turn from tan to red. "You have almost twenty rings, and I have never had more than thirteen. So I have not felt certain struggles."

I glance up. "Thank you" is all I can manage.

Thank you for your kindness when I do not deserve it. My anger and shame splinter under her compassion.

Eli approaches Death for his turn. He gets his remaining faerie on the board. Kassandra rolls, swearing.

A gentle tug on my stained dress, and I move backward, past Lila and another square until the fabric falls to my side once more, Kassandra letting go.

I am on a black square.

I trudge back to the starting line, passing Briar, who moves back one—onto the golden square. Her face breaks into a soft grin, and despite what this will mean for Benji and me, my chest feels lighter as she moves four steps forward, now standing where I was, in front of Lila.

I reach the starting line, where the Unluckie and Benji wait. He shifts, not looking at me.

"I haven't seen you fight in a long, long time," he says after a moment.

"I'm sorry," I whisper.

The boy shrugs. "It's okay."

Then he yelps, flying forward onto the fourth square once more, the black one. My jaw clenches. Under the tent, Dominik grins. Picking himself up, Benji retreats to the starting line once more.

"You okay?" I ask.

"Asshole."

"Don't say that, they might hear you," I scold. "Where did you hear that word, anyway?"

"Around the Nest."

"Be careful about—"

"Jae-jae is dead," he says flatly. "You are gone, and I am an Unluckie."

"I'm not gone," I say. "I'm right here—"

"I don't care."

My heart splinters at his hopelessness. *It was supposed to be different for him,* I think, blinking back tears. *Jae gave so that it would be different for him. So that he would have a chance.*

Lila advances in the lead, and Carter lands on Briar's square.

"Another match-up!" the executioner shouts. "My king, will this fight include magic?"

"Yes." He waves his hand.

A bucket of water plops down between them. The sun presses against my neck, my hairline growing damp.

"You may begin!"

Carter holds up his hands while Briar flicks her fingers. "Don't worry, I'm not gonna hit an older—hey, ow!"

He grabs his cheek, his palm coming away with a line of red. The sliver of ice drops to the grass as Briar lowers her hand.

She smiles. "For a boy, you're pretty slow."

"I'm not a—planes." Carter steps away, shaking his head. "Respect."

She laughs, giving him a pat as he walks away. Although Carter should seethe, should rage, he just continues to shake his head, joining the king. After all, he only has four rings total.

After Eli's turn, Kassandra rolls, and I feel the pull on my wrist again.

"I'll see you at the center, Bee," I say.

"Whatever," he says. My throat tightens, but before I can say more, Kassandra's unseen hands lead me to the silver spot right before my superior.

"That was quick," I say to Briar. "You were quick."

"Of course I was." And there's a sparkle in her eye.

During Dominik's turn, Benji moves forward onto a silver square.

"The child will switch places with Lila," Dominik announces.

"Lila's on a red," Maxian shoots back, his voice tinged with tension. "She's immune."

"Fine—with the Healing faerie, then."

Benji is dragged across the lawn. I bristle, balling my fists, grinding my teeth. There is no point in interfering. Benji is now second behind Lila, followed by Briar, then me, then the Unluckie, and the Healing faerie in last place.

When Kassandra comes to me between rounds, I tell her: "My lady, place your big bet on Benji. Dominik is using both pawns now for a greater chance at winning."

She glances at the center of the board. "And why should I bet against myself?"

My blood burns with fury. "Then win with him."

"Didn't you listen to the rules?"

"*Whichever High Fae can get their faerie of the same House.* You and Benji are of the same House, technically."

She twists the parasol. "Why him and not yourself?"

"Because look at him."

Kassandra does. She stares at his limbs for a long time.

"I tried to revoke the complaint," she finally says to my shock. "The one about destruction of property. But I'm only allowed to file complaints, not retract them. Dominik can retract them, and he will not. I pleaded anyway, but he never listens."

Powerlessness chokes me. Something small and bright dims inside me, and only then do I realize it was ignorant hope. It's time to lay my only card on the table. For Benji, and his spirit. He needs that golden coin.

"If you win with Benji, I will tell you a way around the oaths," I say.

Kassandra whips to me. "There's no way around the oaths."

"Then how do the rumors always slip out?"

"Are you mad?" Her nails sink into the flesh of my forearm. "There is no way around the oaths."

I swallow. She has never touched me with her own hands before. The daggers of her nails nearly break skin.

"You would have a double-sworn faerie, able to witness the secrets of two Houses—and relay it back to you."

She shakes her head. "This is— No. I will win this fairly because I can, and I will use the hundred thousand to bargain more financial freedom. I do not need to resort to treacherous things."

Your brother always acts in treachery.

"One more minute!" the executioner calls.

"You're a fool, you know," she seethes. "Most High Fae would have you killed for such talk."

But not you, I think. Instead, I say, "I would not risk my head for a lie."

"Shifty thing." She glares at me, but her grasp on my arm gentles.

Then she is gone.

I rub the crescent moons imprinted on my arm. Will my gamble work, or will it backfire?

As the sun climbs higher, the High Fae drink and laugh, and we sweat and shuffle around the board. Only one match-up occurs, between Briar and the other Healing faerie, where Briar wins again, eliminating Healing from the game altogether.

There are no gold squares in the final spiral. After an hour, I stand just two turns over from the Pith. Before me is Lila, and several squares behind me is Briar. Benji and the other Unluckie are behind her, on the previous leg of the board.

The High Fae use only one die now. Dominik rolls, and the Unluckie takes the lead. Benji remains where he is. Dominik has chosen the other faerie to be his winner.

Before the next round, Kassandra darts straight to me. "It would pass the rules. I asked Death. But the consequences will be great."

Lila takes the lead back, turning a corner. Her eyes gleam as she lands on a silver square. Maxian orders House of Death to move backward next round. Briar moves up onto a red. I stay on mine.

Benji moves backward—on a black square.

The child lets out a sob. A groan ripples through the lawn.

He shields his face as he trudges back to the starting line. Flopping down, he weeps the uncontrollable shudders of a child.

Again, Kassandra returns to me first. "I'll do it. I will win with the child. But you'll have to force Dominik's hand to get Benji back on the board again."

"How?"

"You'll know," she says.

Lila has to move backward this turn, a previous request.

Kassandra rolls. I take two spaces forward—and bump right into the Unluckie. The phantom hand from Kassandra drops.

No, I think. *Not this.*

As the Unluckie turns, he startles—and so do I. It is the Unluckie I gave High Fae food to, only weeks ago.

"You," he breathes.

The blood drains from my face. "I—"

"Where have you been?" he gasps.

"Please," I whisper. "Not here."

The executioner declares a match between us. The Unluckie just stares, limbs long and collarbone jagged under inked skin.

"Why wouldn't you meet me? Rats had gotten into the sack you left two weeks ago. And then last week, there was nothing at all." His voice cracks. "Do you know how hard it is to stomach the food now that we know it's rotten? Do you know what it's like to see rats eat better than you?"

Kassandra declares the use of magic in this fight.

"I can explain," I say, but really, I can't.

Do less alone, Jeremee had begged, and I thought at the time it was selfish to pull others into my thieving. I have done what the High Fae do; I centered myself instead of the people in need, and now my work of the past few years disintegrated on a whim.

The executioner begins the countdown.

"I'm not ready," I say.

"So?" the Unluckie snaps. "Someone has to take the coin."

The coin.

Oh planes, if I lose, so will Benji. If I win, I will screw over this Unluckie. How can I levy someone's pain against another's? We fight over so little when the High Fae have so much.

The whistle blows. Time is up.

I send a request along the plane to a sharp rock at my foot. The rock declines, silent and stubborn. My genius pushes downward, finding a small root whose origins I do not have time to discover. Nature accepts this time, letting my energy collide with its own.

Hello, the root seems to say, and my genius sings in recognition.

Power floods me in a torrent stronger than any I have ever known.

The Unluckie lunges.

I sidestep, flicking my wrist.

The root shoots up from the ground like an extension of me, scraping against the Unluckie's ribs. He thuds to the grass, scrambles, and stands. He reaches for me again, but the executioner is whistling once more.

We glance down at ourselves, each other. A small dot of red stains his thin shirt. There wasn't even a fight.

"No," the Unluckie says.

The power fades, the root returning to its rest once more. I feel cold in its absence.

"Illusion has won the match-up!" the executioner shouts.

Dominik yells something crass. A glass breaks. He has lost out on a hundred thousand debt rings, unless he wants to use his other player, Benji.

"No," the Unluckie grits out again, shaking. "But you have so little debt compared to me!"

My throat thickens. "I'm sorry—"

"This isn't fair," he moans, tears streaming down his exhausted face. His eyes flick to the gold coin in the center.

He leaps forward, shoving me to the ground. Shouts erupt across the field as the Unluckie sprints to the Pith, diving for the coin. He lifts it up, crying out in joy, like a starving male who finally found a grape to savor.

The king reaches him a moment later and waves his fingers. The faerie flinches, opening up his empty palms to the sun. He drops to his knees once more. Sobs bubble up as he rakes into the ground with bony fingers.

"Where is it?" he wails. "Where is it?"

Tears roll down my cheeks. Someone sniffles beside me.

"Where did it go?" the male croaks. "It was right here!"

The king crouches down next to the faerie, placing a hand on his shoulder. He murmurs something soft, calm. I hold my breath, waiting for the faerie to strike or scream or spit, even if it means death. Instead, the faerie and King Maxian rise together, arm in arm, the dozens of tattoos of one clashing against the untouched skin of the other. The king holds up the debtor like he would any friend, gentle and patient. My jaw drops.

When they stride past me, the king is saying, ". . . but it wouldn't be fair to the others. However, I appreciate your participation and for that, I can offer you this silver."

The faerie holds it to his chest. "Thank you, my king. Thank you."

"Thank you for your service."

"He should be whipped for his insolence." Dominik stalks up to them. His white tunic is askew, strands of hair falling from the ribbon that holds it up.

The faerie trembles.

"He will not be," the king says, moving beyond his friend and toward the tent.

"He broke the most important rule!"

"Rules can change."

"Then what's the point, Max?" Dominik yells.

"Of what?"

"The game!" he snaps. "If you can change the rules whenever you want?"

"The point is that I am your king," Maxian bellows. Energy crackles in the air, the plane flooding with the power of his genius. "I am your king and can do what I please."

My knees quiver, body aching to drop to the shuddering grass in primal submission.

Dominik steps back, bowing, lowering his gaze. "Of course, my king."

"Now," the royal says, patting the Unluckie. "Todd is going to work as a Reign Base from here on out."

The Heir of Illusion raises glinting black eyes.

"Yes, Your Magnificence." Dominik retreats as the king brings the Unluckie over to Carter, doling out instructions. Carter leads the faerie off the garden lawn and toward the servants' entrance into the building.

The plane settles, but my nerves do not.

Kassandra is tight-lipped as her brother bends over her, snarling something. She steps away from him, joining Maxian and Eli by the executioner. The Illusion heir grabs another drink. Dominik rolls and Benji steps forward, landing on a silver near the start.

Something shoves me to the ground. The force grips my hair, yanking, and I stumble to my feet, eyes stinging, as Dominik uses his magic to swap us.

Benji takes my spot in third place, and I his, in last place. My supervisor strides to her spot in second place. I think of the family that awaits in her future, her joy put on hold for decades. Misery washes through me.

The last round begins with Lila in the lead, Briar only a few squares behind her, then Benji, covering his sunburned face, as I remain at the starting line.

Lila enters the inner spiral, only a few paces away from winning. Briar strides forward, landing on Lila's square.

"A match-up!"

A bucket of water appears.

I squint, trying to read Lila's body language from this distance. I've rarely seen her magic outside of lacing and inventing. I don't know which element she excels in or how quick she is.

But she gazes between her arms and Briar's, and although Briar has so few for an Illusion Crest, Lila has even fewer. When Briar forms an ice needle, Lila only holds up an arm in a flimsy attempt, and the older faerie pricks her palm.

Briar steps back, astonished. Lila nods her way, then she—and the House of Reign—leave the game.

The plane does not react. Instead, the king watches his future bride, a lopsided smile gracing his lips, and I think that even if Kassandra loses to Dominik today, she may be winning the war.

Dominik rolls and Benji steps onto a silver square, one spot behind Briar, both of them only a handful of spots away from the coin.

"Illusion will need to move backward on their next round!" the executioner declares.

Kassandra rolls. The king whispers something to her. She shakes her head, not looking his way. A small pull on my dress moves me back two spaces until I am once again at the starting line. Dominik leans into Death.

"Illusion's turn has yet to finish," the executioner booms.

The lord glowers.

She's going with Briar, I realize, heart sinking. The sun hurts my eyes. *He needed this. Benji needed this—does she not see?*

But can I blame her? She must choose between Briar, a servant she's cared for her whole life, who has raised her—or a child she doesn't know.

So I watch Briar and wait for any sign of Kassandra's magic urging her forward. But my supervisor does not move at all.

Murmurs under the tent.

A thought sinks through me like a river stone. Kassandra is delaying because moving back means that Briar will need to match up with Benji.

Benji spins around, facing me, confused. *It'll be okay*, I try to convey. My only hope is that Briar will pity him.

But then he takes a step back, moving closer to the Pith.

Dominik lets out a laugh. "What are you—"

The boy moves backward again, landing on Briar's spot. He moves back again and again and again, spiraling inward, closer to the center.

I understand. The rules say the faerie must move backward. But they never specified that they had to be facing forward when they did it.

Benji retreats backward into the Pith. The boy clenches his fist, trembling as realization dawns. He bends down and wraps his small fist around the prize. He holds it up—the golden coin glinting in the sun.

He won.

Kassandra won.

We won.

But under the tent, the males do not stir, even if the plane does. Maxian and Dominik stare at the board with tight jaws, though the king tries to laugh his off.

Kassandra strolls to congratulate Benji—the least-titled among them winning with the weakest of faeries. For even with crowns and callings like head of House, they are not a worthy opponent of hers.

Then the plane floods with furious energy, like a raging river, and I sink to my knees beneath its surface.

Chapter Eighteen

THE OTHER FAERIES DROP WITH ME. THE GRASS IS SCRATCHY, poking through my skirts. In and out, I breathe, head swarming with the sudden rush of power, the world spinning. Beneath the tent, Maxian laughs loudly, forcefully.

"Don't be a sore loser, Dom."

"She cheated," he snaps.

"Technically, she followed the rules," the executioner says.

"Pull in your genius," the king says. "That's an order."

The spinning slows, then stops. I clutch my stomach and exhale through the dark spots blotting my vision.

"Faeries," the king calls. "Join us under the tent for some well-deserved water and cake."

Sugary cake is the last food I crave at this moment, instead aching for bread or a ginger tea. Still, I brush off my skirts.

"I won," a small voice says. "I won."

Standing, I take in a shocked Benji, blinking, showing me the coin.

"You did." I smile.

"How?" he asks. "Why me and not the other lady?"

"I . . . don't know."

Kassandra does much that makes little sense.

The boy turns the coin over and over in his palm, his neck red from the sun.

"How do you feel?" I ask.

He looks up, suddenly sheepish. "Sunburned."

I laugh. "Let's get some water."

When we approach the water station, the High Fae males are still debating. Briar and I exchange a look, but I break my gaze off first, ashamed. While I will always choose Benji, it had to come at the cost of her future today. My heart squeezes when Benji accepts the mug of water I offer him, and we both drain our cups, the water sweet and cool on my parched lips.

"Give me that coin, boy," Dominik demands, stalking closer. My hand falls on Benji's shoulder, moving him behind me.

"Dom, let it go." Kassandra steps between us, chin raised.

"What's this?" he scoffs. "The Heart of Illusion finally feels something?"

"Let it go," she repeats, but standing just in front of me, I see her shaking.

"Fuck you." He shoves her aside, and she smashes into the ground. I push Benji farther back, the other faeries forming a protective half circle around us.

"Stop this!" Kassandra cries. "Stop—"

Dominik jerks back like a marionette, slamming against the grass. A grunt escapes his clenched teeth, his body locked stiff, eyes darting from side to side.

"What did I just see?" comes a voice, smooth and dark like a death shroud.

No one moves. No one but the king, who steps toward the scene, hands behind his back, face cold and eyes piercing. He bends over Dominik.

"How drunk are you?" the king growls. "To touch her in anger."

Dominik seethes something unintelligible.

The king crouches down. "Tell me. Explain yourself."

Spit slides out the side of the fae's mouth, unable to move his tongue to form words.

"That's right, you can't. Since you do not heed my commands, maybe you will heed my magic. Maybe that's the only language you can understand. So let me be clear: If you ever touch her, or any other lady, like that again, I will come for you." King Maxian stands. "It is only because of our friendship that I am giving you this warning."

Then the king turns, releasing Dominik, and approaches us. I flinch, pushing Benji back again, but the king helps Kassandra to her feet.

"Are you okay?"

"I'm fine," she says, trembling, looking away. I know that look. She is ashamed not that it happened, but that others saw. "I'm so—"

"Don't you dare apologize," he murmurs. "I apologize for everything, truly. I'm sorry you saw me like that, that I had to be that."

"Sometimes the animal only responds to the whip," Kassandra says, face falling back into cool indifference. It makes me shiver. The pair glances back at the Illusion heir, propped up on his elbows, muddied and flushed and brimming with rage.

"I'm quite impressed by your cunning, Lady Kassandra," the king says. "It's quite a royal quality. I think you should be rewarded for it, even if my ego is a little bruised."

A light laugh between them.

"I declare both you and the boy the winner," the king says. "Shall we make it official?"

A piece of parchment pops up in one hand, a quill in the other. He jots down the notes, then laces them away. Benji sucks in a breath. I pat his back, heart clenching.

"Thank you." Kassandra curtsies.

"Let's have dinner tonight," Maxian says, then gestures to the High Fae. "We have much to celebrate now and in the days to come."

This is it, I think. *He will propose tonight. We have won. We will be safe.*

Benji tugs on my sleeve. "Will you come with me to deposit this?"

I take in the true purpose to this all, the meaning of my life now—this boy. My only family left.

"Of course."

As the High Fae and faeries break up to rest and prep for tonight's dinner, I lead Benji through the cool, dark tunnel of the Nest. The boy wraps the coin in his fist, shoves his hand into his pocket. The silence is tense until we reach the creditor's counter.

Benji hands him the coin, and the halfling gasps.

"His Magnificence sent the paperwork through," I say. "It's a tip from Reign."

When the teller pricks Benji's finger, words scrawl across parchment. He nods.

Then Benji laughs. "It tickles!"

Rolling up a pant leg, we watch as ring after ring disappears from his ankle, his shin, his knee and thigh until only one remains. It's a miracle, the coin erasing more than just one tattoo. Perhaps it is that the tattoos were smaller, having been inked on a small body. Perhaps they didn't have time to thicken with interest. Either way, it doesn't matter.

What matters is that he grins at me, and I grin back. Pure joy sparks at the sight of that unmarked skin once more, the light that returns to his eyes. It was all worth it. He won, we won, and soon we may both be free.

I wish Jeremee were here to see it.

Something must give in my expression, for Benji's face falters. He pushes down his pant leg. The moment skitters away like a spider.

"Jae-jae is still dead," the boy says.

"I know," I say, reaching for him, but he flinches away.

"Avery!" Briar shouts. "Avery!"

She rushes toward us, hair undone, shoving others out of the way. There is a cut on her cheekbone that wasn't there before.

"What is it?" I ask. "My planes, are you okay?"

Her mouth open, only the sound of choking escapes. The Illusion oath.

Something has happened in the House of Illusion.

"Benji, I have to go," I say, turning.

But the boy is already gone.

Chapter Nineteen

The parlor is destroyed—the settee overturned, a broken mirror on the floor, the curtains ripped, as if a wild animal tore through the room.

Briar leads me to the bedroom, tears rolling down her cheeks. Kassandra lies limp in the bed. The room feels cold, far away, and I stagger forward, falling at her bedside, gaping at her black eye.

"I tried," Kassandra says. "I was not strong enough."

"I don't understand," I gasp. Briar sniffs and props up Kassandra's head, tipping a vial of tonic into her mouth.

"Lord Eli," I say. "We must tell Lord Eli. He can bear witness to what has been done, and he can Heal—"

"No," my mistress rasps.

"We must."

"He did not break my arms this time."

"So? Any harm is unacceptable! The king said—"

"No!"

"Why not?" I ask. "Why not ask for help?"

"The House," she whispers. "The House cannot appear divided."

"Fuck the House," I snarl. Kassandra bares her canines.

"Avery!" Briar scolds.

"Punish me for saying this, for it needs to be said. Lord

Dominik is an unstable, abusive, violent male. He needs to be stopped."

"My father is dying," Kassandra snaps. "My mother is dead, I have few friends in this court, and the laws are not written in my favor. What do you suggest?"

"The king," I repeat. "The king just said—"

"I canceled my appearance tonight. I have already sent word. I want to be alone."

"He *will* propose."

"And I am to stake our safety on the whims of another male?"

Our safety. I promised to become her spy, confessed to knowing a way around the oaths. She's merely protecting her newest asset. Right?

We stare at each other, the pause unsettled.

"Perhaps we speak to the Council of Keepers," Briar suggests softly.

"Hearts of Houses do not get a vote on the council unless they're pregnant with an heir. We don't even get a seat."

"What of the debt you won?" I ask.

"The debt?" Briar echoes.

"It goes to House Illusion," Kassandra says. "Even if it's in my name, I do not own it."

"Write to the advisor," I say.

"Dominik reads every letter I send."

"Then let's—"

"Do you think I have not tried for two centuries, Avery? Do you think so lowly of me that I would not fight at every turn? Because I have. I have and it only makes things worse and I am so tired. I'm so tired."

I blink, feeling numb.

"But we won," I say. "You won. Today."

Kassandra scoffs. "Only because the king allowed it."

"But—"

"It's rigged, this game. If I win by following the rules, they change them. If I win through subterfuge, I am punished. The point is not their victory; it is watching me lose. As long as Dominik is heir, he will always use his strength to hurt me. If I say anything to Maxian, Dominik will make sure I will never speak again. Not even as queen will I be safe."

"You don't know that," I say weakly.

"He told me so. I do not want to test it."

"Today, the king said he would protect you," Briar offers. "You don't have to tell him. You can show him."

"Again, so I can exchange one pair of grabbing hands for another? Tie my safety up in sex? I've already kissed the kissing king, and look what good that did." We say nothing. Kassandra sighs. "Briar, can you get some broth from the kitchens? And ice. My jaw hurts."

My supervisor departs without a word.

"Change into your Reign outfit," Kassandra says. "Then return to me."

I do what she asks. When I return, the bowl of broth remains untouched by her bedside, and Briar is finished helping her into her nightgown. Kassandra drops into bed once more, Briar pulling up the covers. Kassandra then dismisses her, so that it is just us two.

"Oil, Avery," my mistress says. "The silver-topped yellow bottle."

I survey the dozens of pigments and glass bottles on her vanity and collect a pale gold one with a silver cap.

Pulling out the dropper, I guide it toward her, but she says, "You put it on."

"Me?"

"Yes, you."

"Why?"

"Just do it."

I drop the oil onto my collarbone. It smells of vanilla and jasmine, musky but gentle, before finishing off with a twinge of something sweeter.

"Rub."

I spread the oil across the hollow of my throat. She watches it drip between my breasts as I massage my chest. My skin gleams in the fireplace light.

She gestures to my exposed midriff above the gold pants. *What the planes is going on?* The king isn't visiting tonight. What game is she playing now?

Kassandra parts her mouth, her eyes widening.

"Are you making fun of me?" I blurt.

"Yes," she rasps. "Waist."

Suppressing a grunt of frustration, I rub my midriff with the oil, the scent heady but a touch sweet, an intoxicating aroma I can't identify. It's . . . sensual.

I will never admit this. I should never even feel this. But a small part of me relishes in the thrill of her instructions and my deliverance. As if it's a private show, a meal, a secret. In the way she wets her lips, eyes trailing along my exposed skin, as if we explore my body together. Even in her weakness, I feel her demands.

"Done," she says, waving me off.

I stop, hands slick with oil. My face flares with heat and suddenly I want to wash, to change, to pretend it never happened. I feel empty now that she has taken her fill.

I recap the bottle and return it to her vanity. I force myself to stand in front of her once more, feeling cumbersome and dirty, like a greased pig.

Kassandra just surveys me, her expression unreadable.

"Was this truly necessary?" I ask.

"Yes," she says. "Peach. For Dominik, tonight."

My blood turns to ice.

For Dominik.

She is not done playing the game. She has just swapped our places.

Chapter Twenty

That evening, three violet gazes watch Lila and me set up service in the red-draped dining room. Behind the head of the cherry table hangs the royal portrait of Wilhelm Vandorne the Uniter, founder of the Amyrian kingdom thousands of years ago. He wears an enormous black beard and a leopard-trimmed cape, the Golden Whip clutched in one hand. A giant eagle perches on his other arm, dwarfed by its owner's massive frame. To the right is the portrait of his son, the late Gregor the Great, similarly dark-haired, wearing intricate armor, the whip now inlaid with spikes. To the left is a rosy-cheeked Maxian from his early two hundreds, lounging in a loose white tunic and holding a bitten apple. So soft and golden in comparison to his father and grandfather. A kissing king, indeed.

Next to me, Lila muddles together lavender sprigs, honey, and lemon in a goblet. Even with the array of herbs and fruits on the serving cart, the scent of oil on my skin lingers.

"To sparkle the water, you need to infuse it with your breath," Lila says.

"My breath?"

She pours water from the carafe into the goblet. "The specialty drink has bubbles, but it isn't fermented, it's mixed. So I exhale into the water, infusing it with my breath."

I scrunch up my nose. "Is that clean?"

Lila laughs. "I don't know. And I don't think they care. They just like the bubbles. Here, watch."

Cupping her palms, she breathes out, and herbal magic drifts into the plane. The air in her palm shimmers, the candlelight catching its movement, and she drops it into the glass, then stirs. The water fizzes.

"Done." She smiles, turning to me.

"How did you discover this?"

Those rich eyes, like rain-soaked clay, slide to mine, and she lifts her chin. "If they can wield their magic to destroy . . . why can't I use mine to create?"

I suck in a breath. "Lila."

"I mean it. As long as they choose to ruin, I choose to build."

Tears prick my eyes, and I blink rapidly. "But what if they will always destroy everything we build?"

A demolished parlor. The Unluckie keening as the gold vanished from his grasp.

"Then I will always rebuild," she says, jaw set. "If we don't, there will be nothing."

I pick up the cool, fizzing drink, her granular act of protest. "You are powerful," I state.

Before she can reply, the plane stills. The door clicks open.

Lord Eli enters, dressed in a trim emerald tunic, followed by the cloaked figure of the king's executioner, the wide hood falling to his shoulders, a stretch of skin visible behind his mask. Lila smiles, soft and natural like the rising sun. If I did not witness the transition, I would not see it for what it truly is: armor.

"Good evening, my lord." She curtsies.

In Illusion, she would be punished for speaking first. But in the House of Reign, we are entertainers, company. Eli's gaze flickers over Lila before landing on the set table with only three spots. The executioner retreats to a corner, arms clasped behind his back.

"Hello, Lila, Avery," Eli says. "When will Lady Kassandra arrive?"

My throat tightens, and I curtsy. "Lady Kassandra has had too much sun today."

"I'll have a balm sent over."

"My lord, would it be possible to send over a pain tonic as well? I know she suffers from a terrible headache." I wince, knowing she will not be happy.

"I'll let a Healer know to prepare something."

For a moment, the coiled tension loosens from my muscles. It's small, but it's something.

"Are you okay, after today?"

The shift in Eli's tone has my head snapping up. Softer than before, though he's always been somewhat gentle. Yet the Head of Healing is watching Lila, his brows knit in concern.

"Of course!" She smiles wider. "It was nice to be outside."

"The game was crude. I apologize." Eli glances away from us, as if embarrassed. I try to hide my surprise, but Lila does not falter.

"No need. Now, what would you like to drink? We have non-liquored options."

"Whatever is available."

The doors slam open on a gust of icy wind. Dominik prowls inside, beady eyes pinning me in place, and his lips curl into a lupine grin. In an instant, the plane swells toward him, sinking onto his skin to store for later. I curtsy.

"Lower."

Phantom hands shove down my shoulders. My curtsy deepens, my legs straining.

Pointy boots. I stare at his frilly, pointy boots, lacquered like the floors.

"Avery," Eli interjects. I look up as Lila hands Eli a drink, her expression worried. He frowns, eyes cutting to Dominik. "You may stand."

The hands disappear, and I almost stumble with the sudden lack of pressure. "What can I get you this evening, Lord Dominik?" I ask, straightening.

"Where is my darling sister?" He bares his teeth in a passable smile.

"Apparently, she doesn't feel well," Eli says. "I'm sending over a tonic."

"No need, Eli. The faerie is misinformed."

I bite my lip, grasping for a reply that will keep Kassandra safe but keep my head on my shoulders, too. Eli beats me to it.

"Can't hurt," he says.

"She's fine," Dominik snaps.

"Are you a Healer?"

The Heir of Illusion turns, facing the Head of Healing. "What did you just say?"

But the other fae remains unruffled, calm. "I said, are you a Healer? I think not. Besides, Kassandra seems to suffer many head pains, so having an extra tonic on hand can't hurt."

"Then you do not know my sister. She's the type to swallow the whole vial for an afternoon of attention."

"Then I'll give her attention," Eli answers. "Anyone who harms themself still needs help."

The pair watch each other, tense, the plane pitching and rolling, warming and cooling. I clench my jaw to keep nausea at bay and, in the silence, scrape together my courage.

"Would you like a strong drink, Lord Dominik?" I ask.

"Fine."

I'm tempted to spit in his cup. Lila joins me at the bar cart.

"What was that about?" she whispers. I shake my head, and she says, "I can deliver drinks if you'd like to gather the small bites from the Mouth. They won't sit until the king is here, but they'll snack."

She's giving me a way out. My eyes fall to the lavender drink.

"For the king?" I ask.

She nods. "I'll add ice when he arrives."

If they can wield their magic to destroy . . . why can't I use mine to create?

I pick up an orange from the cart. "I can prepare and serve. I'd like to try a new drink. Something of my choice."

Lila's expression relaxes.

"You're powerful, too." She pats my arm before slipping through the servants' door.

The males are wrapped in conversation on the far end of the room.

". . . and what of the vote in the coming months?" Dominik is asking. "Do you know how Reign will decide?"

"I'm not sure even House of Healing agrees fully. Among our two seats, we are divided."

"Mm," muses the wolf. "House of Death always votes down the line. They must have graves for brains as well as homes."

The executioner doesn't move.

I chop up a strip of orange rind, toss it in the grinder along with clove, cinnamon, and cardamom. I pour the mixture into a glass of water to let it absorb. From the second shelf of the cart, I pull out the smoky amber liquor distilled in the white oak barrels in the Nest.

Flipping through my knowledge of plants like a deck of cards, I find the herb I need. The closed-bottle gentian. Indigo petals form an oblong shape, the edible root bittersweet. It has an earthiness similar to tarragon, a smell like fresh soil, like faerie magic.

It's not in the bar cart.

Staring down at my golden moth ring, a new idea occurs. What if it's too much for me to lace myself and food at the same time? What if the trick is lacing the food alone?

The servants' door opens and Lila glides in, a tray of goat cheese and fig pastries in her hands. She quirks a brow at my work. "Everything okay?"

"Just making a drink for Lord Dominik."

She nods on her way to the High Fae. In a moment, her light laughter bubbles into the space, followed by the rumble of male jokes, the scrape of plates.

My attention hovers on the golden moth ring, my mind's eye seeing a map of the Illusion courtyards, the winding paths and shifting hedges. The little pops of indigo petals from an emerald bush near the western wall. The ring warms, energy buzzing, as my genius unspools through me and twists with the borrowed Reign magic.

I push the energies onto the plane, reaching, stretching toward that bush. My consciousness flattens, squeezes through mounting pressure, before bursting out on the other side. I feel it then, a piece of my genius hovering before the bush like a wraith, a small thread tying back to me, anchored in my finger.

After I thank the flower, my genius tugs on the shoot until it comes free, root and all. Cradling the shoot in my mind, I strain the plant through the compression, reel it toward me like spinning that thread around the spool once more.

The chatter of males titters in my ears, my focus blurring, chest tightening as the panic sets in. I am in the plane and I am here; I am nowhere. My grip falters on the mental limb, and I yank it toward me before it's lost altogether.

My consciousness slams back into my body. Trembling, one hand gripping the cart, I gaze at the other, a white-knuckled fist. Uncurling my fingers, I take in the closed-bottle gentian in my palm.

I did it. I laced *food*. How much food could I lace to the tunnels, to the Peri, with this ability, while I wait for Maxian to approve my proposal? I could cry. With shaking fingers, I cut off the root, grind it with the mortar and pestle, drop it into the mixture. Straining the herbed water into a glass with the brown liquor and sugar, I garnish it with a thin slice of orange skin. The concoction should come out bittersweet, tangy, a little smoky.

A headache pulses behind my eyes, but I feel proud, no matter Dominik's response. I bounce toward the males and Lila, drink in hand.

"My lord."

"Took you long enough."

"Consider this a thank-you for sending me to the House of Reign." I smile at his pale, cold face, the silver hair that brushes his shoulders. "No one else in the kingdom of Amyria has had this drink before."

"And how do you know that?"

"I created it now, just for you."

The Illusion lord curls his lip. What is he thinking? That I am stupid or devious or both? Perhaps I don't mind the glint of suspicion in his eye, as if I am a threat to be noticed.

"I'm happy to give this to Lord Eli instead," I suggest.

"I will have it." Dominik snatches the glass and brings it up to his nose, inhales. He sips the concoction, rolls it across his tongue. He blinks. "It . . . is satisfactory," he says, passing the drink to Eli.

"What's in it?" the Head of Healing sniffs. "Orange, cinnamon, clove. But also something herbal?"

"Closed-bottle gentian," I say. "From the Illusion courtyards."

Dominik's icy stare burns into me. "And how did you acquire *that*?"

I grin. "Magic."

"I'll have something different." But when Dominik shoves the glass into my hands, it is empty.

The plane rumbles. Tumbling power fills the space, followed by a ripping noise. A great, awful, shredding sound of thick fiber.

The grandiose royal portrait of Wilhelm the Uniter splits open, and from the torn canvas steps out King Maxian.

"My lords!" he says. "Let's have some fun tonight, shall we?"

Dominik swears. "Must you always act like that? Are we not too old for your hauntings?"

"One could argue we've only just lived long enough to start collecting ghosts." Max laughs. "At our age, our fathers were killing Death fae in droves. No offense, Executioner," he adds, throwing a glance to the shadow in the corner.

The shadow doesn't move.

"Our fathers couldn't find the clit," Dominik murmurs to himself.

Eli cleans his glasses. "Who says you can find it now?"

Lila giggles behind her hand and I elbow her. Eli finds us, smiling. The look the Illusion heir throws his way could ice over lakes.

"Yes, I would've quite liked to make your sister turn pink, but it seems the sun beat me to it," the king drawls.

Dominik groans. "Where's my fucking drink?"

I can't help it. I cough in shock. Maxian's gaze slides to Lila and me, grinning. What has gotten into these males? "Shall we see what the ladies have prepared for us this evening?"

My neck and chest flush, to my horror. No one's ever called me a lady.

Lila giggles again next to me. "You are too good, Your Magnificence!"

"As are you, Lila."

Their pleasantries should grate, so at odds with what is happening in the Illusion apartments, though I know that this is the power of Lila's armor: shine and shine and shine until all the High Fae can see is a reflection of their best and most adored selves.

The king steps toward the table, rapping his knuckles against the wood. "Now, since it'll just be the boys and I for dinner—I say let's move to the lounge."

"Shall Carter bring some vices?" Lila wonders.

"As long as only you and Avery deliver them."

Goosebumps bud across my skin, for I have no idea what that could mean.

"How about some tobacco sparks?" Dominik suggests as Lila heads for the door.

"Terrible for the lungs," Eli mutters.

"But your favorite."

"Yes, even Healing fae have vices."

"We all have many," the king says, gaze sliding to me again. "Even the ones I hate, I love to hate them."

"Avery," Dominik snaps. "My drink?"

The rapping on the table stops.

I glance at the king, but he is watching Dominik. That beaming smile of white, straight teeth does not reach his eyes.

"Please," Dominik adds.

"Of course, my lord."

The king waves his hand, and the ripped painting of Wilhelm

the Uniter stitches itself back together. I watch in awe and horror as what is done is undone, like changing history.

"Wow, Your Magnificence," I breathe, and for once, it is genuine.

"*Matter and Mind.*" The king shrugs. "We only repair by hand what is sentimental to us. Now, after this round of drinks, we'll head to the lounge."

"How are we traveling to it this time?" Eli asks.

Perhaps I've ingested the drugs meant for the royals, because nothing they say makes sense. After handing the king his lavender drink, I layer together ginger and lime for Dominik's concoction. He frowns as he drains the entire glass. He likes it.

"The lounge is ready for dinner service," Lila declares when she returns.

The king nods, passing his empty cup to me. His fingers brush mine.

"Thank you." He holds my gaze. Then he steps up to his own portrait, flushed with soft youth—and rips it in half with his magic.

"Come on, boys," he calls, pushing through the parted canvas. "Girls, you can come this way, too."

"They change the lounge entrance for the fae after every use," Lila whispers to me, giddy, as Eli and Dominik file in after him. "I've only served in there twice before. The first time, the king broke through the rock. Another time, we had to submerge ourselves in a fountain and swim out to the other side!"

I gape at her. "They alter how the entrance looks?"

She shakes her head. "They alter what the entrance *is*."

"How?"

"*Matter and Mind,*" she says. "The Vandornes shape the world. And they want the other fae to remember that."

Chapter Twenty-one

DESPITE ITS EXCLUSIVITY, THE LOUNGE ITSELF APPEARS AS ANY grand fae room. Wood-paneled walls, a lush green rug, and brown leather chairs. The fae eat around the table, and the executioner hovers by the door. Dominik demands a new drink from me. Then another. I create a reflection of his taste over and over and over. My genius isn't tired; rather, it is exhilarated. When he glowers at me, I raise my chin, hold his gaze.

I see you, I think. *I know who you are and what you've done.*

It is the curse and the power of the prey, to know the predator better than he knows himself.

After the meal, Lila delivers water to the fae, and I take out the wooden box from under the cart. Lifting the lid, I trace the velvet cushioning, the thick, short sparks like rolled fallen leaves. Next to them is a round clipper.

First, I bring the box to the king, who plucks up a spark. Using the clippers, he shears off one end, then snaps, and a tiny flame ignites from his index finger.

A gasp escapes before I can help it, for I've been trying and failing at the same trick. Those violet eyes find mine, flickering with the reflection of the fire. His lips quirk into an uneven grin, and I wonder what he would've been like had he not been born a royal. If he had been born a faerie, if we worked together in the palace, we might have been friends. Or not. Or something more.

"It's not as hard as it looks." He holds the flame to the tobacco, wrapping his lips around the other end. He puffs until smoke streams from the clipped side. "Tell me your thoughts."

"It was the speed that shocked me," I say. "As if it were as easy as breathing."

"It was." He leans back in his chair. "Perhaps one day it will be for you, too."

"My magic is done maturing."

"Is it?" His gaze roams over me like a lazy lover's. "You used it tonight to make the drinks. I can scent it on your body as clearly as that oil."

"Oh, I . . ." Heat creeps along my chest. *It reeks!* Kassandra would say, but the half-lidded look Maxian gives me is anything but disgust. Smoke curls from his mouth.

"You've never worn oil before."

What the planes is going on?

"Well . . ." I stop. "I purchased a small vial at the last Full Moon Festival."

When he smiles, I know I have blundered. Reign fae—like the old fae of bedtime stories—can detect a lie.

"Who's it for?" he murmurs.

For Dominik, Kassandra said from bruised lips. My heart thuds, my tongue thick with fear. Hector once asked which oath my body would submit to if forced: Reign or Illusion? I do not want to test it.

"Don't be nervous, Avery, dear."

"I'm not nervous."

His grin grows. He's condescending, sheltered, conceited. He is everything wrong with my world. The reason my best friend is dead. Yet I can't tear my attention away as he wraps full lips around the spark, his broad chest expanding on an inhale, his corded forearms flexing where he's rolled up the sleeves.

"I like both on you," Maxian says, smoke streaming. His gaze dips to my abdomen. "That oil. And the smell of your magic. Like spring rain."

He's drunk. He's bored, as Lila warned he would become, and he wanted Kassandra here tonight. Something in me curdles.

"My magic is nothing compared to my mistress's," I say. "Lady Kassandra's magic is like wind and crystals."

The crooked grin melts away, and Maxian nods, swallowing. "Go to my friends. But come back to me afterward. I want to talk."

When I reach Eli, he peers into the box of sparks I offer.

"I shouldn't." He sighs.

"You could, my lord."

"Not all desires should be indulged." He looks at me in that quiet way of his.

The king snaps a flame to life, then extinguishes it. Over and over.

I hope the king hurts you, Benji said. *I wish for it.*

But I see Benji, too, holding up a golden coin, his face splitting into a grin as part of his body returned to him once more. *It tickles.* There is no length I will not go to for my little brother.

So much has happened in such a short time. Yet only now do I realize that the game is just beginning.

"Perhaps just for tonight." Eli grabs a thick, short spark and cuts it. He snaps his own flame, and in a moment, smoke coils up from his tobacco. His gaze falls to Lila across the room at the bar cart, and his expression softens.

"Where's my spark?" Dominik snarls from his chair.

I jump. Eli blinks and the look is gone, replaced by wariness.

"Dom." The king's voice slices the air. "What did I say about speaking to my faerie like that?"

I stiffen.

"Your faerie?" the Illusion lord sneers, eyes bloodshot. Silver hair falls limp over his face like overcooked noodles. "She played for Illusion today."

"And you played for Death." Eli sighs. "But you're too loud to ever be mistaken as that."

"Shut up, you self-righteous prick!"

"Drink water, Dom," Maxian replies, calm. "You're making a fool of yourself."

The plane jerks in one direction, then another. Dominik simmers in his chair, and Maxian and Eli tense. I wonder if a fight between the highest of the fae will break out right here.

The grout was pink.

Blood that had soaked into the floors during the Dark Rebellion.

The plane buzzes in my ears like a swarm of wasps, and I feel the vibration through my teeth. The executioner shifts in his corner.

"A smoke for Death?" I blurt. "Or do you consider sparks your cousins?"

It isn't a clever joke, but the males in the room startle anyway, and the pressure eases.

"You are incorrect," the executioner says. "On both counts."

"I'm shocked Death is so serious." The sarcasm slips out before I can reel it back. I cover my mouth. The king smirks, and Eli huffs a laugh, and I can finally breathe as the plane rights itself. Lila gives an impressed smile.

"Apologies," I follow up, face burning.

"You are brave to jest with a Death fae." The king twists the spark between his thumb and forefinger. "They're not exactly known for their humor."

"I got a laugh out of Death once," Eli pipes up. "When was that? Seventy-five years ago?"

"Eighty-one," the executioner amends.

Maxian laughs. "I'm convinced he wears the mask so we don't see how much he smiles. Isn't that right, Executioner?"

Eli giggles—*giggles* like a child, the king joining in. The executioner just folds his arms.

Perhaps there's more than just tobacco in these, I think.

"Shall I bring some dessert?" Lila offers.

"Lovely!"

"My spark?" Dominik whines behind me, the sullen fae almost forgotten. I hold out the box. He grabs one, clips and lights it. An invisible hand presses against my back, pushing me closer to him.

"What game are you playing, little faerie?" he hisses.

"Game, my lord?"

"No wonder my sister enjoys your company. You have even less wit than her."

" 'Than she.' "

"What?"

I stare down at him. "In this context, I believe it's *You have less wit than she.*"

He grips my hip with a cold hand. I yelp, but an unseen hand covers my mouth, and another spins me so that I stand by his side, facing the others.

"May I borrow her, Max? Only for a moment," Dominik calls across the room. His shift in mood stuns me. The king glances up, his pupils dilating.

"Avery?" he asks.

A phantom hand squeezes my throat.

"Whatever Your Magnificence requests," I say past the presence pushing against my windpipe. Sweat dampens my neck.

"Which do you prefer?"

The hand tightens, and my knees almost give out. Maxian squints at me through the haze of smoke, blinking. Perhaps if he weren't drunk, he could see it. If he wanted to use his truth magic on me, I would welcome it, just this once. But no, he just watches, and my heart sinks as he considers that he must be the exception to the rule, that I would choose truth for integrity's sake, and not a lie to save my skin.

"Avery," the king repeats.

"Illusion."

A muscle tics in his jaw, but he nods, puffing a spark and looking away. "I see."

My insides crumble as Dominik pulls me onto his lap, banding an arm across my midsection like the first time we met. My body shudders as my spine presses against his torso. His breath reeks of the alcohol I fed him.

"We're going to talk, you and I."

Lila glances our way, biting her lip. The king puffs and dishes out cards on the table between him and Eli, who rests his chin on his fist. The Healing fae mutters something to Maxian, who just shakes his head.

"About what?" I ask, breath coming in tight.

"How quickly you wrapped your lips around the king's cock."

"I—"

A phantom hand returns to my throat. I watch in horror as the males across from us exchange cards. Do they not see the assault happening, or am I just unworthy of saving?

"You think the king will protect you, just because he fucks you? He's done that to a thousand other faerie whores. You won't be the one to change him."

Taking a breath, I think about what I can use. What do I have? *Information. Access. Influence.*

"You fear I will tell the king what you do to his future bride," I say.

"I fear nothing," he snarls.

"Then why prevent her from joining tonight? Why resist—"

"You know nothing of our politics."

I bite down, teeth scraping the Illusion of flesh, the trick so advanced I can even taste the salt of sweat. Dominik curses, the Illusion dropping away.

"Explain it to me, then," I urge, reaching for my genius. "So that I may better encourage their engagement."

"The king needs a *wife*. Not a wild thing."

My mind stutters, slips along a frozen pond of horrifying images. It is easy to rage in my room alone; out here, I am trying to pry myself from the predator's grip as he whispers how I will be eaten.

I need time.

"Then let the king tame her," I say.

"The king doesn't even know himself," he hisses. "He thinks he wants a wild fae to whom he can sell submission, but he needs a wife who can take his temper so that the kingdom does not have to."

"Temper?"

"It worked for Gregor the Great and his queen."

What the planes is he saying?

Dominik misunderstands. Maxian seeks change, even if he fears it, or fears the talk of males like Dominik. The king needs someone strong by his side, someone like Kassandra.

"What do you mean?"

"A wife does not win, even if she could," Dominik grits out. "And never in public."

Across from us, Maxian leans forward in his chair, gripping its armrest. He stares at us, adjusting himself. My fear curdles to disgust. Does he interpret my breathing as lust?

Is it scared or turned on? Dominik asked all those weeks ago. Perhaps to these fae males, they are one and the same.

Yet the plane shimmers between us. Hardly noticeable at first but like a heat wave, once level with the magic, I can see it swirling in the air. Gathering what little awareness I have left, I reach out to the plane and feel Dominik's power not just surrounding us but extending outward like a spider weaving his web.

An Illusion.

Dominik has shrouded us in an Illusion.

Can Maxian not smell Dominik's magic? Unless the fae has layered another Illusion on top of the primary. This, I realize, is his grand gesture. This is why he siphoned the plane. And I spent the night feeding into his anger, willing him to store only more power.

"Do you understand now, little faerie?" he whispers. "They cannot see you. Well, not the real you."

Maxian glances away, clearing his throat. My thumb rubs against the golden moth ring, but I can't lace away and leave Lila alone. The three figures move around the room undisturbed, like actors in a play.

"I understand," I breathe. "I promise."

"Promise what?"

"That I will make her docile." The words are like ash in my mouth, but I have no intention of seeing them through.

Dominik tsks. "Remember, this is what happens when you try to win."

His incisors pierce the crook of my neck, breaking the flesh. Agony rips through me. Crying out, I thrash, but more flesh tears.

"Help!" I shriek through the pain. "Help, please! Help me—"

The king's attention flicks toward us, then back at the cards.

Dominik clamps down harder, like a wolf. Blood gushes from my neck as another wave of pain erupts. I scream and scream. He rips out his teeth.

"Do you need a reminder?"

"No, please—"

His teeth sink into me once more, lower, severing tendons, and I cry out again, twisting. Fire rips up my neck and down my arm. Darkness blots my vision.

I think of my father.

I slam my head back into Dominik's nose. He swears, his magic loosening its hold. I fight harder, scratching nails against real flesh raking them down phantom hands, elbowing him wherever I can, stomping on his feet. The grip falls away. I collapse to the ground, clutching my neck. Blood spurts onto the carpet. So much blood, it makes my head swim. How deep did he bite?

The world blurs.

"Help," I moan. "Please—somebody."

The king slowly turns his head, brows furrowed, cards still in hand, eyes unfocused.

"Is everything okay?" he asks Dominik in the chair.

"No!" I shout.

Yet an echo of my voice replies, a hollow imitation. "We're wonderful, Your Magnificence."

"No!" I cry again.

Dominik crashes into me. I twist, swinging a left hook at his temple with all my weight behind it. His head snaps back, eyes bloodshot. Body bleeding beneath the fae, the only weapon I have left is magic that is too powerful for a faerie. That I should always hide and that has never protected my loved ones before. All it has ever done is rot.

So I let it rot.

"What are you doing?" Dominik rears back, disgusted.

I release my genius and it contacts the plane, oozing stink like a decaying corpse. My anger and hatred and grief permeate the air around us. Heat erupts in my palms, singeing the carpet, but no flame comes.

"Stop that!" The slap comes hard and fast.

The Illusion flares, covering the smell. Cheek against the carpet, I stare up at the king, only feet away. He tilts his head, cheeks flushed and hair tousled. His gaze cuts between the carpet and the chair, his grip on the cards tightening.

"Please," I beg. "Please."

"What's that?" Maxian demands.

Dominik pauses, still pinning me down, my neck gushing blood and the world spinning. His pale chest heaves, clavicles poking out from his undone shirt, hands and mouth red. His thighs bracket my torso, as if he is about to offer himself to my mouth. His lip forms a tight, flat line, sweat rolling down his temples as his Illusion shimmers in the plane all around us, covering the entire room.

"What's what, my king?" Lila asks, still turned from us.

"There's something strange about the plane," Eli observes, sitting up.

"Dom, are you seeing this?" Maxian asks the empty chair.

"Yes, quite strange," Dominik answers—but it's too late. He used the wrong voice, straight from his own mouth, from on top of me, and not the Illusion of us cuddling.

The king's eyes cut to us on the carpet, and he squints.

I buck, throwing Dominik off center. The room flickers in and out.

"You'll regret this," he snaps, eyes wild.

"I regret everything," I say. Then in a low and deep voice, I demand, "Maxian."

The plane quakes.

"An Illusion," Death says. "There's an Illusion in the plane."

King Maxian leaps to his feet, slapping down the cards.

"What did you do?" the king bellows, glasses rattling, lights winking. Dominik only coughs, a failed attempt at clearing his throat. Maxian tears across the room, reaching through the Illusion to grab him by the tunic and haul him up. "What did you do?"

Dominik drops the Illusion. The concentrated energy dissolves into the plane, like sugar in water.

A gasp, a thunder of footfalls. Someone grasps my good shoulder, and I cry out, blackness threatening once more. Eli crouches before me, surveying the damage.

"He bit muscle," he says.

The king shoves Dominik up against the wall, the stone cracking. "What is wrong with you?"

The Illusion fae spits, the coughs worsening. "What is wrong with *you*?"

"I said if you ever touched a lady like that again—"

"It's just a faerie." Dominik hacks up spittle. "Or are you getting confused? Don't eat where you piss, Max—"

The king punches him in the stomach, and the fae drops to the ground and vomits.

"We need to stop the bleeding," Eli tries, voice low and calm. "Please."

I hiss, showing my own incisors, an immense disrespect, but I need to get these High Fae away from me. I hate them, I hate all of them, and I would rather die than—

I'm gazing at the white ceiling, the rug against my back. Before I can comprehend what's happening, a warm hand clasps over my wound.

"Just a moment," Eli says, his face coming into view. The fire in my neck and arm eases, cools.

"Lila." Then he's shifting me against another body, a toned arm supporting me.

"You're okay," Lila whispers, resting my head against her shoulder. I cry at the sound of her voice, cry harder when she dabs a napkin on my forehead and harder still when I realize that Lila is becoming my friend. She cradles me, and if I had the strength, I'd hug her back.

Eli leans over Dominik, who sputters for breath.

"Leave him," Maxian grits out through a clenched jaw, pacing.

"I'll take him back to Illusion," the executioner offers, eyeing a wall sconce that rattles with the plane before crashing to the floor.

"Leave. Him."

"Max," Eli cuts in, grabbing Dominik's face. "Max, something else is wrong. He's not breathing."

Eli yanks Dominik up from his hands and knees. The fae's face is gray, lips an eerie blue. He wheezes for breath that won't come.

Maxian stops. "I didn't hit him that hard."

Dominik falls onto his back, convulsing. Eli reaches forward, turning him on his side as the fae seizes, prying open his mouth.

"A reaction to overexerting his magic?" Death asks.

"No, this is physical," the Head of Healing states, ripping open Dominik's shirt. Hives break across his flesh from mouth to fingertips. "Something is killing him."

"Poison?" the king asks.

"I'm not sure." Eli runs his hands along Dominik's spine. "I can't cure it if I don't know the source."

The High Fae swing their attention to me, still in Lila's arms. We both shiver as the executioner stalks toward us.

"What did you do?" he demands.

When Dominik inhales, it sounds like a broken whistle.

Eli forms a circle with one hand and presses it over the heir's mouth, wind rushing past my ear.

"Airways are closing," he says. "We need answers now."

Reign magic seizes me.

"What happened to Dominik?" the king asks. My tongue prickles, yanks forward as if someone has reached into my mouth and grabbed it. A new kind of magic I have yet to experience, Reign magic of the mind. The sentence flies from my mouth.

"I don't know," I gasp.

"What poison did you use?" Maxian bellows, the room shaking. My tongue pinches, mouth forced open again.

"None."

"Max, has this happened before?" Eli demands.

"What?"

"This reaction. Did it ever happen in childhood?"

"Once, I think. After we went peach picking in the outer farms and ate a basket together. But I don't know how—"

"He doesn't need an antidote. It's not poison." Eli flips Dominik onto his back. Death helps hold the fae down, and suddenly Eli is rubbing his hands together, static sparking between them. He presses a hand to Dominik's thigh and jolts him.

Dominik gasps. Eli once again forms a circle with his fingers and frames the fae's lips. Air pours down his throat, and his chest expands, his body going limp with relief.

"Adrenaline and air," Eli says. "We need stinging nettle to reduce the reaction." By the time he finishes his sentence, Maxian has laced stinging nettle leaves into his palm from the Healing garden. "Moisten them, please."

A water glass flies across the room, landing in the king's hand. He drops them in the water, handing it to Eli, who warms the liquid. The executioner sits Dominik up, and they serve him the tea. As he drinks, Eli pulses Healing magic across his skin. The hives reduce. The rash recedes.

Dominik lifts his head, his silver hair plastered to his clammy forehead. His gaze finds me, sprawled on the floor across from him.

"You," he spits. "How did you know?"

"I—"

"No one knows of my reactions."

"I d-didn't," I say, the words wrenching out of me from Maxian's magic.

"There weren't any peaches on the menu tonight," the executioner says.

I think of Dominik's hands, his mouth, the hives. As it dawns on me, the king voices my thoughts.

"Your body oil," he says. "It smells of peach."

My mouth dries out.

Peach, Kassandra said. *For Dominik.*

My body trembles as new meaning recasts her instructions. She wasn't priming me for Dominik. She was using me to stop him, to end him so that she could be free and I could take the fall.

House of Illusion is ripping itself apart. And they're using me to do it.

Chapter Twenty-two

I STARE AT MY BLOODSTAIN ON THE FLOOR. THE BANDAGE scratches my skin, the ointment cooling the wound. Eli took Dominik to his chambers to watch over him while Lila cleaned up, and the executioner and the king interrogate me.

"I truly did not know of his reactions," I repeat.

"And the contents of the oil?"

The king forces the truth from my tongue. "I didn't know."

"And where did you find this oil?" Maxian asks beside me, rubbing at the scowl on his face.

"A . . . room."

"What room?" Death grits out.

I don't reply at first. Then the magic yanks at my tongue—

Pebbles fill my mouth and still, the Reign magic rips at me, the sensations clashing. I gag, spittle dripping down my chin. When I wipe with my hand, it comes away red.

"Shit." The king paces.

"Your magic conflicts with an oath," the executioner mutters. "Can you push through it?"

"It'll shred her tongue," he says, then faces me. "You took it from an Illusion room, then?"

I remain silent, afraid.

"Most likely Kassandra's," the executioner says.

The males glance at each other.

Fuck. If she's caught, if they find out, we will both be severely punished. If I don't make it out alive, then what will become of Benji?

"Did you steal the oil?" the king asks, his magic yanking my tongue.

"No," I say, and it is true.

"Did you steal the bottle?" the executioner asks.

"No!" I cry, and I realize my mistake. This time, I could have lied—and I should have. The executioner cannot force the truth from me, but if I go back on my word, they may realize the fault in having two alternating interrogators.

I cannot look panicked—just ashamed.

"Not the bottle," I amend. "Just a few drops."

Pressing my knees together, I wrap arms around my waist, my body trembling.

Do not cry, I think. *Do not cry.*

My vision blurs.

A speck of orange zips past me. A small, floating orb of fire drops into the hearth on the far side of the room. Flames dance in the fireplace, a gentle heat warming the air. In a few moments, some of my shaking has eased, cutting the chill against my back. Maxian is watching me, frowning. He runs a hand through his dark-honey hair.

"You were cold, were you not?"

I look away.

Maxian crouches in front of me. My instincts scream to move back from the large male, but I dare not. He rests his elbows on thick thighs, hands clasped.

"Avery," he says. "We ask these questions to ensure that the palace—and you—haven't been infiltrated. Stealing a few drops of body oil from your mistress is harmless compared to treason. So I need the truth from you one last time."

Do not ask me of Kassandra, please. Not you.

If he does, I will cough up more blood, revealing a hole in their approach.

"Avery," the king repeats. "Why did you do it?"

I exhale. His forehead is pinched in concern; whether real or not, I do not care. Relief flows through me, for in trying to come across as kind, the king was too vague. Tears pour down my cheeks. The truth magic tugs the words out of me, and I redirect my thoughts to the moment I decided to obey Kassandra and rub the lethal oil into my skin. I just open my mouth, and let the truth tumble out.

"To feel pretty," I say. "I wanted to feel pretty tonight."

The executioner scoffs. But before me, the most powerful male in Amyria lowers his head, a gentle laugh escaping his lips. He stands, pivoting to Death.

"I think we're done here."

"So the Heir of Illusion almost died because your servant felt insecure."

The king sighs again, looking my way. "It's a shame, really. Especially since the oil was never necessary."

I bury my head in my hands so that they do not see my disgust, my shame that it's working, that I am getting closer to the murderer of my friend so that I may free his brother. It is the seediest of ways, and the most effective.

"I'm sorry," I cry. "I'm so sorry."

"Me too," the king replies. "Take a few days off. Eli will see you for the wound, and I promise that Dominik will pay for this."

BRIAR GAPES AT me from the service entrance. I glance down at myself, taking in the bloodstained silk. The bandage scratches against my neck. She steps into the hall and shuts the door. "What the planes happened to you?"

"I need to talk to Kassandra."

"Not looking like that."

"I look like this *because* of her."

Briar's eyes widen, then she swears. "May I?" she asks, tilting her head to my injury. I nod.

For the briefest moment, she lifts the bandage, and her eyes soften and glaze. It was a look my mother used to give me when the teller added another ring of debt to my body.

"What are they doing to us?" she whispers.

My throat thickens with an unnamed emotion.

Us.

All of us.

"She's in bed." Briar steps back. "See if you can brave the sleeping beast."

I nod, and Briar leads me into Kassandra's quiet, dark chambers. Lighting a candle, Briar passes it to me and exits back into the parlor. I've taken only one step toward the bed when Kassandra's calm voice floats toward me like a breeze.

In the hours since, her bruises have yellowed, the minor cuts closed. Briar has braided her silver hair. Still, Kassandra remains propped up against pillows.

"Avery." She frowns. "What happened?"

The flame flickers before me, and it's only then that I see my shaking hand. But I'm not scared. I can't feel terror in her presence anymore. Just blood-red, unbridled rage.

"You." I round the bed, reaching her side. "Your brother."

She clicks her tongue. "Oh, yes."

"Did you forget that he's deathly allergic to peaches? Or that you oiled me up to kill him?"

"I've never tasted this emotion of yours. It's like frustration but much more pungent."

My hand twitches to throw the candle at her. It wouldn't do anything—she'd douse the flame before it could fall onto her blankets. But just to show her I would, that I am capable.

Her eyes flare in surprise.

"You are furious," she says.

I do not reply.

"So you want to live?"

I blink, and some of that choking anger stutters in its tracks. "I—what?"

"I couldn't tell, after your faerie friend died," she says, "if you wanted to live or not. I just thought you wanted the boy to live."

My eyes squeeze shut, the flood of memories overwhelming. Jeremee's moss-green eyes. Benji's debt-riddled body.

"Please, don't." I press back the sting of tears.

"You're growing stronger," she says. I open my eyes, watching the flame grow brighter. "The rot is still there, but so is freshness, too."

I hesitate, then say, "I haven't been holding myself back."

"That's how it begins."

We lapse into silence.

Finally, she says, "It was a moment of desperation."

"The king questioned me afterward. I was forced to speak truths, and I could've spoken this one. I could've revealed what you had done."

"But you did not. You are too intelligent for that."

I can feel my fury beneath my skin, like a fire spreading through a forest. But Kassandra collects hers in an icy stare: a calm defiance that has me shivering.

"Dominik banned peach from my wing," she says. "I managed to buy that perfume from a smuggler decades ago."

"Where's the bottle now?"

"I've hidden it. I couldn't give you any magic tonight. Couldn't call you back to the House of Illusion. And I couldn't be there. So I drenched you in harmless body oil, a poison made just for him."

Perhaps Kassandra is redacting her reasoning. Perhaps this was her true intention all along. Either way, I do not care.

"I could have died," I say, and to my surprise, I sound . . . hurt.

"I know." She takes a shuddering breath. "And for that, I am sorry."

"I do not forgive you," I say, then bite out: "Mistress."

Her eyes narrow. "It is not forgiveness I truly seek."

"What do you seek, then?"

"Relief."

I blink, stunned at the emotion in me she has also named. Exhausted, the candle flame dies. In the dark, there is our breathing, the patter of light rain outside. The wounds on my shoulder throb. The moments stretch on.

"You were right, earlier," she says. "He must be stopped."

It wasn't the worst plan I've ever heard of—but I'll never admit that to her. I am tired of being a pawn, thinking I can see the entire game from my spot on the board. Only the High Fae can see everything, all at once, for they drew the lines. And I think I am being clever by walking those lines and trying to make a pawn out of my mistress in turn. It hasn't gotten either of us very far. Perhaps it's time to swap pawns for partners.

"Do you truly want to stop your brother?" I ask.

The covers shift, fabric against skin, and Kassandra reaches for my arm.

"Say what you want to say." Her nails graze my skin.

"Why did you win with Benji when you could've won with Briar and not faced so many consequences?" I ask.

"Very demanding."

"I risk my neck with this conversation."

"So do I," she says, and it is true. She sighs, her hand retreating. "I won with the boy because he needed it. Because Dominik would've punished me for winning either way, so I thought, may as well win as egregiously as possible. And because you asked me to."

The boy giggling as rings dissipated on his skin had been the most beautiful thing I had seen and heard in years. If there is any chance of that happening again, then it is worth it. Jeremee and my mother would warn against teaming up with my tormentor, playing against the High Fae using one of their own. Yet I have already made enemies of the Upper Court. Perhaps it's time to become their enemy, too.

It would be a reluctant alliance, no better than a debt collector, aligning with the fae. But I am out of options.

"You won with Benji today. So it's time to hold up my end of the promise," I say.

"A way around the oaths."

"I'll collect the secrets, and you use them as bargaining chips for blackmail."

"Tell me how."

"Riddles," I say. "You speak in riddles, but you must picture those riddles, too, so that your tongue and mind seem nonsensical."

"Show me."

"The wolf breaks two limbs of the silver cat at night."

A quiet intake of breath. "Another one."

"The golden eagle and the silver cat may share a nest."

Silence, save for our breathing and the light drumming of spring rain.

"Who else knows?" she asks.

"Just me." I will not give Briar up in this, even if Kassandra is protective of the faerie.

"How'd you figure it out?"

"My friend is dead. I have time to talk to the walls in my room."

"So you bring me secrets, and I'll use them to barter our freedom," she says. "Do we have a deal?"

I don't trust Kassandra, but I trust the motivation of escaping her brother. Despite our differing statuses, we have a similar goal: to be free. If it were just my fate at play, I would risk it. So I think of a suggestion as rare as a fae and faerie working together, one I only heard once in the first year working for Kassandra, and when I asked a cook about it, she told me to never speak of it ever again.

"What of a blood bargain to enforce our pact?" I ask.

Kassandra coughs. "Do you even know what a blood bargain is? How it differs from an oath?"

I bite my lip. "An oath is when one party swears fealty to an institution. It uses blood to bolster the magic that enforces the loyalty. A blood bargain is sworn between two individuals. Both parties must deliver on the agreed-upon terms."

"And if they fail to do so, one or both parties will lose their geniuses," Kassandra hisses. "Do you want to be without magic?"

I suck in a breath. "Like a Molder? But High Fae can't be Molders."

"No," she agrees. "But they can be losers."

Scoffing, I roll my eyes. "How would it work? Losing your magic in a blood bargain?"

"The fuck if I know! I've only ever entered one, and that was a century ago. I refuse to join in another."

Another time, I will pull on that thread, unravel the tapestry that is Kassandra. But not tonight. So if a blood oath is devotion, a blood bargain is damnation.

"How will I know you won't just use me?" I ask. "How can I ensure my own freedom?"

And that of my friends, I think but do not say.

"How do I know you won't tell the king I find no interest for the thing between his legs, or between any lord's legs?" she counters. "How do I know you won't turn to Dominik, as the House and staff always do? He is the more powerful one, the stronger ally. I may be your mistress, but both these males are our masters."

My mouth drops open. "I would never reveal another creature like us."

"And how can I know that?"

"Well," I stutter. "I—"

"Exactly," she cuts in. "We are bound, you and I, by our indiscretions."

It hits me again; in being played so often, I have come to know their hand. Their tells, their strategy. There is power, too, in bearing witness. And I have witnessed much.

"We have a deal," I say, extending my hand blindly in the dark to shake.

Soft fingers wrap around mine, tugging me forward with shocking strength. Kassandra grips my palm in hers, clutching it as if I were a memory onto which she desperately wants to hold. She has held me twice today when she's never touched me before.

"We have a deal," she echoes.

The candle flickers awake once more, a small spark that illuminates her satisfied face.

"How did you do that?" I ask.

"I didn't," Kassandra says, the fire shining in her eyes. "You did."

"I've never properly spoken to fire before."

"Perhaps it's never listened until now." She shrugs, dropping my hand and leaning back.

Kassandra is stark naked. The flame flickers, crimson and peach and gold light painting her shining hair and taut pink nipples. Indigo shadows cup her breasts and pool between her thighs. I cannot look away from the power, my power, especially not as it bathes every inch of her in a brilliant portrait.

For once, my magic doesn't smell like festering hate. Rather, it smells like the tang of upturned soil for a fresh grave. It is not the aroma of rot; it is the aroma of ruin.

"What's changed?" I breathe.

Kassandra smiles, slow and deep, like a cat with its cream.

"Everything," she says.

And the fire burns brighter and bigger and hotter.

Chapter Twenty-three

DAYS LATER, MY HAND HOVERS OVER THE DOOR. *KNOCK*, I WILL myself. It's been three shifts since I nearly murdered Dominik in the lounge. In between Healing sessions with Eli in the king's private library, I took advantage of the time off by lacing as much food to the bloodstained tunnel as my genius could manage. Now the scab itches, and I will return to work in two days. I haven't had a chance to see Lila or thank her.

If they can wield their magic to destroy . . . why can't I use mine to create? She is a strong, admirable faerie, someone I want to create pockets of joy with, to call a friend.

So I knock.

Lila opens the door, her coiled hair framing her face like a halo. Her eyebrows shoot up in surprise before a smile breaks out across her features.

"You're okay!" she exclaims. "I was so worried—"

I throw my arms around her neck. We stumble against the doorframe and when she laughs, I'm shocked that I do, too.

Lila pulls back, scanning my face. "Are you okay?"

"Much better."

"There was a lot of blood."

My eyes water. We could talk about what happened, what she saw when Dominik curtained us with an Illusion. I should apologize for all of the disruption, for making her clean up alone. Instead, I just hug her again.

"Thank you," I mutter.

"For what?"

"For being my friend."

Lila stills in my arms, falling silent.

Oh, I think. *I've already messed up.*

My arms drop as I pull back. Lila frowns, chewing on her bottom lip.

Something sinks in my chest. "Sorry, I didn't mean to assume... We don't have to be friends, if that's not what you want." The words are stones in my heart.

"It's not that, it's—Avery." She plants her hands on my shoulders, looking me square in the eyes. My discomfort urges me to look away, but I don't as Lila takes a breath and starts again. "No one has ever called me friend first. Usually, I'm the one who cares more."

The one who cares more.

"Well, I care," I say. "A lot. In fact, I was hoping we could..." I clear my throat, my pulse pounding. I feel like a child again, asking if I could sit in an open spot on the long bench. "We could spend time together, whenever you're free?"

Lila grins, nudging the door open. "I'm free now."

A cacophony of color jumps out as I follow her in. Swatches, fabric scraps, and pieces of parchment are arranged in various shapes and colors in spiraling patterns, forming a collage that resembles a stained-glass rendering of a meadow, and in its center, a grand tree.

"Lucan's Tree," I whisper, studying the collection. Every piece has been intentionally and intelligently placed to appear as accidentally beautiful. I face her. "Lila, you're an artist."

She flushes. "I'm not sure about that."

"Where did you find all of this?"

She shrugs. "I collect colors in the trash. Scraps from the seamstress, spices from the kitchen. The High Fae expect perfection, so that leads to an exorbitant amount of waste. But it's not truly waste—it's just not perfect."

"I prefer imperfections," I say, my eyes trailing to a piece of parchment stuck to the wall. It's a sketch of different blocks, with labels scribbled inside. In the top right corner are two words: *The Pith*.

It's the royal quarters in isolation, a simple square divided into four quadrants, to represent the different apartments. The top two are labeled *Sun Salon* and *Moon Salon* for the king and queen, respectively. Reflections of each other, they consist of linking chambers that, starting from the outside in, are the antechamber and reception room, the dining room, the lounge, the private library, the bedroom, the wardrobe, and a large bathing suite that connects the two salons. The two southern apartments are both labeled *Salon of Stars,* with fewer rooms and labels. My finger traces these apartments.

"For the royal children," Lila says behind me.

"How did you figure this out?"

"My father was a Reign Scarp—he cleaned and stocked the chimneys, oiled door hinges, wiped windows, cleaned tapestries. There are fireplaces, doors, windows, and tapestries in every room." Her voice deflates with each word.

"You miss him."

Reaching for the parchment, she peels it from the stone, caresses the etchings. "He would take me on his rounds. Tell me Unesse legends as I passed him the wrench, the rag, the oil. He painted the most vivid pictures."

"And you're continuing his legacy."

"Perhaps."

I nod, understanding the wound in her voice. It's not something to argue or gloss over. Instead, I ask what I always wish faeries would ask about my mother.

"What was his name?" I say.

Lila gives a small smile. "Dorin."

"May Dorin wander well."

"May he wander well," she replies.

Leaning forward, I notice that the intersection of all four apartments has been scratched out, redrawn, and scratched again. "What's that?"

The next thing I know, Lila is pushing the parchment into my hands and crossing the room. She presses her ear to the door, checks the lock. Checks the lock again. My spine stiffens, cold air wafting off the stones. I say nothing as she reaches her cot and pats the mattress next to her. When I sit, I force my fingers to loosen from the crumpled paper.

"Is . . . everything okay?"

"Yes," she whispers. "I think there's a hidden room—at the center of it all. I just don't know what's inside it."

Goosebumps pinch my skin. *A secret,* I think. *Follow this secret. It may be useful.*

I observe the map once more, the very center of the Pith, unknown even to a faerie who's lived here all her life. "How do you figure?"

"For one, Reign has no inner gardens."

It was one of the first differences I had noticed—that the rooms had no windows, the only natural light pouring in through glass squares in the roof. I'd assumed it was the trade-off for the privacy of the Pith, its placement as the core of power.

"But maybe they do. Maybe a garden exists, but even the servants aren't allowed to enter." Lila's expression brims with a naked curiosity that brings extra color to her cheeks and a spark into her eye—something she rarely shows beneath the armor of laughs and smiles.

"That's not all, is it?" I ask.

A grin splits her face. "One time on a cleaning shift with my father, I noticed that the wall in the king and queen's bathing suite curves into the space, cutting down the size of the bathing pool by half. It's not a smooth curve, either. It's as if the chambers are built *around* something."

But nothing in Versara is built around nature, for the entire point of the palace is to dominate the elements—the gardens of trees sheared into unnatural shapes, the right angles of the archways and columns, even the tapestries and painted ceilings. All of it designed to say that *we render our world and everything in it.*

"And what is important enough to cut into the space of the king and queen?"

"Part of the old building?" I guess.

Lila shakes her head. "King Gregor—may he wander well—used to gut and rebuild rooms with the change of the seasons. My father called him the Bored General. He's redone every part of House of Reign, even the servants' quarters, except for the royal bathing chambers, which are even smaller than ours. Why allow something to be inconvenient? The High Fae never do that, especially not House Reign."

My finger drifts to the two southern apartments for the royal children. "And the Salon of Stars?"

"Their shared bath also curves into the space. As if it's a mirror of the parental suite."

I glance up at her. "And the two half-moon walls form a circle. A giant, empty space at the center of the Pith."

"Yet there are no doors into it, and it's not an Illusion." Then she shrugs. "I asked my father and his generation what it could mean, but they all say the Pith is the oldest part of the palace. It's bound to have a few odd walls."

"But it does seem a bit strange for the royal family to give up space in a palace as sprawling as Versara, and then not to correct that oversight. Most faerie servants only ever see one House's wing. That's why the coronation was such a large event for the staff."

Lila nods vigorously. "We know it's not for lack of wealth or resources. And that's not all," she says, scooching closer. "Why is House Reign nicknamed 'the Pith'? No faerie today is old enough to remember why, but we all call it that because my father's generation did. But they didn't remember, either."

"Why would a palace of stone and gold be called a pith? If you pry apart a stem in some plants, it's the central tissue inside. That's what it's called."

"Wow, okay," she breathes. "Do you know what to pith an animal means? Fern told me once that it's an old term that describes killing an animal by severing their spinal cord."

Perhaps we fixate on a detail that means nothing. But again, why must only *night servants* take oaths of silence? Day Crests experience their fair share of terror at the hands of High Fae. What secrets are they afraid we'll discover during the twilight intimacy that forms when helping a High Fae to bed and hearing their nightmares?

"I believe you," I say.

"But you haven't seen the curved walls."

"But you have."

"Perhaps it's something they perceive as more important than themselves. Though I don't think their egos would ever allow that."

I snort, then think on this. "You're saying it could be a relic? Something sacred?"

"Yes!" she whispers. "For if it were a resource, they would send faeries to mine it. If it were favorable with the other Houses, Reign would show it off in ceremonies. If it were unimportant, they would destroy it."

We lapse into silence. Lila takes the parchment, folds it, and slides it under her pillow. Climbing to my feet, I reach the window on the back wall, the spring air warming this time of year. My eyes scan the concentric buildings that ripple outward like water, rendering the Pith as the point of contact. The spine of the palace, the central nervous system.

I'd spent so much time looking at the barren state gardens from my room, I forgot to look beyond. From Lila's room I can see the peaks of the northern mountain range, and perhaps at night, she can even spot the city lights of Cont to the north. I learned, secondhand, that there is a river to the north and another to the south of us, but even from this distance, I cannot see them through trees and rolling hills.

"Perhaps this is about more than just the palace," I say. "Maybe it's about all of Amyria."

My friend approaches. "How so?"

"Of all the hills in this valley, why choose this one? Why not build the capital closer to the fertile lands of the riverbanks and fresh water supply like the other cities? In a kingdom surrounded by sand, what is more important than access to fresh food and water?"

Lila sucks in a breath. "Whatever brought them here. Whatever they built Versara around."

"But you say there are no entrances into whatever may lie at the center of the Pith."

"That we know of." Her eyes widen. "Like . . . like the way the Reign fae hide the lounge."

"So no one can access it. Except for Reign fae."

Lila cups her hand around my ear, despite us being alone, for fae hearing is too sensitive. "Perhaps that is the point. That the thing at the center of the Pith can also no longer access us."

When I shiver, she leans into me. I lean into her in return.

Our lives may be short, but memories pass along, inherited, reshaping into legends with time. Someone must know something.

It may be useless to Kassandra. Or it may be the biggest secret of all, the best piece of blackmail.

In this moment, sitting in contented silence with Lila, I suddenly don't care. Panic and hope entwine painfully in my chest like sharp ivy, for today I feel less alone. I will work to strengthen this connection with Lila night in and night out, something I have not made the effort to earn in a very long time.

Today I made a friend.

A friend who wants to wander into the dark of the maze, too.

Chapter Twenty-four

I EXIT THE STORAGE ROOM, CLUTCHING THE NEW UNIFORM TO my chest, to see a stout halfling in a black teller's tunic waiting for me in the hall. Only a day has passed since Lila and I spent all of her free time chatting before she departed for her shift. Eli and I met for one more Healing session to fully repair the wound. My shift restarts tomorrow, and the bloodied silk of my other uniform had been beyond saving.

The halfling clasps his hands behind his back. His tan skin has only just started to mature, with crinkles around his bespectacled silver eyes, matching the silver threaded through his dark hair.

"Avery, Night Crest of both House Illusion and Reign?"

"Yes?"

"You may call me Silas. I'm a teller for the creditor's counter at Illusion. There's been atypical activity on your account, and I thought it best to go over it with you."

"Oh." I clutch the unstained silk to my chest. "Yes, of course."

With his own golden ring, Silas laces us from Reign to the Nest back at Illusion, the smell of watery broth curling in the air. We pass the creditor's counter, a short line of faeries waiting to check their balances. The teller stops before a plain wooden door around the corner. The lock clicks, opening to a small office.

Inside, the space has a few cabinets, and a table and chairs in the center, with a blank piece of parchment. I force myself to exhale, fingers tightening around the fabric.

"Was there some sort of mistake on my part?" I ask.

"Oh, not at all." Silas reaches for the cabinet on the opposite wall, taking out a tray with teacups and herbs, and gestures for me to sit. I catch a glimpse of small pantry items and think it pays to be a teller—to have a private lunch.

The chair squeaks against the floor as I settle into it. The sweat on my palms leaves faint imprints on the gold fabric. I wipe my hands on my cotton dress as he hands me a cup.

"I'm afraid we don't have a kettle in here," he says. "So you'll need to heat the water yourself, or I can do it, if your magic doesn't extend that far."

"Thank you, but I've been practicing firework."

Every hour that I'm alone, and since I haven't gone back to work yet, it has been many hours.

I reach for the cup, conjuring the feeling of ire; a rush of breath, and my tea warms. "So what's this about, may I ask?"

"Sometimes we speak to faeries in private when there are several deposits and withdrawals happening in their account at the same time."

My back stiffens. "But I haven't . . ."

"Yes, so let's start from the first deposit."

The teller slides his tea aside and holds out a hand, a quill in his other. I offer a finger to prick, and as he touches the nib to the parchment, letters and numbers scrawl across it. He analyzes the information.

"So." He glances up. "You've received a bonus payment from House of Reign. It's categorized as a tip, though the amount is quite large. We've triple-checked with the House, and it's the correct number."

My mouth dries. I take a sip of the tea, a mint concoction.

"How much?" I ask.

"Ten gold coins."

The cup slips from my grasp. Silas shoots out a hand, magic

bending the plane around the cup to catch it midair. Reign magic.

"I-I'm so—"

"It's all right."

"I didn't expect—"

"It's okay."

My trembling hands pluck the cup from his, and his hand retreats back through the plane. I gulp down the drink, the liquid scalding my throat. *Ten gold coins? That's—that's* . . .

I think of that glittering gold coin that the debt-ridden faerie sprinted toward during Prize of the Pith. The hours in the sun sweating, burning, the false starts and punishments, and all of it worth it for the one gold coin that eradicated half a small limb of debt on Benji.

Swallowing, my throat tight, I realize my cheeks are wet. I am crying silent, awkward tears that I swipe away. "Sorry."

"It's a shock, I know."

The table and my tea blur before me, my face burning. In a moment, a sun-spotted hand holds out a handkerchief. But not even embarrassment can stop the stream of tears, so I take it.

"I never thought . . . I didn't realize it was possible," I say after wiping my face.

The teller nods, pushing up his sleeves. Like most halflings, he has one debt tattoo on each wrist. "It *is* quite rare. Usually after a particularly good night, the servants sometimes receive it in the form of thanks."

"Oh, I'm not—I didn't—"

"It's not illegal." Silas clears his throat. "Just an uncommonly large pay."

He thinks I spent the night in the king's bed. When I shift in my chair, I shudder at the memory of teeth ripping into my skin. Is that the reason for the tip? Because of what I endured?

"What would you like to do with this payment?"

I want to give it to Benji, but the king might notice. Safer to keep the boy off his radar.

"All toward the debt," I reply. "Save for ten copper coins to spend."

He nods, and as he scratches something across the parchment, he asks: "Would you like to be relieved of your debt rings now?"

There's no question. Offering my finger again, he pricks once more. I feel dizzy and take the deepest inhale I've taken in months. Then I watch my arm.

Benji is right. It tickles.

The first tattoo tingles, then fades, then another. Eight rings on each arm, the least I've ever had. But it doesn't stop there. The rings continue to dissipate on each limb until both of my forearms are visible.

My debt has been halved.

My fingers graze the unmarked skin from wrist to elbow. There is the occasional freckle, a little birthmark there, a small nick of a scar. Now each upper arm only bears five rings, ten total. A month ago, I had twenty.

This, I realize, *is true power.*

One stroke of the quill to dissolve another's debt or damn them with more.

"Congratulations," Silas says. "Before we move on, do you have any questions?"

My attention flicks between the first tattoo—cut across my elbows—then to his on each wrist.

"Why are our tattoo placements different?" I ask. "My debt disappeared from the bottom up, but it looks as though yours was erased from the top down."

"Ah, great question." He leans back. "Each ring represents more than just a certain amount; it also embodies the debt owed to that specific House. Any money paid to you from a House will first counteract the balance owed to that House. So while the rings look all the same to us, the magic is specific."

"So the debt that I just paid off could've been the ring from House of Reign I received at birth, and the years since for maintaining the kingdom?"

"Absolutely."

I think of what Kassandra revealed in the state garden during the game. *It's about who owns whom, and for how long.* In all the commotion later that evening, this crucial epiphany slipped by me. If members of the Upper Court can buy and sell one hundred thousand debt rings for an afternoon game, what do the Houses do? Could they trade millions in just one afternoon?

The thought feels sickening, gluttonous.

I clear my throat. "Or could it be debt from Illusion that Reign later acquired?"

Silas adjusts his glasses. "Oh, um—I am unsure of that."

I'm not ready to drop the subject. His silver eyes spark as I twist the gold ring on my finger.

"I didn't realize all tellers, even those in Illusion, have a gold ring."

"They don't." He clears his throat. "Though highly unusual, you're not the first attendant to serve more than one House."

He tilts the engraved signet toward me. Feathery, spotted wings.

"An owl," he says.

"A moth, for me."

"Perhaps you were always meant to be a night faerie."

I take a breath, hoping that because I have now inquired more about his background, he may give me something else. "I just want to better understand what I've overheard. The king sometimes asks the opinions of his faeries, and I don't want to appear ignorant."

"A progressive habit of the late queen." Silas pours us more tea. Wrapping my fingers around the cup, I feel the heat transfer to the liquid inside, steam curling up. The water starts to boil, the glass burning. I let go, stunned. Same effort, greater result.

My magic is done maturing, I told the king only a few nights ago. But it isn't.

With every debt ring off, my body fills with renewed vigor, with energy.

"Hope." Silas smiles. "Quite a powerful thing. It can impact not just our minds but our bodies, too."

"First, I want to better understand why the Houses buy and sell debt. They already collect interest from their own faeries."

"Think of purchasing swaths of faerie debt like buying a piece of a greater trade. A sliver of a business. Say you purchase the debt of ten faeries who work in the mines. You do not just gain their payments and interest—you are profiting off their labor. You don't need to own the mine to make money off it. You just need to own the workers."

I sit back in my chair, hands falling to my lap. Glancing down at the new uniform paid from my own pocket, I wonder who owns this portion of my debt, who owns me.

"It's very confusing, I know," Silas answers.

I'm not confused, I want to say, but I bite my lip. Let him read my revulsion as befuddlement. He was kind enough to explain; I will be kind enough not to because *I understand perfectly*. There is an invisible economy on top of the one we participate in as workers. It is the bigger game, the great game, the one you must buy your way into at a cost so large, only those with inherited wealth can do so.

"Can faeries purchase the debt of other faeries?" I ask. "So that the indebted faerie makes payments to the other?"

"Theoretically, yes. But it's difficult for a faerie to front the sum all at once. And the House would have to be willing to sell the debt in the first place. It's improbable, but not impossible."

I keep my expression from souring. It feels dirty, perverted. It feels like the trickery of fae, and while I am not above blackmailing the High Fae, I do not think I could exploit a fellow faerie. The thought feels comforting, to know that no matter how much I change to venture further into this labyrinth, I still hold some core values.

"Are you ready for the next transaction?" he asks.

I sit up straight. "What do you mean?"

"There are two more transactions we must settle." Silas pulls the parchment closer. "First, there's a fee owed to you from Illusion for a recent assault. The payer is offering the legal minimum."

My stomach plummets.

"I didn't report an incident," I say.

"It was reported by a third party."

No, I think. *No, not this.* My hand finds the ghost of the bite mark on my shoulder.

"I don't want to report it," I say.

"It's already been verified by House of Healing."

Eli? My head drops into my hands. *How? How could he be so ignorant?*

"Can we scratch it from my record?"

"I'm afraid not."

"Then at least allow me to deny the payment."

Silas sighs. "I'm sorry. Once it was verified, the fee was already withdrawn from Illusion. When you're ready, I'll take your hand."

I lift my head, groaning. Dominik has been charged with this fee, knowing it was from me, fueling and justifying his malice. I offer my finger. Whatever the assault fee is, it's not enough to thin a debt ring.

When I'm sure there will be no change in my tattoos, I ask: "And the final transaction?"

Silas nods, pushing my tea closer to me. I shoot him a look. He clears his throat. "There's been a complaint against you from the House of Illusion."

I jerk back. "For what?"

"It says for endangerment."

A laugh bursts out of me before I can stop it. Although Silas looks appalled, I scoff again. *No. No, this can't be happening.* Dominik gets to harm me, threaten to kill me, assault me, and pay a menial fee. Yet he can level any complaint he wants without question.

No matter what protections lie in place, the faeries will pay the price.

I have no words when Silas pricks my finger one last time.

There is nothing to say as the balance slams into my body, the pain ripping across my skin. I double over as new debt rings swallow up my freckles and little birthmark and that nick of a scar once more. Will I ever see them again?

A month ago, I had twenty rings; a minute ago, I had ten. Now I have sixteen.

Just like Benji's new limb of freedom after the Prize of the Pith—even if I pay everything off, a fae could levy him with restrictions once more. I could do everything in my power, I could pay off all his debt, and they could just add it back.

My hands begin to tingle, my mug of tea boiling.

"I count down from ten backward," Silas rushes to say, eyeing the bubbling drink. "Anytime I need help breathing."

I follow his suggestion, taking breaths until I can see straight again, and the heat calms. Finally, I ask, jaw clenched, "How can we stop the complaints without being High Fae? How do the halflings do it?"

"The only way is if a House grants you the status of legal protection. Any complaint against you would need to be explained and justified, not just automatically accepted."

"And how do I get that?"

"Only a head of House can grant it."

My heart sinks, because I already know what I must do. Kassandra's and my plan for financial freedom isn't enough. I must secure protections, and to ensure that Benji will be as safe as he could be, I must barter with the head of the most powerful House.

The king.

Chapter Twenty-five

WHEN I RETURN TO MY ROOM FROM THE VISIT TO SILAS, A letter laces into the air. Stamped into the parchment is the royal crest—an eagle clutching a whip in one talon, a branch from Lucan's Tree in the other. Undoing the wax, I parse out the looping instructions.

To my training halls.
Wear something comfortable.

I return to work tomorrow, but there is no denying a request from the king. A chill slides down my spine that he knows exactly where I sleep in Illusion.

Kneeling, I tug the small basket of belongings from under the bed and dress in a long-sleeve cotton shirt and trousers—a black pair I sewed to fit my hips. The trousers are tight against my muscles. Thanks to the Healing sessions, I am finally back to full strength after the bite. It feels good.

I lace to Reign and venture to the training halls, a part of the palace I've only seen on Lila's map. The mighty room stretches before me, the walls lined with racks of swords, daggers, arrows, whips, and strange weapons. Mats lie scattered across the floor, sunbeams spilling over them from the openings in the ceiling. The vastness of the palace always stuns me.

A large padded platform rises from the center of the room, occupied by two males who circle each other, muscles glistening with sweat. One wears a white shirt, stuck to his skin; the other is in black. Maxian and the executioner. Memories of another ring flash through my mind's eye: my father beating another faerie to a pulp, long ago. I knew he had only stopped harming others the day I woke up a decade ago with searing pain on my wrists from his leftover debts. May he wander lost.

To the side of the platform is Carter, next to a table with towels, boxing tape, and a pitcher of water with glasses. I cross the space to join him.

"Haven't seen you in a few days," he says. His face gives away nothing, and perhaps he does not know of the incident in the smoke room.

"Miss me?" I try.

Carter smiles. "Only a little."

My gaze follows his. The executioner swings at the king, who dodges and twists, wrapping thick arms around Death's waist, and tackles him to the ground. The two grunt and swear as they wrestle.

I drop my voice. "How long before they find a bed?"

"And miss out on being exhibitionists?"

We snicker. The groaning and grappling of limbs continue.

"No magic?" I ask.

"Not the same as grabbing your buddy, I guess."

This time, I let out the laugh. Smiling, Carter turns to grab the pitcher of water behind him, filling up two glasses.

"Avery," a smooth voice calls. "Glad you joined!"

When I glimpse the ring, Maxian has the executioner in a choke hold, stomach to the ground, squirming beneath him. For a moment, I am a visitor admiring this new royal portrait of the king—brawny Maxian triumphing over everything, even Death itself. Then the executioner grabs the golden forearm barred across his throat and heaves. The king pitches forward, landing on his back with an "Oof!"

Death stretches to his full height, looming above the fallen king with a preternatural stillness. His eyes glint with something I've only ever seen in beaten faeries, in Kassandra's eyes, in my own reflection: hatred.

In a blink, it's gone. From his back, Maxian flips up into a crouching position. The plane hums with energy, the back of my neck tingling.

Carter throws two hand towels over his shoulder, grips the glasses of water. The towels and water lift from his hands and glide along the plane to the king and executioner.

As the king approaches, I take in his wide shoulders and disheveled hair, his cheeks flushed, eyes shining. His bunching muscles look well fed, well tended, a male with time and magic to sculpt his body into what he wishes. His beauty is almost blinding, like trying to stare down the sun.

The king's executioner wipes himself down. He is towering and dark and corded in muscle formed from years of physical labor, and any female would—and should—pool with heat. But Jeremee dissolving before my eyes will forever prevent that. Shame at my misplaced anger floods me. Even Death itself cannot truly defeat Reign fae. None of us can, and it's infuriating and demeaning.

"Avery! So glad you found your way here. I wasn't positive you could read, seeing as faeries aren't interested in books," the king says, drawing my attention back to him.

For the briefest moment, my eyes find Carter's. *Uninterested in books?* The valet's face gives nothing away, not even the mimicry of this conversation later tonight in the Mouth. I can hear it now. *Then—get this, Fern—then the king said faeries don't like books! As if we have the time and coin to waste.* The cook will cackle at that one.

"I learned the basics during my service to Illusion," I say. "It was nice to be challenged once more."

"Because you are clever," he answers.

Clever. Clever. Why is it always *clever* and not *intelligent*? Clever like a pet who picks up tricks quickly.

You are too intelligent for that, Kassandra said days ago. Only now do I register that my mistress complimented me.

"Thank you, Your Magnificence," I say.

"I brought you here so that the executioner and I can assess the extent of your injury. See if there will be a permanent crippling, though I doubt it with Eli's skill sets."

Carter's attention weighs on me, but this time I do not return it. My hand twitches, aching to cover the healed wound beneath the bandage.

I take a step away from the king.

He tilts his head in confusion, spine rigid. Does he desire me to drop to my knees and weep? Thank him profusely and apologize for my loss of control?

It was his friend who harmed me, his almost-betrothed who caused it, the game he set up that triggered so much pain. As if the Avery of his mind would willingly and gladly worship the male she's blood-bound to serve, like a whore who refuses payment because the fucking was so good.

"Avery." His teeth shine in a tight smile. "You heard what I said, did you not?"

Do not insult him with your slowness.

"Oh!" I gasp. "Yes. I'm so thankful."

"It's settled. It's about time she defends herself. Besides, there's some fight in her—isn't that right, Avery? Your reflexes were quick during the game."

"Thank you." I grimace, unsure whom he is truly addressing.

"But it's no wonder! You were hiding the most interesting part about you. Nothing that couldn't be discovered with a little digging." He steps toward me, eyes sparking.

Everyone's attention turns to the king and his sly expression. My palms feel clammy. Does he know about my arrangement with Kassandra? "What is interesting about me, my king?"

"Your father was the pit fighter Red the Ruthless."

My mind detaches from my body, feelings of the hall falling away.

"When I turned two hundred, Dominik, Eli, and I snuck into the Peri in disguise and saw him fight. Even *I* was afraid; he truly earned his title."

The bloody mash of faeries' faces that begged for mercy before falling silent forever. My mother pleading in a tiny kitchen, my father beckoning me to come out from under the table because *Daddy is sorry he got mad, he had a hard day and you're hurting Daddy's feelings by hiding, if you don't come out I will drag you out by your hair and give you a reason—*

"What do you say, Ruthless daughter?" the king asks. "Care for a match?"

Carter huffs a laugh. "My king—"

"I'm serious."

"I'm not a worthy opponent for you," I try.

"Oh, enough of that. You wound up your hits so they'd lose power and time during the board game. You were holding back with the other faeries. Well, I'm not a faerie." He quirks a brow.

So he noticed that. The king understands technique. Yes, he's more powerful than I am, but that doesn't matter in a fight, not really. What matters is precision.

"Your Magnificence, her shoulder, as you said," the executioner answers.

Maxian spreads his arms wide. "Afraid she's a better fighter than you, Death?"

Death is holding back, too, I realize.

I haven't worked out in a few days to give my shoulder some rest, but now I'm restless, itching for activity after only Healing. I'm at the disadvantage in every other way. Except perhaps one.

No one has ever pulled their punches when punching me. Has Maxian ever been hit with the full force of someone's hate? I doubt it. Like any faerie, I have—and often had to work full shifts afterward, too.

"I won't hold back," I warn.

I'm aware of everyone looking at me, but I only look at Maxian. A smile splits his face, the spark in his eyes brighter and sharper.

"Why do you think I picked you?" he says, ducking under the rope. "Brutality is in your blood."

My vision blurs with rage, and I quell the heat that rises. Beside me, Carter sucks in a breath. I kick off my shoes so that we're both barefoot. I want to take off my shirt, too, and fight in trousers and the band around my breasts, as the long sleeves of my shirt can be yanked. But those sleeves cover up the new tattoos placed there by Dominik, and I'm not ready for that conversation.

"If you're going to do this, you need a ref," the executioner mutters.

"Thanks for volunteering," the king says.

I step over the ropes and onto the padded platform. Maxian runs fingers through his bronze hair. The son of the Sun King, and I, the daughter of Red the Ruthless, the unmarked and the marked, in the same ring. Bending my knees, I raise my fists to my chin and tuck in my elbows.

"Nice form."

"Better than yours."

Laughing, he lowers himself, light on his feet.

"Perhaps no magic as one of the rules?" Carter says from the sideline, approaching the ring with a tight expression.

Maxian shrugs. "Sure."

"First to surrender," Death confirms.

"What's your safe word?" the king asks me.

I watch him, never looking away as we both start to circle. I think of the very first time I wanted to hit a king—the day the halfling guards tortured my mother for giving me slices of—

"Apple," I say.

The executioner sighs. "Surrender will be three taps to the ground, not a word, since words may not be possible."

"I'd like to see you speechless," the king says as we circle closer.

What is going on? Has every fae lost all sense? But from the look on his face, the king does not see another prospect to be won, more like an accessory to have. An extension of Kassandra. Perhaps he wants us both, together.

Closer still, I can hear his breathing.

My gaze drops to his shorts, then back up again. Our eyes lock, heat smoldering in his, and I know I'm caught looking. Those lips pull up in a crooked grin.

"Start," the executioner says.

I advance, a small step forward with my left leg, a quick jab with my right arm. The king blocks. I duck his counterpunch and weave beneath his outstretched arm, then swing an open-palmed left hook toward his jaw. He's quick to block, pivot, trip me. I stumble forward, find my balance again.

We orbit each other once more.

"Faster than I thought," he remarks. "For a faerie."

"Slower than I thought for a High Fae."

His expression flickers, smile dropping.

So that was too far.

Maxian lunges. I sidestep. He grabs my shirt, yanking me toward him. *Damn sleeves.* Breath puffs out of me as my back slams into his torso, and he wraps large arms around me.

Trapped.

"So we're grabbing clothes now," I gasp, squirming.

His mouth drops to my ear. "Too bad yours cover so much."

I shiver.

Maxian shifts, one hand reaching up to the neckline of my shirt, his other arm still banded around my front. I freeze, unsure what to do. To smack him when he's off guard is dirty fighting, and for as much as he's teasing now, I don't think the king would appreciate an elbow to his pretty face. Worse yet, if I succeed, I'd knock out the royal in one hit.

So I guess I'm like every other opponent of his: holding back.

Unacceptable.

Maxian's fingers tug on my neckline, gentle. Cool air tickles the raw skin of the bite, the bandage site itchy where it adheres to my skin.

"I'm sorry," the king says, low, his thumb grazing my neck.

I don't move, feigning uncertainty. "It's okay."

"No, it's not." His voice is so soft it makes me shiver again. My heart knocks against my ribs, and I'm sure he can feel it where his thick arm binds me to him. His nose is in my hair, curling wildly with sweat, and I hear him swallow. He adjusts to give more room between our bodies, as if he's changed his mind about his front pressed against my back.

I have the advantage.

I twist in his loose grip, one hand clamping down on his arm as the other snakes beneath his pit to find the small of his back. He braces, realizing what I'm doing.

"Wait—"

Tipping us forward, I push my tailbone into his quad to lift him off his feet. The move would flip his body over my shoulder so that he slams onto his back on the ground. I would keep hold of that one arm so I can control how he falls and ensure he can't get up, maybe jab a pressure point and twist his arm so he'd surrender.

But I don't.

Not because he's the king and I could win with this move.

But because there's something on his back, rough like tree bark. My palm slides under the hem of his shirt, feeling the expanse of gnarled—

Reign magic tumbles through my legs, bringing me to my knees. It's so abrupt, my own genius flails, a moth trapped in a stony room. His power shoves me away, and I sprawl across the mat as it releases me. My head spins, a protest rising to my mouth.

"We said no—"

Breath seizes in my chest. The king towers over me, panting, fingers twitching, gaze unnaturally bright and shining. Something has died in him; something new has come alive. Power thunders into the plane like a rockslide. On the other end of the room, a shield crashes to the floor.

No one says a word.

He takes a step forward, plane rippling. I scrabble back.

"Never do that again," Maxian says.

Then he pounces.

I roll to the side, but it's too late. The king's arms bracket me, and his body descends, the full weight of him pinning me to the mat. Wriggling, I try to knee his crotch, but Maxian's thick thighs spread mine wide. Too late, I slap palms against his chest to shove him off. His hands circle my wrists and push them down on either side of my head.

Our breaths come ragged and fast; our skin is sleek with sweat. The king's scent fills me, musky and sweet, his heft all encompassing. My chest pushes up against his with each swallow of air, but it's not enough to slow my slamming heart.

His face shifts once more from aggression to awe.

"Your eyes," he breathes. "They're gold."

"Maybe we should leave," Carter murmurs from the sidelines, but neither the king nor I look his way.

"They're brown," I correct, but blood roars in my ears.

Maxian shakes his head, leaning closer so that we're almost nose to nose. He examines each iris, gaze flicking side to side in minuscule movements. I turn my face, hide, as heat flushes up my chest and into my cheeks, but he shifts my wrists into one hand above my head. Then his other thumb and finger hold my chin, turning my face back up to him. I stare off to the wall of weapons, glinting and beautiful in the light. It cannot assuage this feeling of display, spread like a star under him with others watching. It does not feel alluring and powerful to have this attention. It feels like the stripping of armor and skin.

"Look at me," he commands, and I do.

A noise gets trapped in the back of his throat.

"I've never seen this on a faerie before," he marvels. "Your eyes are the color of sap."

I shift under him. "Can we . . ."

"If you want something, ask for it." The king smiles.

His thumb strokes the skin of my wrists. I try to tug them out of his grasp, and his focus slides up, watching me struggle. The plane stirs.

"Avery," he says, voice smooth like rich cream. "What's this on your arm?"

"What do you—"

Then he's kneeling back, yanking me onto my knees in front of him. His grip on one wrist tightens to the point of discomfort while the other rips at my sleeve.

"Wait—" I struggle.

"My king?" Carter asks, bending under the rope to get onto the raised mat. "Is everything—"

"Not another step," Maxian barks.

The faerie freezes, meeting my gaze. Behind him, the executioner shifts. "Your Magnificence?"

"Show me your arms," the king growls. We kneel knee to knee, but still I try to twist away. The training hall booms with power as he shouts: "Stop resisting!"

He doesn't even give me a chance to obey.

Reign magic crashes through my entire body once more, forcing me to hold my forearms out to him in silent supplication. It is the violation of the coronation once more, what little agency I had yanked away from the inside out, like a hand up a puppet.

His attention roams over the rings, mouth moving without sound, brow furrowed.

He's counting. He's counting my debt.

"I checked your books. It should've been enough to take off half your rings," the king snaps.

The ten-gold-coin tip.

His magic releases my tongue, demanding an answer.

"It—it was," I stammer. My genius batters against the rocky wall that blocks me from my own will. It beats and beats, printing bloody wings across the surface. The stony façade shrinks tighter around my genius until it is nothing more than an insect dying in a jar. Until all it can do is cling to the shelter of a darkened crevice.

A crevice.

A crack in the wall means a crack in his own genius, in his ability to wield magic. My wounded genius spasms to life, one last time, and begins to burrow.

"You didn't give it away, did you?" he seethes.

"I didn't," I force out, my genius digging deeper, deeper into the crack in the wall.

"Then why do you still have so many rings? Did he also not pay the assault fee?"

"I—well—"

"Avery," he bellows. "The truth!"

My attention snaps, my grip on my genius slipping. The moth drops to the stony ground, stunned. I take a breath, eyes stinging at the loss of control, as Reign magic clamps down on my tongue, as it roots through my mind looking for an answer I'm not willing to give, snagging on the memory I wish to hide.

"A complaint," I hear myself say. "A complaint from House Illusion added the rings back."

Maxian closes his eyes, forcing air out his nose.

"My king . . ." Carter tries again. "Shall I get a glass of water?"

The king seizes both of my elbows, his magic all encompassing.

"Your Magnificence," the executioner starts. "What is—"

The king of Amyria laces us into the plane.

Chapter Twenty-six

My knees sink into plush carpet. A medallion of coral and cream, a border of pink roses. The vibrancy stuns me, like the color of my mother's cheeks on a hot day. A female screams, a gruff male voice shouts: "Maxian! I—"

"Hector."

"—what are—hon, can you—"

I scramble to my feet, taking in bright walls, azure drapery, and a wide four-poster bed. A naked female with sage skin and long limbs stumbles from the mattress like a doe. She clutches the bedsheets to her breasts, grappling for her dress on the floor. She appears familiar and in a less shocking situation, I could place her. Instead, my attention moves to Hector Vandorne as he sits up in bed, gray hair curling across his chest.

For a moment, I'm not sure what shocks me more: that the king's advisor has a nipple piercing or that his centuries-younger mistress just had her tongue around it. Or that the king just laced us into his bedroom "to interrupt."

Maxian turns to the female, who's bowing, apologizing, fixing her hair. In her movements, I catch a flash of silver. Not a coin, but a ring. She's married, too.

"Was it consensual?" he asks.

The female blinks at him. "I—of course!"

"Speak the truth or I will dig it out of your mind."

The fae blanches. "Yes, Your Magnificence."

"Good. Now, Illusion or Healing?"

"Illusion, my lord."

Maxian reaches forward, touching a hand to her shoulder. Her mouth opens in protest, before she disintegrates into the plane like mist.

"Maxian Cornelius Vandorne!" Hector shouts. "It is inconceivably crass to lace another male's mistress."

"Clothe yourself, Uncle. We need to talk."

"What is so important that you must interrupt me in my own chamber?"

Maxian gestures to me. My face burns and I wish, more than anything, that I could sink into the lushness of this carpet. The plane around me rumbles, warming. Hector's mixed heritage of Healing and Reign. Then comes the rush of Maxian's rocky power.

"Assault laws," he says. "We're going to rewrite them."

Rules can change.

It is unfolding but not in the way I imagined, not in the way it was intended.

The king, the advisor, and I regroup in a gold-trimmed parlor adjacent to the bedroom. The males settle themselves in the two tufted cream armchairs before an oval glass table. Across from them, I perch on a green settee at which the king gestured. My palm presses against the soft but firm texture. My hand leaves a darkened impression on the fabric. I reach down, brushing the threads in the opposite direction; it is once again shiny.

"Something wrong with the cushion, girl?" Hector asks.

Blood rushes to my face, and I keep my chin tucked. "No, sir."

"You have a question, Avery," Maxian states.

How in Lucan's Tree does one clean this thing?

"Lady Kassandra does not own this material," I say.

"Crushed velvet. From Cont."

"And what exactly is she doing on my crushed velvet, Max?" Hector grunts, tugging his robe around his belly.

"She's going to help us close the loopholes in the assault laws."

Hector opens his mouth, but the king cuts him off with a wave of his hand. In a moment, a stack of documents drop on the glass table, fanning out across the top. A pile of empty parchment comes next, two quills and inkpots, as well as more folders of work. The armchair creaks as Hector angles himself toward the king. He drops his voice.

"And why, sir, is she helping us and not the Council of Keepers?"

Maxian stares down his uncle. "You and I are both on the council, yes?"

"Yes."

"Have you ever been a faerie?"

Hector laughs. "My lord, I don't—"

"Have you ever been a faerie serving the High Fae in Versara?"

"No."

"And have you ever been assaulted by a High Fae while serving them?"

I suck in a breath. Hector cuts a look to me, then back at the king. I cringe, keeping my eyes downcast. *Please,* I beg silently, ears ringing. *Do not bring me into this—*

"No," he grinds out.

"Are there any faeries on the Council of Keepers?"

"No."

"So you and I, and the rest of the council, are wholly unqualified to write new laws that will actually protect faeries from assault—no matter the class of the attacker," Maxian says. "That is why Avery is sitting on your crushed velvet."

Hector shifts in his chair once more. "I know you are eager to assert yourself as king and build a legacy worthy of the Vandorne line, but this may only further disrupt the dissatisfied council."

Maxian quirks a brow. "You are satisfied doing business with rapists?"

"Well," the advisor sputters. "That's a bit harsh. I see you want to make your mother proud—"

"Do not speak about my mother."

"Then let's speak about you. You are king. Your job is to stabilize the kingdom with a marriage, not—"

"Yes, I am the king, not a common whore!" The plane quakes, a deep shuddering beneath our feet. "My job is to rule, Uncle, and yet when I try to do that, you discourage me. So which is it? Am I weak or am I threatening?"

"Maxian, you know I didn't mean—"

"You will address me as 'my king' or 'Your Magnificence.'"

Hector jerks back. I can hardly breathe. After blinking rapidly, the advisor collects himself. "My king, while I admire your commitment to protecting all the denizens of Amyria, I fear this type of law will upset certain Houses—"

"Good," Maxian rumbles, dust floating down from the ceiling. "They should be upset. They should be disgusted that their peers are monsters. They should be horrified that the law allows these atrocities to go unpunished."

"I just don't see a way where we can properly protect the faeries while also incentivizing the High Fae not to—"

The room thunders again, the glass table cracking.

"*Incentive,* Uncle? They need incentive? How about the fact that they are Illusion. They are Healing. They are not Reign. They do not rule—we do. If they need incentive, they will do well to remember that the Desert Walk applies to the High Fae, too." Maxian draws up to his full height. "And if they cannot obey my laws, then I will take their Matter and Mind."

My stomach feels as though I've swallowed sludge. This isn't what I meant at all; this isn't how it should go. But if it leads to better for all, perhaps I can compromise and be thankful. Perhaps this is what true change looks like—halting and hard.

Hector bows his head. "We do not need other House support, but we will want it."

"We have never been wealthier, more influential."

"We have never been so few in numbers. We are a dying breed, we Reign fae."

"An Illusion fae cannot assault my faerie in front of me. The *audacity* to do that in front of his king, to my coronation present, no less."

A chill claims me. My fingers dig into the expensive fabric. This is not about me or any other faerie. This is once again using us as pawns—this time, to curtail Illusion's ego for the sake of preserving the king's.

This is about destruction of property. Reign property.

I set my jaw. *It doesn't matter,* I tell myself. *It doesn't matter what their motives are if change happens. If my people are better protected. That is what matters most. Impact over intention.*

Hector grunts. "Illusion must have an outlet for their malice, Healing for their experiments. Better the faerie servants than you."

Maxian paces, the stony surge of power retreating from the plane like thunder rolling away. He runs hands through his hair until finally he stops before his advisor.

"We will increase the assault fee by five silvers and ban complaints against the victim for one sun cycle, at which point the High Fae can choose to file one or not. Eli will bring me the data at the end of this year, and we can reassess."

My chest feels so tight. *High Fae don't blink at a few silvers. This is nothing. This is worse than nothing—this is an insult—*

"And while you're here, you must know that this food waste redistribution proposal is preposterous," Hector says, grabbing at a parchment on the table.

I go still, attention falling to the king, whose hair is messy, square jaw clenched. He plants hands on his hips.

"Why's that, Uncle?" This time, Maxian's voice is deadly quiet.

"If the Unskilled are going hungry, then they shouldn't have spent all their coin on drink or theater or trinkets in the market. If they aren't earning enough, they should work harder, like the rest of us. We don't give handouts to the ill-behaved, addicted, or foolish. If we did, they would never learn their lesson."

The muscle in Maxian's jaw feathers. "And what's that?"

Do something! I want to scream at the king. *Why aren't you doing something?*

Hector doesn't even have the decency to ask me to leave when he leans forward, saying: "That the Unskilled need to take it upon themselves to become skilled."

I flinch, something in me breaking. The Unluckies are worked beyond the bone, for even their bones are not free from debt, nor the whites of their eyes from the involuntary ink. They are skilled, even if they don't work, though many do. And how can they step out of immense poverty when there are no stepping stones?

"A hungry people are an angry people," the king tries.

"And a fed people are a strong people."

"But wouldn't that be better—"

"To give up your way of life? Trust me, you do not remember what Healing had to quell in the west in the years following the rebellion."

In Remiti, we do not make windows so large, and the High Fae especially do not purchase this much glass, the faerie from the coronation had said. *Windows can be shattered.*

The High Fae stare down each other, the plane pulling taut, neither male blinking. Finally, the king looks away, and something in me sags.

"Shall I do with this what I do with all of her proposals you bring me?" Hector says, voice like iron.

Her. Lila. Lila's proposals she writes to the king, the ones he asks for—

Maxian doesn't even look his uncle in the eye when he nods.

Hector snaps his fingers, a flame on his thumb, then touches it to the parchment. In the silence, the thought and effort and hope for a better future shrivel to ash.

That's it? I want to snap. *You're going to lie down so easily?*

I should've known. He's the kissing king, after all.

When he looks my way, he almost looks chagrined.

Maxian does not want to be good. He wants to seem good. He wants to seem good so much that he is malicious enough to waste Lila's heart and hours.

My eyes water at the images that play through my mind. Lila, staying up all night trying to envision a better world, an artist at work, drafting page after page to give to the king who signs his own name, to a council who will never read them, all for the vicious ruse of hope. Lila, befriending those around her and trying each day like a schoolteacher to make the king better. As if he were a troubled boy in need of love. As if he did not perceive her as a decent dog that never pissed inside, withholding everything but occasional pats on the head for good measure.

"Here." Maxian crouches before me, voice calm. My body goes rigid, though not with his magic. This time, however, the royal does not seem insulted by my self-preservation, merely sad. He pushes a strand of hair from my eyes, his fingers leaving a trail of rot behind.

Cool, heavy metal presses into my hand. I glance down at the glimmering myth in my grasp. A gold coin. My fingers trace the rays of the sun, turning it over. I read the words printed above and below the Reign crest: *Matter and Mind*.

The rising eagle, spread wings, each claw clutching an item. One set of talons holds a branch from Lucan's Tree, a peace offering. In the other, the bird clutches a whip.

The question never was whether to bring a sack of food to one Unluckie each week or try to change the law for all. It was never about getting a menial raise for the illusion of safety. Not when the answer was always going to be *no*. I have been begging for shallower wounds to a general who will never release his grip. The High Fae will never grant us anything, even when they already have everything. And the king—the head of this violent system—has the most to lose.

The House will never risk its foundation.

My fingers wrap around the money as I meet his violet eyes.

"Thank you, my king," I say.

He nods, patting my cheek. "Clever faerie."

Chapter Twenty-seven

Immediately upon lacing back to Illusion, I find Briar in the kitchens, apple in hand. Tugging her into the pantry for privacy, I pass over the small purse, swallowing the lump in my throat, steeling myself against my own emotions. She crinkles her brow, untying the cord.

"What's this?" she asks.

"What you should've won," I say, but the words stick in my mouth, for no one truly deserves to lose or win.

"Where'd you get this?" she hisses, face blanching at the gold coin.

I point to my throat. My oath.

"No." She shakes her head. "I can't take this."

"In a few days, exchange it for silvers. Start adding a coin to each deposit for your debt. The record will say Illusion has increased your salary with tips. But wait until I get confirmation from Kassandra. Either way, on the record, you'll be safe."

Only three rings tattooed on each wrist. After centuries, she is so close.

"I don't understand." Her voice cracks.

"It can't free you completely, but it will set you on that path quickly, within a year or so," I say.

"And your debt?"

"With the Reign Crest salary, I will find my freedom soon enough."

Briar looks up. "Avery, I . . ."

"For that family you have been waiting to start."

"I can't accept this," she rasps.

"You and your descendants can be free. Your family could even build wealth one day. Please take it. Please."

Tears roll down her cheeks. Then her face cracks, and she weeps desperate, broken sobs. Reaching forward, I cradle the older faerie as if she were a child once more. It is so simple to care for her as she has cared for me, for Kassandra, for countless others. It is so simple, and yet her cries stamp themselves forever on my soul.

IN THE EARLY hours before dawn, I am exhausted, but sleep eludes me. Kassandra was not in her apartments when I stopped by earlier. I do not know where else to go. So I scrape together the last of my energy to lace to a familiar sight, even if just an echo of a life I once shared with my mother. I walk to the empty training halls.

In the dim light provided by the stars above, I take in the racks of axes and crossbows and swords and clubs. Why must the High Fae craft beautiful weapons for such horrible acts?

Walking across the cushioned fighting mat, I reach its center, lowering and crossing my legs. My fingers trail along the seams of the mat, cleaned by some faerie—perhaps Carter—in the day since I was here last.

Why? Why him, Mama?

It was a question I asked her many times as an adolescent, in the years when my rage poisoned every interaction we had, a delayed fury I felt on behalf of the child I was, and because my father was not there to take it, my mother did.

Why him? I would scream. *Why did you not leave him sooner?*

She chose to love a monster and I did not, and yet he consumed us both.

Because I loved him, my mother would say, crying. *Because it was hard to leave.*

Every time she reached for me, I would shove away her hand. *Don't touch me.*

Okay, I won't.

We did not touch for years, and then for years after that as our shames and secrets drove us apart. Only her dying brought us back together again. Only when her skin was paper-thin did I feel how easily it could bruise. Only when she soiled herself did I bathe her and understand it as a simple, reverent act, to keep a loved one clean. Only when she shivered did we share a cot once more, her bony body sheltered in mine. Only in those final days did she whisper childhood dreams and childish hopes, and I dared not beg her to stay, not as she moaned in pain and struggled for every breath. All I did was listen and cling to her essence as if I could keep her from death itself.

But sitting on that fighting mat in the middle of the royal quarters, I reach clarity. After hearing the king's weak protestations before ultimately conceding to comfort, I understand. In a kingdom of killers, my mother chose a fighter in the hopes that he would fight for us.

"I'm sorry, Mama," I say, tears pouring down my face. "Please forgive me."

Something shifts in the air around me, an enveloping and a letting go, an old guilt finally laid to rest, and I draw a deep breath. And although it may be foolish, I believe, once more, in my mother: that she has come to listen to the words that only now I have the humility to share.

The plane stills, almost reverent. On silent feet, the executioner circles before me. "You grieve for many. May they wander well."

I wipe my face. "Why are you here?"

"Why are *you* here?"

"I'm too tired to return to Illusion."

"You do not have a room in Reign?"

"I don't."

A pause. Then, "Do you want me to take you?"

I could go to the Mouth, to the singing and drinking and laughing, and ask either Lila or Carter to take me. But it would cut their evening short, and my dark mood may dampen their lighter ones.

"Maybe," I venture. "How do I know you will . . . bring me back to life?"

"Your time is not now, and I do not believe in early deaths."

"I don't trust you."

"If any harm were to come to you, I would make enemies of the king and possible future queen. I do not wish to do that."

I had planned to rest here until I was strong enough to return on my own. But perhaps Kassandra is back in her room. It must be tonight, as I've already given Briar the coin.

"Okay," I say. "Please."

When Death extends a gloved hand, I once again side with the monsters around me in hopes of preventing those jaws from finding my own neck.

When Death folds me into him, shadows drawing around us like a cooling curtain, I clench my teeth and let him. We dissolve, and it is peaceful and quiet. We emerge into the earthly plane again, in the hallway outside Illusion.

I twist from his grip. "Thanks."

"Of course." He nods, smoke curling around his feet.

"Why help?"

The executioner shrugs. "I am from the House of Death. We welcome anyone who wanders to our doors."

Then, in a plume of smoke, he's gone.

I FIND KASSANDRA on her balcony, overlooking the moonlit Illusion courtyards, a discarded novel next to her. The curtains of the doorway flutter in the soft breeze of spring dawn, and she stares across the shifting maze to the northern building, to the darkened room of her brother.

"For a Reign Crest, you have spent much of your time in my apartments these past few weeks," she says.

I lower myself onto the cool stone bench opposite hers on the balcony.

"I have a secret," I say. "An important one."

She quirks a brow. "Already?"

"My price, first."

She sighs, then gestures for me to continue.

"Briar's deposits will grow under the assumption that you are tipping her extra. The difference is being covered by someone else, so it will not show up on the Illusion accounts and Dominik won't see it. But I need you to write a note to the tellers that the tips are coming from you."

"Did it come from my account involuntarily?"

"No. It didn't come from Illusion at all."

Kassandra tilts her head. "The tip is coming from your pocket."

I should deny this, but it is better she knows the source than dig up unwanted information. Besides, we have a pact now and this will just have to be my leap of faith.

"I'm passing it along."

Kassandra reaches for the novel. "Still, someone may pick up on the discrepancy—that she is getting extra coin while extra coin isn't being taken from my account. The Illusion advisor, Lord Tomas, is keen. He's one to notice, even if Dominik doesn't."

"With this secret, things will change."

We cannot beg a kingdom of killers to kill us softly. We have to act as they do: nefariously.

"Whose is it?"

I bite my lip. "The eagle wears the crown but listens to the older pig."

She laughs. "Hector."

"The pig rolls in the mud with another from a different pen."

"Disgusting but not surprising. So, the old bastard is sleeping with a wife—just not his own?"

"She's from the farm that . . . does tricks."

"She's House of Illusion."

My eyes cut to the building diagonal from us. "The pig has green skin and dark hair. Her pen is with the blue pig."

My mistress jerks back. "Are you sure?"

"Yes."

She retreats between the billowing curtains. I follow as Kassandra waves a hand and various candles throughout her chamber—on her vanity, on her bedside table, by her looking glass—come to life.

"Hector is sleeping with Clara Roche," she declares. "He's sleeping with the Illusion advisor's wife! Do you know what this means?"

"We have leverage." I shut the balcony doors while Kassandra fumbles through the drawers of her bedside table.

"Where's parchment?" she asks.

"Bottom shelf."

Her silver braid falls over her shoulder as she bends down to scratch a quill against the paper. "This means that I need to invite Clara to tea."

"You never invite anyone to tea."

She scowls. "I do."

"When?"

"Avery, I simply cannot keep track of every obligation and event I have! There are so many."

I roll my eyes. "So tea?"

"Yes, tea. Clara helps her husband keep the books. Our books—which means I can grant Briar her raise, set aside a safety net for myself, and start giving out more tips. If Clara doesn't want to give me what I want, that's fine, too. I'll just send this note about the affair to her husband. We're in the game now, Avery."

It should feel bad, manipulating another female like this, but the repercussions mean so much more. Kassandra straightens. "I'll let Briar know when she can deposit the extra coin."

"Thank you." I nod, falling into silence.

We stare at each other in the candlelight, and my mistress opens her mouth, then closes it. As we come down off this high, knowing our plan is working, we are left with the distance between us once more.

"Is there anything else, mistress?"

Kassandra clears her throat, looking away. "I was wondering . . . I'm trying to learn how to do my own hair. The way you used to. I suppose gaining some agency over my life has sparked the need for more."

"I can offer you tips."

"I'd actually like to . . ." She huffs, hugging herself. "Could I brush your hair?"

"You want to *what*?"

"Is it so shocking to you that I would like to learn?"

"Yes!"

"Just sit at the vanity, okay?" She gestures behind me. There is the faintest tug on my clothes, a gentle request but not a demand. Swallowing, I pull out the chair and perch on the soft cushion. When Kassandra comes over, comb in hand, I stiffen.

"I'm not going to stab you in the back with it," she seethes.

"You used to throw it at my head!"

"Lucan's Tree, you're dramatic. Now relax."

I sit ramrod straight. Her fingers pick up a plait of my hair, gently untangling its knots. Then, starting at the ends, she begins brushing.

She massages my scalp between the knots, working her fingers in circles. It's rhythmic, gentle. It reminds me of being a child again when my mother would dress me. I try to keep my shoulders tense out of protest—I will not be Kassandra's doll.

But I am so tired. My bones feel weary. It takes everything in me to stay upright. Soon I feel phantom hands drawing a blanket around my shoulders, and I lean back into the chair, into her touch. She keeps working, hands moving to a predictable pattern. The stress of the day slides off my shoulders, even the one that still aches.

"I always wished my mother would brush my hair." Kassandra sighs. "I was thinking of her tonight."

I was thinking of mine, too. Keeping my eyes closed to afford her some privacy, I say instead: "Tell me of her."

A slight pause. Then, "She was brilliant—much more than my father. If head of House were granted on merit, she would win over any male, any day."

I look at our reflection. I've been tucked into the chair, wrapped in furs. Kassandra sways behind me, eyes focusing on my locks. "But she was not head—she was just a wife. So she turned her boredom on us. We were her playthings, my brother and I. And the servants."

"What . . . what do you mean by that?"

Despite her blank expression, tears gather in her eyes. She runs the brush through my hair gently. "I was never good at it. The servants' screams confused me. For many years, I refused to hurt them, despite her unpleasant reactions."

In the reflective glass, my face pales. Perhaps it is my oath, our pact, or the loneliness of the twilight hours. Whatever the reason, Kassandra seems to be unburdening herself from something long held, just as I had done tonight. I stay silent, offering space.

"It came easier to Dominik, hurting them." She shrugs. "Or maybe he just loved her more."

The brush stops, a lock of my chestnut hair trembling between her fingers. I ache to reach up, clasp her hand in mine. But she has gone somewhere else, eyes glazed over, and I fear the consequences, like waking a sleepwalker. So instead, I sit in the nightmare with her.

"One night, they came for me—my brother and mother." Tears pour down her otherwise stoic face, and it is like watching a garden statue weep during a rainstorm. "My mother instructed Dominik to break my arms. He was crying, I was pleading, but she wouldn't budge. She said we both needed to learn this lesson: that family does not mean protection. We must learn that we can only protect ourselves, and if we cannot, then we deserve the harm that comes our way."

My fingers grip the blanket.

"So Dominik broke them," she states. "But because he cried while he did it, Mother made him come back again the next month after they had healed. And the month after that, and every month until he no longer cried. It took years, but eventually he stopped weeping, and she stopped attending. But the lesson had been ingrained: He started visiting me on his own volition, and every month, for the past two centuries, he has returned to break me.

"Every faerie who witnesses it quits or is harmed themself. Some became crippled, some just disappeared. And how can I blame them? But you and Briar stepped in, even when I did not deserve it." Kassandra blinks, as if returning to herself once more, and those bloodshot eyes find mine.

She holds my gaze for several moments. I remain in the chair, staring up at her as a storm of emotion roils in me. Sadness, fear, hatred, and empathy—it is a tempest that crashes into my swamp of grief, disrupts the stagnant waters and shifts the shorelines.

"You're crying," she says.

"Everyone deserves to be protected."

She hiccups. "I have been cruel to you."

I turn in the chair, facing her. "Mistress—"

"No, listen to me. Listen to me, please," she cries, clutching my hand. "I have been cruel and callous. I have been like my mother to you. I am sorry. I am so sorry. I want to be better—I just don't know where to start. I don't know what to do. All I know is that I am angry and tired and this is the true rot in me. This is my rot: that I am my mother's daughter."

I could say she's been nothing but kind, but we both know it's a lie. I could tell her it never mattered, but it did. I feel everything: layer upon layer of conflicting thoughts; the storm has swept us both away.

"Kassandra," I say, and her given name from my lips shocks us both. We stare at each other, and I wait for her to punish me. Instead, she just watches with widening eyes. I clear my throat. "If cruelty is learned, then it can be unlearned, too. I don't believe Dominik wants to, but that doesn't mean you can't."

She looks away, wiping her face. "What if it's too late?"

I think of Maxian, giving up on protecting faeries. But the king is not female; there are certain pains he will never understand. Kassandra is . . . complicated. Complicated, but perhaps different.

"As long as you breathe, it is never too late to become better," I try.

Grief is what I felt that day lined up in Kassandra's chambers. Grief is what she recognized in herself.

She looks at me. "We should get to bed."

I rise, folding the fur blanket and resting it on her bed as she scrubs her face with a cloth. We move around each other in silence for several moments, not saying goodbye as I leave.

Later, in the loneliness of my cot, I brave that storm of emotions once more, picking out her pain, so raw and visceral, and tucking it under my ribs and beside my own. In the dark, the two hurts look the same.

Chapter Twenty-eight

My genius won't move, exhausted. My shift started a few moments ago, but I still hover outside my Illusion room. Panic climbs my throat. With the uniqueness of my situation, no one in the Mouth has approached me about getting a new room, and truthfully I haven't wanted to ask, nervous at the potential rejection. Now I wish I had. The Reign ring warms with magic, then—nothing.

Lila insisted on helping me lace when I rejoined Reign service halfway through last week. She was worried about my shoulder. I didn't protest because—well, as I worked that third week in Reign, scrubbing, cleaning, clearing, serving, I became worried about my genius. Stunned from the clash in the training halls with the king, it only twitched when called upon.

"Shit." Ten minutes late, I pace the hall, trying to coax my genius to no avail. It has never taken this long for my magic to return to me after an illness or injury. Then again, I've never battled a king in magic before, either. Is this the start of Moldhood? The thought churns my stomach.

Footsteps freeze behind me, and I whirl to see Benji, his face pale.

Before I can open my mouth, he blurts: "Why are you here?"

"I still sleep in Illusion."

His eyes dart to my door. "I know this is your room. I meant, why aren't you gone yet for the night?"

"Well, I . . ." I pause. "Is everything okay? I've never seen you up here before."

The boy shrugs, looking at my door again. "I don't know."

"Okay. Do you want me to help you find Glenn?"

"Why are you so nosy?" he shouts.

"I'm sorry," I say, softer now. I step forward, and Benji doesn't react. He lets me draw closer, blinking, I see now, angry tears away. "It's okay, Bee."

He groans, covering his face, turning away. He whines something into his hands.

"What was that?" I ask, crouching so we're the same height but not daring to touch him. I'm already so late for this shift, so very much in the king's disgraces. It can't get much worse than this. Who knows, maybe he's fed up with my service and will release me back to Kassandra.

Benji mumbles into his hands again. "I come up here every day and sit outside your room and pretend I'm telling you about the horses."

My chest shatters, throat tightening. "I'd love to hear about the horses. If you want to tell the real me."

He peers through his fingers. "Yeah?"

"Of course."

Dropping his hands, he frowns, looking over my shoulder. "You were at the game we played on the lawn."

I spin around to see Lila emerging from the dark.

"Hi!" Lila smiles, nervous. "Sorry to interrupt, but—you weren't coming so I wanted to check on you." Dust splotches across her white shift, and her hair springs out of her protective style, which twists from the sides of her head to the nape of her neck. Dirt smears across one cheek.

"Bye, Avery," Benji says, then flees down the stairs. At least he said something this time.

"Bye!" I call, then groan, turning to my friend. "What happened to you? You need to wipe down before we go to the king—oh planes, we're so fucking late."

"I came to tell you that he dismissed us for dinner." Lila offers a palm, her ring already illuminating. "But I want to spend time with you."

She laces us to her room.

"So," Lila starts, barely giving time for me to catch my breath. "Ever since you said you believed me about something at the center of the Pith, I can't stop thinking about it. It's like a flood of memories, entering the chambers with my father. I remembered the word he used for access."

"A word?" I ask.

"Like a spell woven into the very essence of an object. A verbal way to unlock it. And I know which door we'll use. The king's apartments connect to the queen's, so that's the riskiest route, especially since we don't know what time he'll be done trying to forge the dagger."

"What are you saying?"

"Who was Maxian before he became king?"

"A prince?"

"And where do the royal children reside?"

"The Salon of Stars. But—"

"It's empty, since Maxian has no wife or offspring."

"And how are we going to get there?"

Lila grins. "You forget I am a chimney cleaner's daughter."

My friend steps up to her collage wall of fabric dyed with spices: a swaying meadow, a swath of flowers that surrounds a rendering of Lucan's Tree. Lila hooks a fingernail into a knot in the trunk and tugs. The fabric rips—and so does my heart as my friend tears a gash in her own art.

"No!" I reach for her elbow. "What are you doing?"

"Look." She nods to the wall.

The fabric curls from the dark stone beneath it, like a shadowy pit. It's a niche in the thick wall that has been scraped away, dusty layer by dusty layer. Lila reaches into the space, and when her fingers draw back into the light again, they clutch a thick iron ring of keys.

"I think he wanted to leave me more than just his debt. This was all he had," she whispers.

"A great gift," I say. "The ability to enter spaces that exclude our kind."

"And yet I've always lacked the courage to do it. I was never afraid to enter the apartments before. I always had my father."

"And he had you."

"Perhaps the real key is not courage but company." She meets my eye. "Let's go now, while we're not needed."

Lila wants to search the labyrinth, to stand where we're told we cannot. A growing urgency sweeps over her face, a desire to traverse like Lucan. I have secrets to collect like a creditor with his coin. And like a creditor, I do not feel like asking for permission.

So I smile at her and say, "I will wander—"

The building shakes. A violent quaking that shudders even the thick stones, dust billowing through cracks, the ceiling groaning. Then it all stops, as if the entire force were a passing earthquake.

I slowly unpeel my fingers from their vise grip on Lila's forearm. My heart hammers in my ears.

"What was that?" I whisper.

Lila grips the wall. "The king."

The plane quakes harder this time, and it doesn't feel like a rockslide. It is more sentient than that. It feels like an ancient creature roaring from the depths of the earth.

The hairs on my arm stand up. "Is this why he dismissed us?"

"He's trying to forge the diamond dagger again," she says. "Carter told me he's been at it all day."

"He told me—"

"No." She clasps my arm as pebbles tumble around us. "Maxian's *trying* to forge a diamond dagger. And he cannot."

I jerk back. "Is this a jest?"

"He tries every day, and every day he fails."

I think of the cuts on the king's hands, his questions to Kassandra of the dagger as an Illusion, and Hector confirming that it is not.

"He has the technique wrong," I guess.

"His failed approaches are making him . . . volatile."

I bristle, remembering the way he clutched me with Reign magic during our clash despite agreeing not to. The way he shoved my limbs around like a doll's, his grip hard and bruising.

"Then he's not siphoning enough from the plane," I say, but Lila just shakes her head.

But why would the most powerful fae in Amyria need to borrow energy when he possesses the strongest genius? He must be doing something wrong. He is Maxian the Mountain, son of the Sun King, his testament bending an entire ballroom to his will. The last pure Reign fae.

The walls shudder again.

"We need to get out of here!" I shout to Lila over the thundering.

"Now is the time!" she yells back, holding up the key ring.

I shake my head. "He's already furious."

"He's distracted, and so are his other attendants. Come on, let's be quick."

LILA LEADS US beyond the Mouth, down an unlit corridor I thought was storage. My fingers trail along the wall on my right, the other hand clasping my friend's. Even after five minutes of walking, my eyes do not adjust to the darkness. In fact, the opposite is happening as the torches fall behind us. The temperature plummets, the stone cold. The palace rumbles again, this time fainter.

Lila halts in front of a large bronze door and fumbles with the keys.

"It's too dark." She curses.

"Hold on."

I rub my hands together, reaching for my genius. It lies twitching at the bottom of my mind, and despite prodding, the magical organ remains asleep.

In the far distance, behind our backs, there is a thud, thud, thudding. Or maybe it is my heart in my ears. I swallow.

"Can you summon flame?" I ask.

"The smallest one."

"Why don't I try the keys while you hold a light close?"

The weight surprises me when she passes the thick, cool ring into my hands. I grope for a proper grasp. Then Lila snaps.

The sound claps through the silence, bounces off the stones. My spine goes rigid, my breath held. We listen for the sound of footsteps. None come—and neither does a flame from her skin.

"Shit," she mutters. "Okay, we're only going to try that once more."

She snaps again and this time, there's a spark from her fingertips, the smallest bud of a flame. Crouching, Lila levels it with the lock. I examine the brass keyhole, select a large ring that's turned green.

It doesn't fit. I try the next bronze ring, then another. Glancing at the keys, I determine that there must be at least ten of them.

"What was that?" Lila whispers next to me, a hand on the wall. Her light begins to fade, the lock and keys slipping into the dimness once more.

"What was what?"

"The screaming."

I drop the keys. They clatter to the ground, and Lila's light goes out. Blood pounds in my ears, and I force myself to breathe until my heart calms. The only noise that greets us is a faint drip-drip-drip deeper in the Pith.

After a moment, she mumbles: "I thought I heard screaming. I'm sorry."

"Could've been the quaking. Maybe we should leave and try again."

"When will we have another chance such as this? With Maxian distracted and you here to help me?"

She's not wrong. It's been almost a moon since I started working in Reign, and while we have another together before I temporarily return to Illusion, when will Maxian be once again occupied?

So I pat around for the keys. My fingers find dirt and the ridge of a small leaf, peeking through a crevice in the structure. I suck in a breath. How is it possible? In a dark place with no room to grow, no rich soil, and still, a little life has begun to flourish.

I find the keys. By feel, I eliminate several we've already tried. Lila and I determine that the sound of the snap isn't worth so little light, so instead, I guide a new key into the lock. Something clicks.

Moving aside, I hear her grasp the key and whisper, "*Etoles.*"

The entrance creaks open, a high-pitched whine, as if a creature has been resurrected against its will. Lila grapples for my arm; her touch is damp with sweat, as is mine.

"Ready?" she asks.

"Never."

Together, we wander into the abandoned bedroom.

The smell greets me first, musky and full. The scent of abandonment. Twinkling lights scatter across the floor like faerie lights. Not powerful, but plentiful, and it's enough to illuminate the room.

I bend down, seeking to brush one with my finger. But my shadow descends, and that's when I understand that the lights are not embedded in the floor. In fact, they're not tangible at all.

"Look up," Lila says.

When I do, my breath stops. The room itself is three levels tall, with no windows on any of the walls. Yet the entire ceiling is made of glass, displaying the brilliant, speckled night sky above us. It gives the illusion that we stand at the bottom of some giant well.

"It's beautiful."

"It always was," my friend replies, gaze scanning the chambers.

I survey the space, a rectangular bedroom with tapestries, a four-poster bed in its center, a desk pushed up on the far wall, an empty weapon rack on the other. Across from where we entered is another egress, a passageway to another chamber.

"I was picturing a child's bedroom," I say.

"He was the child of Gregor and Elise, so technically, you're correct."

"Somehow I forgot he has only been king for a month."

"He expands like that."

"What do you mean?"

She shrugs. "He took over some of the governing years ago when his father started to decline, so it hasn't been as big a transition as it seems on the outside."

We wander to the weapon rack.

"He hasn't spent time in this bedroom for years now?"

"No. King Gregor—may he wander well—moved to the royal chambers in the House of Healing, where he could receive the best care. He was there about a decade before he passed, and so Maxian moved into the Sun Salon."

I do not comment on how strange that sounds—settling into his father's space before he died. Running his father's kingdom before he's king.

Starlight washes the tapestry and its intricacies in a glittering waterfall. A meadow of an apple orchard that extends to the horizon. A little boy plays in a tree, an adult in a plain tunic looking up at him. A nursemaid. Several paces away is the dark-haired queen, adorned in a rich red-and-gold gown, patched to add a train behind her. My hand reaches up, strokes the fabric of a bronze-haired faerie nursemaid.

"They included her," I utter. I have never seen a faerie captured in any art before, neither portrait nor sculpture nor official song. To see one of us up on a wall, even in an abandoned room, shifts the entire world. As if we are worth noting. As if we are worthy of preservation, of history.

"I'm sure the rumors have warped in the century since the fever took the queen, but . . ." My friend stops, glances at the royal.

I look at her. "But what?"

"Apparently, the queen adored her faerie. It's why she was kind to all the servants. Supposedly they were friends."

I laugh. "Were they truly friends or did the queen just think that?"

Lila tilts her head to the tapestry. "Enough to memorialize her."

I look to the faerie again. "Perhaps they were lovers."

Now Lila laughs.

We cross the chamber and enter a closet three times the size of my room, full of mismatched tunics and shoes of varying styles. Another key, another *Etoles,* and we enter the bathing chamber, the innermost part of the Pith.

Light still pours in from the sky above.

A looking glass lines one wall completely, doubling the image of the room. I catch my reflection and truly examine it for the first time in over a month.

The dark circles under my eyes have faded, and my irises—as the king observed—are brighter, like the color of sap. The appearance of my collarbone has now softened with another layer of muscle and weight, and my chestnut waves shine thick and lush thanks to the soaps from Lila and Fern. I stand a bit taller, skin clearer, like Lila's. It's as if even in my grief and the games of the fae, the shorter hours, the fresher food, the higher pay, the better soaps, and the more rigorous exercises have performed some sort of magic on my body. In the reflection, Lila comes up to me, leans her head on my good shoulder.

"You okay?"

The king was right. Kassandra was right. The stranger in the glass answers. "I look . . . different."

Better.

"Rest, I have found, is the greatest resource of the fae."

"Maybe there is another."

Both of us glance at the large, empty bathing pool on the other side of the room. With no water, the floor slopes down, a large drain exposed at the bottom.

Lila's account proves correct. The wall opposite the looking glass bows inward dramatically, cutting into the bathing pool, halving its potential.

She starts forward, feet padding down the slope of the bedrock, placing a hand on the wall. "On the other side, the king and queen's bathing chamber also looks like this."

Yet her words barely register. My muscles lock up, my mind reeling with a rush of a floral, warm scent, like inhaling a perfume that becomes a drug. It's not the sickly sweetness of the fae wine, or the brightness of the stars. It is deeper, earthier—balanced and unknowable.

"Avery?"

But I cannot speak, cannot move or even stay with Lila, as my consciousness turns inward, to the genius that lies like a stunned moth at the bottom of a well. When I inhale, the earthy scent pours down that well. It is strong and rounded and natural, like the scent of a lover's skin, like the damp earth dug to bury the dead. This is life and this is death and the two suddenly seem the same, two halves of one circle, a current that flows into itself.

Hello again, say a thousand voices.

My genius twitches, its wings vibrating. Then it's snapping to life again, flapping and fluttering up and up and up, the surge of energy so powerful I feel the tingling spread to my limbs, to my fingers and toes, sparking outward, connecting once more to the plane. Sounds and colors and smells flood my senses as I access the plane of magic once more.

"The magic is strange here," I breathe.

My concentration falls to the floor, and I freeze. My sandal lies across the drain, a whispering blackness under the grate, like a sighing mouth. I step off it. The rush abates.

"There's something down there."

"Has something happened?" Lila asks, glancing at the drain, then startles when she looks back at me. "Your eyes—they're glowing."

"I . . . I'm not sure what happened."

We ascend out of the pool, and I stop short at my reflection, again. Transformed into a creature brimming with power, I stare at the two flames that fill my gaze. An aftereffect of my genius reawakening, perhaps. A slip of control on my fire ability. Blinking only slightly dims the light.

She glances at the sky. "The hour is late. We can return another time."

My friend takes my hand.

As we wind our way out of the Salon of Stars, I cannot shake the feeling of that magical exhale, that sighing creation that slumbers at the heart of the Pith, which was powerful enough to animate my hibernating genius and set my eyes aglow.

It is something other than Reign magic. Something ancient. Something *alive*.

As we close the door once more, cutting out the light, Lila struggles with the keys. My genius buzzes with the strength of a swarm. All I have to do is think, and a roaring flame erupts from my palm.

It's as easy as breathing.

Chapter Twenty-nine

L‍ILA HAS JUST PLACED THE KEYS IN THE NICHE WHEN THERE'S A pounding on her door. We share a glance, and then she's pressing the fabric over the hole and leaning against the wall.

"You answer," she says. "And do whatever you can to make them go away."

On the other side of the door stands Carter, in a rumpled shirt, laces undone at the top. The moment he registers it's me, standing in Lila's bedroom, his mouth goes slack.

I raise my brows. "So you're the competition?"

"Avery!" Lila yelps.

I keep the door tucked close to my shoulder. Carter coughs. "No, I— What's with your eyes? You know what, never mind." He holds out an envelope. "From the king. He laced it to the Mouth, and it's addressed to Lila."

My friend squeaks behind me.

"Is she okay?" Carter leans to the side, but I lean with him.

"Yes, she's just spent. How's the king in general? We felt the . . ." I glance up at the ceiling.

"It's fine. He found a new outlet." He shrugs, then departs, and I close and lock the door. Lila comes away from the wall, crossing her arms.

"Was that necessary?"

"Was what?" I smile.

Lila gives me a look as she plucks the letter from my hand. Her exasperation disintegrates to a darker emotion: dread, fear, resignation. Each time my friend rereads the note, her light dims just a bit more, frown deepening.

"What's wrong?" I ask.

"Nothing."

Before she can tuck it into her pocket, I snatch it back.

"No," she says. "No, it's fine—"

Scrawled across the parchment is just one word.

Bedchamber.

It yanks the air from my lungs.

Bedchamber?

My vision blurs with rage. My head snaps up, and I try to meet my friend's eye, but she just hugs herself, staring at the floor.

"This is not fine," I snap. This is worse than not fine.

For all his drama and noise and pity, the king acts as those he condemns.

"It's not what you think," Lila snarls.

I take a breath. "I do not judge, Lila. I just care for you."

"You misunderstand. He's brought a new fae into his bed."

"What do you mean?"

Lila shifts. "He makes me watch sometimes, for an audience. His guests like it, too. They seem to enjoy my discomfort—perhaps believe it turns me on."

"And they make you—"

"I've never joined. Sometimes the guests request it, but the king always declines."

The strange feeling congeals in my stomach. I remember Maxian's warm, honeyed words the night I wore the oil.

Who's it for? he murmured. *Don't be nervous, Avery, dear.*

I am nervous now—nervous for Lila. For myself, I feel pent up with new power, like a dam ready to burst. I think of the look the king gave me in the training halls. His full weight pinning me. His bruising grip on my arms.

Something swells up in me, an emotion I can't identify.

"I'll go," I say.

Lila grabs my arm. "Do not."

"I'll say you weren't feeling well and so I've stepped in."

"No."

"Lila." Now the nerves are for us both. "How many times have you stepped in for me? Let me do this for you."

"It's not just that." She bites her lip. "It's your disdain. Lately, it's been leaking through."

"My disdain?"

"It's dangerous. It's the one emotion Maxian cannot handle: when a faerie looks at him with disgust." Shaking her head, she says: "You cannot slip once, not even for a second."

"I won't." Taking a few deep breaths, I rein in my genius and emotions. "How are my eyes?"

"Normal again. Brown."

So there is a connection between all three—my genius, my emotions, my eyes. I'd rather the king not ask questions for which I have no answers, even if I want to inquire after his features. I remember during our clash feeling the skin on his back, ridged and knotted. How the king had turned into someone else afterward. *Never do that again.* I can't fight the intuition that there is a secret there to uncover. And perhaps learning whoever is in his bed can be useful to Kassandra.

Most of all, the king made me feel powerless. And now it is my turn to do the same.

LILA BRINGS ME to the door in the servants' hall that leads to the king's chamber.

"Please don't do this," she begs.

"How many times have you done it?"

She doesn't answer.

"I can handle it once," I say. "Now, get back to your room—you're ill and need rest."

Lila gives me one last look, squeezes my hand, and disappears into the hall. I do as she instructed. I bite my lip, bringing color to the skin, grip the knob, and speak: "*Solil.*"

The normally sealed door glides open, revealing a glowing chamber and warm parquet floors. To my right blazes a veined marble fireplace carved with leaves, berries, and a rising eagle in the mantel's center, clutching a branch and whip. A sultry glow comes from above, and I expect the night sky again, only to find hundreds of floating candles, their collective radiance like that of the sun itself. Yet there's no faerie around to maintain them—only a fae.

There's a huff to my left.

As I pivot, I take in the enormous white-and-gold tufted bed, stories-tall drapes crowning the headboard. A tray of sparkling wine and two glasses rest on a side table.

Sprawled across the bed is a dusty-rose fae with pert features, magenta curls tumbling over one shoulder. Though she wears a thin shift, her curves press against the white fabric. When I meet her glittering black eyes, she sighs, rolling over.

"Max," she whines. "I wanted the pretty one."

A deep, soft voice slides along the plane: "What, you don't find Lila—"

The king's head rises from behind the female's shoulder, then stops. His cheeks are flushed, hair plastered to one side, lavender tunic askew, cock thick against his thigh. His eyes flash in shock, brows pinching, and then he smooths his expression into one of cool indifference.

"Avery," he says.

"Your Magnificence."

His eyes flick to the fae in his arms, then to me. I give nothing away, schooling my expression, and wait for him to speak.

"I sent for Lila," he says eventually.

"She's ill."

The female fae sighs again. "I think I'll leave."

"Come on, now." The king wraps an arm around her back, drawing her closer. "We can still have fun."

I wonder whether the tunic will come off. Perhaps he always hides whatever is on his back.

A giggle. "Yeah?"

"Yes, my love."

"Love?" More giggling. "I do like the sound of 'Lady Reign.'"

"I do, too."

Lucan's Tree. I feel queasy at the talk alone. Maxian dips his head, capturing her mouth in his. He pushes her onto her back, climbing on top, mostly clothed. They lie facing the foot of the bed, facing me.

As they grind, she squeaks out empty sounds. I push down my disgust. *Is this what they have Lila do? Just stand there and stare?* I guess it works for some. If I wanted to put on a show, I'd at least make it entertaining. Distracted, I let my genius unfold in my mind, frenetic and frenzied, energy prowling beneath my skin. The plane shifts, picks up in vibration.

When I refocus on the act before me, my breath catches.

The king watches me. As his thumb twists the nipple of the female, he watches me. As his mouth finds her neck and sucks, his eyes search mine for any sign of desire, any heat that he is the greatest lover in the land.

According to the forceful, pitchy moans of his bedmate, I know he is not.

I keep my expression dull. As the king pushes harder, his touches growing desperate and sloppy, his partner tires of her own performance. They wanted to be seen. They never specified in what light. I stifle a yawn.

The king crawls off, and his lover pushes herself up. "Why'd you stop?"

"Just wanted a change of pace." He meets my eye. "Avery," he snaps, the sound cracking through the space like a whip. "Come closer."

I circle the bed until I stand at its side.

"Kneel," he commands.

I drop to my knees, lean back on my heels. The fae's attention flits back and forth between us.

He nods. "Good. Shall we continue?"

The fae hesitates, then gives way. She pulls her nightgown over her head, shaking out her sunset hair. Her nipples are hard, hips curving into thick thighs. She is beautiful, and regardless of what she's said about me, I feel for her. She needs something, wants something, and also must put up with Maxian to get it. I do not judge using the king. He uses everyone.

"My turn on top," the fae coos, and Maxian grins, leaning back against the pillows and headboard. She climbs on top of him, bracketing his legs with her own. He runs his hands up her thighs, and she flips her hair to one side.

They dive into their show again, smacking and groaning, the sounds and gestures growing more exaggerated, more desperate, but not for each other—rather, for a gaze they attribute to me, one that is only really in themselves.

Planes, no wonder his litany of lovers can stretch around the palace thrice over, something males always like to brag about. No one came back for seconds.

As they flail, the power of the fae deflates before me. These statuesque, striking creatures—the most alluring in the land—cannot enjoy pleasure. Even in their desire, the fae will not messy themselves, will not grasp and beg for and earn the body of another. They will never worship and never be worshipped, and so then, what is the point? To value the look of sex over its feel is to misunderstand it.

And the king never takes off his tunic.

They steal glances in my direction, distractedly, and fumble with each other, and suddenly it is not enough. It's not enough to know that I am a better lover than the king.

I need him to know it, too.

I let my bored genius stretch its wings, buzzing, unsatisfied, along the plane.

The female breaks apart. "Okay, I can't do this with her staring at us."

"Is that not the point?" I ask.

"It's the way you're staring."

"How's that?"

"Like a dead fish."

It takes everything in me not to laugh. Maxian frowns furiously, and I feel a thrill. Not of desire but of the game. If I cannot spill the blood of those I hate, why not heat it? There is a little death in that still, and their shame ensures I can get away with absconding their control.

They take and take and take. Perhaps I should take, too. My genius hums at the very idea.

"I can do other things besides play dead," I venture, then glance to Maxian, remembering the official laws that contradict the private behavior of fae and faeries alike. No pledging to the same sex, no public displays, no asking, no telling.

He shrugs, fighting a smirk. "It's not illegal to play with each other. Only to marry."

Male desire is so predictable.

"Besides, you're the king," I say. "You can play however you want. Even as a spectator."

His gaze narrows.

"What do you mean?" the fae asks, her expression wary. Maybe they want someone to messy them so that they can indulge without claiming responsibility.

"Come to me," the king commands.

"Ladies first," I reply. "Then, if you'll still have me, I will."

A small rumble in the room, yet from the flash in the king's eye, I know he likes the pushback. It riles him, makes him feel stronger when he'll get me to submit. Like thinking me a scrappy opponent in the ring, the Ruthless daughter. But here is what he gets wrong: Just because I serve him does not mean I submit. After everything the king has done and allowed, I will never submit. Not to him. He has not earned it.

"I don't want you to touch me, if that's what you're saying," the fae says.

"You don't?" I rise forward onto my knees once more.

She jerks back. "What are you doing?"

"Do I have your permission?"

The plane rumbles again. The fae won't look away from me.

"For what?" she demands.

"To ruin you."

Her cheeks deepen in color.

"No," she sputters.

"A lie," the king says.

"That's okay," I answer. "You can look, if you prefer. But if you want to feel, you say so. And if you want to stop feeling at any point, you can say a word."

She watches me. "Even after we've started?"

Again, my heart twists for the fae in front of me, for the oppressed oppressor.

"Especially after we've started. It is all up to you."

The room groans with the vibrating of the plane, a mingle of all our magics, the flicker of a thousand candles. The king's ire spikes my own, but his is not a true anger. It's a desire to be acknowledged. So I look at him, and he is *brimming*. Brimming with frustration, with tension, with hatred and lust.

"See those drapes behind you?" I say. "Tie your hands in them."

One side of his mouth tugs up. "No."

"Fine. As long as all you do is watch until I decide you can join."

He gets everything he wants, he gets to win every time, everywhere, outside this chamber. But not in his own bed. Not anymore.

The fae surveys me. "You cannot speak of this to anyone."

"I am blood-bound. The king will confirm."

"It's true," he grumbles.

She flicks her gaze to him, then back to me. She swallows, her throat bobbing.

"I heard . . . I heard the faeries fuck like animals."

Desire sings in my veins, and I loose my genius, drenching the plane with the scent of spring rain. They both startle, look to me, the air heady and heavy.

This. This is power. This is control, if even for a moment. This is that feeling I have been chasing ever since Jeremee died. This glorious and painful reality, like the shallow nick of a blade against skin. Something to remind me of my own body. Something to reclaim.

So reclaim I do.

I prop my elbows on the edge of the mattress and take in the gorgeous fae sitting cross-legged before me.

"Your word?" I ask. "Utter it once and everything stops."

"I-I'm not sure," she stammers.

I glance at the king. "How about 'apple'?"

Heat glints in his half-lidded gaze, his cock flexing.

" 'Apple' it is," the fae says.

Taking a breath, I search for someone, an ex-lover, a beautiful stranger, to envision as I service the fae once more. But as my mind flicks through the possibilities, it keeps landing on the same one, no matter how much I abhor and abate the image.

My mind magnetizes to a silver-haired female.

Something twinges low in my gut. I push down the panic, the self-hatred that comes with this realization. *You cannot slip once, not even for a second.*

So I stoke the fire of my own desire that I will never share with another. I think of her in her nightdress, the neckline slipping down one shoulder. I think of her sleek skin, the cutting glances, the sharpness of her tongue. I imagine it on me. I imagine those blood-red dagger nails scraping down my sides as she gets on her knees before me, this time in her lingerie of gems.

When I open my eyes, I drink in the pink fae, imagining a silver one in her place. I know my gaze exudes lust. And the fae knows it, too. She sits up straighter, her breath catching, her own eyes widening. Has anyone ever looked at her like this before? A creature to worship. For her sake, I hope so. For her sake, I hope this is not the first time someone will break her apart with care.

"You wish to be ravaged by a faerie," I hum.

She hiccups.

The plane vibrates around us.

"Shall we make it so?" I ask.

"I . . ." She wets her lips. "I don't think so."

But she does not say *apple*.

"You do."

Sinking hands and knees into the mattress, I crawl toward her. She shifts. As I slink closer, she leans back on her hands, her expression both terrified and thrilled. When I reach her crossed legs, I wrap delicate fingers around her ankle.

"What are you—"

I kiss her ankle bone, unfolding her leg. She gasps in disgust, jerking. But she doesn't signal me to stop, so I do not. I pin the limb to the mattress and brush kisses up the inside of her calf, her knee, then her thigh. She squirms toward me. My face descends to her upper thigh, my mouth sucking in her stunning skin, my left hand holding down her other leg.

I kiss and inhale and lick the area around her hip bone. Her pelvis bucks and I brace my forearm across it, strapping her down. Trailing fingers over the shivering skin, I bite her round hip. She gasps again. Heat radiates from between her legs, as she tilts her sex toward my mouth.

I do not indulge. Not yet.

She whimpers as I plant gentle kiss after gentle kiss along her navel, up her center. When I reach her chest, I prop an arm along her spine, brace my hand on the back of her neck, holding her in place. Into her skin, her luscious stomach, I murmur:

"You will not make a sound."

She whimpers again. I give the sides of her neck a small squeeze.

"What did I say?"

"To be quiet."

"Good girl."

Then I lick the space between her breasts. Her body heaves. With my free hand, I trace circles around her nipple, never touching it. She tries to push it into my palm, and every time, my touch turns to a whisper. Goosebumps bud across her breast.

My mouth descends on her other nipple, warm and wet, as I will my fingers to cool. My magic shimmers along the plane, earthy and strong. The fae groans as I work her, icy fingers coaxing one peak, and enveloping my mouth around the other, teeth tugging.

I feel it building, deep in her throat. She fights it, and so I push more.

"Quiet now," I say.

But she moans, a deep, guttural sound that vibrates against my palm on her neck. I squeeze, listening as her breath hitches, and roll her in my mouth, tease her, drive her higher and higher as she moans lower and lower and lower.

I slide my legs over hers, use my weight to hold her down, so that her torso is suspended, only held up by my touch, as her lower body moistens beneath me, bucking and bucking and bucking—

She cries out, body spasming. I pinch harder, tighten my grip on her neck as her orgasm rolls through her, all-consuming and messy. I keep going as she shudders, my grip more a reminder than a hindrance, as I know this feeling; the nerves sparking throughout her body, everything sensitive and raw and reeling.

The last of her spasms cease and she goes limp in my arms. I lower her to the mattress, the fae gasping, eyes closed, a stupefied grin on her face. Then I reach for the king, still not looking at him. His hand guides mine low, but I grip his wrist instead, tugging him forward.

"Again," I say. "You're going to come for me again."

She throws an arm over her eyes. "I can't."

"What's your word, then?"

She just shakes her head, and heat gathers between my thighs.

When I glance to the king, my fingers still clasped around his wrist, he is staring, mouth agape. The veins in his neck bulge, and his other hand is fisted around his throbbing cock.

"You ready?" I ask him.

"They're golden again," he breathes. "Your eyes." Then he leans forward, as if to kiss me. My head turns to the side on instinct, heart pounding. My breath hitches as I realize my mistake.

"Avery." The plane creaks with fury.

You should've just let him! I yell at myself, but my chest hurts so much. There is only one male I have ever wanted to kiss, to let kiss me, to run tattooed fingers through my hair. And while I will give any other part of myself, I somehow cannot give away this.

"What's going on?" the fae asks, shifting her arm.

"Don't move," I tell her.

She huffs in mock protest, then shimmies deeper into the mattress, nipples hard. I drag my gaze back up to the king. He frowns, biting his lip. I tighten my grip on his wrist to ground him, then catch his other hand, the two of us knee to knee, his arms in my grasp now.

"What are you doing?" he murmurs, but the anger in his voice falters.

"Asking you to join."

He raises a brow. "You seem to have it handled."

If this were another male, I'd roll my eyes at his petulance. But it's not, and besides, Jae would've never said something so inane.

"Your hands are bigger than mine," I say placatingly. "They'll feel better."

The plane rumbles in pleasure.

There you go, I think.

He says nothing as I guide his palm to cup her wet pussy. The fae moans.

"One finger, first," I say.

We sit between her legs, side by side. The violet of the king's eyes flickers, darker then lighter, as he gets to working her. Perhaps powerful creatures react like this. Perhaps I am one of them now. As he slides a finger inside her, I brush his thumb over her clit. The magenta lover shivers.

But Maxian grinds in his thumb.

"Lighter," I say, pulling it back. "Softer. That's how you build, and you have to build until she's ready to burst."

He turns his face to mine, inches apart. "And then?"

"Then you go harder."

When he drops lips to my shoulder, I let him, eyes slipping closed. It's easier to see who I want this way.

"Open your eyes," he demands. "I want to see the gold."

I blink, swaying. "It's the candlelight."

"It's your strength."

This is getting away from me; he's getting away. I can't allow it. I nod to the fae grinding against his hand, his thumb pressing her clit and finger pushing in. The plane feels hot, heavy like smoke.

"Another finger," I say. "She can take it."

The fae whimpers, arching her back. Her breasts push up into the air, and she is a glorious sight, even if she isn't mine.

"And what are you going to do?" he whispers back.

I slide away from him, crawling across the mattress. His attention is heavy on me, but I need the distance.

"What are you doing?" the fae gasps, pulling back her arm. My thighs bracket her face, and I look down at her.

"This."

My fingers wrap gently around her neck again, tilting her chin back so that she can see only me. Then I lean down and kiss her. I kiss her through her gasps, through her heaving chest, hand still cupping her chin so she can't see what he's doing.

"Apple?" I ask, pulling back.

She yanks on my hair, bringing me down again.

I kiss her as I watch the king, kneeling between her thighs, stroking her how I say. I kiss her as he watches me over the body between us. I kiss her as he grabs himself with his free hand and works himself, works her at the same time. I kiss until my eyes droop closed.

"Look. At. Me," he grits out, and I do with my strange, glowing eyes, and my sinking heart, my body rocking against the mattress, nothing beneath it, my mouth claiming another lover who never really was mine, and I should not like this, no one should, stealing others.

But I do.

As the plane undulates, as the beautiful fae writhes, I swallow her cries, pet her hair, tell her how perfect and pretty she is, my little slut, listen to them both groan. I do not stop claiming her, watching him, uttering things that make them thrust harder into his hands, both swept away in a wave I conjured.

Candles drop from the ceiling, the plane sings, my spring scent all around us, until finally, finally, the fae lets out a scream, back arched, and the king doubles over, spilling onto his hand.

I sit back, wiping my mouth as they pant. With another faerie, I would want my due, seek repayments, matching release for release, just as how Jae and I stole prospects from under each other. Normally, he would be right: It would not be enough.

But here, with the High Fae undone and powerless under me, my pride soars. I slip off the mattress, fix my hair. The king stares down at his sticky palm, confused. When he looks up with wild eyes, chest expanding, he struggles.

"You . . ." he starts, then stops. "You . . ."

Yes, I think. *I fucked you, too, with words and looks alone.*

"The pleasure was all mine," I say.

Then I turn and walk out, leaving my spent lovers alone without a master.

Chapter Thirty

Four days later, Lila and I eat herbed potatoes in the Mouth before our shift. The kitchen is warm and fuzzy, the clatter of the next meal filling the space. It feels like a new normal, one that I want to resist but feel relieved exists. Carter trudges in, holding a sack of towels, his face grim. He collapses into a chair opposite us at the center table and groans.

"That bad, is it, love?" Fern asks from the stove, cheeks ruddy from the steaming pot.

"They've been at it all day."

My fork screeches against the plate. A passing errand boy giggles.

So they're still trying to find what I brought to the bedchamber that night. When I returned to Lila's room four days ago, she asked not what happened. Instead, she gave me a change of clothes and we passed out in her double cot, both too exhausted to lace me back to Illusion. Still, she did not inquire when we received word the next morning that we were dismissed for two days. When it happened again, my smugness spoiled to regret.

"So, the king is enraptured by another female," Fern says, following up.

"You think he has moved on from Kassandra?" I ask, but in truth, I had been wondering.

"Maybe he'll just marry another Reign like they all do," a laundry Scarp adds, grabbing the bag from Carter's feet.

"Think we'd all go deaf if this is the one," he says. "They're so strangely loud."

"Aren't they always?"

Lila clutches my leg, whispers that we can talk in her room. It feels as if we are the couple and I have cheated. An emptiness washes through me. I shovel the last of the meal into my mouth, collect my plate, and stand.

"Where are you going?" she asks.

I feel several gazes on us. "Just need to handle a few financials back in Illusion. I'll meet you under the stars tonight. I promise."

"Okay!" But Lila's bright, pleasant tone disrupts me.

It is the one she gives the king.

FAERIES WATCH AS I weave through the common room in the Nest. My hand tugs down the hem of my golden Reign uniform. *I'm taking it off next week,* I want to tell them. *Just one more week, and then I'll be Illusion again.*

I join the line at the creditor's counter. A raven-haired male faerie shakes a finger at the teller, who puts down his quill and adjusts his glasses. I recognize the weathered face, the calm demeanor. Silas, the halfling who spoke with me.

"This is the most outrageous complaint against me!" the faerie screams, face beet-red.

"I understand—"

"I didn't even do it."

"In three years, the Council of Keepers will vote on a law that allows faeries to dispute complaints—"

"How the *fuck* does that help me now?"

"Well, I just—"

The faerie spits. Saliva splatters against Silas's glasses, his face.

"Hey!" I yell, grabbing the faerie's shoulder and yanking him back. "What's your problem?"

The male blinks in surprise before his face distorts with rage once more. He jabs a finger in Silas's direction again; the halfling pulls out a handkerchief and wipes down his spectacles.

"My problem? That hybrid cunt is fucking me over."

Silas stops cleaning his glasses. My blood turns to ice.

"He's just trying to do his job," I say. "It's not his fault—"

"Fae-fucker!" he shouts.

I groan. "Let's just—"

"I can smell it on you."

My body stiffens. There's no way he could, but it's too late—the faerie's face splits open with glee.

"I knew it," he says.

I wince. Heads turn in our direction.

"You do not deny it?"

I can't. Even if I tried, the blood oath would trap the words in my mouth.

"She doesn't deny it!" he shouts, laughing to the growing number of witnesses, blocking the view to the creditor's counter.

My genius sparks, flaring to life, expanding its wings. I grapple to tame it, but the thing inside me dives and dips from my control. This is not what it was before. My eyes have returned to normal, but the change to my genius has stayed. The routine exercises are laughably easy. It is not just stronger—it feels smarter. It feels like its own creation. It feels alive.

Let me out, it seems to ask. *Let me fly.*

"You're a fae-fucking whore."

Flames erupt from my fingertips, warming my skin without burning it.

Gasps around me. Fire licks up my forearms, and I turn on the faerie, who pales. "Say it again."

His mouth clamps shut.

"Miss Avery," a voice cuts in, calm and gentle. "There's a credit issue on your account we need to discuss."

Silas.

Turning, I see the halfling male, face grave, twin flames in his glasses. He looks like a monster with those fiery eyes. A blink later, I realize that it is my reflection, my power. I am the monstrosity.

"Avery?"

A child's voice. A familiar one. Benji.

The boy gapes at me, at my arms, at the crowd. Something in me sputters out, dies. The flames fall beneath my skin once more.

"How'd you do that?" he asks, his voice touched with trepidation and wonder.

"I . . . don't know."

There's a shuffling as Glenn emerges, putting a hand on Benji's bony shoulder. By now, faeries have backed up, and as Silas gestures, they part ways, staring.

I go with Silas, Glenn ushering Benji away. Only the raven-haired faerie will not move, so we maneuver around him. He spits on me regardless.

SILAS SETS UP the tea and I heat the water for both of us. He pulls crackers and an apple from his cabinet and places them on the table. He looks to me.

"Apologies. I only have enough lunch for one."

"This is great, thank you." I take a sip of the lemon-ginger tea. "Last time I was here, I thought you were lucky for taking lunch in private. But perhaps it's for protection."

Silas stares down at the table. "I wouldn't like tellers, either, if I were a faerie."

"But as a halfling, the fae . . ."

"Tolerate us. Most privileges are just arbitrary advantages established and doled out prior to our birth. It's a system of luck, not morality."

"And we can become Unluckie at any time," I say. Benji was the least tattooed young servant at the coronation. An hour later, he was the most indebted. Observing my own arms, I can still visualize how they looked when the king paid off half my debt before Dominik returned it.

Slipping on my moth ring, I wait until he puts on his owl one—a symbol of our sworn oaths.

"You cannot pay off another's debt until you have paid off your own," I say. "This leaves the fae safe, the faeries controlled. Yet all halflings have about two rings, and still typically thrive." I meet his eye. "Why not just pay off the debt with so little left?"

Silas leans back. "You are astute."

"I am determined."

"The tattoos are reminders of who we are."

"The halflings choose two rings?"

He tilts his head to listen. Despite our oaths, we dance in dangerous territory. He lowers his voice. "They choose not to be targets. A fae who accidentally perceives another fae in place of a halfling can lead to two deaths."

They . . . cannot tell. Without the tattoos, they cannot tell the difference between halfling and fae.

Silas withdraws his hands. "I've said too much."

"Wait." I lean forward. "Please, it's just—I have this . . . brother. He's a little brother to me in every way but blood, and I need to help him. You just saw him."

He looks away. "I did."

"You know the debt will drain everything from him, and soon they may send him to the mines. He's a hard worker, but his luck has turned, as you said. I want to do it legally—provide for him."

"He won't inherit your debt."

"But someone else will, and I'd like to not burden them or Benji. How can I ensure the balance becomes null?"

"You can't."

I deflate, heart sinking. Whatever the next step is, it's too far for him. So I nod, standing. Silas does not look at me. He just stares at the table, wringing his own hands. Crumbs scatter across the surface; the tea has gone cold. His shoulders sag, and before me, I do not see the terrifying teller, the heartless halfling. I see a weathered creature who bestows bad news on hundreds of faeries each day, his only reprieve being a silent lunch.

"If you'd ever want to swap peace for company, let me know," I say.

Those sun-spotted hands stop twisting. "Why would you offer that after I've turned you down?"

"Because you stand with one foot in Illusion and another in Reign. And only lately have I appreciated how difficult that must be."

Silas gives a rueful smile. "Lunch would be nice."

Nodding, I depart, hope blooming anew. While I am gathering enemies in every House, and at every level, I may as well find allies, too.

Chapter Thirty-one

LILA AND I TREAD TOWARD THE SALON OF STARS, THE DARKNESS cold but living. I listen for it now, between the buzz of the kitchen, the list of chores; when I press a palm to the stone and slow my breathing, I hear it. Shifting, beneath the palace. Disturbances. Screams.

Something is down there.

"You mastered that quickly," Lila whispers over my shoulder, to the flame blossoming from my hand.

"My genius seems . . . transformed."

"Can sex impact our genius?"

I stop short, the flame flickering. "What do you mean?"

"I don't know."

"Because of last week."

"I don't know what happened last week."

"I don't owe you that." The flame flares. "I don't owe you anything."

The words ricochet along the stones, slinging back to me like slaps. The fire crackles, dampens.

"I'm sorry," I rush. "That was—"

"You assume parts of me as well."

"I . . ." The flame dissipates. Darkness curtains us. I want to ask what she means again, but instead let space unfold between us.

"I do not enjoy sex," she finally says.

Comforting words, reassurances, rise like heat, but I do not know her years just because I fill her days now, do not know what she's been through and how it's made her feel.

"Okay," I say instead.

"I really do not enjoy sex," she whispers. "But it's always been that way. Even before the king."

I search for the right words, to recall another in my life who feels such as this. But I'm not sure. Sex—and sometimes its accompanying violence—is so prevalent at Versara that I do not know what the absence of it would look and feel like.

"That's okay," I say again.

"I'm not innocent or childish. It's just that I don't think I experience attraction in the ways others describe. I feel other things—love, affection. Just not lust."

"That makes sense."

"And it's not like I haven't had sex," Lila adds. "I've had it with males I thought I liked, ones who were kind."

"Have you experienced desire with females?"

"I don't experience it with anyone. It's not the other creatures—it's me. There is something . . . missing in me. Perhaps I'm not even a faerie—I'm some unfeeling accident."

My knuckles brush against hers. "Just because your desires differ from someone else's does not make you less than. I know we haven't known each other long, but you're the most creative and intelligent faerie I've ever met."

"Avery . . ."

"Listen. The fact that you are also the kindest, most loving faerie, too, is a privilege I get to experience every day. You have—"

My throat tightens. *You have changed me already, irrevocably.* But that is too much, I am being too much. Suddenly, I am grateful for the darkness, too. Lila squeezes my hand, and I squeeze back.

Then her arm finds my shoulder, pulls me into an embrace. A dam has been broken, and the emotions of the past weeks, the past month, flood through me, and I tremble. We still cannot see each other but I tremble—not for what has been said in the dark, but for what Lila has made me feel in the light.

"You're my friend and I am yours," she says, rubbing my back. "The first day you started, we laced to the Pith together. Do you remember what you said when you realized the rings let us borrow Reign magic?"

I rack my brain. Though it was just over a moon ago, it feels like much longer—so much has happened in that time, so much has changed.

"What did I say?" I ask.

"You said, 'How lonely it must be to carry this knowledge around, unable to share it with anyone.' Every faerie before you commented on feeling powerful, scared, excited, confused. But you . . . you saw me. Even when you didn't know me, even when you were lost, you saw me."

"I see you now, too," I say, then pause. "Well, not truly because it's so dark in here."

Lila laughs and so do I. It strikes me then that if I had perished after Jeremee's death, by my own hand or another's, I would not get to experience this. I would not have stumbled into the warmth of Lila's friendship, the kindness of her character. The waters of my grief subside, revealing more solid ground to stand on. Rather than replacing Jeremee as I feared, my heart has expanded to hold them both.

"Well," Lila says. "Shall we wander under the stars once more?"

"Where you wander, I will follow."

"No, you're going first into the strange, abandoned bedchambers."

I roll my eyes, smiling. My smile doesn't last long.

The bathing chamber is silent and cold when we enter, a primordial stillness like a grave despite the moonlight pouring through the glass ceiling.

Lila grabs my arm. "Look!"

Something small and shiny flickers across the far wall. A glint of metal, of brass. We creep forward, the glow of my flame falling on a door. How did we miss it before?

"This must be a door to the second Salon of Stars," she says.

"Did you ever venture into it with your father?"

She shakes her head. "There was no need to clean fireplaces that were never lit. Perhaps, if Maxian had had a sibling, it would've eventually been used."

Lila places a hand on the brass and tries each key. Nothing clicks—until the last one, a small, rusted thing.

"*Etoles*," she whispers.

Nothing.

"*Etoles*." She takes a breath. "*Etoles*."

"Maybe the issue isn't the word, but the key?" I suggest.

"The key definitely fits."

She tries *Solil* and *Lune* to no avail. Finally my friend steps back, wiping her forehead. "It's no use."

"We could try breaking the door in, but . . ."

"We aren't destroying anything."

My genius twitches with a pulsing energy that is not my own, exuding from the door itself.

"Perhaps we can speak to the wood in the door and request it to move," I wonder.

"Once the tree was cut down, it would've died."

"Let me try something," I say, pressing my palms to the grain.

A ripple of energy.

My genius sparks, rising through my mind, down my arms, contacting the plane. Magic crackles around me, a tapestry of nerves and feelings, currents of life that weave throughout the entire space, brushing against the stones, the door, down the drain behind us.

My genius works against the current of magic under the pads of my fingers, pushing, pushing into the door. Then a rush of information, a flood that washes back into me, overtaking my senses in return.

Chestnut wood. The door used to be a chestnut tree, eight

hundred years old, blooming full and tall and lush in a grassy meadow. Columns of cream flowers sprout from branches, clusters of spiky spheres holding sweet nuts. The drop of leaves, then snow, the burst of new life and warmth. White, slender birds building nests in its crooks.

The sound of a child laughing. The feel of little hands, pulling on branches, a chubby cheek against the trunk.

What is your name? the child asks.

Baffling, I have none. I do not need one; I am many things, I am a leaf and a forest.

Will you be my friend? the little creature requests.

What is a friend? I wonder. *What are you?*

A faerie, the child says. *A friend.*

The child remains in the shade, collects nuts, insists on planting along the meadow. Saplings spring up from the grass. A growing network, a family, someone with whom to share roots.

The creature and I grow together, expand. One time, the child brings water in a dry summer; another time, it cries in my boughs. The child brings its child and so do the birds. A circle of little lives, woven around me, through me, spawning outward—

Pain. A visceral, deep cutting. Dragging, stripping of the skin. Pressing, grinding, sawing, sanding, harnessing together, nails driven into nerves. Screaming.

So much screaming. But no other creature to hear. No other life to feel, to harbor, to speak to along roots that rot under a meadow, an old faerie, an old friend weeping over stumps.

Slamming.

Pounding.

Strange magic pushed under the grain, burrowing and sprouting like fungus. The others shove a word in me to command, a word that does not ask, a word that cannot be refused.

It spreads its spores through me.

The strangers slap me, feeding the fungal magic, letting it fester each time they command. I become infection more than life, and still, I cannot die. The magic has intertwined with my essence, a parasite keeping a host alive so that it can always feed.

Creaking when opened, and still, they ignore the last of my protests. Generation after generation, that word, the hated word, a violation each time they conjure it, the blight twisting around remaining nerves. Then silence.

Years of silence.

Darkness.

Never peace, as the blight remains and so do I. Never the birds and chestnuts sprouting, the earth cradling and connecting. Never my friend again.

Silence, until the touch of magic once more.

Now, a wiggling insect, worming into the grain, grasping for what the others hooked into my pith. It pokes at the darker magic, the word clamped to my core.

Don't say it, I beg. *Please.*

The little creature, the moth, wraps small, fuzzy legs around the dark magic. It tugs. The last of me rips. I scream for it to stop—screaming, screaming once more.

And it does. The moth moves back, waits. It sends a message along the threads, but not like the others. It is a gentle ask, a quiet one. A request, instead of a demand.

How should I help you?

A spark of light in this night. Help? Why would this flittering thing want to help?

What are you? I ask.

A faerie, the moth says.

A faerie. A friend once, who built my family and hers. A creature that I had forgotten ever loved me, it has been so long, and I no longer look like something to love.

Take it, I say of the festering magic.

That will harm you, the moth replies.

I am already harmed.

You will die.

I will be free.

The moth beats its wings. *I will think of this in the years to come. Your story has shaped mine.*

It is an acknowledgment, an invitation back into the tapestry of woven lives. I no longer have chestnuts to grow or shade to offer, but I can speak this, as they give me my ending.

Everything has a voice, I say. *You must learn to listen.*

The moth flutters, landing on the last of my living fibers, forever squeezed by the dark magic. It brushes a leg against me—me, not the disease I've become. It is startling and gentle. It is a goodbye. The moth waits as I gather myself. Finally, I send my last message.

I am ready, faerie.

The moth flares with brightness, with warmth. As it flies toward the fungus, it transforms into a fiery creature. Then it descends. The parasite recoils, shrieks. The moth descends and descends, scorching off the disease, burning through the fever that's ravished me for a millennium.

As the dark magic squeals and putrefies, it falls from my being and I am growing, expanding. I am floating, wandering, breathing, tall and lush and full again; I am life. As I waft away on a celestial wind, like a seed in a spring breeze, I say goodbye to this new friend.

And then I am cupped, held, in the familiar hands of my oldest friend once more, and we are together and we are content.

Chapter Thirty-two

Legs buckling, I slide down the door to the ground. Magic spills away from me, returning to the plane, my muscles and genius depleted. Chest burning, eyes watering, I hang my head between my knees. It's as if I've emerged from a long dream where I lived another life and loved and hurt but have no proof of any of it. Lila's face enters my vision, and it is jarring and grating, this faerie whom I know, and I'm not sure why.

"Avery?"

I pant. "Where—"

"You were in a trance. I didn't want to wake you."

"The tree—"

"What's in your hand?"

I glance down at my clenched fist. Something palpitates in its grasp, stinking of decay. Reign magic. Old, ancient, corruptive Reign magic, though I don't understand how I know this, only that it doesn't feel like the power that whooshed up from the drain days ago.

I release the magic, and it sizzles back into the plane, the return of something that had stayed away too long. As it evaporates, I can almost hear the word. Almost. But it is muffled and in a tongue I cannot recognize.

"You—" Lila looks at me, then the door. "You removed the magic that unlocks the door."

"I did?"

"How?"

"I . . ." I cringe, the sensation of being stripped down, sanded. "The tree spoke to me."

Lila's eyes widened. "Spoke to you?"

"It sounds moonstruck, but—"

"No. No, it's an old Unesse belief." My friend examines me. "Every living thing is connected through the plane of magic, a giant network of nerves. You just need to learn how to tap into that and . . . you did. But to access the tree the door was made from? How?"

I explain what happened as best I can, thinking of all the enchanted doors in the Pith. How many trees are not dead but trapped? The thought unnerves me, as if surrounded by taxidermy that is alive, the torture invisible and unending.

"We should come back another time." Lila stands, offering a hand. "You look fatigued."

It feels worse than that, like someone has carved my insides out and left the skin behind. The memories of the tree and my own flicker in a dance of two flames that seem as one.

I take her hand.

The door scrapes open, and I scramble back. Musk and darkness roll over the threshold.

"If the chambers are identical, then that must be the closet to the second Salon of Stars," Lila says. "Stay here."

"Wait—"

"I just want to take a peek is all."

My friend lets the dark mouth swallow her whole. Blood roars in my ears, heart thumping against my ribs. I creep toward that shadowed entrance. "Lila?"

"It's not empty," my friend says.

My blood chills. "What . . . what do you mean?"

A pause. Then: "There are a child's clothes in here."

"Overflow from Maxian's closet."

No response. Just a rustling, a fumbling. A swearing. Lila rarely swears.

At the threshold, I snap my fingers. No light springs up; my genius is spent.

From the dark, my friend says, "Then why are all the clothes for a young child?"

"What?"

"If this is storage, then why are all the clothes in there one size? Nothing for the prince when he reached teenagehood? Early adulthood?" My friend melts from the dark, eyes wide, clutching something to her chest. "Why are all the clothes in there for a toddler?"

She holds out a tiny riding boot made of red leather.

"Maxian hates red leather."

"He probably didn't have much choice in how he was dressed."

But my friend is shaking her head. She discards the red boot and stomps into Maxian's closet, then reemerges with a black boot. Maxian's. She crouches down beside me, holding the boots side by side.

"To this day, Maxian labels his clothes. I've always found it a strange habit," she says. "Why would an only child do that?"

"A quirk of his. Sentimental reasons, maybe."

Lila shakes her head again. She loosens the laces of the red boot, unpeeling the tongue. She holds the boot up to the moonlight, thumb stroking over a patch on the inside.

"Everything he receives in life is new and customized to him. And if it's old, it is from his family. So why—"

My friend stops short, color leaching from her cheeks.

"What's wrong?" I ask.

She hands me the black boot, pointing to an ink scribbling on the inside of the tongue.

M.V.

"Maxian Vandorne," I state.

"Like a child claiming their possession around other children."

"He grew up with Dominik and Kassandra. Eli joined them in the summers."

"Then who is P.V.?" Lila holds up the small red boot. I see the initials inked into the top.

P.V.

"A cousin," I supply, voice shaking. "Like Daisy. The one who died in the snow."

Lila shakes her head. "Not even Daisy stayed in the royal apartments. Not Hector and his family. Only the king and queen and . . . their children."

"You think there was another Vandorne child?"

"It might be why the salon was always locked, why this closet is fuller than Maxian's. It could be why all the clothes are for a child of one age."

"But where . . ." My voice falters. "Where is . . ."

We exchange a look, an unspoken conversation, my shock reflected in her visage. As we sit in the starlight, as we hold a small red boot, and a much larger black one, we try to comprehend the unknowable.

"All the royal portraits only show three figures," Lila whispers. "But if the child had died . . ."

Wouldn't they still be featured?

"And Maxian's first betrothed, you know the rhyme?"

Lila nods. "*Daisy, Daisy—in the springtime you grow, in the summer you glow. Daisy, Daisy—winter is here, beware the snow! Daisy, Daisy—why did you go? Poor, poor Daisy—don't you know flowers freeze in the snow?*"

"So surely there would be some record of a royal child," I reason. "Even if the death was too painful to commemorate—there would've been a funeral, a small one. Or a portrait? An engraving? Conversations among nobles about P.V.?"

We sit in stunned silence, attention falling to the red boot.

"Perhaps it's all here," Lila says. "Maybe this is what's left of them."

Something sparks in my memory, the smallest detail from our

first visit. Why did the royal family repair, when they could replace? They have wealth, time, magic. Yet they kept the imperfection. *Why?*

We only repair by hand what is sentimental to us, Maxian said the night he stepped from the ripped portrait of his grandfather. Before I can speak, I am moving through the space, clutching the red boot, a baby's boot, really. It fits in the palm of my hand.

"What are you doing?" my friend asks, following, as we enter the main chamber once more and walk toward the tapestry on the wall, the child in the tree, the queen watching.

I stand close, feel along its edges, squint in the moonlight. My fingers snag on it, the extra layer, the cloth used to patch up the weaving. To cover what is too painful to remove entirely.

I pull.

The fabric rips, and Lila gasps.

"What the planes—"

My breath leaves me, and we stumble back.

Before me is a child clinging to the queen's skirts, baby fist grasping two of her fingers. A male with black hair and violet eyes, dressed in a white tunic and wearing a pair of little red boots. My heart plummets, hands dropping the boot. Lila shakes beside me, breath hitching.

"The king has a sibling," she whispers.

"Or had."

We lock eyes.

"But that's not all, is it?" Lila turns back to the tapestry, fingers tracing Maxian's bronze waves, then those of the faerie standing beneath the boughs. Her hand drifts to the dark-haired toddler with violet eyes, so very much like the portraits of Wilhelm the Uniter and Gregor the Great. Chills rip up and down my arms.

"If I were the artist commissioned by royalty," she starts, "I would not cut corners on the colors used to dye the wool."

"What do you mean?" I breathe.

She looks at me, throat bobbing, voice dropping. "There are

different shades of yellow in this tapestry, in the leaves here and the sun there. Look at the array of browns, too, for the trunks of the trees. So why would an artist use the same color for the hair of the future king of Amyria and a lowly servant? Would that not be considered an insult, that type of association?"

"Maybe their hair was the same color," I whisper, a roaring in my ears, the conclusion on the horizon I do not want to look into directly—like a burning, bloody sunset.

"But why choose truth for a royal rendering? The artists always stylize the subjects, and besides, a true artist is intentional in everything she does."

My gaze darts between the dark-haired queen and the toddler patched behind her skirts, then to the bronze-haired Maxian and servant, both boys sharing the violet eyes so signature to the Vandorne line.

"Perhaps it was the truth," I whisper. "Not that the fae queen and the faerie were lovers, but that perhaps they shared one."

Lila sucks in a breath. "But—that would mean—"

"Please," I beg, terror clanking through me. "Surely we are moonstruck."

"That is someone else's thought, planted in your mind. We should trust ourselves, what we have seen. Look at it!" She points to the tapestry. "Why do she and Maxian *look alike*? Why include a faerie in a piece of royal art at all?"

"The royals include their pets in portraits!" I hiss back.

"She could've still been a pet. She could've been King Gregor's."

A shiver tears through me. "But if Maxian is the result of . . . that," I whisper. "Then that means he's a half—"

Lila covers my mouth, her face stricken with fear. *A halfling bastard.*

She sways with the realization, and so do I. After a moment, her palm drops away.

"It can't be true," she says. "The king is always the strongest fae in the land. And the strongest fae always come from the Vandorne line."

"It can't be true," I echo. "Or else Maxian would not be alive today."

But Hector's words come thundering back to me like a storm over mountains. *We are a dying breed, we Reign fae.* The High Fae birth so few children in general, the Vandornes the least of them. Faeries, on the other hand, are more fertile and populous.

"Let's get out of here," Lila says, and I can't agree more.

As we cross the chambers, I glance one last time at the tapestry, the two boys, the queen, and the maid. Whether the toddler died or was removed, his existence is only carried on in the few scraps we clutch, hidden away in this forgotten place. It's a finality deeper than death.

At the heart of Versara is a secret so great, it could unravel all of Amyria.

PART THREE

House of Healing

*Follow the flow
up, around, below;
offer the final breath
to find a face of Death.*

—"THE RATTLING"

Chapter Thirty-three

I SLAM INTO KASSANDRA'S VANITY, HER POTS AND LOTIONS FLYing and smashing onto the floor.

Kassandra screams and springs out of bed in a pink nightgown, glass of red wine in hand that sloshes onto the carpet.

"What the fuck are you doing!" she shrieks, her magic tickling the plane.

Thank the planes she's here.

I gasp for breath, leaning against the wall. Panic clings to me like spiderwebs. After seeing a shaking Lila to the Mouth for some water, I laced straight to Illusion.

"The king," I try again, but the oath starts to block my throat. "I found—"

"Who gives a fuck?" Kassandra snaps, little invisible hands trying to piece back together a jar of something glittery. "Do you know how expensive this is? It's from a Remiti artist who only releases products once a century!"

The bedroom doors burst open, Briar clutching a fireplace poker. "My lady!"

"It's me," I manage to say, sliding down the wall. "It's me."

Briar lets out a string of curses, lowering the poker. Kassandra tips back the rest of her wine, then blasts the residue with hot air. She places the dry goblet on the ground as bits of glitter rise from the carpet like snow. They collect in a small pile at the bottom of the glass.

"Briar, can you find this a more suitable container?" she says, the cup lifting in the air and floating toward the faerie.

Briar looks between us. "You two are keeping secrets."

"Nothing exciting," my mistress says. "Can you give us some privacy?"

She tuts but follows instructions and departs.

Kassandra looks at me, planting hands on her hips. Her silver hair falls around her, sleek and shiny, while I'm sure mine now looks like a bird's nest. I'd never cared about my appearance in front of her before, but even in the evening light, it's stark, her prettiness to my roughness.

She points a painted nail at me. "Next time, don't talk so loudly about the king like that. I refuse to implicate Briar in this. Now, what did you find out?"

I swallow, standing once more. "The Mountain . . . the mountain is half dirt."

She rolls her eyes. "What else are mountains made of?"

"Rock," I say. "Every mountain is made of rock, no?"

"Okay . . ." She paces. "Maxian is a Reign fae, we know this, just like all the other kings. But you're also saying he's part dirt. Who's dirt?"

"Me."

Kassandra stops. "What did you just say?"

"I am dirt, as you always say. Well, so is . . . the Mountain."

She just stares at me, paling. "How."

"How else are . . . half mountains made."

But she's shaking her head, as if banishing the thought. "Impossible."

"I found the little mountain. The one that's made only of rock but has crumbled since—"

"Stop!" Kassandra flies forward, one hand clamping over my mouth. We stumble against the wall, and she hisses, eyes wide and afraid. "Stop. Please stop."

I tense, peering into her face. Her skin is soft, body flushed against mine. She blinks, then steps away, rubbing her arms as if cold.

"You . . . you know," I say.

"About the little mountain, not the dirt."

"Why didn't you say anything before? This is what we've needed."

Her shoulders curl inward. "Can't."

"You're sworn to a blood oath."

She shakes her head. "Worse."

A blood bargain. In which two parties make a deal and the party to break it loses their magic.

"Who's his true mother, if not the queen?" Kassandra whispers, then looks my way. "Someone like you?"

I nod, my head against the wall. She lets out a curse and paces again.

"How do you know of this?" she demands.

A headache pulses in my temples. I rub them. "I can't explain."

"You have to. Or else who will believe us?"

"We don't need anyone to believe us," I snap. "You need to tell him you know—"

"And risk death? No. No, I will not speak of this anymore."

Pushing off the wall, I start toward her. "But—"

"This is *treason*," she seethes. "To talk like this. If I'm to use this, I need real proof or else it's just his word against mine, or worse, your word against his."

I halt, stung. "You don't believe me."

"I don't know what to believe." She reaches over to her vanity, grabbing a pink pigment that didn't fall. "Now, Briar's coming back, and I want her staying innocent. So that means you can't be."

"What are you—"

Kassandra reaches up, smearing the pigment on my lips. I freeze, throat bobbing, as her thumb smudges it across my mouth, then across her own.

"Let her think this is what you're doing here," she whispers, snapping the lid back on.

"I'll get in trouble!" I hiss.

She raises a brow. "Are you proposing to me? Are we in public? Don't be ridiculous. Besides, you think Briar cares? Now, go and get me proof."

The doors click open again, and Briar stops in her tracks. Kassandra rubs the back of her hand across her face.

"What are you doing back so quickly?" she squeaks, then turns to me. "Didn't I tell you to leave me be?"

Giving a shocked Briar a quick glance, I lace away.

IN THE HALL outside the royal library, I stumble into a body.

"Oof," Carter says, righting me and pulling away. "Where'd you come from?"

I adjust my clothes. My head spins with all this lacing and secrets, and I rub the pink pigment off my lips altogether. "Checking in with Lila. You?"

"She's still in the Mouth. And I'm on my way to clean up all the rejected plates Dominik thought were poisoned."

I wince. "What's he doing here?"

"Guess they're friends again." Carter shrugs, then turns to walk down the hall.

The last time I saw Dominik, I was bleeding out from his bite and he was choking from my body oil. The last time I saw the king, I was making him and his lover come. It would only make sense for me to join Lila now, to make sure she's okay in the wake of learning the truth of the king.

But I need proof of that truth. I need to see the halfling bastard beneath the crown. I need to know why none of us can tell what he is.

I follow Carter. "Here, let me help you clean up."

"Okay, but they're both not in the best of moods," he warns, then falls silent as we approach the door to the dining room.

Conversation dies out. The two most dangerous males in Amyria stare at me. Maxian is seated at the head, Dominik to his right, drumming his fingers on the table. Maxian's gaze drags over me, eyes glinting, brighter and more viscous than they were in the tapestry. Cold sweat slides down my spine, and I rein in my emotions. I pray to the planes that he thinks my nerves are from seeing him for the first time since we were together four nights ago, and not from the weight of the kingdom-shattering secret I now carry. *Does he know that I know?*

He cannot. I would have been killed on the spot if he knew what Lila and I discovered.

Taking a steadying breath, I reach for the dirty dishes and cups, stacking them in my arms.

The plane thrums with energy. My gaze snags on something dark spread on the table between plates, two black lines of what looks like ashy powder.

"You may leave us," the king commands.

Carter bows. "Yes, my king."

The servants' door opens on its own, our cue to hurry the fuck up. Balancing the dishes, we rush out. The two males continue watching us from the shimmering light of the room, their eyes dilating. Then, the king flicks his wrist, and the door slams shut. I nearly sag with relief.

"What was that on the table?" I hiss as we walk away.

Carter's gaze slides to me. "You've seen coca powder before?"

"I'm from House Illusion, of course I have."

"It's like that."

"Carter, coca is white. This stuff was *black*."

"I'm not allowed to talk about it."

"Even with other Reign servants?"

"It was a mistake to let you in there," he breathes, tipping his head back. "I'm going to get so much shi—"

"I'm sworn to both Houses."

"Does that matter now? They've seen you see it."

"But I cannot speak of it."

We trend down the hall in silence, the light and merriment of the Mouth growing closer.

He shakes his head. "You cannot tell anyone. It's . . . different. It's not like other drugs. It affects your genius directly."

My brow furrows. "All drugs impact the genius because they impact our minds."

"It's not . . ." The valet groans. "Never mind."

Why wouldn't the faeries know of an Upper Court's favorite substance, even the most exclusive? We are the ones who bring it out, then hide the evidence.

When Carter opens the door to the kitchens, his somber air falls away, and reluctantly, so do my questions. Lila and Fern sit at the table together, two goblets and a plate of little dessert squares in front of them. At the sight of us, Lila gives a small smile that doesn't quite reach her eyes.

Carter and I bring the dishes over to the sink.

"You ladies have fun." He sighs. "I have to wait awkwardly in the hall until His *Magnificence* summons me to help take off his tight leather trousers."

Fern snorts as he leaves, and for a moment I'm tempted to follow once more.

"Saved you some chocolate," Lila says, pushing the plate forward.

"I'm working on a new recipe, one with milk," Fern says. "I need some taste testers."

From Lila's glum expression, I feel that Fern conjured up the role of taste testers, especially for High Fae dishes, but for that I am even more grateful. When I pop one in my mouth, it's soft and sweet and creamy. "Fern, I've never had something more delicious in my life." I've been at Reign for over a moon, and still the difference in faerie food access amazes me.

Fern chuckles, a pleased sparkle in her eye. "Flatterer."

Lila grabs a bottle of liquor from the floor, clinking it against the table, and pours each of us a glass. She drains hers. "Fern was telling me about her uncle who used to work for a Healing botanist. They studied trees and found out they can talk, right?"

Saplings spring up from the grass. A growing network, a family, someone with whom to share roots.

My pulse quickens. While I was relaying a secret that should've never been unearthed, Lila was poking around and conducting her own investigation.

The cook sips her cup. "In Healing, they do experiments. They tap into the plane of magic and observe pulses of energy sent through the roots. Not just their geniuses, but information in those pulses. Scents that the trees would release to inform one another of dangerous animals that might eat them. When to drop leaves, if at all. The roots, you see, are like the mind. They store memories."

The life of a chestnut tree flickers before my eyes.

"It happens slowly, and so it is not always considered intelligence," Lila says. Then she looks to me with a lopsided smile. "You're very smart, Avery, and even if you weren't, I would still like you. I like you, Avery."

"Fae wine, is it? That stuff is strong," I say, grinning.

"Did Avery ever tell you about how she and her friend Briar got drunk at the coronation?" Lila blurts. "It was—oh. Oh no, Avery, I'm so sorry. I didn't mean to bring up—"

"It's okay," I say. A smile tugs at my lips, for Lila's consideration and because for the first time since the coronation, I remember that moment fondly, and because I am so tired of frowning. I turn to Fern. "We heard the executioner was coming and I was already bored to death."

Fern gasps. "Naughty faerie!"

Lila reaches for the bottle to pour again, and I sniff the floral wine in my cup. "What is this?"

"The king sent it back earlier. Wasn't dry enough for him." Fern hiccups. "We're just sampling it."

I glance between the pair of flushed faces, then drain my glass. They squeal and refill the cups and we clink them together, the air warm.

"Oh no!" Lila gasps. "How are we going to get you back to Illusion? We can't drink and lace. We might end up in a bush somewhere!"

A laugh bursts from me, light and bright. It breaks up the heaviness of the night, the fear and dread churning in my stomach. It's a temporary distraction, and this time not a harmful one.

"What's this?" Fern demands. "You don't have a room in Reign?"

"We didn't know what was going to happen between the two Houses, so I kept my old room," I explain. "I've been going back and forth."

"Sounds exhausting," Fern exclaims. "Why not have two rooms?"

"Is that allowed?"

"I'm in charge of the rooms, so I say yes!" she shouts, wrapping a thick arm around me. She is sweaty and her embrace is warm. "Pour me another drink, will you, Lila? Aw, come on—more than that. After all, no one is drinking and lacing tonight!"

"Would you like that, Avery?" Lila asks, her face shining. "Would you like a room at Reign?"

"I think I would."

"I was hoping you'd say that." She smiles. I smile back.

"Well, then." Fern raises her mug, and so does Lila. "Welcome home, Avery."

They glance at me expectantly, gleefully, hopefully.

I blush. "Thank you."

They squeal in glee again, the sound bright and high and irresistible. For the second time on this long, hard day, I find myself glad I stayed after Jeremee left. If I had followed him, I would not have this. A deeper, darker, more desperate side knows that in the coming days and weeks and months, I will need these friends, this network, and they will need me. Friends are the only thing on this earthly plane worth fighting for.

Chapter Thirty-four

I WAKE IN AN UNFAMILIAR COT. MY HEAD THROBS, STOMACH churns. Groaning, I close my eyes, arm falling over the side of the mattress. It brushes against the cool glass of water Fern and Lila insisted I take with me, still untouched at my bedside.

Lifting my head, I gulp the water and wait until the nausea subsides. My new room is double the size of the one in Illusion. A place to return to after my moon with Kassandra, which starts in a few weeks. Perhaps I'll collect little scraps of color like Lila and render them something new to decorate. I've never truly decorated anything before.

It strikes me then how similar Lila is to my mother, with her consistent care and reliable respect. Though Lila is more effervescent, I wonder, just for a moment, if my mother would've been like that as well, if not tied to my father with pregnancy. My mother spoke of her aspirations only once, in her final days when any formality between child and parent fell away. As I shifted her frail frame to prevent bedsores, she muttered her deepest dream. To one day learn to play the lyre.

I rub my chest, circling the pang there. Perhaps, when I'm done bribing for my friends' debts with the High Fae, I will purchase a used one and start my mother's dream.

The metal cot vibrates against the stone. My head snaps up with the roll of rocky magic through the plane. Scrambling to my feet, I brace myself, staring at the ceiling and wondering if it'll cave in. It's been days since the last rumbling, and late last night, Fern spoke of a royal stable that collapsed, trapping the horses. It didn't take long to dig out the animals and repair, but the palace of Versara does not fall. It never has fallen, not since the Dark Rebellion.

Still, as dust exhales from a crack in the ceiling, I hold my breath until the building has settled once more. A piece of parchment pops into the air, floating down like a feather. I snag it. My brows cinch, my eyes scanning the words:

Library. Before dinner.

The king has finally called upon us. My fist crumples the paper as the full events of yesterday surge through my mind: the door, the boot, the child in the tapestry, the faerie watching Maxian in the tree, the pair so alike.

"Shit," I breathe. "Shit."

He knows. He knows that we know. This is a killing secret, like swallowing a hot ember that burns my mouth and throat and belly. How the planes am I going to find proof of this? And even if I did, what would Kassandra do with it?

What if Lila and I are wrong and now I've included Kassandra in deadly slander? What's more likely—that we misinterpreted a tapestry or that the king is a halfling bastard?

In the corridor, I pass the lunchtime sounds of the kitchen and reach Lila's door. I knock.

"We're on tonight," I call.

Nothing. Her door is locked. She's probably still asleep. Unease prickles the back of my neck.

I head to the shared baths of the Reign faeries for the first time. The antechamber is lined with racks of unused towels, bars, and bottles of soap. The space splits off into private rooms, and picking one, I find an individual empty pool the length of my own height. Pulling the curtain across the entrance, I strip and reach for the nozzle on the side wall and twist. Cool water springs forth and I laugh in shock at the luxury. Once the pool is full, I dip my palm below the surface, thinking of the heat of the sun on my face, fire from the hearth, and soon steam curls around my face. I climb in and scrub.

When I dip below the water to rinse my hair, my ears fill with a roaring. I break the surface and find it silent. Submerging again, I follow the deep, shuddering din, dissimilar to the rush of water. Reaching out a hand, I graze against something smooth. The drain.

Nails prying under the edge, I pull against the pressure. The lid lifts and sound explodes, reverberating through the water.

Shrieking.

A thunderous timbre that shoots up from the ground, as if a creature will crawl out of the earth's center, splitting our world open like an egg.

A thousand voices, screaming a singular word.

Help.

I drop the drain cover, muffling the sound. Kicking to the surface, I gasp, panting for breath, ears ringing. My body shakes, goosebumps pricking despite the heat of the bath. I scramble out, knees scraping the hard ground. After toweling down, I shove clothes over damp skin and collect my belongings. I should drain the bath—later. Later, I will come back. But right now, my body screams to *run,* my genius flying around my mind, bouncing against its constraints.

Let me out! it pleads. *Let me out—*

It is the death at the center of the Pith, not a life, I remind myself. Not the screams of the unheard and unknown. Or it's another chestnut tree, another door. It could be a thousand petrified things, screaming for aid, and only now do I hear them. Vomit slides up my throat.

"Food," I breathe. "I need food."

I took a hot bath on an empty stomach—never a good idea.

In the Mouth, I gulp down coffee and toast before fixing a

plate for my friend. Placing it outside her door, I knock again. Still, nothing. A sick feeling settles in me, my breakfast threatening to make a revisit.

Maybe Lila returned to the tapestry and we just missed each other. Maybe I need to meet her there. I don't have the keys, but with my revitalized genius and ability to free the doors in the Salon of Stars, I don't need them. I just make sure to stuff some hairpins in my pockets.

Reaching the door to the salon, I recall the word Lila learned from her father, the keeper of the chambers. *Etoles*. I will not be using it tonight. No one will ever use it again.

A palm to the door, I call up my fluttering genius, picture it flapping out of the confines of my mind, along the length of my arms, through my fingertips and into the grain of wood.

An oak tree. An oak tree surrounded by others, cut down and stuffed with an oily, parasitic force.

The oak does not scream, only sighs to be let go, so I let it go.

Reign magic sizzles into the air once more.

Still, the door is locked, and Lila would leave it that way if she were inside. Crouching down, I wedge a hairpin into the lock, then repeat the process with another. My father did not bestow on me a set of keys like Lila's did, but he did teach me what to do if you don't have any.

The lock clicks free.

The door to the Salon of Stars creaks open, and for a moment, I'm curious to see it in the sun for the first time. I step inside.

Blood drains from my head, my hand reaching out for the jamb to steady myself.

The entire space has been ripped apart. I rush inside.

"Lila?" I call, not caring how loud I am. "Lila!"

Furniture shattered, clothes shredded and strewn about, large crumbling gashes on the walls as if a giant beast raked its claws against them. Whatever—or whoever—did this is full of unspeakable power and violence.

And it was not my friend. *So where the fuck is she?*

I sprint out of the apartments.

I sprint back toward the light.

I slam into Fern outside the Mouth, carrying a tray. "Whoa, there—"

"Lila," I gasp, tears streaming down my cheeks, lungs burning. She tries to steady me with one hand. "*Where is Lila?*"

"In the library, of course. With the king," Fern answers. "They've been in there all day."

No no no—

The secret has risen, finally, to the light of day. What will the king do to bury it again?

This is the end. This is the end. Terror claws at me like at the coronation, but this time I can move, I can fight, I could save a friend.

Pivoting, I race down the hall.

"The king asked for privacy!" Fern calls after me. "It's been locked for hours!"

As if I don't know what to do with a locked door.

Chapter Thirty-five

I KICK THE SERVICE DOOR OPEN WITH ALL MY POWER, FLIMSY lock shattering, and it slams on its hinges into the wall. Maxian leans an arm on the mantel, staring into the darkened firebox, his back to me. Lila pours water from a pitcher, unharmed. For a moment, I want to sink to my knees in relief, cry, and hold her as I never could hold Jeremee that one last time.

Yet the muscles in her neck strain. She is fighting Reign magic; the king is controlling her. Her arm shakes. Water overflows the cup, spilling onto the floor. How many hours has she held this position? How long has he been torturing her? And where have I been? Soaking in a bath.

"Your Magnificence," I grit out.

My mouth clamps shut against my will. The shuttering magic tumbles through my jaw, piles stones behind my teeth; I can taste the minerals. As his genius pushes inward, it forms rocky walls around mine, a moth trapped in a well once more.

The door behind me slams shut.

We are trapped, the three of us now, in this. But if that's where I need to be to have Lila's back, then I will stay until we can both leave.

The king turns, something clasped in his large hands.

A small red boot.

My stomach plummets, my legs almost giving out. When I

drag my eyes up his heaving chest, to his distorted, beautiful face, I find red-rimmed eyes. Red and violet and sorrowful and wild.

"Why?" he croaks.

Pebbles grind down my throat. A fire crackles to life in the hearth. The ground rumbles, and water splatters to the carpet.

"Why would you dig up my brother like this?"

My heart twists. Shame burns me as tears pour down Maxian's face. He lowers his head, presses the boot to his chest, as if clutching an exposed heart and willing the organ back inside him.

But he has said nothing of his heritage.

Movement catches my eye. Lila trembles, an endless stream of water cascading from the pitcher into the overflowing cup in her purpling hand. He must be lacing the water from another source, for it keeps flowing. Pain etches across her features as her raw hand shrivels, rivulets soaking the carpet at her feet.

He hands back my voice.

"Please," I manage, throat tight.

"Please what?" he spits.

A low whimper escapes my friend. Her hand has cracked, bleeding, the water tinged pink, her skin leaching color. Wherever he laces the water from, it must be an icy stream in the north.

He is killing her hand. He is killing her.

"Please spare her," I rasp. "She does not deserve this."

Something punches my stomach. Stars blot my vision. I grapple on the carpet, wheezing for breath that doesn't come. My vision wavers and I cough blood.

"I decide what she deserves," the king says, approaching.

"Please." I cough again.

The king crouches before me, gripping my chin, a painful, twisted echo of another time.

"Look at me when I'm speaking."

Oh, how I believed myself a thing with claws just because my thoughts had teeth. But they mean nothing now, as my friend moans in pain and the king holds my face in his killing hands.

Still, I say, "What can I do to—"

"Tell me," he snarls. "Tell me what you know."

But my mind spins, my stomach throbbing with pain. I do not care, at this moment, what the greater game is. I only care that my friend lets out a closed-mouth cry.

"The tapestry," I gasp. "Your brother."

"What else?"

My genius spasms, the creature surrounded by a stony façade. But there is something else in the façade, something I discovered that day in the training hall, when our magics collided, something so small, only a moth could fit into it. *A crack.*

"Avery," he seethes, shaking me until my teeth rattle. "What. Else?"

Does he know that we know?

No, Lila would be dead, then, favorite or not.

"I don't know." My voice cracks with fear, something in me giving way. I almost wet myself.

"You must understand," he whispers, pressing his forehead to mine. Blackness edges out his beautiful irises. Has he taken more of that black substance? "You have to understand the position I'm in. I must do this. To keep the kingdom safe. It's the only way to keep the kingdom safe. You must tell me. Who are my parents?"

My genius flies in erratic circles, its legs brushing against the walls of that stony closet, sensing the vibrations beneath the surface: wrath and shame and disgust and fear and sorrow.

These emotions are not mine, I realize with a shock. As if in entering my mind, the king left the door to his propped open, a crack small enough only for faerie genius.

"The late King Gregor the Great and Queen Elise—"

"You're lying." He twitches, pulling his face from me though we still kneel, knee to knee.

Lila whines in pain.

"I am not a killer like my father. But you force me to do this," he says. "You force me to keep her here, like this, for days on end until there is nothing left but a shriveled, blue shell of a creature. Then I will send her to the mines with four limbs of debt and special instructions—stamped with the royal crest—for the halflings to keep her alive at all costs. As the ash fills her lungs, as the dark and cold weaken her body, as her hands and arms tingle with the pain of a pick against rock over and over and over, even in her sleep, she will live. She will keep living for hundreds of years more and she will know it was you who sent her there. All because you wouldn't tell me who my parents are."

"I don't know who they are," I cry.

Maxian pulls back, cocking his head. He tsks, then looks at me. "You aren't lying this time. Just like Lila."

Because I don't truly know, not really. I don't know the name of the faerie who birthed him.

I sob, my stomach splitting with pain. "Please."

"Did I say I was done?" He pinches my chin, and I open my eyes. "There you are, golden faerie."

Yet his eyes fade in and out of focus. He is fighting to keep his attention split, just like me—between the magical plane and the earthly one. I think of the niche in Lila's wall, the slow carving out of the thickest stones in the palace. I don't need to take down the mountain before me. I just need to put pressure in the right place.

"Stop that," he spits. "What are you doing?"

It started without warning. My genius wedges into the crevice in his magic, picks up a speck of rock, a shaving of mineral, then drops it to the floor below. It does this over and over, scraping away dustings of the rock, removing it on the most minuscule level, deepening the crack ever so slightly. It has become automatic, like breathing, and I do not give it all my concentration to remain undetected. In the dark well, I give my genius what it wants: permission.

Do it, I think. *Do what you must.*

Because what can a moth do to a mountain? It can erode it.

He shakes his head, coming back to me once more. "You haven't heard the most important part."

"What's the most important part?" I gasp, giving my genius more time to work.

"Do you know which stable the silver mare is kept in? Yes, that one. From the coronation. You see, the mare may be Illusion's, but the babe is mine. So, in a way, mother and child are both mine. Now, where is the silver mare kept?"

"Reign?"

"Come on now, you're cleverer than this." He pulls me forward by my face, and I fall off balance, into his arms. Maxian tucks me in close, rearranges our bodies so that I sit on his lap like a child. Cradling my head, my cheek pressed to his chest, he leans down, whispers in my ear. "The silver mare is in a very special stable to me. Yes, it's an Illusion stable, but do you know why it's special?"

He yanks on my hair, tilting my head up. My throat dries. "Why is it special?"

Now he smiles. "Because it's Benji's stable."

My mind goes blank.

The room pitches.

He pets my hair. "Yes, my golden faerie, yes. You understand now. You were a gift from Illusion, but I've decided something today. Nothing could ever convince me to marry Kassandra Morella, even if she is extremely powerful. Even if it means saving this kingdom. But I will never return you."

"What . . ." I try to focus, keeping the words even. "What are your plans for us?"

"Stop digging," the king hisses, his eyes dilating.

My genius scrapes and scrapes, dust billowing around it. But it is not enough; erosion takes years and I only have a few minutes, and the magical organ inside me is spasming, the walls around it trembling, screams filling my ears.

My attention snaps back to the library, to the shaking fae. I have a hand around his throat, a bruising grip, and his eyes are glassy. His arms have fallen limp at his sides, the effort too much to hold me anymore. We are both split between our inner and outer battle, only he must also keep Lila in place and lace the endless stream of icy water into the pitcher.

Even if the king is the most powerful fae in the land, it may not matter, for his mind is more splintered than mine in this moment.

The room around us quakes, and books slide off the shelves. His magic retreats from my limbs, focusing instead on our battling geniuses in the back of my mind.

I have control over my physical body once more.

But it will have to be quick, lest he realizes.

Taking a breath, I slip from his lap. The king cocks his head, eyes flashing black to violet, brows furrowing, as if checking each environment to find the source of change.

I sprint to Lila, whose lips turn blue as she stands in a puddle, feet bare.

Bare feet? Why are they—

A high-pitched whine escapes her gritted teeth. I try to pry her hand from the pitcher, but it remains frozen solid as rock under his Reign magic. Instead, I grip the pitcher, an ice block.

"I'm so sorry for this," I whisper, and yank.

Bones crack. The fingers jut out at odd angles. The arctic water splashes across my torso, my heart seizing with the shock of a thousand needles. I toss the pitcher to the floor, water soaking into the carpet.

The Reign walls quake in my mind, my genius shuddering. I shake my head, my focus fragmenting. Lila remains rigid, though her eyes close, unconsciousness taking her, cheeks bloodless. It's a terrifying image, like a corpse stuffed and dressed to be displayed.

Her hand holding the overflowing cup is worse. Blotchy gray and blue and black, digits swollen. A dead limb. I pull the cylindrical glass up through her grip, the bottom narrower than the base. It comes easy, a small miracle. Yet could she be removed from this puddle? Could I lift her legs to slip on my shoes or will I break more than just a few fingers?

I have seen this freezing once before. A kitchen boy accidentally locked in the ice room. When a cook found him, his pulse fluttered weakly in his neck. My mother urged me not to cry.

There is always hope, she whispered. *There is always hope until they are stiff like an animal found after a snowstorm.*

To get Lila out of this frozen puddle, I must break the king's grip on her. There is no choice in this, for I refuse to watch another friend die.

Grasping the pitcher from the floor, I throw it across the room with all my strength into the back of Maxian's head. The king groans, sliding forward, and I feel the smallest blip in his control. The walls in my mind crumble, his Reign magic retreating.

Lila collapses, and I catch her. As the plane vibrates like scattered sand shifting into a storm, I haul my friend over to the lit fireplace and drop her into a leather chair. Stripping off her soaked cotton shirt first, I tug the warm shirt off my back and over her head. She groans. When I lift an eyelid, I find a large, dilated eye.

"Lila?"

Nothing.

It's not enough. I peel off my pants and rub the silk against her arm. The material begins to fray, fall apart. I need something stronger, more absorbent. I need cotton, better if it's warm. I unwind the band of cotton from my breasts and wipe down her damp torso and legs, cup hands around her frozen feet, urging life into the skin. I can't lace her out with my genius occupying the king.

Then time runs out.

An arm drags me backward.

"No!"

I kick, fingers scraping the strong band around my waist.

"Faerie cunt," Maxian seethes.

"No!"

I twist as another forearm brackets my neck. In that moment, I feel my nakedness, and how I am dizzy and reeling and bleeding. I scratch harder, the king slamming my spine against his torso. My breath stops as I feel it against my lower back.

He is hard.

My body goes slack in shock. My hands drop away, the fight paralyzing in me. It's over—it's all over, and all I can do is stare at my frozen friend, slumped in the chair by the king's fire, struggling to breathe, as he presses himself against me. As he pants, unmoving, we both understand his arousal. He is disgusted and excited by me.

The king lowers to his knee, shifting to hold me to his chest like a bride. My body heaves, my eyes trained on my friend, until I feel a soft caress on my jaw. He turns my face up to him, hand coming away wet with tears and blood.

"Avery," he breathes. His eyes dip to my exposed body, upturned to him, pulsing with pain, falling into the shadow of the Mountain. Heat rolls off his golden skin as he takes in my body, a sight he requested in his bedroom, then was denied.

"Yes?" I manage.

And here we are, streaked in each other's sobs and sweat and blood. As he clutches me like I am life, I feel my own self slip away: a knowing. When he takes me, it will hurt. When he takes, I must give and give some more because maybe it will satisfy him, just for a moment, maybe it'll be enough to return him to the caring façade he sees as himself. Maybe Maxian the Magnificent will not allow his favorite faerie to freeze to death. He wouldn't because he is not his father and I will not fight him because I am no longer mine.

"Avery," he croaks.

I close my eyes, let the tears fall, will my face into placid femininity. I am not Avery and this is not the king. This is a stranger in a tavern who stands in front of the door. Whose approval I must receive so that I can cross the threshold.

I become female; I become nothing.

An empty parchment pressed of dead matter, waiting for the ink to spill.

"I thought you were different from the rest," he breathes. "I need you to be different. I need . . . something from you."

To reach that door, to be able to carry my friend through it, I betray my own kind, faeries, females, servants—we are all the same. I open my eyes, blink up at his beautiful, garish face.

"I am different," I say.

He shakes his head. "You have to know. You have to understand my mother and father because I need you to do something for me. Please, you must do this, and never tell a soul."

"What is it?" I whisper.

He shakes his head, clutching me tighter to his chest, squeezing his eyes shut. For a flicker of a moment, I hear the screaming again. That awful, animalistic wail inside his head. My fingers reach up, stroke his cheek. He leans into the touch like a starved predator. He kisses my fingertips, his lips soft, and I brace myself for the violence of the act that will seem gentle to him. Maxian the Mountain, son of the Sun King, our first kissing king, the kindest lover in the land.

"Forgive me," I breathe.

"How can I?"

"Then punish me."

I beg you, punish me instead, Jeremee cried on coronation day.

Hurt me, I think, just as Benji wished. Enough hurt and maybe it'll balance the scales, maybe I will have paid enough, maybe it will set things right.

Another voice, not unlike my own. *Please. Please, don't do this.*

An iron grip, a large hand wrapped around my entire arm. I am screaming as a child, struggling against the fighter who lost a match and came home determined to win another. My mother pleaded, throwing herself at his feet like an offering, a concession. As if the only option when living with an angry male is to redirect him. As Briar learned and so did my mother and grandmother and now, me.

I am an adolescent, screaming that I will never be weak like her.

I bent to avoid breaking, my mother told me once. *It was all I could think to do.*

"Please hurt me instead," I cry now, sobbing in the king's arms as he cradles me, as my friend lies dying, as he knows the location of the boy I'd do anything to protect. "Please, I beg you."

"I don't need to," he says, eyes bloodshot. "They are your punishment."

I flinch. He flips me, my bare stomach sliding against carpet, pain blooming in my abdomen. Bile threatens as his length presses against my backside. But before me is another horror.

Lila. Stiff, damp legs sticking straight out, spine bowed. Stiff, like an animal found after a snowstorm.

"You did this," the king hisses in my ear.

"No." I thrash. "No!"

I search for that fluttering pulse and there—I see it, at the base of her throat.

"Lila!" I shout. "Lila, please—"

"I am not my father," he mutters like a child with a toy. "I am not my father. I am not my—"

I am not my mother, and still, we act out their roles in a play a thousand years old. All I can do is weep for the faeries in my life that I have failed. I cannot carry Lila through that door with me. I cannot get to her. I have run out of options. I have run out of strength. But I have not run out of friends. It is a decision that could either kill or save her. But anything may be better than the fate he promised, and in this, I do believe him.

"I will do it," I say to him, ceasing my struggling. "I will do what you need, but you have to trust something first."

He stops. "What?"

"Trust that I will return to you."

Then I kiss his cheek and lace into the plane.

Chapter Thirty-six

Knees slam into stone, then palms. My lungs drag in nothing. I scrabble for purchase, my magic depleted with the lacing outside my room. I need to tell someone. Anyone. I need to get someone to Lila, while there's so little time left.

I crawl. Dragging my exposed torso and legs across stone. As I gasp for air, little comes. The servants' hall stretches before me, a scaly dragon I scrape my body across but cannot conquer.

A hand grabs my shoulder.

"Please!" I scream.

"Avery?" Benji gasps. "What—"

"Lila is—"

Pebbles fill my mouth. I try to wedge the words through the Reign oath because if an oath can be sworn with blood, perhaps it'll take blood to break it.

"From the game, you know her. She needs—"

I gag as the stones tumble down my throat, drop deep into my stomach. My belly button aches as it distends with pain, as I push and push the words: *Lila needs help, Lila—*

Blood sprays from my mouth.

Benji screams for help.

Footsteps pound.

"A Night Crest!" a voice calls.

"Gone mad, I think!" another says, somewhere behind me.

"No," I wail, ripping off my golden ring and offering it up. "Lila n—"

My tooth cracks. *Help her! Help her, for planes' sake, help—*

Someone throws fabric across my back, a scratchy cloak. The heft of it collapses me, the ring pinging against the stone and rolling away. Still, my fingers dig into the grooves between stones, and I heave toward it.

Hands cover me, a gentle voice begging me. No, I will not stop. I need to go—I need to get to Lila, for this was a mistake, coming here.

"Lila," I scream again. My body ripples, blood splattering against the walls. "Needs—"

Another spray of crimson.

My arms drop, head lolling to the side. I need to tell someone, I need—

Briar.

Briar holds me, a crowd growing behind us. Faces once familiar now look on, horrified.

"Avery, honey—"

She whispers calming words, though her eyes dart around the space. She caresses my face, just like he did, the monster in the Pith, and I recoil, hissing. I hiss and hiss at her, but my body feels so heavy. It is the only fight left, to show my canines like the day I swore the blood oath to Illusion. To let her know that I hate being touched.

"Please be still."

Tears pour down my temples, hot and burning like the blood from my lips.

"Lila," I weep. "My—"

Briar clamps a hand over my mouth, cutting off the words and the surge of blood magic rising up from my throat. I sob harder, wincing in her grip. What is she doing? What the fuck is she doing? Does she not see? Can she not understand that something has happened, something terribly, terribly wrong? The greatest offense, the sickest act: the Mountain crushing the warmth from the strongest among us, the kindest, the best of us. The best of us. He has killed the best of us.

Not yet, a voice whispers. *Not yet.*

I thrash in Briar's arms. Still, she holds a hand over my mouth, blood seeping through her fingers.

"Please stop," she begs. "You're killing yourself—"

"No," I groan against her hand. "That's not—"

If she knew, if she understood—*I thought she'd understand*—she would try to break the oath as well. Someone kneels beside her, beside me, almost glowing in the dark of the corridor.

Kassandra.

Kassandra, impassive, lips pursed, pale eyes on me, in the servants' space. Unfeeling, uncaring, expressionless Kassandra. What does she need now? Does she not see that there are more important matters at play? I hate her. I hate her, I hate Briar, I hate them all. I hate Versara, I hate Jeremee for dying, I hate myself for living. But most of all, I hate the king.

My limbs grow heavy with despair, drooping. My head pounds and the hallway wavers. Kassandra is ordering extra cloth and water, then snapping at someone for parchment as Briar wraps the cloak over my exposed chest. She is telling Benji to leave, to go to the Nest and stay with a friend.

"Not the stables," I moan. "Anywhere but the stables."

"Avery," my mistress says, voice solid and firm. Not gentle or cooing or dismissive or angry. Just a robust sound, a sturdy foothold in my roiling fear. I grapple for it. "We have your ring. But remember, riddles."

Riddles?

Her eyes flick to the space around us, the faeries who scrabble away. Delicate hands slide beneath my back. I squirm. I am too heavy, too tall. I am a large faerie and Kassandra is a small fae. Then phantom hands join her own, and they lift. For once, I do not resist. For once, I lean into the solid force and cry as Kassandra and her magic carry me from the servants' hall. Briar runs ahead, grabbing the door.

Kassandra carries me to her room, to her large bed and crisp white sheets.

No.

No, I cannot dirty them with my blood and saliva and nakedness. No, I try to twist out of her grip, but she holds me firm, lowering me to the bed. No, I do not belong here, I cannot be coddled while Lila is suffering so, and still, no one knows despite how much I try.

"Her face," Briar whispers. "It's scratched up—"

"Lila," I try again. "Lila, she—"

Blood fills my mouth, and I try to swallow it, I try, but it surges up, hot and explosive. I lean over the bed and vomit red onto the floor. Then my shoulders are being pinned to the mattress, cool fingers bracketing my forehead.

"You will stop that," Kassandra says. "You will stop trying to break the blood oath or I will knock you unconscious, and then we won't be able to hear your message. Do you understand?"

I think I see fear in her eyes, but perhaps it is mine. She brushes hair from my forehead like Maxian did and I wince. Her eyes scan my face. "Do you understand, Avery?"

I nod through my tears, my head pounding with pain.

"Where's that fucking parchment?" Kassandra calls over her shoulder. A day servant trips over something in the parlor, silver clattering to the floor. "Planes-pickled idiots," she mutters, looking back at me. "Turns out you're hard to replace."

I hiccup, a pause to my crying.

"That's right. Breathe, Avery," Briar says, but I flinch. Her face goes dark. "I'll grab water and medicine." As she turns, she mutters to Kassandra, "This is an assault."

"I fear this is not the worst of it."

"No," I cry. "He didn't put—"

"Quiet, Avery," Kassandra says. "That's an order."

This is about Lila—

Briar swears, then exits as another faerie comes in, handing Kassandra parchment and a quill. My fae scratches out a note, and when she is done, she crumples the paper in her hands, closing her eyes. When she opens her fist, it's gone.

I stop crying altogether.

"Mistress?" the other faerie asks.

"Leave."

When they do, Kassandra turns to me. "Turns out you were right. I can send an experience along the plane, an Illusion that does the job, but sometimes I need help from the real thing. A hobby I've picked up recently since you're not around to excessively annoy me."

I want to ask her how and when someone taught her. But my throat is raw, my tongue cut up, my teeth aching. In slowing down, my awareness has shifted, less a cornered animal and more an exhausted one. The aching in my stomach increases. My mouth feels full of drying clay.

Kassandra ducks her head, leveling her eyes with mine. She wipes a thumb across my chin, across the tender bruise.

"He grabbed you in many places, didn't he?" she whispers.

New tears spring to my eyes.

"But that's not all," she says. "Something has happened to Lila. Do not confirm it, it will only hurt. Something has happened to Lila, but help is almost here. That is what we're going to focus on now. We will figure out the rest later."

When Briar returns, she cups a hand under my neck, tilts my head. Still, my muscles give out as blackness spots my vision.

No, I think. *I must hold on.*

Briar dips a cloth in the water and squeezes it onto my lips. It burns, but enough times, and the drying blood gives way as they work in tandem, Kassandra blotting while Briar rinses. I swirl water in my mouth and when I spit it out, a tooth comes with it. I blink in shock, but Briar pockets it and they move on.

Finally, I try riddles. I think of Lila's gold ring, the wings that represented her spirit. A hummingbird.

"The hummingbird..."

Kassandra and Briar do not glance at each other, though they both believe they're the only ones to know up until now.

"Your friend, this hummingbird," my mistress prompts.

"The eagle . . . the eagle froze the hummingbird. He, the k—"

"The eagle," Briar interrupts. "Stick to the riddle."

"The hummingbird was shaking from the cold. The hummingbird wasn't the right color. I think she stopped breathing—"

Someone moans in pain and when Briar brushes hair from my eyes, I realize it's me.

"Then what happened?" Kassandra asks, face grim.

"The moth," I gasp. "The moth saw the hummingbird flutter. The hummingbird might still be alive but doesn't have much time."

Kassandra does not push me for more details. She knows why.

"We need to be strategic," she says instead. "Maxian's father quelled the Dark Rebellion and rebuilt Versara, and his father before him united Amyria. We cannot have Maxian leveling the city in a fit of rage just to show us he can."

Just to show that he's still powerful, even if a halfling.

"Kassandra is right," a voice says from the door. Eli stands on the threshold. "What has occurred? I felt rumbling from House Reign."

"Do you know of the Reign Crest Lila?"

Eli stops in his tracks. Then his eyes take in my bloodied body, my pallor, my tears, and I see something I've never seen on him before, a darkness like shadows between trees, the tensing of his shoulders, the narrowing of his eyes. Fury.

"What. Happened," he grits out.

"The king has tortured her. We need to get to her now before the cold takes her to the celestial plane," Kassandra answers.

Eli's gaze lands on me once more. "*Why?*"

I offer the only truth that comes to mind, the shame and hatred I feel.

"To torture us," I say. "But he's the . . . kissing king. He wasn't going to—"

The oath stops me.

"But there are worse things than death," Kassandra finishes.

"Does not every creature need to be invited into House Reign?" Briar asks. "Is there another way to access Reign?"

"My ring—"

"You've lost half your blood trying to talk," Kassandra snaps. "However your ring works, we don't have time to learn. Is there any other Reign servant who could help us?"

"Carter," Eli says. "The king's valet could grant us access, but he may be with Maxian. We need someone else from the Pith, someone who may be powerful enough to lace Lila here."

There is only one option left, and he is not a friend.

"Death," I say. "Death could bring her."

"Will that not—" Briar glances around. "Tempt him into taking her?"

"No, this Death is strangely moral," Kassandra says.

"We're wasting time." Eli unties his cloak, letting it fall to his feet. He turns to Kassandra. "Shall we perform the Rattling?"

"Does it work with halflings?"

"It should. He is the closest one with Death blood around."

"I'll circle the water, you warm the coal. Briar, a coal from the hearth?"

Briar rushes out of the room into the parlor. I shift in bed.

"Stay as you are," my mistress states. "You'll need energy to speak to the executioner."

"We're not on the best of terms."

"Of course you aren't."

"It'll require strength and concentration," Eli tells her as she grabs the water pitcher next to the bed and places it at her feet.

"I find those traits easy to summon with the right motivation."

"And what's your motivation for helping a Reign Crest you don't know?" He watches her, his tawny gaze hardening.

But my mistress is watching me with glassy eyes. She blinks, glancing at him.

"Perhaps the sweetness of Versara has become sickly to me," she says. "I do not have an apartment in Remiti to escape to when needed."

"I haven't been home in decades."

"You still have one."

They lapse into silence. Briar enters and places the coal into Eli's hand, her fingers coming away covered in soot.

The two fae face each other at the foot of the bed. Kassandra pulls the water from the pitcher with ease. Maybe it's the practice she's been doing. Maybe Dominik has not bothered her in a while. Whatever the cause, my mistress grows confident, and so do I, in her.

Kassandra moves the water around her like a ribbon, coiling it up into the shape of a ring, a circular, ever-flowing river that feeds and devours itself. The room warms as the coal in Eli's hands rises. It burns a deep red, sparks flickering around its edges. It bursts into flames, then burns brighter, taller, more ferociously. Then the two fae begin to chant.

Follow the flow
up, around, below;
offer the final breath
to find a face of Death.

The ring of water and the burning coal shrink, rising in the space between the fae, until the water circles the flame entirely. As the coal burns brighter, it becomes smaller, darker, more compact. The water steams, the fire smokes, and together the elements bow into another, transforming into vapors that dance in the air.

It is beautiful and eerie and ancient. It is something I have never known, another layer to the winding labyrinth; a map given only to the fae, while faeries stumble in the dark. Finally, there is the last sputtering breath of the coal, the last path of circling water, until both elements, and the chanting, end.

No one says a word.

Smoke pours into the room, a dark figure materializing out of the shadows.

"Death," Eli says before he's even fully formed. "Can you tell us if the Reign Crest Lila lives?"

If Death is surprised, he does not show it, does not react.

"She does."

A sob escapes me. Eli pushes forward. "There's been an incident. We need you to retrieve Lila from Reign, bring her to House of Healing, where I will tend to her injuries."

The Death fae's eyes scan the room, flickering across me, before falling back to the Head of Healing.

"This is not a command from the king," he states.

"No, but it is from his oldest friends," Eli replies. "He acted out of anger, and in torturing his favorite faerie, he may have killed her. We want to salvage the situation so that he may choose his desired path when of sound mind."

The room quiets, the plane paralyzing. "You accuse the king of madness?"

"His magic is still maturing, which makes it unstable and vulnerable. As a Healer, I've seen this before. He's not mad but rather struck with a passing illness."

"If he truly wants Lila dead, he can kill her after he's rested," Kassandra says, and Eli stiffens. "But if she dies as an unintended consequence of his moment of weakness, then it will be a tragedy come light of day. We are not asking you to disobey him. We're asking you to give him another chance to decide her fate when he has calmed."

The executioner tightens and loosens his grip on the sword hilt at his hip.

"Okay," he finally says. The room lets out a collective breath. "But I will inform the king after it's done. Lord Eli?"

Death holds out a hand. Eli grips it, then glances at us. "I will order another Healer here."

"Charge it to my account," Kassandra says.

He nods. "We will send word."

Then, with a plume of smoke, both males are gone.

We wait in paralyzing silence.

One minute.

Two.

After five agonizing minutes, a scroll drops into the room on a puff of smoke. Kassandra retrieves and unfurls it.

She reads: "Lila is safe and alive at House of Healing. She's being treated in the royal center, where her care will be overseen by Eli." Kassandra looks up. "I've never heard of a faerie receiving such treatment."

The answer is not far off. It lies in all his lingering looks, the tenderness I have never seen from a fae male before. His soft questions and attentiveness to her dip in mood in wintertime.

"He loves her," I say.

"And yet he questions me." Kassandra closes the scroll. "Rest for now, Avery. Your friend is safe."

Chapter Thirty-seven

FIRE BLOOMS FROM MY BELLY, SPREADING TO MY PELVIS AND down my legs. I writhe and flail, desperate to put out the flames. Hands reach through the blaze, and I shriek as they grab me, hold me down, let me perish.

"Stop!" I beg. "Stop, please!"

He has come for me. The king. I told him I would return. I told him I'd do what he asked. I just needed more time. But time is gone, and he has come to reap me and my friends.

"Get off me!" I thrash. "Get—"

A voice cuts over the roar, sharper than a diamond dagger. "Where the fuck is that Healer?"

Another voice: "We need help—"

"He was supposed to be here by now—"

"Avery!" a friend says. "Avery, you—"

But everything hurts and it's too hot and I can't breathe in the smoke. I roll over and vomit red sticky flames. Someone swears, then a cloth descends on my forehead and it feels like ice.

"Lila," I cry.

"She's—"

I retch again, and suddenly I'm staring down at a puddle of blood, so much blood, the air is metallic and thick.

"She's bleeding from the inside!"

Everything hurts. Is this what Jeremee felt in his final moments? Did the cold that poured over Lila turn to fire on her skin? How my friends have suffered—and I have not understood it until now. Finally, after all these weeks, the reckoning has found me.

I hope Jeremee didn't wander too far and that we may find each other again.

I hope Glenn takes good care of Benji. I hope Benji is safe, always, and loved.

I hope Lila recovers fully.

I hope Briar frees herself and her descendants with the coin.

I hope Kassandra defeats Dominik. I hope she finds happiness and replacing me is not as difficult as she said it has been.

I hope to see my mother. I hope to hold her once more without the illness between us. I hope and hope and hope as the inferno consumes me.

A DARK WEIGHTLESSNESS. Far off, a spot of bright light that grows into a gliding white bird. It perches on my chest, though I do not feel it. Smaller than a swan, lither than a dove, brighter than a phoenix. I know this creature. I have seen it before, recently, in another life, or was it a dream? The bird cocks its head, glowing.

Faerie, it seems to say.

I do not know your name, I answer. *Yet I know you.*

I was sent here by a friend, the bird says, and there is a memory we share of building nests in branches in another life, on a hill somewhere.

Why? I ask.

To return the favor.

Where are we going?

Home. The bird shakes out its wings. *Now hold still.*

The long white bird walks to the base of my throat. I tense.

You are not alone, little moth.

But I've made mistakes. I keep making mistakes.

And yet they still wait for you.

The bird bends its slender neck and touches its white beak to the center of my forehead. At first, nothing. Then the fiery pain retreats from my legs, leaving behind a cool trail. The bird on my chest glows brighter. The anguish pulls back from my pelvis, my abdomen, a weight peeling off my chest. My skin calms, my breathing evens out as the sickness withdraws, pooling in my head. The pain concentrates to a singular point, then is drawn out of me altogether.

The bird is luminous still as it folds my sickness into itself. I gasp with renewed vigor.

"But you will grow ill," I exclaim.

I will heal. And now you will, too.

The bird spreads its glorious wings and takes flight. As it soars higher and higher into the darkness, its glow disseminates, and the plane around me gleams and glitters as the light envelops me, lifts me, delivers me.

Chapter Thirty-eight

I WAKE IN A SOFT BED ENCLOSED IN DRAPES. MY MOUTH FEELS DRY as the desert, my limbs aching and sore. Yet I'm no longer struggling in the tempest of pain. In its aftermath, I assess the damage.

I lift the covers to find a patchwork of bruises along my legs, and I fear what is beneath the cotton gown someone dressed me in, especially with the deep ache in my stomach.

When I drop the covers, a new sight shocks me. Kassandra, slumped in a chair by my bedside, her head resting on the mattress beneath her arm, the other resting against my knee on top of the blankets. Fast asleep and still, her face crinkles in worry, shadows under her eyes.

Lila. She's in the House of Healing now, but how does she fare? What is the extent of her injuries?

"She's okay," Kassandra mutters, pushing herself up, scrubbing her face. "Lila is okay. I get reports from Eli."

My gaze wanders over the curtains. "Briar?" I rasp.

"Resting. Now, you need to take water and a pain tincture."

Before I can protest, Kassandra dips between the curtains, and when she reappears, she holds a glass of water. Gentle, ghostly hands prop me up against the pillows. This time, I do not fear them. Kassandra tips back my head and slips water between my chapped lips, cool and soothing, coating my tongue and throat. I lean forward to gulp more.

"Not too much at once, or you'll be sick." She retrieves a small vial from a pocket in her tunic. "A pain tincture. May I give it to you?"

Nodding, I do not meet her gaze. Kassandra drips the warm tincture into my mouth, an echo of another night with a brother and broken arms. Warmth blossoms on my tongue, filling my chest, leaving my head fuzzy. She lowers me back to the pillows, frowning.

"I'm sorry," I mumble.

"For what?"

"I didn't get the proof." My voice cracks. "I didn't get the proof you asked for."

"Hush now," she chides. "He'll still be a halfling tomorrow. We'll figure it out." But her mouth pinches tight.

"You're angry." I sound like a child, but I feel like one now: terrified.

"The Healer said your genius and body were equally harmed," she says. I wait, unsure if there's a question in her statement. Kassandra sits on the edge of the mattress, eyes burning into me. "You battled with the king, both physically and magically."

I nod.

"Why would you do that?" she seethes. "His genius could've crushed yours."

"It didn't."

"But it should've."

"You think me so weak?"

"You could've died!"

"I know."

"You have always been careless with your life! And so you are careless with others."

Anger roils around in me. "What was I supposed to do, Kassandra?"

"Live!" she shouts. "You are supposed to want to live!"

Why do you care? I want to yell, but the words disintegrate on my tongue. Neither of us is brave enough to name why she cares.

Maybe the Heart of Illusion is not so unfeeling. Maybe she bleeds for only a select few.

"I do want to live," I say, and for the first time since Jeremee's death, it is not a lie. Yet she is not convinced.

"Then act like it."

"If I stay here and hide from the king, will it matter? He will just find me. If he wants to silence me, he will. But . . . he didn't. He wants something from me. We can use this to get the proof we need."

She falls silent, then surveys me again. "Your magic smells different. It's . . . richer now. And it was rich before."

"Finally tolerable to you?"

"I never truly hated it," she mutters.

"No, you just humiliated me for it."

Kassandra looks away. "I was a fool, and I'm sorry. I'm sorry for everything I have done to you. I'm sorry for the actions of my brother. I'm sorry he sold us both to the king, and that you were so greatly harmed. There is little I can say to make it up to you."

"You're right—there is."

My mistress doesn't flinch, just slides off the mattress.

"May I roll up your sleeves?" she asks.

"What are you doing?"

"I was going to explain when you had fully recovered."

I glare at her, but curiosity takes hold. When she bends over me, I smell cinnamon and ginger and the faintest hint of peach. Kassandra slides delicate nails under the fabric of the nightgown and rolls the sleeve up to my shoulder. I gawk at the unmarked skin of my biceps. To the other arm, she does the same.

So much untouched skin. All that remains are four rings from my wrist to my elbow on each arm, put back there by Dominik's complaint. Just like before, my debt has been halved, and I only have eight rings. I stare at the skin, waiting for the tattoos to return like last time. They do not.

"I could only forgive some debt," Kassandra says. "So I chose the debt of the other Houses, as to not flag Dominik's attention. I'm trying to keep these transactions low profile."

I glance up at her, gratitude and vexation swirling in me. "How?"

She smiles. "Remember Hector's mistress? The wife of Illusion's advisor? I had her to tea."

"How'd it go?"

"It was pleasant despite the blackmailing. Well, pleasant for me, at least. She agreed to my terms and helped shift the books, which means I now have my own account Dominik does not know of."

"Has he been here?"

"Not in over three weeks. That's why I've been able to practice."

The last time I saw Dominik, he was in the Pith with Maxian, a strange black powder on the table between them.

"You know something," Kassandra states. When I say nothing, she huffs. "Tell me everything you learned while there. In riddles. Maybe it'll help us come up with a new plan."

"The eagle calls to the wolf."

"I know that."

"They . . . play with a powder."

She snorts. "Coke?"

All that comes to mind is the image of the black powder on the table, and so my tongue cannot get around the oath. So I shift to different images, as if she's asking a different question: What color is Eli's hair? What color does Death wear?

"Black," I sputter.

"I don't know it." Kassandra makes a face. "What else?"

"I don't know why, but the eagle wants to keep the . . . moth."

"No."

I wince. "But the eagle—"

"Not happening. Next secret."

"The eagle mated with . . ." My face burns and I look away.

"Go on."

"The eagle mated with a pink . . . eagle."

"You're very eloquent today."

I shoot her a look. "Do you know who the pink eagle is?"

Kassandra shrugs. "There's only one magenta Reign fae at court. So how does the king feel about me now that he's found a cousin to fuck?"

I grimace. "The eagle is no longer interested in the silver cat."

Her eyes have gone hazy as she rubs her temple.

"What's—"

"Be quiet, I'm thinking."

She slips through the drapes, and I yank one back. She rifles through her desk drawers, pulling out parchments.

"Where'd you put my notes from my tutoring?" she calls.

"You never took notes."

"The ones the tutor gave me." She glances up. "Where are my notes on the marital laws of Versara?"

"In the storage box in your closet," I say. "Bottom shelf."

Kassandra disappears through the door that leads to her bathing room and closet. When she emerges, she's shuffling parchment, eyes scanning the pages. "Why are only males the heads of Houses? Why is it the females who always marry into another?"

"Because . . . they have archaic views?"

She taps a nail against a parchment, moving closer to the bed. *The Head and Heart must never share a body, only a bed. One must lead, and the other must wed.* It's a system of checks and balances on the Houses."

"What does that mean?"

"To prevent institutional alliances, a head of one House cannot marry the head of another."

"But the fae marry between the Houses all the time."

"That's between individuals. Every heir must marry a female who is below him in rank. Even if there are two sons and the second son is the Heart, he must marry a lesser noble female."

"So it's a law that keeps the Houses, the heirs, and all females of the court in check. It also prevents same-sex marriage, since the heads can never marry," I say.

"Exactly. It's why I was set up to marry Maxian. Or Eli as a backup."

"I didn't know that."

"I have my secrets, too," she says. "A marriage between two families can be used to ensure the fulfillment of business contracts used as the dowry. But the Head and Heart law prevents the Houses *themselves* from merging, pooling assets, and becoming one big House."

"So, Dominik became the heir and you the Heart. One leads, building wealth, and the other marries to expand the wealth."

She nods. "It's why most fae try for two children, despite it commonly killing the mothers. Each family desires a Head and a Heart."

My stomach curls. Despite wearing the crown on its head, the entire House of Reign is vulnerable. It lost its second child, its Heart. Its heir may not even be—

We are a dying breed, we Reign fae, Hector had said.

Kassandra continues. "Now that Maxian does not want me, and Eli and I do not want each other, it means something else. It means I will be neither the future queen nor the Lady of Healing." Her eyes brim with tears. "It means I have no marriage prospects. That I have failed as the Heart of Illusion."

"I'm sorry," I say. "I know that was your way out."

She shakes her head. "These are happy tears."

My heart breaks a little as I watch freedom dawn on Kassandra's face. She blooms with a joy I have never seen before. She laughs and my chest hurts, imagining telling this to my mother as a young faerie, before she married my father, even if it means never having me.

You don't need to marry, I would say. *You are enough as is.*

"I'm free," Kassandra gasps. "I'm free."

Tears sting my eyes, my throat thickening. "You are."

"At least until Dominik finds out. He may try to marry me off to another noble."

My joy stumbles. *Does he already know?*

No, this can't be. For all of Kassandra's faults, I would never force a freed creature back into a cage. Something given once, then taken away, is the greatest torture. My mind spins for a solution while hers spirals into despair.

"Kassandra," I breathe. "If you are no longer the Heart of Illusion—at least not for now—then that means you could be the heir. The head, one day."

She blinks. "Dominik is the heir."

"What does it say of sex in the doctrine? If second sons can be the Heart of a House, could a daughter be its head?"

Kassandra reads. "It's more of a practice, I think. If there are no sons . . . they usually find the oldest one among the fae families, and the control of the House switches to a new lineage."

"Do you have any older male cousins?"

"No, just a younger one." She looks up. "There is no distinction of the sex in the laws."

"So you could be heir if Dominik is not."

"The other Illusion families could still choose Ranicus, my cousin in Fraulus. A male child is more valued than an adult female."

"But then House Illusion would need a regent and be further destabilized."

"Why are we talking about this?" she snaps. "Dominik is heir. He is the first male and he's stronger than I am."

But she has spent two centuries being beaten, insulted, and told she is nothing. How large could she loom, if allowed? Would she surpass a mountain? Perhaps she already has.

I think of Lila whispering to me the day we thought Versara would collapse. *He tries every day, and every day he fails.*

Of the king's own confession. *Nothing could ever convince me to marry Kassandra Morella, even if she is extremely powerful.*

Of his lineage. His true lineage. *About where I come from. Who I come from.*

Wouldn't a powerful wife help hide Maxian's secrets? No, she threatens something larger and more fragile than lineage: ego.

"Kassandra, you've already shown yourself to wield great power."

She glares at me. "You're moonstruck."

"Can they do what you did at the coronation?"

"The dagger?"

"Maxian can't—" My mouth fills with the oath, and I groan. "The eagle tried and failed to build what the silver cat did."

Kassandra winces. "It's a specific technique."

"What if it's not?"

What if he can't? I wish to say around the oath. *What if he can't because he's not fully fae, and even if he were, could he compete with you? Could Dominik, for I haven't seen him meld the hardest gemstone on earth into a weapon?*

"Why do you care?" she says. "It means nothing."

"What do you want for yourself, Kassandra? If you did not hold yourself back, as others have done to you, what would you choose if you could?"

She lowers the papers, biting her lip. "To never be a wife. To be powerful enough to never be harmed. To . . . to be untouchable."

To be untouchable.

I flip the sentence around in my mind, examine it from all angles. It fits neatly into my image of Kassandra—the silver fae who rode the silver mare. The female who forged a diamond dagger. Her spitefulness, her regrowth after every breaking.

"Untouchable would look good on you," I tell her.

I wonder how it would feel on me.

"So," she says, cutting into my thoughts. A half smile tugs at her lips. "It seems House of Illusion isn't the only House made of mirages."

Chapter Thirty-nine

For the next few days, I am the opposite of untouchable. When the Healer visits—a short fae with curly black hair—he places cold hands on my bruised stomach and closes his eyes. A ticklish warmth flows through me, spreading to my limbs. After each Healing session, he and I are both drained. He informs me that I had internal bleeding, numerous cuts, and a depleted genius. It is nothing compared to Lila.

She clings to life. Eli and his team slowly rewarm her, monitoring her heart and fluids. The few times she's awoken, she cannot comprehend what she hears.

Kassandra refuses to take her bed back, opting for a servant's cot rolled into the bedroom. Briar does not comment, though I know she wants to. The day servants leave supplies and meals in the dining room but do not venture further. Once, I wake to see Benji by my bedside, pale and tired, but it feels like a dream.

After four days, Eli visits, scrubbing a hand over his face as he enters. Briar closes the door behind him, while Kassandra rises from her desk chair to the left of the bed where I lay.

"Lord Eli," she acknowledges. "How does Lila fare?"

"She is stable now, but there will be some long-term damage. He laced near-frozen water, most likely from the Arctic River north of Cont in the mountains."

"What type of damage?" I manage.

He and Kass share a look.

Tell me, I could demand, but do not. There have already been so many lines crossed between High Fae and faeries these past few days.

"Her heart failed because of the cold," Kassandra replies. "But they were able to revive her."

"There is long-term scarring around the heart and lungs," Eli adds.

"She died?"

"Temporarily."

"She died and you didn't think to tell me?"

"You were busy dying, too," Kassandra spits. "For all we know, you two waved at each other during your stint in the celestial plane!"

Quiet settles around us for a moment. Eli takes a breath. "We couldn't save her left hand."

My mind stutters to a stop. "But . . . you're the best Healing fae . . ."

"I can only Heal what is still alive."

"But she's an artist! She needs her hand."

"Our first priority was her heart."

"And you didn't seem to do that, either," I whisper.

Eli flinches, and I almost feel guilty for forgetting how good their hearing is. The cool touch of Illusion magic brushes against my forearm. I swat it away. *They will keep more from me—because I am not one of them. I never will be, even when I sleep in their beds.*

"We will know more when she wakes," Eli says. "But for now, I want you to know that there are faeries and fae out there who are born without or lose a limb, and they go on to live and experience and love. It will be difficult, but she is not alone. We are all here, waiting to support her."

"When may I see her?"

"When she is awake."

"Why?" I croak. "Why can't I see her?"

Eli watches me with a detached curiosity. "Your injuries were also severe, and yet you're practically healed."

"Your Healer came."

"To Heal is to know, and I do not know you, Avery. And you are not willing to share."

"Eli." Kassandra crosses her arms. "I don't know if that's fair."

"Isn't it? Ever since Avery showed up to Reign, there has been much violence. Lila has served Maxian for decades and she's never been on the receiving end of—"

"Do not pretend to care for her!" I snarl. "How dare you—"

"Quiet, both of you." Kassandra rubs her temples.

Face and eyes burning, I grumble an apology.

"It's been a long few days," Eli mutters. "I'm grateful you got her out."

"I'm grateful you took her in." I pause, thinking of the white bird that visited me in my dream, the same bird that built nests in the boughs of the chestnut tree. I clear my throat. "It was not just your Healer."

"Who visited you?"

"We would've known if someone else were here," Briar says.

I exhale. "It was while I slept. A white bird in my dreams drew the illness out of me and into itself. We spoke. It . . . spoke to me."

Eli's arms drop by his sides. "You were visited by the calabris."

"The calabris?"

"The bird of House Healing. A myth, practically, for it only visits the dying in their dreams."

"She had a very high fever," Kassandra says flatly.

He turns. "We have reports of the calabris going back thousands of years. The same visions of the same bird, Healing a select few, helping them return to the earthly plane." Eli faces me again. "It would not even visit my father, no matter how much I prayed at his side. No matter how many fae he Healed over his many centuries. So I suppose I am confused as to why it would visit you."

The room falls silent, the air thin, the plane warming. As the two fae watch me, I should claim confusion, or perhaps confess that my genius now connects to consciousnesses that others do not know exist in the wood of a door, in the screaming beneath the palace, in the darkness of the king's mind. But then, Briar speaks, low and gentle.

"Avery is a faerie," she says. "We are nature, like soil and the roots that grow in it. Creatures of the earth, it's where our magic excels."

The fae miss her implication, a compliment I cling to—not that faeries can only perform root magic, but that we are better with root magic than they are.

Eli slowly nods. "I shall be back in two days to take you to Healing, but only if you swear the oath to the House. I cannot have you revealing our protections and methods."

Kassandra starts. "She already has two—"

"The Healing oath is not violent like the others."

"I'll do it," I say.

"How are you sleeping?"

"Fine."

"She's not. Can we get a tonic?"

I glare at Kassandra as Eli produces a vial from his pocket. He hands it to me. No one says a word as I uncork the bottle and drink the entire tincture.

WHEN MORNING COMES and I wake once more, head aching, despair and guilt greet me. Briar throws open the blinds, sunlight pouring in, while Kassandra does her makeup, plopping down vials and bottles loudly, as if the pair are determined to disrupt me. She quips that I look treacherous.

"Thanks," I say.

"Hungry?" Briar asks, bustling around the bed.

I shake my head.

"You should eat anyway."

Reluctantly, I do, and I feel better. I can't go to the House of

Healing yet, or Reign, but I can't sit in bed anymore. I drag my feet over the edge of the mattress. Kassandra dabs cream under her eyes while seated before the vanity.

She turns. "What do you think you're doing?"

"Tending to some business." I peel away the covers. "You can have your bed back."

"Who are you to order me around?"

"Do you not miss your silk sheets and queen-size mattress?"

Then Kassandra does something I've never seen her do. She blushes.

"Well, I—" she sputters. "I mean, who wouldn't miss those things?"

Briar snickers from her corner, now dusting a bookshelf. Kassandra whips around.

"You have something to say, Briar?"

"Absolutely not, mistress."

"You're awfully interested in that bookshelf."

"Very interesting titles, mistress."

"Anything else?"

"I think you may do well with some beauty sleep before your guests come tomorrow." Briar bites her lip. "You're awfully cranky."

Kassandra gasps and the faerie laughs. It strikes me now that perhaps the two of them are always like this in private together, having spent two centuries side by side, and it is their relationship to me that's changed. As if I am included in their private lives now.

"It's hard work taking care of someone, day in and day out." Kassandra sighs, combing knots from her hair with her fingers. This time, I laugh. My mistress glares. "Especially when the patient is so stubborn."

"I'm not stubborn."

"Yes, you are," Briar and Kassandra say.

"Well, I'm better now thanks to your care." I reach for the robe at the foot of the bed and slip it on over my nightgown. Kassandra wrinkles her nose.

"You may want to bathe."

"I did yesterday."

"You sweat in your sleep."

Briar lets out a giggle. I shoot her a look. "Whose side are you on?"

My friend raises her hands. "The side of truth."

I roll my eyes while Kassandra snorts, turning back to face her reflection in the glass. She scoops out cream from a glass pot and rubs her hands together.

"You invited guests over?" I ask, my mind finally catching up.

"Just for dinner." She doesn't look at me. "Are you well enough to walk?"

So she doesn't want to answer questions, only ask. Perhaps it's the advisor's wife again, or another lady of the court. Perhaps Kassandra is finally open to making friends.

"I'll lean on the railings," I tell her. "I just can't sit here and do nothing anymore."

"Avery, you aren't doing nothing. You're Healing."

"It's not enough."

"Perhaps it should be."

"Before the coronation, you were siphoning from the plane. Even with two broken arms, you were layering its power along your skin."

There is a pause. Then, quietly, Kassandra says, "I am fae."

"I know." I clutch the bedpost. "How could I forget?"

"Avery," Briar admonishes. "Watch your tongue."

But my vision wavers, my mind flooding with an unrelenting rage. A moment ago, we were jesting with each other like peers, almost like friends. Yet I am not allowed to challenge Kassandra as one? So the High Fae can indulge in familiarity when they are lonely, but slip back into superiority when uncomfortable? They cannot have both—yet that is what they seek. That is what Maxian sought—to feel the love of friendship without earning it. To have ultimate obedience with the visage of choice.

I am in the library, being cradled by the king.

I am in the lounge, being torn open by Dominik.

Perhaps I am performing complex magic, just as Maxian did that day, splitting my consciousness. Lila would find a way to paper together this collage of memories, and find a greater image, a larger meaning, from this experience. But I can only feel the jagged lines, the pieces of me that remain in Reign, and the longing is stretched far, as if I am a trunk severed from its roots; I exist in both places, I am both the chestnut door and the decaying stump in the meadow.

"Avery!" Kassandra shouts.

I blink, the images dissolving before my eyes. My good hand grips the bedpost, knuckles white. My body leans against it. I reach for my genius, requesting it to seek out the tree that made this furniture. But my genius is depleted, and the bed is not enchanted. The wood is dead.

"Why don't you sit?" Briar says.

Lifting my head, I take in Briar clutching her duster, Kassandra gripping the back of her chair. The pair watch me as if I am an animal about to bolt. Their attention makes me want to hide.

"You saw me naked," I say.

Briar furrows her brow. "We had to in order to—"

"It was the only way to save you," Kassandra says.

"I didn't want that."

My mistress cocks her head. "You didn't want to be saved? Or you didn't want us to do the saving?"

"Both." I straighten, releasing the bedpost. "I don't know."

"Tend to your business, if you must," she says. "But do not speak to Briar with such disrespect. She has tended to you every hour since you arrived dying in that hallway. You've always been prideful, Avery, but do not be cruel."

"I'm not—I don't have—"

But was it not my pride that spiraled this entire situation out of control? Kassandra returns to brushing her hair while Briar looks at me with a fatigue that makes me wince. She points to the floor near me.

"I gathered them yesterday from your room," she says.

My pair of tan slippers, worn and molded from years of use. I haven't put them on in months, and the sight is odd, like finding a well-loved recipe I don't remember cooking.

"Thank you," I say, voice cracking, as I slip them on. She places a hand on my forearm, guiding me toward the servants' exit. When we are out of my mistress's earshot, I speak again. "I'm sorry for everything."

"Kassandra has been at your bedside even more than I have. She has been relentless."

"As she is with everything."

Briar squeezes my hand. "Saving your life is not a balance you must repay, but if you can only think in those terms, I will remind you that you saved both her life and mine in different ways."

My bitterness slides away. In its bedrock remains something unnamable until now.

Unworthiness.

"I will make it up to you," I insist.

"You don't need to." Briar nods to her forearms with only three rings total. "Besides, I wouldn't have hesitated to help. I care for you."

I am a child again, confused. "Why?"

"Oh, Avery." She touches my face, and I feel my mother's cool palm against my cheek, a ghost of the past, a promise in the future. "Because you're you. And I like that person very much."

I am speechless.

"You are not alone in this," she says, her tone final.

An echo of another voice. *You are not alone, little moth,* the bird had said.

But I've made mistakes. I keep making mistakes.

And yet they still wait for you.

I thought the bird meant my mother and Jeremee, but now I

am not so sure. Now I wonder if Kassandra and Briar had been waiting for me to wake.

Then a new thought blooms, a radiant, enveloping thought, and with it, the sweetest pain growing in my chest.

How wonderful it is—how lucky am I—to have family waiting for me on every plane, in every existence. How beautiful it is to be loved, then and now, and in the next. I will never bargain it for anything.

Chapter Forty

I SHUFFLE THROUGH THE BUSTLING ILLUSION KITCHENS AND steal a jar of jam from the end table, where a faerie is bottling an array of preserves. A loaf from the breadbasket by the door. Glancing up, I see the red-haired cook staring at me. The one who ratted out my mother years ago for five copper coins.

She grips her wooden spoon. As I stand in a worn robe over my nightdress, pockets bulging with stolen food, hair uncombed and face bruised, I know what she sees. Another night servant gone mad.

I raise my chin and stare down the cook, unblinking. "Hello."

Her gaze flicks to the food in my hand, to my bulging pockets.

Do it, I think. *Report me.*

The cook takes a step back.

"Avery—" she stutters. "How—"

I leave the kitchens before she can finish.

I reach the Nest quickly. Leaning against Silas's office door, I wait for the teller to return. After a few moments, he rounds the corner in a collared shirt and wool pants.

"Lunch?" I ask.

He stops. "What has happened to you?"

"I'll let you infer."

Silas stares, shaking his head. Then he is trundling toward me, unlocking his office, and shooing me inside.

I start pulling out the jams and cheeses and bread. "Do you have a knife and some plates?"

The halfling circles the room to take out utensils from his cabinet and joins me at the table. After several beats of quiet save for the scraping of metal, he asks: "Can you speak of it?"

I shake my head, scrutinizing the seeds of the raspberry jam that stick in the divots of the grainy bread.

"You are still woven with the oath."

I look up. "Woven?"

"The oath—the Reign magic. It needs matter to weave into, as it cannot exist on its own. All oaths are a finesse of Reign work."

"Even oaths sworn to Illusion?"

He nods. "That's why every blood oath uses an enchanted item to seal the ritual. Every oath is Reign magic, even to the other Houses."

Stunned, I put the bread down. "Why tell me this?"

Silas sighs. "Is there anything I can do to ease the pain?"

"My injuries are healing."

"I meant from the fallout of whatever has happened."

"I want what the halflings have," I say. "The contract that stops your relatives from inheriting your unpaid debt."

"There is no such thing."

"Then how is it done? How have the halflings stopped debt from accumulating?"

Silas slathers more bread with jam, finishing off one slice, then another. "There's no way to stop the inheritance of debt directly, but there's a way to assuage the balance, sometimes pay it off entirely, but only after their life ends."

"What do you mean?"

"Halflings set aside some of their income that, once deposited, cannot be withdrawn in their lifetime. It can only be used by the beneficiaries on their account to pay off the debt after their death."

"A savings account for coin that will never enter your pocket, only the pockets of those you've left behind?"

"A risk that many faeries cannot afford."

"One that they do not know about."

"This is true." He nods. "Most halflings maintain a savings balance similar to their debt. Part of the account must go to family, but the rest can go to anyone."

"Let me open one."

"It requires an up-front deposit of ten silvers."

My heart sinks. I could borrow the money from Kassandra, but that'd put me in more debt that some distant cousin will inherit. I will never ask Briar for the gold coin back, but for a moment, I wish I had saved some for myself.

Then I remember—I slept through payday. I have not collected my last Reign paycheck.

"Let's check my accounts," I say.

Silas collects parchment and quill. The enchanted objects have me shivering—can the bird still feel its feather being used? Can the plants feel themselves being scratched again? It is all Reign magic. All of it. Like learning that the massive forest is really just one giant fungus.

"There should be one last payment from Reign," I say as he presses the bloody nib against the parchment. His finger slides against the writing.

"There's only a complaint."

Sweat breaks out across my brow, and I close my eyes, breathing through the nausea. I should've known. I did know. The fallout from Reign will break apart everything I have managed to salvage these past few months.

"It's just a copper coin," Silas says, his words blowing out my despair like wind to a candle.

"What?" I open my eyes.

"There's an attached message, addressed to you. One copper coin is the minimum fee needed to file a complaint."

My spine prickles. "What is it?"

Silas furrows his brow. "*Soumeter.*"

My body stiffens and suddenly I am being skinned alive, my nerves sanded down, coated over with thick lacquer, squeezed into a tight space. The wriggling, black parasite burrows under my grain, contorting around my essence until we are one and the same—the blight and me.

And the word. The word they shout as they slap me, the command that feeds and feeds the leaching magic as it clamps further into my pith, as it rips me into forced movement. The word that steals my will.

Soumeter.

"What is that?" I hear another voice ask—the voice of the moth.

Your voice, I tell the fragmenting mind. *That is your voice. You are in the office with the creature that may be half a friend.*

"A word from the old Reign language," Silas says. "The language used to enchant all objects."

"*Soumeter,*" I repeat, the friend repeats, the others demanded, all cards shuffled in a deck of time that now stacks upon itself, thousands of moments happening all at once. "What does it mean?"

"Translated directly, it means to bow," the half friend says, the stranger.

Maxian wants me to bow to him—I have done that hundreds of times.

"Is that all?"

The teller shifts. "More commonly, *soumeter* is a command. It means *submit.*"

My mind shatters, screams.

Soumeter.

Submit.

Submit to me.

Hands. I imagine delicate, familiar hands with red painted nails, calloused hands that push aside my hair, dark hands that craft beautiful things, tattooed hands that hold me, long strong hands—the original hands—that molded me.

Together, they sift through the splinters of two lives, the tree's and mine. They pluck up and sort the memories in a meadow, memories outside a fighting pit, inside a golden palace, beneath one fae and on top of another, fragments of the sharpest feelings. And I would do the same for their owners—that is what I'm here to do, after all. To repair what I have shattered and soothe what I have not.

"Avery?" Silas is asking.

Avery, yes I am she. Avery, the Night Crest. Avery, the Mad.

"There is something else here in your account."

"Yes?" I say, and as I say it, my mind comes together, a complete, if disorganized, creation. I am here, even if I am hurting. I am here, through the work of others and myself and that should be celebrated. I no longer feel that my mind is fully my own. That there is something else out there, calling to me, and I to it. But it is not terrifying, like an oath in my mouth or tattoos on my skin. It's not ownership at all, but rather companionship.

"A tip from a Rose Tunes."

I blink, my mind quieting. "Do I know a Rose Tunes?"

"She's from Reign. She left you a tip of three gold coins."

"*Three* gold coins?" I balk, slamming fully back into my body. "Is there a message?"

Silas squints. "It seems like nonsense."

"What does it say?"

"*Three gold coins to Avery. I never did say apple.*"

Your word? I asked a naked, rose-colored fae beneath me. *Utter it once and everything stops.*

I-I'm not sure.

How about "apple"?

"Apple" it is.

My face flames.

Silas looks up. "I know this is overwhelming. If applied to your debt now, you could be free of all dues in a few short years."

A sentence that I've craved my entire life. The game has declared that I'm special; I worked hard enough and earned this freedom. But it is like the Prize of the Pith—a glittering distraction for the few. What is liberation, if not for all?

"It's also enough to open the account," I say. "And then some."

"Are you sure?"

"You said I could assign multiple beneficiaries?"

"As long as a percentage goes to a relative, yes."

"Must I know the name of the relative who inherits my debts?"

The teller shakes his head. "You just need to specify in the contract that next of kin will get fifteen percent."

"Draw up the contract."

Silas does. Once the account is opened, I request that the money be placed into it, then half my income from now until my death. Any remaining unclaimed income will also be placed into the account. The longer I live, the larger the account grows.

I had to flee Reign, but I had somewhere to land, somewhere to send Lila. Perhaps it is pride, or a desire to repay balances. Yet it feels like something else, something more solid. It feels like security. Security, as all of the money goes to my loved ones, save one silver toward my current debt, and one for art supplies for a friend.

I will aid my family for as long as I live. And I will aid them after I die—no matter how near that fate is.

Chapter Forty-one

Hours later, I return to Kassandra's bedroom only to be greeted by steam flowing from her bathing chamber. *Where's Briar?* Why isn't the faerie laying out Kassandra's clothes for tomorrow night? Checking the fabric and cleaning the jewelry our mistress will wear for two dinner guests?

"Avery."

The voice floats from the bath. I should slip out now while I can, allow Kassandra to think she imagined I was here.

"Come here, Avery."

I swallow, my skin prickling.

In the glittering silver-tiled bathroom, a sparkling inlaid pool stretches out before me, steam rising from the surface. The space is quiet, heady. From the fog emerges a naked figure. Kassandra.

As she wades through the water, it swirls around her hips. Droplets roll off her curves and splatter into the bath. Her hair falls in plaits around her shoulders, cheeks pink with heat, lashes dewy with condensation. I say nothing, only wipe damp palms on my thighs as she glides toward me.

"You said Briar and I saw you naked," she says. "Need I remind you how many times you've seen me unclothed?"

"That's different. It's my job to dress you."

"And undress me, no?"

"Yes," I say.

Little raindrops roll off every part of her. I tear my eyes away to find hers again. Heavy-lidded and glinting, she smiles, and I know I am caught.

"Briar's off for the evening," she says, rising onto the first step that leads out of the pool. Her thigh emerges from the water. Another step, and the surface flickers just below her center. Another step, and it's fallen to her knees. Again, I drag my eyes up to her smirking face.

"What's changed?" I ask, not for the first time. "Between this morning and now."

"I needed a bath and Briar is gone."

"So I guess I'll just have to bathe you myself."

Kassandra wrinkles her nose. "Not smelling like that, you won't. You'll get me more dirty than clean."

"Is that your desire?"

My mistress blinks. Then she's stepping back down, the pool swallowing up her thighs, her hips, her waist. She sinks lower, her breasts cupped by the water.

"You're bold," she chides, voice smooth. Pink blushes across her chest, from heat or words, I do not know. I do not care.

"Am I?"

"Are you attempting to be mysterious?" The ends of her hair float around her like a siren's. As she moves deeper into the pool, I take it for what it is, what I have been denying since I entered the bathing chamber: an invitation.

She wants to play? *Let's play.*

Gripping my damp nightgown, I pull it over my head, dropping it to the tiles beside me.

Kassandra straightens. "Avery, what are you doing?"

"Being bold."

"What if someone comes in?"

What if someone comes in? Not *No, don't. Stop that. What is wrong with you? You're disgusting. Get out.* No, she asked, *What if someone comes in?*

My blood sings.

"Briar's off, like you said. And anyone else will see a faerie bathing her mistress."

"Naked!" she yelps.

"That's generally how bathing works."

As warm water laps at my thighs, slips over my stomach, I feel the borrowed indulgence of the glimmering baths and the expensive soaps that line the pool's edge. To be naked in the same pool as a nude Kassandra is exhilarating—nothing akin to the sick cot that has become her bed.

She turns away. A reaction that causes a sinking feeling. She is questioning it; she is ashamed. *The law says nothing about looking,* I told her once. But even that may be too much for her.

I stop, the water circling my waist. The entire pool stretches between us. It was too much, too soon. So I reach for a soap bottle resting on the ledge.

"Wait," Kassandra barks. "Not that one."

I watch her, untwisting the cap and inhaling. "Lavender."

"It was a gift."

"I see." Then I dump the contents on my chest and lather.

"Avery!"

"Yes?"

"Wipe that stupid smile off your face."

"Shall I frown instead?"

"The soap was a gift from my mother!"

"You hated your mother."

"Why do you have to be so—"

I laugh, and Kassandra huffs. A phantom touch caresses my forearm.

"I have a solution," she says. "If someone comes in, they won't see anything."

That ghostly finger trails along my upper arm, goosebumps budding across my skin.

"Are you cold?" she asks from the other side of the pool.

"No."

"Oh?" The unseen hand trails over my shoulder, sliding down my chest, between my breasts. It slips below the surface, the water rippling, as it circles my belly button. I don't move. I stand half in the water, upper body exposed, my nipples hardening.

Her unseen hand brushes against my inner thigh, and I feel myself clench.

"Is this what you desire?" she asks.

I cannot deny the deep ache anymore, the feeling that if she does not touch me, I will not recover from this moment, I will not move on. I will remain in this pool, repeating this feeling over and over, wondering what I have done wrong or right in my life to end up here, in the hands of my mistress, desperately waiting for her to mold me anew.

"Yes," I breathe.

"Is that the truth?" The water swishes with her walk, those hips I have slipped fabric over day in and day out for two years, gliding closer now.

"Yes."

The ghost of fingers, threading through my hair. A phantom feel clutching my hip.

"After all," I gasp as her magic tugs me closer, "you aren't truly touching me."

She stands only a few feet away, head cocked like a cat, eyes narrowing. Only her chest betrays her, flushed and heaving. One hand grips the edge of the pool, the other twitching by her thigh. We are bared to each other like throats to knives. We are a feast of silver and blue and brown and tan, of her curves and my muscles, of rough hands and sharp nails and a pink mouth I want to grab and swallow whole. Her voice comes low.

"The law says nothing about looking."

"Nor your Illusions."

Her eyes flash. "Do you want to feel all of your senses all at once?"

"I want to feel all of you, everywhere."

The Illusion in my hair gives a gentle tug, baring the column of my throat to her. I swallow, staring at the ceiling. She could slit my neck with a fingernail.

"Are you sure?" she whispers.

"Do your best."

My nose fills with the scent of her skin, as if she were under me now, her gasp tickling my ear, my tongue dragging on her neck, licking the salt of sweat. On the ceiling is the prettiest picture, a mirror to this moment: her magic coaxing my legs open, and her real hand between her very real thighs, stroking as she watches my pupils dilate, my mouth part, my chest blushing. Unseen hands tease down my body, circling my nipples, sliding lower, my abs flexing. She circles around where I need her most, again and again and again, and I should have known she would be perfect at this game, too.

A breath hisses between my teeth, pressure building higher, higher. I am cupped by her Illusions, overloaded and overwhelmed and overtaken in every sensation.

No wonder she failed as the Heart of Illusion, for she should be its queen.

A moan builds in a throat, but in whose I cannot say, we are one and the same, every part of her indulging every part of me.

"Is this," she pants, "what you want, my love?"

"Yes," I cry in the rising crescendo. Illusions stream through my mind like water. Her on her knees before me, my thumb pressing into her neck, my body pinning hers to the mattress, her nails scraping my back, and it is her fantasies over the years setting my very essence on fire. Steam rises from the bath, hotter and hotter.

"But is it—" She swallows, leaning against the pool as her body tremors, and I see it all on the ceiling above me and in my mind's eye, and hear her very real gasps around me. "Is it what you need?"

I groan in response. The tide is taking me away, everything hot and shivering, and if I do not burst now, I will die.

"Can you . . . can you say no to me?"

"*Never.*"

Everything stops.

Everything. Stops.

The images die out, the sensations yanked away like a tablecloth under a feast, and everything scatters, ruined.

"No," I sob, slumping forward.

Water swallows my torso, smacking my mouth; I sputter. Delicate hands, much weaker than their magic, grip my shoulders, hauling me up. Kassandra, her flushed face pinched with worry, mouth set in a tight line.

"What is wrong with you?" I snarl, shoving her away, humiliation burning every inch of me where heat just was.

She flinches, eyes wet, almost afraid. Then she's reaching for the ledge, hauling herself out of the pool.

"Wait," I say, reaching. "I didn't mean that."

Her feet slap against the tile. "Yes, you did."

"I didn't—"

"This was a mistake. I made a mistake."

This time, I flinch.

No. Not this, not now—not when I was so close to a release, to feeling something that is not rejection and failure and fear.

"Why?" I demand. "Because I am female or a faerie?"

"Because I am your mistress." She reaches for a robe draped over a hook on the wall. "I'm sorry. I should not—will not take you like this."

As Kassandra ties the robe around her, I stand naked in the water, my entire body burning with hatred and unspent pleasure.

"So now you care how you touch me," I mutter.

She glares at me. "You're still covered in bruises from Maxian."

"And now a scar from the brother you offered me to."

Kassandra crosses her arms, standing on the ledge above me, the light glinting off her silver features like a glittering statue. She is incandescent and horrid—and she is silent. She knows I'm right, and this knowledge only propels my rage.

"Where were your morals when you spit on me and called me names and insulted me every day for two years?"

"I know!" she cries. "I know you've experienced the worst of me."

"So forgive me if I don't believe that you've suddenly changed."

"I'm trying to be better. I'm . . . trying."

A small voice in me screams to stop as her eyes fill. But her tears, her guilt, are nothing in the face of the pain and servitude and grief my people have suffered, and my desire curdles to disgust, but if I were to look too closely, I would know it is disgust in myself. So I don't look this time. I point.

"You're just like Eli," I say.

"Explain."

"Never mind."

"Go on, say it. It's what I always liked about you, after all."

"That I'm a bitch?"

"That you're not a coward, even if you are foolish enough to let your feelings slip along the plane."

"You fae dangle dignity in front of those you deem fuckable. Then you rip it away once you're done with us. But we all deserve rights and respect—whether it serves you or not."

"Eli is a good fae."

"Would he have taken Lila in if he didn't love her?"

"I do not know." After a moment of silence, she speaks again. "I will not report you for your insults or send you to the executioner, if that's what you desire."

"I do not desire it."

"Then why say such dangerous things if you do not have a death wish? Most fae would harm you and I tell you this, and still, you are insolent."

"Because," I snap. "Because—"

Because it's you.

She watches me with her sharp, feline eyes, and somehow this makes me wilt, covering my bruises and blushing with the hot pool.

"A part of you trusts me," she states. "And you hate that about yourself."

I say nothing.

"Well, there are parts of me I hate, too. Most of me, actually," she says. "I am sorry for everything I have done to you and to the other faeries. My own pain clouded my privilege. I do not expect forgiveness or kindness. You can stop serving in my apartments, too, if you'd like. I only ask one thing."

I raise my eyes to Kassandra, shimmering Kassandra, power and authority rolling off her in waves I have never felt so strongly before.

"What is it, my lady?"

"Weeks ago, you told me that if cruelty must be learned, then it can be unlearned, too. So please—scream at me all you'd like for what I have done. Flog me for it; planes know it is deserved. But do not indict me for trying to be better. I falter every day, but I am still stumbling toward good. I would very much like to be good. So please, let me be good."

The smallest crack in her voice on the last word.

I lower my gaze, cheeks burning. "Okay."

Kassandra sighs. "I laid out some clothes for you on the bed, but you will not be joining me in it. You smell like my mother, and lavender has always given me a headache."

I raise a brow. "She gifted you her own scent?"

"Is it really that surprising?"

"Did she not know how much you love peaches?"

Her sharp gaze finds mine. "Careful, now."

"Another way you are unlike her, then."

She turns away. "Avery?"

"Yes?" I sink lower until the water is lapping at my throat.

My mistress keeps her back to me. "I should never have even dared, and for that, I claim full responsibility. I will never again take you. Not like this," she says. "Not when your only option is to give."

She departs, and I am left alone in the echoing pool, my body buzzing, my mind teeming with questions. When did it start for her? Those Illusions that flooded our minds included images from our early days together.

As I stride, dripping, to her bedroom, and pick up the clothes she purchased, I notice her stealing glances in the looking glass. As she wrings out her hair, as the tunic slides over my curves in a way cloth has never fit before, I wonder if she has memorized my body the way I have hers.

"Good night," I say.

"Good night," she echoes.

Later, in the dark of my room, I slip a hand beneath the sheets to try to finish what we started. But shame and humiliation swell forth, tugging up other times that made me feel this way. Days after my mother died, when I pressed myself, drunk, against Jeremee, and he held my wrists, kissing my forehead before helping me to bed. The slew of half-hearted prospects in the decades of adolescence and early adulthood, young love and old games.

Why now do I cry in a cold bed as an adult? Why do those who claim to care for me the most want to touch me the least? Others were willing to grab, to strip and take and swallow. It was not all bad, all pain. It was power; it was the price placed on my tongue at three gold coins and not just an oath of loyalty. Why should I be ashamed of victory? Of reclamation? Of pleasure? I am not.

But they are. Kassandra and Jeremee are the only ones who deny what spiced their blood and mine. *Why?* If I cannot be a creature to love, why can't I just be their creature to covet? Even if only for a few moments.

What felt like power before now feels like broken pride.

Curling up on my side, I feel empty.

Chapter Forty-two

I OPEN MY DOOR THE NEXT MORNING TO FIND A FIGURE LEANING against the wall. When I step forward, something dark catches my eye. Black splotches cover the ground and smear across the walls. Not just any marks—bloodstains.

My bloodstains.

I halt, breath dragging in and out of my chest, the flame dying on my fingertips. The figure approaches—and he is small, with curly hair and big eyes. Benji.

I stare at the skinny child whose face has lost its chubby innocence. I take in his hollow cheeks, his calloused hands, and the debt ringed from fingertips to neck, suddenly looking so much like his brother.

Benji crosses and uncrosses his arms.

"You returned covered in blood," he says. "Whose blood was it?"

Still, I cannot say. This time, I meet his eye. "When does your shift start?"

"I can do what I want."

"You can . . ." I start. "I just don't want to cause you more trouble."

"I saw the fire spring from your arms. Remember?"

The day they called me a fae-fucker. "I'm sorry if it scared you."

"But it didn't. I just didn't know you could make fire."

"Not until recently."

"Did you do that to the king?"

"What?"

"When you came back covered in blood. Was some of it the king's?"

I do not speak.

"Remember when . . ." He looks away. "Remember when I wished for the king to hurt you? I didn't think the planes would listen—"

"Benji, this is not your fault."

"I didn't think the planes would listen after ignoring me every time I begged for Jae-jae back."

I close my eyes, throat tight. Oh, how he has grieved, how he will keep grieving, and how distraught Jeremee would be to hear how the mind of a child has warped the world's indiscretions into his own.

"I'm so sorry, Benji, for what you have been through and for the role I have played in it. But you are utterly blameless."

"I wished for you to be hurt, and then you came back hurt."

I shake my head. "Those around us can impact our lives more than some unseeable plane."

"You do not believe in the power of wishing?"

"I believe in our actions."

"But I saw you in the bed when you wouldn't wake up. I waited for you to wake up."

"I'm awake now."

Quiet, for a moment. "This was you, wasn't it?" he says, bunching up his pants to reveal two unmarked knobby knees and legs. He is no longer an Unluckie, merely a palace faerie with two arms of dues like the rest of us.

The Illusion debt was forgiven.

"How did you do it?" the boy asks. "I didn't deposit anything big, but the rings just disappeared when I was eating breakfast."

Kassandra did. I shake my head—I cannot say.

"I know it was you. Who else—" His lip quivers. "Who else would help me?"

"Glenn," I say.

"It's different with him."

"Has it been okay?"

"It's not you."

I grimace. "I'm sorry. I should've—"

"Did you kill someone to do this?" Benji gestures to his unmarked legs. "Is that how you released that debt?"

So he can see the monster lurking in me, even when I cannot reckon with it myself. If it weren't for the oath—if I could deny this—would he even believe me?

He pushes down his pant leg. "Good."

"What?" My head jerks back.

He looks up with watery brown eyes, and suddenly the stony face of a hardened faerie cracks into that of a child of only ten years. "I said *good*."

"You don't mean that."

"I do. They killed my brother. All of them." He shakes his head, his curls bouncing. "If they all get to be killers, why can't we?"

"Benji!" I look over my shoulder, but no one is there. "How many times must we remind you who may be listening?"

"Let them listen—I don't care!" he yells. "You can cut them down. You can conjure flames from your arms and battle the king in magic and *live*. So let them." His voice breaks, and his soft brown eyes spill over with tears.

"Oh, honey—"

"Let them come for me," he shouts louder, face reddening with the passion of a child. "My big sister can protect me. My big sister *will* protect me. Won't you?"

Then he is sobbing, and I am rushing forward. Benji holds out his arms, reaching for me, and I hoist him into an embrace. Slender arms cling to me with a shocking strength, tattooed fingers balling up the fabric of my tunic, and I am crying, stroking his hair.

"Of course," I gasp. "Of course I will. I will always protect you."

"Even when—" He hiccups. "Even after I—"

"Shh, don't start with that. There is nothing you can do to stop me from caring for you."

"Why?" he cries.

Why? The same demand I made of Briar. She has taught me so much.

"Because I love you and that will never change."

"But *why?*"

"Because you're you, and I like that person very much. Because you're my brother, my family. Because—"

He sobs harder and my legs buckle and we sink to the stones stained in my blood. And although it is dark in the hallway and we cannot see the mess, although we cannot look each other in the eye, we cling together with our remaining strength and do not let go.

I can only hope he can forgive me when I return to the king. I hope one day he understands, that Kassandra and Lila and Briar understand so they will not blame themselves. I know what I must do, not because I loathe myself but because I love them more.

But first, the final pieces must slot into place.

Chapter Forty-three

I PACE BEFORE THE INTRICATE IRON GATES OF THE HOUSE OF Healing. The vine-covered iron stretches beyond my sight on either side; even the metal cannot seem to contain the deadly botany of the Healing gardens.

A screech whines through the air, the gates scraping outward. I walk into the mist and chill and the smell of vegetation, and plod under an arched, ivy-covered tunnel. The haze rolls out before me, obscuring my boots. The temperature drops. Somewhere overhead, a bird caws.

The murkiness deepens, the ivy above weaving together tighter, thicker, blocking out the sun entirely. The dark unfolds its cold embrace, but I press forward.

Something snags the toe of my boot. I fly forward, arms outstretched into the moist undergrowth. When I scramble for purchase, I sink lower into the dying vegetation.

A scream claws up my throat, but the more I thrash, the deeper I sink. So I stop. I cease moving, the control one of the hardest instincts to fight. It takes a moment once I swallow down enough terror to register.

I have stopped sinking.

Panic dissipates, my mind clearing. I call on my genius, a hesitant request. The little moth inside me flutters awake, beating its wings—and energy surges through my limbs. As my fingers brush against petals and leaves, they zap with energy, minuscule sparks of power like little gasping breaths.

I think of my mother, whispering to fruits and vegetables as the Base faeries brought them into the kitchens, the tender way she'd hold each one. The phrase she'd utter before eating, quick and gentle like a ladybug.

"Thank you," I breathe. "Thank you for giving your life so that I may live mine."

Pressure sloughs from the plane. The ground rises to meet my body, solid as rock. I lie against the sturdy surface, panting.

A test, I think, staggering to my feet. One I seem to have passed.

At last, the air brightens to a dove gray until the mist is once again colorless and thin. Sunlight spills toward me from the far end of the archway until I am stumbling into its warmth.

The herbal aromas flood me first, revitalizing my mind, soothing my nerves. Soft and smoky lavender, cool mint, floral chamomile, and bright garlic. A circular courtyard materializes around me, surrounded by thick trees and bushes. Gravel pathways divide the space into four wedges, exploding with herbs, and converge in the center, surrounding an enormous, foggy-glass greenhouse. Birds chirp nearby, a breeze slipping through the leaves. While the Illusion courtyards echo a maze with trickery at every turn, the Healing gardens feel like an emerald oasis, a spot of serenity amid the labyrinth of Versara.

I approach the greenhouse and lift the latch on the door with ease. The tremendous room bursts with a rainbow of plants, brighter and more vivid than any I have ever seen. In its center is a curving banister that disappears into the floor.

I descend. A gasp flies from my mouth when I discern a figure standing in the stony corridor. I grip the iron railing and breathe, waiting.

"Lord Eli?" I ask.

"Hello, Avery," Eli says. "Welcome to the House of Healing."

After treading down the tunnels, we ascend into a grand gallery with leather-bound titles crammed into shelves that reach the soaring ceilings. Iron staircases coil up to a mezzanine, where the occasional fae walks along, stack of books in hand. It is silent, save for the sound of footsteps.

I did not know so many books existed. My fingers itch to snag a volume, tuck it under my shirt, and later examine it by firelight. House of Healing has plenty of knowledge—they wouldn't notice one small piece of it missing. Yet as I gaze at the soaring shelves, a new thought blooms.

Ahead of me, the Head of Healing slows, rubbing the back of his head. "Do you have a question?"

"No, my lord."

"I swear I can feel your confusion nudging me."

"Apologies, my lord."

"Never apologize for curiosity."

"Where are all the sick patients?" I ask.

"In their homes," he says. "But rest assured, Lila is in the royal ward."

I scowl. Typical fae, thinking I would be satisfied with this because my own are cared for. "What of those without a home?"

"There are Healing programs they can go to in the Peri."

We take a right at the end of the hall, lined with tapestries and portraits of Healing lineage.

"Would the plants in the tunnel have killed me?" I ask.

"Could we call ourselves House of Healing if that were the consequence for failing our entrance test?"

"It would seem fitting. In nature, we are either growing or dying."

Eli pauses, chuckling. "You wouldn't have died. There is another state we can occupy with the help of magic—stagnation."

I think of the chestnut tree, forced into a frozen state by Reign magic.

"And how would that look?" I ask.

"If you had not answered properly, you would've fallen asleep, and we would have delivered you back to your rooms. You would have to attempt the oath another day. But you passed, and now the oath is around you."

They let the plants decide, I discern. *But isn't that similar to an Unesse belief?*

I dare not mention it. Interesting, how every fae and faerie born in Amyria must be delivered by House of Healing—for a price—and yet only a few are deemed worthy of salvation.

"How does the oath work?"

"You physically may speak of what you see here—but we will learn of it and put you on trial."

What an odd system of enforcement, one that starts on the back end. We head down another corridor lined with doors, until Eli stops before one.

"Here we are." He knocks, and after a moment the door swings open.

Deep olive-green walls embrace me in a moody, intimate bedroom with exposed beams, brass sconces, and a red brick fireplace opposite a full bed. Propped up against cream pillows is my friend, gazing out the one arched window to a private garden.

"Lila," I breathe, stepping forward.

Those rich brown eyes remain on the garden beyond, her shoulders caved inward. Eli perches on the end of the bed, and the gesture feels so familiar, I bite down on my cheek to keep from hissing.

"Lila, if you've changed your mind about Avery visiting, that's okay," he says.

I bristle. She doesn't react.

My hand slips into my pocket, touching the parchment I brought. I move forward. Lila doesn't seem to notice, attention trained on a pair of bluebirds twittering around a birdbath in the center of the courtyard. After learning that the plants listen, I am hesitant. But anything that may bring my friend some relief is worth it.

"Would you like to sit out in the garden?" I ask.

Eli stiffens but says nothing. Finally, Lila turns her head. Her face appears gaunt, skin dull. Yet she gives a small smile, and it is the most soothing sight.

"I think I would like that," she says.

The Healing fae directs us to a stone bench in the sun. After some fussing, some questions—*Do you need water? More pain relief?*—he finally departs.

Lila sits beside me in a cotton gown and a sweater, her left arm tucked into a pocket. We watch the chirping birds splash as they clean their feathers.

"I want to be angry with you," Lila finally says. "But it doesn't feel natural."

"It would be understandable if you were."

"I heard you almost bled to death."

I swallow. "I heard your heart gave out."

"Well, we're a morbid pair, aren't we?" The corner of her mouth upticks.

"We like to do everything together, it seems."

Lila gasps a laugh this time.

"And how are you doing now, or is that a foolish thing to ask?" I venture.

"Eli is nice." She has dropped his title, like I have with Kassandra. She takes a breath. "But there are some things he cannot understand."

"Like what?"

"The king has released me from his service."

A spike of loathing and loss plagues me, but I am not surprised. Maxian has not just taken her hand, but her current and future livelihoods.

Her eyes fill with tears. "Eli has offered me a place in his kitchens. It would be a Scarp position, but it's something. I'm thankful, but . . ."

My friend will not look at me. I brush my shoulder against hers. It feels like the greatest of leaps when she leans against me.

"I was born in Reign, have never lived anywhere else. My mother walked those halls, my father fixed up those chambers, so what will become of them now? There are no markers to visit, no records save for debt I paid off years ago, as if I were ashamed of them. It was all I had left of my family, to exist where they did, and now that is gone."

My arm wraps around her shoulder, and Lila cries. She cries and I pull her closer and cry with her.

"They cannot understand," I say. "These spaces—they are our only inheritance."

To the High Fae, we are a rotation of *stuff* they want to always keep current. Yet for us, our lives and livelihoods are ripped up and planted somewhere else at the whim of a cruel gardener, always cultivating an aesthetic, with little regard for the roots we attempt to put down.

"And the king . . ." Lila swallows. "The things he said!"

"I know."

"I didn't even know he *thought* like that."

"I know."

"And he kept . . . going. He kept going, but I didn't break."

Now my heart breaks again for my friend. "Oh, Lila . . ."

We sit in silence for a moment, hugging each other, before I dig into my pocket.

"Here." I pull out a folded blank parchment paper and a small tin. With the push of my thumb, the top springs open. Inside, a small, thin paintbrush lies next to four spheres of clay, each with an indent at the top. "It's paint. You can take it wherever you go and just moisten the tops of it—the pigment will remain in the indent here."

"But . . ." Lila blinks. "Paint's expensive!"

"I had the coin." I pass the tin onto her lap and she grips it. Her severed arm emerges from the folds of her skirts, the end wrapped up in bandages. I force myself not to stare.

"Avery." Lila looks at me. "You know you did not have to bring something for me to still want to be friends."

"I know."

"But I appreciate it." Lila leans in once more, closer this time. "I grow tired, but you must visit me again. Tell me: How are you faring?"

"Better," I say, and I mean it, hugging my friend once more. "So much better."

"Have you returned to it? The . . ."

I scan the garden, quiet and yet not vacant. Shaking my head, I reply: "We should not speak of this."

"Listen to me."

"Lila, look what has happened! You have lost—I mean—"

"Do not use my injury for your narrative," she seethes.

I close my mouth, blinking. Looking into her face, I do not find fear or even anger, just the hard lines of her conviction.

"Yes, look at what has happened. We have been burned, badly, and what does it mean? That we are closer to the fire than ever before. I don't just mean the tapestry and its truth," she whispers. "It feels as if everything has unraveled around us. As if there's a larger picture than just his . . . heritage."

"The king is always the most powerful fae in the land." I echo the old adage, and we swap a look.

Lila is not wrong. She is rarely wrong, and she's brave enough to look it in the face. Reign power corrupted that chestnut tree, kept it alive to co-opt its strength. Is Maxian intrinsically the strongest in the land? Or does his power come from something else? And where do we faeries fit into this picture, if at all?

"We still didn't make it to the very center," she says.

The empty circle on the map. The odd curved walls of Reign that seem built around something. The energy surging up from the drains, the voices wailing to be heard. The strange magic that felt more right than anything ever before. We uncovered the truth of Maxian that night, but that does not mean we learned the truth of Versara.

Hello again.

"You heard the screams, too, the first time we went into the salon," I say. A shiver ripples down my back.

"Something is there," Lila urges.

A thousand voices, screaming for help.

"Or someone."

That afternoon, as Eli leads me out of the House of Healing, stuffed with our world's knowledge, forever gatekept from faeries, I think that Lila and I are so close to the center of a labyrinth that keeps our kind wandering aimlessly in the dark. But mazes must be built around something. For what is a game without a prize?

What do the High Fae play with the most?

Our freedom.

Chapter Forty-four

"I WOULDN'T GO IN THERE," BRIAR SAYS. "THE GUESTS JUST arrived."

I stand on the threshold of the servants' entrance into Kassandra's dining room while my friend pushes a cart of fruits and lettuce and bread by me. I glance at my old cotton dress I changed into after Healing. "I'm in uniform."

"Kassandra requests that you stay in your room. You're still Healing, and I can handle a party of three."

"Depends on who the party is," I mumble.

Briar arranges three tea sets, saying nothing.

"Does she not want me to know who—" I stop as it dawns.

"Avery, no—"

I swing open the doors with an unexpected rush of strength, my power spooling away faster than I can rein it in. It hums along the plane of magic, sparking when it comes into contact with three other pooling energies: the twinkling cold of Kassandra's, the deadly darkness of Dominik's, and a third I do not recognize, a quiet rumbling.

Dominik lounges in a black tunic at the head of the table, facing my direction. He splits into a slow, lupine grin. His silver hair falls loose around his shoulders.

Someone drums their nails against the wood. Kassandra sits at the head closest to me, stunning in a powder-blue gown that plunges to her belly button. One long red fingernail taps against an empty wineglass, while her other hand digs into the armrest. When she faces me, her eyes narrow for a moment.

Idiot, I can see her thinking.

"Mistress," I say, curtsying.

She turns away, bored. "As you were saying?"

"The king has extended a marriage proposal to our guest. I thought you should like to know, Kass."

"Congratulations, Lady Rose."

My breath catches. Seated along one side of the table is the pink-skinned fae who had been panting in my arms in the king's bed last I had seen her. Had given her two orgasms and shared her with a royal, telling them both what to do. *Rose Tunes.* Heat rushes up my face.

"Thank you," Rose says.

Briar rolls the cart into the room, and after moving to her, I reach for the basket of bread. Does Kassandra know I coupled with Rose? Is that why she's here and my mistress told me not to be? No, it can't be that. It must have something to do with . . .

"You and Maxian know each other through the Reign reunions, no?" my mistress asks.

Rose perks up. "Yes, we are—"

"Cousins."

"Distant."

Kassandra drums her fingers, watching Rose. "Do the Reign halflings come to the reunions or does that dampen luncheon conversation?"

The breadbasket slips from my grasp, and Briar shoots out a hand to grab it.

"You should listen to the lady," she mutters.

But I am. I'm listening to Kassandra *find another way* to gather proof of Maxian's heritage. I just didn't realize she'd be so bold. Then again, it's Kassandra. Then again, I kicked down the king's door.

"Halflings?" Rose guffaws. "Why would they?"

"Considering how many half siblings must be running around—"

"So you're accusing our guest and her family of either being a faerie-fucker or a cousin-fucker? Have some decorum, Kass," Dominik drawls. "Besides, who cares? The late king and queen were first cousins, and they had one lovely son."

I suppress my shiver. *One. Lovely. Son.* None of those words are true, are they?

"Careful, now," my mistress says. "I wouldn't want you to lose your genius, brother. You have so little to spare."

So Dominik swore a blood bargain to keep the secret of the second Vandorne child, I understand. *Does he know of Maxian's mother, too?* Something tells me that if he did, Illusion would have already pried the throne from Reign.

"Maxian truly is lovely," Rose tries.

"Is that why your skin is so pink?" Dominik asks, and she gasps. My mistress clicks her tongue.

"He sent me an informal proposal as well. The day after I won the game."

The plane thrums with a tight, anxious energy. Even the hairs on Briar's arms rise.

"What a relevant piece of information you failed to mention," he draws out.

"You were busy dying from the bite of a peach."

"Kass."

"What?" she sighs. "As you know, nothing means anything in Amyria without a contract. I was waiting on the formal letter of intent, the contract itself. Then I would've come to you and asked which companies you'd like included in the dowry."

The Illusion heir cocks his head. "Have you received a formal letter, Rose?"

"No, not yet. But . . ."

So the king promised marriage to two females of two different

Houses and has delivered on neither. He told me he wouldn't marry Kassandra even if it saves the kingdom. Does he feel the same way about Rose Tunes?

"Faerie, my sister's cup is empty and so is mine," Dominik barks.

Briar starts. "We have tea, coffee, sparkling—"

"Wine."

"Avery, I would like my glass filled first," Kassandra cuts in, her eyes glinting with fury.

Briar and I share a look, then swap the bread and the decanter. As I approach, my mistress slides her cup to the opposite side of the place setting, out of my reach.

"Go on." She motions. "Pour."

My eyes flick between the two fae females. Rose has yet to notice me, her face turned toward Dominik in a strained smile. I lean over Kassandra to service her. With the distance between us closed, Kassandra hisses, low and cutting, "When Briar gives you an order, you *listen*."

I tilt my head, taking in her kohl-lined eyes and berry lips. "Yes, my lady."

"After you pour the wine, you'll be dismissed for the night. Foolish creature."

"Yes, my lady."

She narrows her eyes. "I mean it, Avery. This is not one of those times where I want you to . . ." Her eyes drop to my mouth, and she glances away, drawing the glass to her lips and swallowing.

To what? To disobey?

"I'm parched," Rose whines.

Kassandra nods in dismissal, and I circle down the table to Rose. Dominik's inky eyes trail across my neck, to where my scar is hidden beneath my clothes. Rose's attention returns to her food, which Briar plates and presents. While she's distracted, I pour wine into her cup.

"I believe you two know each other," the lord announces. "Intimately."

I stiffen, the wine sloshing over the rim.

"Ugh, clumsy faerie!" Rose snaps, glaring up at me. Her face falls, deepening to a maroon shade. "Oh! Oh, it's . . . you."

"How did you two meet, again?" Dominik asks.

"The House of Reign, my lord," I say, drawing back. I need to leave.

"What are—" Rose clears her throat, voice dropping. "What are you doing here?"

"She's my Crest attendant," Kassandra answers flatly.

"Yes, Avery—why are you no longer in House Reign?" the Illusion heir drawls.

"I, well—"

"Rose, how does Maxian fare in his week of grieving?" my mistress asks. "Is it not the anniversary of his mother's death tonight? Or was that yesterday?"

My heart pounds.

"I believe it's tomorrow, but he's unavailable for the whole week, as you know—"

"You'd think the future queen could break him from his stupor," Dominik mutters.

"No contract, no crown," Kassandra says, looking to Rose. "It's a declaration not of your character but rather of his indecision."

"I do not think him indecisive in this matter."

"No?"

"I have frequented his bed lately. Have you?"

I tense up again, almost dropping a plate of fruit. Rose has opened the door, one that Dominik now waltzes through with a smile on his face.

"If that truly mattered, then Avery would be the next queen," he says.

All eyes in the room fall to me—Dominik with his smug expression, Rose and Briar with looks of horror, and Kassandra . . . My stoic mistress does not even purse her lips or flare her nostrils. Instead, she takes a sip of wine, glancing at her brother.

"'Avery' does mean 'queen' in the old Illusion tongue," she says.

Rose chokes, bringing a napkin to her lips. "Pardon," she whispers. "I feel I may have overstayed my welcome."

"You all have."

"You." Dominik points to Briar. "Escort Lady Rose to her chambers."

A beat of silence. Kassandra picks at her nails, yet I spot the nervous fluttering in the hollow of her throat.

"Go on," she says to Briar, and then to me: "We'll have the dessert now, please."

My heart sinks at the resignation. She's not just giving in to Dominik—she's trying to clear the room so that the threat does not strike anywhere but her.

"My lady—"

"Return with our dessert and depart immediately. That is an order, and if you disobey, I shall release you from my waiting staff."

I nod and restrain every muscle in my body to walk slowly—so slowly—toward the servants' exit. As I swing it open, I steal one last look at the siblings who sit on either end of the opulent table, the plane brimming with unspent energy. When Dominik meets my eye, he grins.

The moment the door closes, I sprint to the kitchens.

Chapter Forty-five

THE NEST JAMS UP WITH DAY SERVANTS FINISHING THEIR EVEning chores and night servants starting theirs. I slip between the bodies. In the kitchens, I snag the two dessert pies under Kassandra's name and push through the masses again. Someone calls for me as I reach the stairs. I take two steps at a time, my blood rushing, pulse thumping in my throat.

"Avery!"

Glenn.

I stumble, catch myself. "Yes?"

The faerie stands a few steps down from me, his wide face upturned and open. "I just want to apologize for—"

"It's okay—"

"No, it's not. I pushed you away and we should've grieved together—"

"That's sweet to say, but I need to go."

"Do you need help?"

"I can carry these, thank you." I glance up the winding staircase.

"Is something happening?"

I open my mouth, then close it when the Illusion oath pricks along my tongue.

"If anything happens, you take care of Benji," I say.

"What's—"

"I mean it, Glenn. You protect him."

"Of course."

I glance down again at the dessert before me.

Peach pie. I huff a laugh.

That spoiled brat didn't tell me she was doing this again. There is fight in us both yet.

"Thank you," I say.

"Be safe!" Glenn calls.

In the Illusion apartments, the plane is plucked tight like the strings of a bow between two energies. The twinkling magic and the unfeeling one: fallen snow and an empty sky.

The two siblings swallow wine in silence, passing the decanter over the table on a magical wind. Kassandra beckons me, still not looking my way.

"Both, please," she says, and I place the plates before her. I try to catch her eye, but she waves me off. "Depart."

"Stay, little faerie."

I linger, glancing between them. Two months ago, I hesitated as well, unsure of who was the top master. Now I battle within myself: To obey Kassandra would be to abandon her here, with her brother.

"It's confused." Dominik barks a laugh.

"Avery. *Leave.*"

My legs move despite my screaming thoughts. *Coward,* I think. *Stay for this fight.*

"Seems like disobedience is another trait you two share," the heir jeers.

"I do not disobey, brother."

A peach pie lifts from the table, floating across the room. It drops in front of him, the plate cracking, the dessert crumbling. His nostrils flare, pupils dilating. The chair flies across the room as the fae leaps to his feet, body heaving with rage. The plane swirls around him, drains into him, as he siphons its power and lays it across his skin.

"Then what do you call this?" he screams. "What is this?"

Kassandra meets her brother's gaze. "An act of war."

"You declare war on your own House?"

"I am declaring war on you, Dominik. The title of Heir of Illusion belongs to me, and this is your last chance to hand it over peacefully."

He slams the table, the dishware rattling, crashing to the floor. Yet he doesn't reach forward with invisible hands, doesn't strike out at her. There isn't fear in his eyes, only fury. Something is off. More than usual. Something is missing.

My attention sweeps the room but can't pick out any Illusions. But when have I ever been able to discern the sophisticated fantasies they spin? Bending over, I slip a shard of glass up my sleeve as pieces of wood splinter beneath Dominik's grip.

"You're a delusional cunt whose little rebellion has gone on too long," he snarls.

"Avery, out," Kassandra says. "Now."

"Guards! It is time for my sister's gift!"

Before I can move, Kassandra's chamber door flings open. A line of Illusion guards files in, clad in silver armor and bows. Five, seven, ten march in, more than any number I've seen before outside of Illusion events. As they form a straight line, the hairs on the back of my neck rise. My genius panics, fluttering along the plane for a source of nature to call upon and finding nothing. I could conjure flames along my arms, but to what avail?

The soldiers draw their bows, notching silver arrows, strings pulling taut. Ten Illusion archers aim at Kassandra.

"Excuse me!" she yells. "What is the purpose of this?"

"To remind you of your place," Dominik says. "They will follow who they know will win."

"Guards, I demand you lower your weapons."

No one moves. One exhale and ten arrows will rain upon her—could she survive it? One would pierce an organ. The arrows would reach her before I could. My broken piece of glass seems pathetic, but I grip it with everything I have.

Two Illusion halflings tramp in, each holding a fae in their grip. A familiar sky-blue male and a sage-skinned female twist to free themselves, each sporting a black eye and scrapes along their shackled arms. I recognize the female fae from Hector's bed all those weeks ago—his mistress. And the male—Lord Tomas Roche—Illusion's advisor, her husband.

The fae Kassandra had to tea. Clara Roche.

Something drops in my chest.

Lord Tomas's gaze falls to Clara's belly, and I spot it there, a faint but important detail. The swell of her abdomen. She is with child.

I take a step forward. Dominik's eyes slide to me, a smile creeping along his thin lips. The monster took the time to lick his wounds, and now he is unleashed.

"Oh, little faerie," he says. "You haven't seen the best part yet."

The last guard enters, a gruff, burly male whose large hands hold a faerie. Briar.

Kassandra stiffens at the same time I do. Neither of us moves as the guard raises a blade under Briar's chin. She squeezes her eyes shut, lips moving in an unheard prayer. A knife also appears at the advisor's throat, another poking at the pregnancy of his wife.

"Please," the mother, Clara, whimpers.

"Please what?" Dominik says.

"Don't hurt the baby. I'll do anything."

"Anything but stay loyal to your husband and the head of your House."

A flash of movement, a gurgling sound. Kassandra jumps to her feet, but it's too late.

The advisor collapses to his knees, clutching his neck, blood spurting between his fingers. He drops prostrate on the marble, a pool of crimson teeming beneath him.

Horror descends as the buzzing in the plane intensifies.

Dominik just executed the third most powerful fae in the Illusion House. Tonight, he's not just merely stalking us. He is hunting.

My fingers tighten around the glass, its edges biting into my flesh. I could throw it at Dominik, but it would need to hit the target directly, or else there's no going back. Even if I do succeed, there is no guarantee that his guards won't let the arrows loose. The act wouldn't save anyone, not even Benji.

"A shame, really." Dominik clicks his tongue. "He was so good with numbers. He even noticed the little inconsistencies in the reports as of late—the little debts forgiven here and there. He just wasn't smart enough to realize that it was his wife's doing. And yours."

"I don't know what you mean."

"Are you truly that foolish, Kass? Money is my domain, not yours."

The advisor's body twitches one last time, his skin clearing. Then four rings of debt snatch across the pregnant fae's arms, like black shackles that weigh her down. She cries out in pain. Briar jerks forward, but the guard yanks her back. He slaps her hard across the face.

"Don't move," Kassandra says.

Still, Briar hisses with her canines and the guard slaps her again. The other guards shift on their feet, their arrows quivering.

"Briar!" Kassandra barks.

Briar flashes her teeth, cheek red. This is sliding sideways faster than I can blink. My best bet is to pick one path and pursue it: getting the guard off Briar and the pregnant fae.

"Dom," Kass utters. "We can discuss this, just you and I."

"Ah, did you forget, sister? A war is fought with bodies," he says. "So you must be willing to sacrifice some."

Shifting, I catch it—a translucent shimmering that surrounds me—and only me. A protective wall of hardened air, or the beginnings of an Illusion? I'm unsure. Yet with the way Dominik squints in my direction, head cocked, he's deciding, too.

"Run, little faerie," he grins. "This is your chance."

A falter in the shimmering air despite Kassandra's impassive face. She extends magic toward Briar and the pregnant fae, but it's not enough—ten arrows are trained on her, and Dominik hasn't even touched his magic yet. She cannot battle and protect us all and herself, and he knows this. We need to fight together, she and I.

Suddenly the hardened air falls away from my back, giving me an exit to the servants' door but maintaining a shield before me. Now is the chance to run.

I turn inward for the pulsing pride she accuses me of—my insolence. It tastes bitter and sharp. Instead of letting it spill onto the plane in a poor attempt to ignore it, I embrace that bitterness and focus it down my arm and into the piece of glass in my hand. Wrap it with my obstinance, my pride in her. Then I press that broken shard of glass against the shimmering air to my right, willing my message to transpire through the plane.

I am here, I think. *I will fight with you.*

Kassandra straightens. "Is this your true desire, Avery?"

"Yes," I say.

"I wish you well."

Footsteps. The clopping of my own boots, an echo of the sound. The false creaking of the servants' door, the slamming of its hinges.

An Illusion.

An Illusion in which I have left her.

Briar begins to cry, and despite the cracking in her voice, I am grateful. It seals the deal. Dominik throws his head back, laughing. He sees what he wants.

"You *fool*!" he shrieks. "Did you really think your favorite toy would stay? After everything you and I have done to break it so that the other could not have it?"

"I don't know," she says.

As I creep across the room, her magic glimmers around me, mimicking the view from all around, an apartment that Kassandra knows in meticulous detail—she has been jailed in it for years. She must also quiet my footsteps, for as I approach the guards with drawn bows, they do not budge.

I slip behind their line, pausing. I could nick the neck in front of me, but it would draw immediate attention. So it can only be one neck. The halfling twitches; I hold my breath. Dominik is too preoccupied to notice. Instead, he just crosses his arms.

"You have options, Kass," he says. "Carry the king's child, married or not. If you refuse to be his wife, then you can at least be his whore. With Maxian's family madness and Reign growing more restless by the day, they may even welcome a bastard to secure the line."

I am halfway down the line of guards.

"Speaking of bastards—guard?"

A high-pitched keening. Clara falls to her knees, an animalistic wail ripping from her. She clutches her abdomen as it gushes blood.

Even the other guards flinch.

Bile rises in my throat, the air in the room thin. I take tiny, shallow breaths, my heart bursting against my chest, demanding more, but if I concede, I will gasp, I will cry, and we will be found out.

The wailing blooms in the space, the fae mercilessly alive. All color drains from Kassandra's face, and Briar bites her captor's arm once more. He rips her back by her hair.

"End this," Kassandra pleads, grabbing the table for support.

"I ended your competition," Dominik says. "It's important you remember the sound of disobedience. And she may live yet, even if her Reign bastard doesn't."

The Illusion around me flickers, falls for just a moment. A guard turns his head, and the shimmering air snaps up again. I inch behind the guard holding Briar, the mother howling on the ground before us.

"And my other option?" Kassandra asks. "You said I had some."

"If you cannot convince Maxian to put a baby in your belly, then I will put one there myself."

The Illusion around me drops.

Clara spots me first from her fetal position on the ground. She shrieks in shock.

"You!" she screams.

Guards whip around, mouths dropping open. Someone releases an arrow.

"What the—"

I yank Briar's guard down by his collar, slicing the shard across his neck. He goes limp in my hands, dropping before me. There is no time to dwell on my first kill.

Someone tackles me into the blood.

I think of fire. Of the deepest fury a male could never know. It stretches before me, around me, back generations: my mother losing her life to young motherhood, my grandmother shouldering the failure of the fields on her back. The endless experience of big hands grabbing little girls and the malice that adult males inflict on adolescents—oh, that hatred had to go somewhere, did they ever consider that? Did they think we'd just absorb it like how they want us on our backs, passively?

No, it is in me. Compacted down into my core, for there is so much of it, and now, *finally*, I get to draw up that ferocity from its fathomless, yawning pit.

It is either the halflings or me, like starving rats in a bucket with no food but one another. And I will not be eaten. Not today, not ever.

So when the guards grab me, I let them.

Multiple sets of hands, a male body, then another, yank at me, punch me, a boot lands into my stomach. There are at least three bruising me. Only then do I let the heat and wrath and anguish loose.

Flames explode, consuming everything in their path.

Chapter Forty-six

SCREAMS.

The guards stumble away.

I rise, naked and bloody, radiating a furious, fiery tempest. Around me, the guards burn alive, shrieking, clutching their hands, their arms, their feet.

It should not feel good to watch them cower. Their fear and pain should not feel right.

But they do.

I flick my hand, and flames blast the nearest guard, smoke curling up through the chinks of his glowing armor, the male inside screeching. The smell of burnt flesh fills the air, but I do not stop. Discarding the charred shell, gone silent, I reach for the next.

The nearest guards wail and wail until they stop.

Briar battles with another halfling, a flow of water dancing around her like a current, slinging ice needles into his exposed neck above the chain mail. He goes down.

Next to her, the mother struggles under a halfling. I reach for his neck, singeing his skin. He cries out, stumbling back. The fae grapples for something in the growing ocean of slippery blood. She grips something between her fingers—the shard of glass—and whips it across the jugular of the guard.

I survey the scene. Six dead bodies, four remaining guards. Arrows stick out of the far wall, the ceiling. The siblings are gone.

Yet we still fight like rats in that bucket. We must, for we do not know when someone will drop the entire thing in a river, all of us drowning.

A guard charges me through the flames, knife in hand. I dodge his swing too slowly and find my shoulder nicked. His weight drops down on me and I hiss, incinerating the arm bracketing my throat, and he screams, then goes limp. The weight lifts, the halfling unblinking with two of Briar's ice picks up his nose.

A mirror cracks, crashing to the floor on the other side of the room. The siblings tumble into sight, seeming to materialize from nothing, as if they laced. As they wrestle, both of them flinging out bands of power that cut down furniture and bodies—another guard falls—I understand they are not lacing; they are rendering themselves unseen.

The remaining two guards assess their movements. I help Briar to her feet.

Someone grabs my arm. Clara, her face drained of all color. She glowers at me with hollow eyes, her entire bottom half dripping with crimson.

"We'll call for a Healing fae," I say.

"You," she says. "I remember you from that day."

"I—"

"You have condemned us all."

Then she draws the glass across her own throat. Her blood spits, hot and metallic, in my face, and Briar cries out. I grip Clara's elbow as she falls, lowering her next to her husband. The family of three no more.

In total, ten bodies soak in the carnage. The air is thick and wet and full of iron. I swallow back vomit. The plane roils around us, and Briar heaves next to me. Kassandra and Dominik struggle in and out of our perception. Power explodes outward, unnatural and sickening, sending the two guards to their knees.

My body rolls with nausea, and I sink to the bloody floor, aware that I have burned away all my clothes. Briar sheds her sweater, handing the dripping cotton to me, and I throw it over myself.

Dominik stands over Kassandra, her face pressed against the ground. Both of them are covered in cuts and bruises. Dominik grabs her arms, fitting both wrists in one of his hands.

"No," I croak, but my mouth burns with that strange magic. The bizarre, unnatural power. I gag.

"Guards," Dominik calls.

The two stumble to their feet.

"No!" I shout, slipping in blood. Beside me, Briar lurches forward.

"I want you to remember this," Dominik says.

"Kassie," Briar cries, and it is almost the sound of my mother. *Not this again. Not this.*

Anything but this.

"Any House member you buy from me, I will just buy back," Dominik says.

A glint of silver in his hand, a flash of his arm. Before I can reach outward, Briar is tackling me to the ground. I scream, thrashing—until I hear the thudding.

The guards collapse, two daggers across their throats. As they fall away, blood splatters and leaches into the oak floor. From the mass of bodies, Dominik stands tall.

"There were too many eyes in this room anyway."

Beside me, Briar yelps, sputtering. A force wraps around my neck, dragging me to my feet. My fingers spark with little heat, my genius spent.

Dominik wraps a hand in Kassandra's hair and jerks her head up so she's looking at us, her face cut. I scratch harder at the hands that hold me, hiss, flashing my teeth.

"Spare them," she begs, tears rolling down her cheeks.

"Even if it means you will be harmed instead?"

Her eyes flick to him, and my heart grows heavy.

What is he saying? My sluggish brain cannot put it together.

"Whose arms shall I break tonight?" he asks. "Theirs or yours?"

"Mine."

"No," I cough. I snap my fingers over and over but there is no air. I cannot find my fire.

Dominik glances between the two of us. "A lovers' quarrel? Interesting."

The only sounds in the room are our choking.

"Since you two can't decide . . ." he starts, flicking his wrist.

Briar's left arm snaps, the white bone jutting out from her tunic. She screams, then goes limp, head rolling. Kassandra cries out and I kick outward, ripping at the force around me.

He drops his grip.

I crash into the floor, gasping for air. Briar falls facedown in the blood. I drag myself on hands and knees, but Kassandra is already kneeling, flipping over the faerie, wiping blood from her pale face. She cradles Briar with a care I have never seen in her before, have only ever known from my mother, from Lila and Briar. It is the tenderness with which a female holds a life in her hands.

"Consider it a mercy I only broke one," Dominik says, stepping over us. "Every night you go without being in the king's bed will be another night I shall break limbs. And when I am done with Briar, I will move on to Avery, then you, Kass. Remember, faeries do not heal as quickly as you. You have three days."

He navigates the ring of dead bodies, the finished family by the table. As he reaches the door, he glances back at us.

"Remember your options, Kassandra. Either Maxian will sire the future Illusion king, or I will."

With the slam of the doors, Dominik is gone, leaving Kassandra and me in the carnage of blood and bodies and our broken friend.

Chapter Forty-seven

I REMAIN QUIET IN THE DARK ROOM. CURTAINS DRAWN, HUSHED voices, a four-poster bed occupied by a shriveled fae: the Head of Illusion. At his side, Kassandra kneels, hands clasping the withered, spotted ones of her father. Their conversation stutters in fits and starts.

"Papa," she urges. "Do you understand what has happened? Dominik has slaughtered a dozen fae and halflings."

"Guards," the Head of Illusion says.

"Yes, and Lord Tomas, his wife, and her unborn child. Our advisor is gone."

"Mostly guards."

I wince as Kassandra gapes at him. "We need . . . help. I need help. What should I do?"

Dry lips smack together. "Speak to your brother."

"He will not listen."

"Then stop him," he says. "If he needs to be stopped, then stop him."

The air in the room plummets, my mistress shifting, blinking.

"I . . . tried."

Then, Iros Morella, the Lynx of the Lowlands, lifts a large head upon a withered throat. He looks his daughter in the eyes with a sudden clarity that takes my breath.

"The title of head of House belongs to the strongest fae." His voice comes out deep and loud. "If you are too weak to stop him, then you must accept your role as its Heart."

KASSANDRA AND I march down the marble corridor for the Illusion fae. The hall is empty of halfling guards, scarce of servants. I open and close my mouth, unsure of what to say.

"What is it?" she sighs.

"Nothing, mistress—"

"Stop calling me that. Please."

Please.

Spare them.

The images flicker through my mind, the blood still drying into the lines on my palms.

"We must contact outside help," I say. "Lord Eli—"

"No," she cuts in. "Illusion cannot look weak, not at a time like this."

"Illusion is weak."

"You think I don't know that?" she seethes, wheeling to face me, teeth bared. "The advisor is dead, the head dying, and the heir murderous—"

"Then you must—"

"You heard my father. I tried—and I was not strong enough."

"Dominik is half a century older. He has spent two centuries breaking you with your mother's encouragement."

Kassandra flinches. "Stop."

But I can't. Not when Briar's bone is being set in the servants' quarters, not when an entire family line has ended, not when a dozen people died, some by my own hand. My own hand, which burned and cut under the idea that it was a necessity, that violence such as this must have a purpose and not merely justifications, but grappling for either, I only come up empty.

We walk in silence until we reach the grand door to her apartments. But I am not done.

"Let's break Dominik back," I whisper. "Then we'll see if he's a worthy opponent of yours."

Kassandra glares at me. "We're not speaking of this again."

The truth in the tapestry. The bronze-haired faerie with her bronze-haired boy, Maxian.

The diamond dagger, I think. *That was the beginning of the end.*

"The coronation," I say. "Your power—"

"People have died." She throws her hands up.

"And they will continue to die unless you take action."

"Why me? Why do I have to be the one to do it?"

"*Because,*" I spit, my heart wilting. "You are in the most privileged position—you have more power than any faerie. More power than most High Fae."

"No," she grits out, voice tense. "You barely survived this past week. Have you ever thought that perhaps we females get fucked because we're meant to?"

But I refuse to accept this—not anymore, not after the oily feel of Dominik's power, not after the king's genius cracked at the right angle, not when the males have been trying so hard to push us down down down.

"Why are we on the bottom?" I snap. "If we are truly weaker, lesser, why do they create laws to enforce what is supposedly natural? Why harm and kill us over and over? Why does Dominik want you—yes, you, Kassandra—to bear his child?"

She covers her mouth, no doubt holding back vomit. I feel it, too. But a plan falls into place in my mind that could save us both, that could free Benji and heal Briar, and prevent war between the Houses, avoid more bodies. We won the game, even when it was rigged, and faced consequences. We tried to rig the game back and faced more consequences still. What if the only way to stop them is to *become* their consequences?

"Because he's sick," she says.

"Yes, and he's weak," I push. "Why hasn't he married you to

another? He could write up the contract tomorrow. If not the king, why himself?"

"He enjoys torturing me."

"Why?"

"Because my mother told him so."

"And what did they both see in you that threatened them so? If you are truly foolish and weak, why expend so much of their energy curbing yours?"

Kassandra watches me, eyes flicking to her hand on the door. "I don't know."

"You told me only last week that you seek to be untouchable."

"And I have failed!" she cries. "Many lost their lives because of my desire to do more, be more. Dominik proved he will always control me."

My heart aches for her. With my battered body, my exhausted genius, and the sea of blood on the other side of the door, I want nothing more than to curl up in bed and never move again. Yet Lila's words come to mind. *We have been burned, badly, and what does it mean? That we are closer to the fire than ever before.* I think of a moth in a mountain, chipping away away away at the right pressure points. I think of Lila's niche that she carved with years of patient, relentless work. We cannot give up now.

I try again, softer this time. "If you did not expend all your energy healing, then how large can you loom? Dominik said so himself—if there is ever to be an Illusion king, it will be because you have birthed one."

"I don't want to birth one."

"So become one."

Kassandra's face blanches.

"Stop this," she hisses. "This is treason."

"This is truth."

"There have already been enough deaths for tonight."

Then she grips the handle and jerks it open. The metallic smell washes over me.

Death, in his cloaked garb, has cleared the bodies, but a room of blood remains. He directs faeries to clean up the broken furniture, the shattered mirror, the cracked dishware.

"Everyone out!" Kassandra shouts. "Please."

The faeries begin to scatter.

"Do you wish for some aid?" the executioner asks.

"I do not care."

There is no more anger left, only exhaustion. I sigh, gesturing at him. "Would a day like this not fuel you in some way?"

There, in the corners of his eyes, is an almost imperceptible tightening.

"Just because I am a Death fae does not mean I enjoy it," he says. "I detest stolen lives."

The feel of armor growing hot under my touch. *They would've killed you. They were going to,* I tell myself, but it is little comfort.

As the apartments clear, Kassandra strides to an abandoned bucket.

"Do you wish to wash up?" I ask.

She doesn't answer. Instead, she summons water from the pitcher, a dripping river around her, and kneels in the drying blood. She dips a sponge in the water and slaps it against the tile. My mistress scrubs the floor.

I kneel, drawing out my own water, adding soap left behind by a faerie. I reach for a rag in my pockets—my clothes borrowed from Briar, I realize with a pang—and I wipe at the crimson, streaking the liquid across the floor and dyeing the rag.

We work in tandem, in solemn concentration, even when Death unclips his cloak, draping it across a chair, and grabs another bucket and rag. Kassandra only gives him the smallest nod, in that moment, then returns to work. Even when the sober silence washes away to sniffing and salty tears taint the soapy water, we rub at the spots.

It was them or me, I tell myself. *The guards were choosing themselves. So I had to choose myself.*

I had to.

I had to.

A refrain, a desperate chant with which I torture myself to keep from thinking about what I could've done differently. It's alarming how easy it was: to take a life.

We dip and wipe and wring and wash again, over and over, an endless rusty river. As the twilight hour lifts to scarlet and finally, a golden wash, even when the silver room sparkles once more, we clean. We clean and clean and clean, and still the grout remains dyed pink.

Afterward, I lean against the wall, sipping water from a canteen that trembles in my raw fingers. My mistress sits cross-legged, pushing hair from her face. The executioner crosses his arms.

"When are the funerals?" Kassandra asks, voice hoarse. It is early morning, and we have not spoken in hours.

"This afternoon," the executioner says. "I've delivered those whose wills state they must be buried in certain family plots. As for the unclaimed, I've cleared a spot in the Illusion grounds, as requested."

"Paid for by my family, of course." Silence. "Executioner?"

"We need approval from the head, the heir, or the advisor. We cannot proceed with the ceremonies until one of them has given permission to release the plots and the funds."

My stomach twists.

"We don't have an advisor," Kassandra says numbly, rubbing her forehead. "My father may be able to give permission, but his lucidity is inconsistent."

"We could wait on Dominik's word."

"How else can we accomplish this?"

He shifts. "If the funds cannot be paid for up front, then they can be put into the debtors' system as an individual balance."

"I will assume the debts."

I gawk at her. "Mistress, I—"

"I said stop calling me that."

Shoving up a sleeve, I protest: "You do not want this debt. It may be difficult to pay off, especially if Dominik is unwilling. When the interest collects—"

"Do it, Executioner. I will take on the cost of the funerary expenses personally."

"Can House of Death forgive this one time?" I ask him. "Must we charge in a tragedy like this?"

The executioner's amber eyes sharpen.

"Speak," Kassandra demands. "Whatever it is, your secret will be protected. She's under oath and I don't have the energy to share."

He clears his throat, shifting. "The . . . the House of Death does not dole out or reap any debts."

I lean forward. "What did you just say?"

"House of Death protects us from the creatures in the borderlands and the Amyrian Desert, does it not?" Kassandra asks.

"It does."

Blinking, I point to a ring by my elbow. "What's this for, then? Who do we owe?"

He opens and closes his mouth, an oath silencing him. An oath to his own House?

"House of Reign," Kassandra answers. "House of Reign charges and collects the military fees."

The executioner says nothing.

"It can't be." I toss the canteen aside. It seems that everything is House Reign—*everything*. The four Houses are like a shimmering mirage that even their leaders fall for, an illusion of choice and diversity. "Is your House truly banished to the borderlands?"

His head turns slowly in my direction, like a surveying owl. "Yes. Where else would it be?"

"I don't know, buried?"

"Avery, will you stop bothering her with these mindless questions?" Kassandra sighs.

My mind halts like a rearing horse. *Her?*

"Who?" I demand.

She glowers at me, gesturing at the executioner. "What do you mean, who? The executioner."

Between us, Death has gone still.

"But the executioner is a male."

My mistress groans. "Are you not the one always bemoaning how the High Fae favor one sex over the other? Why is it so hard to understand that Death can be menacing and still have tits!"

"I don't understand, because I don't see that."

"How—" Kassandra stops.

We look to the executioner, crouched, hands flexing on thighs. Their figure seems to flicker. An Illusion? But Death laced me back to this House weeks ago, held me in his arms, stood before all of Versara to execute my friend, and has been at a king's side for over a century.

Death is watching us.

"You understand now," they say.

My mistress's magic reaches across the plane, fluttering the executioner's cloak. She frowns. "You aren't an Illusion."

"No, I'm not."

"I don't care what's under your cloak," I say. "I just want to know why we perceive you differently."

"It's part of the oath I took to represent my House. To become as faceless as death itself."

My mistress shifts. "So what are you?"

"What you fear most," Death says. "Usually, a loved one who did not know how to love."

"I do not seek the approval of males," I mutter.

"No, you just seek safety in them."

I flinch, eyes burning. *There is no safety in them*, I think, and finally understand.

"*Enough.*" Kassandra stares down the executioner, face smooth and unreadable. "You claim your House collects no debt, yet you still protect Amyria. Why?"

"Because it is needed."

"And your House grows with anyone who survives the Desert Walk. You must be the biggest House at this point."

"Few survive the Walk."

"But some do?" I wonder.

"Yes."

"But the scorpions and carnivorous sand turtles? The winds of the Amyrian Desert?"

"Are you a child?" Kassandra sighs. "These are ghosts you fear."

"They exist," Death says, "but we do not harm the creatures if they do not harm us."

We fall silent for a moment, the air thick and full of iron.

"Take me to the king," Kassandra says.

"I can't do that," the executioner replies, hands flexing on their—his—thighs, the visage of a male once more to me.

"I'd like to speak to my creditor."

"He's . . . indisposed."

Kassandra rubs her face, swearing.

"Why?" I ask.

"The anniversary of his mother's death," she replies. "He drinks himself stupid for the entire week."

"Well, if the king can drown himself for his mother, surely he could understand that we—"

"I wouldn't finish that sentence," Death mumbles. "It would not be wise."

Kass glances around. "Could you issue the debt on behalf of House Reign?"

"We would need a teller with Reign blood."

My ears prick up.

"I know of one," I say.

SILAS SITS WIDE-EYED in Kassandra's parlor. His gaze keeps lowering to the floor, then back up at my mistress.

"Are the terms of the agreement acceptable?" my mistress asks.

"Yes, it's just that this is highly unusual for a fae. Are you positive, my lady?"

"Yes."

I shift. "I don't think there's a need to self-flagellate—"

She cuts me a look. "The funerals are happening today, no? If it does not fall on my wrists, then it shall land on those of the families—whoever remains. I will not have it."

Silas scribbles on parchment, reaches for Kassandra's hand.

"Wait," she says, putting her palm to her chest. "What of my dowry? Could I pay with that?"

"I'm afraid not, mistress. It's under your brother's name."

"Her apartment allowance?" I supply. "Does that need approval?"

"Dominik doesn't care about which drapes I order. Besides, what good would that do?"

"Your . . . your floors needed cleaning," I say.

The room looks at me, blinking, the tile shining.

"You withdrew money to pay for your floors to be specially cleaned."

"The money in this account cannot be withdrawn, merely transferred. And the note attached must clarify for what services," Silas says. "I'm sorry."

There is another moment of silence as realization dawns. Kassandra faces Silas again.

"I'd like to tip my Illusion Crest attendant Avery for hand-cleaning my floors," she says. "And the executioner in their assistance."

Death straightens. "My lady, that's unnecessary—"

"Use all of it," she says.

The teller blinks. "This account hasn't been touched in years. There's quite a sum."

"Then split it down the line and pay what is owed."

"It—" Silas swallows. "I see."

"Kass," I start. "You—"

"When that is done, I would like to set up my personal loan to House of Reign for the funerary expenses. Will that do?"

Silas nods again and pricks her finger. Three rings wrap around each arm, her skin reddening, and it strikes me that it has never been marked; it is not used to it. She hisses in pain, clenching her teeth.

"Apologies, mistress," Silas says.

"You are only doing your job." Kassandra stands and faces me. My heart stops, my throat thickening with emotion. *She looks like a faerie.* With her small stature and angular face, she looks more like a faerie than I do.

"Your turn," she says.

I seat myself next to Silas and offer my finger. He pricks and the information scrolls across the page. "Congratulations," he says. "You have a tip from Lady Kassandra in the amount of five hundred silvers, or five gold coins."

I choke.

"Would you like to withdraw, apply toward your current balance, or deposit into your . . ." His voice trails off. My savings account that will be given to my loved ones upon my death.

"Apply to what is left of my Illusion debt," I say. "Then deposit the remaining, please."

Silas exhales, relieved in not having to expose our arrangement. When it is time to prick my finger again, I do not want to feel excitement, a lightness in a time like this. Yet as the Reign magic unlatches its hold of my balances, I feel it as much as I see it.

My rings dwindle to just two on each wrist, the least I've ever had. With a cursory glance, I resemble a halfling, especially with my height.

Then it is Death's turn.

"What do you see when you look at the executioner?" I ask Silas. "If you don't mind me asking."

He startles. Death doesn't move, a hand outstretched to the teller.

"Um," the halfling stutters, looking down. "Oh, nothing."

"Please," Kassandra nudges, brows drawing together. "Who do you see?"

Silas adjusts his glasses, stealing a glance at the executioner. "Apologies, it's just that you remind me of the first fae I worked under. He was . . . well, it's your eyes, you see. They're violet like his were."

Gregor the Great.

"How long did you work under him?" I ask.

Silas shifts. "My entire life, until a decade ago. I was . . . demoted to teller in Illusion when he began his decline—may he wander well—and moved to House Healing for hospice. But before that, I was his valet."

The air in the room seems to dry up. Kassandra covers her mouth.

"His personal valet?" I gawk. *To King Gregor?*

"It was an old tradition in House Reign, to have halflings serve as personal valets and ladies-in-waiting for the royal couple. Only when the administration started to transition over to the prince were the faeries brought into those roles. They typically serve the royal children, yes, but never the king and queen."

Kassandra and I look at each other.

"How'd you end up in Illusion?" she says gently.

He coughs. "The current administration wanted me gone, said I wasn't young enough to be progressive. But the late king wanted me . . . taken care of with salary and retirement. It was a favor, really, to the king. A favor granted by the Lynx of the Lowlands."

Kassandra sucks in a breath. "My father took you in, in exchange for what?"

"I don't know." Silas squirms. "I wasn't allowed in that room."

"Apologies, we shouldn't have pried," I say.

Silas collects his things. "It's okay. It's nice to talk about it. My old life."

Kassandra thanks him and he nods, bowing, and departs. She

gives me a look that I know means *An in*. We might have an in on proving Maxian's heritage.

"Who else knows about your changing appearance?" I ask Death.

"Whoever asks." But he stares down at a body obscured by black robes. He shakes his head. "My lady, you . . . my . . . my debt is now gone."

"Good. I'm glad to hear it."

"I owe you."

"You do not." She glances down at her own skin, tracing a finger along one of her six tattoos.

"I cannot take you to the Pith, as there are wards in place that prevent it," he says. "You would need to be formally invited."

"I understand."

"But," he says, turning to me, "I can take you. Your invitation hasn't been revoked yet."

"Oh," I blurt. "Well—"

"No." Kassandra shakes her head. "The king is too unpredictable right now."

"I don't need to see him to collect Lila's belongings."

Another point of contention between us. While I still have my moth ring, my genius hasn't been strong enough to lace to Reign. The only reason I was able to summon enough energy to fight was from adrenaline, and now that it's gone, I feel drained.

"I could smother her genius so that the king can't detect it on the plane," Death says.

"*What?*" I cry.

"Using Death magic, I could mask your genius for about an hour. That way, you can still slip in through the wards without anyone detecting you once there."

I shrug. "An hour is long enough."

My mistress studies me. She throws up a hand, and a sparkling wall of air surrounds us. An Illusion or force of some sort. On the other side, the executioner drops his shoulders in a sigh that we cannot hear.

"What are you on about?" she asks.

"I have an idea."

"That's why I'm worried. Tell me."

"It would allow you to become head of House. It would . . . require it."

Kassandra's eyes spark. "Dominik's death may lead to war between the Houses."

"He does not have to die to lose his spot as heir."

She stares at her tattooed arms, rotating them. "I didn't expect it to feel so painful. So . . . heavy. Yours used to go up to your shoulders."

"I am one of the lucky ones. Most palace faeries are."

"The boy," she says. "The little brother of your friend Jeremee."

I blink, shocked to hear his name on her lips. "Yes. What of him?"

"How many debt rings does he have?"

"They spanned all four limbs," I say. "Until the game. Then you forgave some . . ." I stop, emotion rising.

"I forgave what I thought we could get away with. It seems I was wrong."

"They only cover two of his limbs now," I say. "Benji's debt."

"But in a few years, it could be back to four again. Yours could wrap around all four if you anger a fae enough. And . . . and now me as well, I guess. It's a rather capricious feeling."

"The head of House can grant legal protections to avoid that," I say.

"But not the Heart." Kassandra chews on her lip. "The head of House can also appoint a new accountant and advisor. One who may have seen personal Vandorne documents in the past."

I raise a brow. "One who was a personal valet to the king?"

She nods, then looks at me. "I harbor much fear."

"As do I."

"So where does that leave us?"

I take a breath. "We can either act while afraid or never act at all."

Before Kassandra drops the wall of hardened air, she tosses a look to the executioner.

"Bit creepy, no?" she says.

"I thought you liked looking at other females."

That gets me a shove, but as my mistress turns away, the faintest smile graces her lips.

Chapter Forty-eight

THE EXECUTIONER BRINGS ME TO THE DARK SHADOWS OF THE servants' corridors. Even after my body adjusts, the Pith vibrates with energy.

"The king," he says.

"I'll stay clear."

He holds my forearm as a dense weight settles in the air around me, the smell of my genius smothered. "Meet back here in an hour," he says, then puffs away.

I creep down the hallway, toward Lila's room. It wasn't a complete lie to want to collect her belongings, especially one. Murmurs whisper across the stones from the Mouth, and after the fading of footsteps, I round the corner barefoot.

In front of her door, I kneel and pick the lock, then slip inside. They haven't cleared her room yet, either. In fact, they've added flowers, beads, anything bright and creative. Scraps of parchment are grouped throughout the room in piles. *To Lila, love, Fern.* Another pile reads *To Lila, from Carter.* Over and over again, I pick up letters addressed to my wonderful friend, from all the friends she made in her time here, squirreling away the notes in my pockets to deliver to her.

Then I unpeel the putty that secures her art to the wall. Exposing the niche, I retrieve her father's keys, securing the art in place.

The door clicks behind me. I whirl around. Fern steps through with a candle. She gasps, pulling back. My heart pounds, but I put a finger to my lips, pleading.

"What are you doing here?" she whispers, placing the candle holder on the floor.

"Collecting Lila's belongings to bring to her," I say. "Please, I'm not supposed to, but—"

"You're alive." The cook barrels toward me, wraps thick arms around me. "Oh my planes," she hiccups. "You survived."

I blink, tears filling my eyes once more.

"When we found Lila—" Her voice falters. "Lila was so—"

"I know."

"My poor Lila. He had *left* her. He left her in the library after doing that to her."

"I know," I croak. "I know and I am so, so sorry."

"No," the cook rushes to say, shaking her head. "No, none of that."

"But you don't understand," I say. "You don't know me."

"Lila does. She trusts you, and I trust her." For the first time since I've known her, her eyes darken with fury. "I see her like that, in my nightmares. Blue."

"She's safe now."

"I heard they took her hand."

I nod. Fern plants hands on her hips, nodding, too. "You sure you two don't need anything? How are you getting out of the Pith?"

I pause, debating if I should reveal it now. The truth of the matter was that I was never going to meet the executioner in our spot in an hour. I was going to wait until my task here was complete.

"Come on, lovely. Tell me."

The more people who know of the plan, the more dangerous it becomes.

Do less on your own, Jeremee had said. Perhaps I need to be like Fern and trust the one who Lila trusts. Perhaps community doesn't need to come just from me. Perhaps I have found an existing one, one that Lila invited me to join, and now Fern, too. Friends are the only reason why and how I've survived lately. They are here for me just as much as I am here for them. All I have to do is accept the help.

"It's a bizarre request," I start.

LIGHT SPILLS INTO the hallway from the Mouth. My breathing slows, ears pricking at the conversation within.

"And when do you think he'll be stopping tonight?" Fern asks.

A heavy sigh. Carter. "Until he can't fit any more in his body."

"Maybe it would do him good to get some sleep. It would do us all some good."

"His tolerance rises each night he binges."

"Then give him the stronger stuff," Fern suggests, then adds: "It'll be a mercy, I think. To let him sleep through the grief this time. Especially without his usual company to cheer him up."

"His own doing," Carter grits out.

"Easy now," the cook says. "You can never let him see that hatred."

Holding my breath, I slide farther into the deep darkness of the Pith, down the halls, and to the Salon of Stars. There has been too much debt and death. While I wait, I may as well free those I can.

I return to the trees, place palms on their petrified wood, whisper my genius into their grain.

A linden tree.

Another oak. Then a chestnut again.

And so on and so forth.

For half an hour, I press against the wood and ask: *What do you need?*

Some choose to be let go; others wish to stay but to have the parasite abated. Some just wish to speak of what they have seen, what they know.

They know much.

And I so little. So I lean against them, and I listen. And with every freed tree, something frees in me, my genius expanding, crackling like lightning beneath my skin.

When the time draws near, I shake myself loose from the final hold, a door in the second Salon of Stars, the child's bedroom that belonged to P.V. The doors in this space speak of a blast of energy, one hundred years old.

As I slip out of the Salon of Stars, my thoughts tangle with many lives. Lila was right. Every enchanted object spoke of a creature at the very center of Versara, one they cannot reach. Although I cannot see the living thing in my mind's eye, I know its depth, the power that surges up from the drains. Something remade, something unrelenting.

Something that will never submit.

It is not a monster; it is merely trapped. I promise that creature—whatever it may be—that I shall return and free it, too.

I HOVER OUTSIDE the king's bedroom door. Death will be here any minute, and still I strain for the sounds within—the snoring, the clink of bottles. The servants' door swings open and I flatten myself against the wall as Carter pushes a cart out, turning his back to me as he moves toward the Mouth.

The snores tumble into the hall.

I have moments.

I slip inside the king's bedroom. Only a few candles float this time, the space dark and moody. It smells of sweat and alcohol and smoke. The chambers have been destroyed—bits of broken glass, food strung about, the curtains ripped down. Pausing, I watch the lump of covers on the bed shift and settle, followed by a snore.

I pick my way toward the grand desk to the left of the bed. Scattered with papers, an upturned wine goblet, and letters, requests. If this were any other time, if Death weren't around the corner, I would snag a few papers, read them over. Instead, I scan the desk until I find it.

His royal letter opener, the Reign crest imprinted on its handle. A solid bar of gold, it is heavier than most platters I've carried. Still, it is not the diamond dagger.

I open the drawers, searching. *Where is that damn thing?*

It has to be here, somewhere.

Opening the bottom drawer, I spot it. Glimmering, translucent, deadly. Yet when I pick it up, it feels too light, dull. I flip it over and notice cracks along its blade. This, I realize, is made of glass. This is fake. I brush aside more paper, and they glitter up at me.

A dozen or so failed diamond daggers. Some have been shattered, others half formed. Still, a pile of loose diamonds rattle around the bottom. *Carter and Lila were right.*

But is it because he's a halfling, or because Kassandra is so powerful?

A noise in the hall.

I close the drawer and retreat from the desk. Moonlight pools on the prone figure among silk sheets.

Maxian. Beautiful, powerful Maxian, with his sharp jawline and bulging shoulders, lying on his bare stomach.

My breath leaves me. A grotesque patchwork of bumpy, cross-stitched scars cover his entire back, gnarled flesh on top of gnarled flesh. I have never witnessed one before, but I know its aftermath, have heard of it from other faeries, know my own grandmother died of it.

A lashing. From the look of it, many.

Someone has whipped the king. Over and over again.

A deep terror trickles through me. *Who would dare whip the king?*

The letter opener feels heavy in my hands. The eagle clutches a branch from Lucan's Tree in one claw, and the Golden Whip in the other. No, it couldn't be—but it must.

The king was not whipped.

Prince Maxian was.

Brutality is in your blood, he said of my lineage, the glint in his eyes not curiosity but connection. This is the legacy of Amyria: led by monsters and murderers. I could end it all now—cut off the eagle's beak and watch the kingdom plummet into chaos.

But that is vengeance, not venturing to something better. Jeremee was right. High Fae will issue orders, faeries will die, and someone worse will rise from the bloodshed. Someone sadistic. Someone like Dominik. So today I will not take the king's life, if only to ensure a safer tomorrow.

If I am to fight the High Fae, it will have to be in their Houses, their bedrooms.

This is the logic I cling to as my eyes settle on a packet of black powder by the king's bedside. An unnatural powder. There is no time—and still, I make it.

Opening a letter addressed to Lila, I drop the black powder between the folds. I take the empty packet to the fireplace and fill it with ash. Death is waiting, and suddenly I don't want to be late. It is only then that I notice the silence.

The snoring has stopped.

Two violet irises glow in the dimness.

I do not move.

"Why?" he rasps.

My heart hammers, body locking up as he coughs.

"Why do you haunt me so?"

I do not dare breathe. My mind scrambles for a response, that I have returned to him to do what he bids, so long as he spares my friends. Yet the leverage they need is in my hands right now; it must be returned to Illusion, and I am not ready. Something tells me that once I give the king what he wants, I will never return.

"Tell me, when will I be free of your death? I know . . ." He trails off, eyes closing. Still, he mumbles, "I have wronged you, Mother. I have killed you both. But . . ."

His breathing slides into a deeper rhythm, and the king is snoring again. My heart doesn't slow. With my genius dampened, he thought I was Death. He thought I was a ghost. I force myself to tread around the destruction. Reaching the servants' door, I crack it open.

The moment it closes softly behind me, I am running again, sprinting down the servants' hall, feet slapping against the cobblestones.

I do not care.

My legs work harder, sweat beading behind my neck.

Ahead of me, I see it—the spot where I shall meet Death. When he melts from the shadows, offering a gloved hand, I leap into his arms, despite his puff of surprise, and cling to his robes.

He laces us away.

Chapter Forty-nine

THE NEXT DAY CRAWLS FORWARD, DOMINIK'S THREAT OF breaking again like a dark cloud in the distance. As hours pass, that cloud grows closer. After having her arm reset, resting, and taking a pain tonic, Briar has settled herself in the Illusion kitchens. She will give the signal.

In the meantime, Kassandra and I practice, our geniuses straining, my body tumbling into the wall, off the sofa. We practice until we hit the target every time. We argue, in hushed tones, over the envelope of black powder that sits on her glass parlor table. I urge Kassandra to sleep, to gather her strength; she refuses, and so do I. She washes in her bath, and I wash in the communal faeries' chamber, finding each other once more, dressed anew.

In the early afternoon, the note from Briar comes, delivered by a red-faced Benji. I pour him a water as Kassandra reads. She thanks Benji, and I hug him and shoo him downstairs again. When he's gone, when we are alone, Kassandra meets my eye.

"Dominik and his bedfellow are awake and have requested tea," she says. "Briar managed to slip in the tonic."

I let out a breath. "It should grant us an hour."

Kassandra kneels beside the glass table, her saffron dress fluttering around her like a tulip. Leveling a stare at the pile of black powder, she folds Briar's note into a square with sharp corners. I crouch down next to her.

"We should take as little as possible. Just to be safe," I say.

Briar's note hovers over the pile of black, then cuts it in half. Kassandra looks at me. "Have you ever had the powder from the coca plant?"

I pause. "Yes."

Her eyes narrow. "When?"

"Two years ago when I was cleaning up after your two hundred fifty-eighth birthday party. There was some left on the dining room table and I wanted to try it."

She leans back. "You jest."

"I do not."

My mistress searches my face, not finding what she seeks. Then Kassandra shakes her head, laughing.

"You're moonstruck," she says. "You don't go around doing random vices off messy tables!"

I quirk a brow, nod toward the black powder.

"This is different," she says.

"Because I wiped down the glass this morning?"

Even before the end of my sentence, my lips are tugging up into a smile. She gives me another gentle nudge, and I quite like being pushed around by a bratty fae in this way.

"Okay," she asserts, wiping her eyes with her free hand, Briar's note still in the other.

"Okay," I repeat.

"We need every advantage," she says, almost more to herself than to me.

It affects your genius directly, Carter had said.

"If they use this to hold us down, then we can use it to break their grip."

Kassandra nods, forming two small lines of black ash. Rolling up Briar's note, she hovers over one line, then snorts. Tipping her head back, she sniffs, blinking.

"How do you feel?" I ask after a moment.

"Fine."

When Kassandra glances at me, her eyes dilated to black, terror pierces my chest. With a sinking feeling, I recognize this expression. How many times have I seen it on Maxian, Dominik, Hector, and other High Fae of the Upper Court? I thought it was simply the look of violence, but now I understand it to be something else: unnatural power.

Kassandra hands me the rolled-up note, and I position one end over the black line, the other by my nose. Then I sniff, too.

My nose burns, as if I've inhaled ash, as if smoke expands my lungs.

"Breathe through it," Kassandra says.

I try, but the thick, oily sensation wriggles up my sinuses and into my brain like Reign magic. My heart pumps harder as my blood thickens to muck, my genius struggling to flap the oily magic off its wings. This is not the merriment of the mirthroot, the giddiness of hemp, the sultry seduction of wine. This isn't even the racing feeling of coca powder.

"Open your eyes," Kassandra demands.

The room bombards me with a myriad of brilliant, sharp colors. I inhale, and I can smell the soup in the kitchens below, hear the pulsing of Kassandra's heart next to mine, feel the spiderweb of veins beneath my skin, pinpoint the crumb of bread beneath one of my knees, crushed into the carpet. When I reach for my genius, it shoots through me, a black raptor with heaving, beating wings.

It is so much *more*.

And I experience *everything*.

Kassandra rises. Her tawny dress now radiates like a star, my black tunic a pit I could fall into.

"Would you like to take a stroll in the courtyards, my lady?" I ask.

"It's such a lovely day." She licks her lips. "I would love to."

THE OUTSIDE IS overwhelming. The emerald trees pop; the red flowers resemble droplets of blood.

Kassandra brings her parasol, shading herself from the sun. I tug at my tunic, thick and dark and entrapping.

"Stop tweaking," she grits out through shining teeth.

"I'm not—"

We pass by an Illusion guard to whom she gives a smile. I smile as well, though it feels more like a grimace. We promenade around a hedge, crunch down a path that winds toward Dominik's wing. We reach the northern wall, which casts a dark, cool shade across the plant life and the garden of Kassandra and the king's first date.

Kassandra takes a seat on the northern bench that abuts the ivy-covered wall. I stand beside her. Her eyes flick up to the top of the walls that surround us, where Illusion guards with bows across their backs patrol the area. I pull out the novel Kassandra requested and hand it to her. She sets down her umbrella and undoes the leather strap.

"I used to come here as a child," she whispers, eyes on the page before her. "I figured the best place to hide from Dominik would be right under his nose. Many guards will remember this."

She doesn't exaggerate.

Halfway up the ivy-covered wall at our backs is the balcony off Dominik's bedroom.

My mistress reads for a few minutes, tugging the plane in bits and pieces toward her. She layers its power along the back of her white-gloved hand. I reach for my genius, coaxing it, explain to the thing what will happen, what is needed. It flaps uncontrollably, its blackened wings heavy and thick.

We should've practiced with the powder in our veins, but there was no time and not enough powder. I extend my awareness to the plane around me, the lush, vibrating energy. The garden hums with life, with strain, as branches are clipped, seeds planted, weeds removed, trees isolated from their root system in individual mounds of soil, carved for the aesthetic of control. It is bursting with life that screams at its confines, and I can sense the ivy sucking the moisture from the brick behind me.

I extend my genius toward it, wishing to say hello.

The plant recoils, disgusted. The rejection weighs down my heart with oil.

"It's time," Kassandra mutters, resting her gloved hand, pulsing with power, on the seat beside her. I lean forward, my fingers brushing hers.

"I'm here," I say.

She takes a breath, eyes never leaving the open book in her lap. Yet her attention distends, a bubble of Illusion magic snapping around me, strong and bright. The black powder is working to boost her genius. Others will see her attendant standing in the shadows behind her—but I will be above.

"Good luck," she whispers, then swallows. "And Avery? I—"

I do not give her time to say goodbye.

Instead, I reach forward, my genius barreling down my arm, sparking against the plane, and I grip her hand. With every ounce of strength I have, I clutch her, our geniuses colliding, slipping over each other like blood, like oil, like the pain I carry in my ribs, an anguish that is all my own, that was wedged there by her, from her, a darkness that did not originate with either of us, a knowing that only we share, a furious, desperate, weeping desire to be good, to fail and try again, over and over—a stumbling through time and life, together.

Magic sparks between our palms, tunneling into the plane, a darkened mass of teeth and nails and pulsing murder, and I dig claws into it, heaving it toward me as she shoves.

Suddenly I am afraid.

In the seconds I have left, I brush my free hand against her ribs. A final goodbye.

Kassandra stiffens, but it is too late.

The mutilated magic descends upon me, and chunk by chunk, piece by piece, it tears me apart.

Familiar sensations rush through my hair, my stomach, my legs as they melt away, my existence woven into the plane itself. As I lace up and up and up, the garden falling away from me, something sticks to my side, something like a chipped diamond wedged into me, a painful pinching when I try to breathe.

So I don't breathe.

I don't speak, not as a scream slams against my teeth, cutting my tongue, as the mangled magic ribbons my body back into existence and I collapse, wheezing, in the shadow of the balcony. Panting, I press myself against the wall. I scan the patrolling guards. A foolish decision to do this during the day, but we refused to go another night of breaking.

Birds chirp in the garden below.

Someone turns a page.

I blink and the book is before me, my gloved hands gripping its binding as my genius—like a slinking silver cat—circles my ankles, its tail flicking an Illusion into the air. I blink, and a part of me is crouched by the balcony banister, rolling a silver ball of magic before the glass doors, another wall of Illusion to hide the brunette faerie, strong and muscular, sensitive and soft, and I hate that I admire her. I shake my head, once again pressed to the brick and glass doors, a faint shimmer of Illusion magic blocking me from the view of the guards.

You idiot! Kassandra hisses in my mind. *Why did you do that?*

My lady?

You took a piece of me with you!

How?

The fuck if I know! But I can't be in three places at once. My head—

The words on the page swim before me, the book almost slipping from my damp grasp. I roll the silver ball in front of the balcony doors to obscure the beautiful brunette faerie.

I can't, she grits out, and I am back in my body, trying to breathe through the pain.

I'll be quick, I think.

I don't know if I can—

I pull the two pins from my hair, crouching before the lock.

Straining, my genius slips under the door, and I gather the faintest sound of snores on the other side.

I am in the garden again, gripping a book I'm not reading. I'm pacing before the brunette faerie, I am the brunette faerie, I am a child with clumsy hands, picking the lock of a basement window, my father urging me on from the bushes.

Remember the coin pouch, he says.

Now is not the time for sentimentality, Kassandra cuts in. I shake my head again, but the pain swells, a splitting of my mind, the galloping of my heart.

I can't keep up three—

Drop the balcony Illusion, I say.

Are you in yet? she asks.

Are you in yet? my father asks. The window jerks in its frame, and I am shoving the pane upward, with all my strength. I slip inside the cool basement, dropping down on a desk.

The balcony doors click open. The snoring inside sputters, then starts again. My mind splinters.

Drop, I grit out. *Drop something—*

The silver ball pitches over the balcony edge, unraveling to a thread that lands before the silver cat. The cat pounces on the prodigal magic, the Illusion sighing in relief. The words on the page fall back into place, and the pain eases.

I am back in my body, my sweaty forehead pressed against the doorjamb, hairpins clutched in my hand. The air is cool and dark, filled with the scent of sex. I am inside Dominik's chamber. Slowly, so slowly, I turn.

Garish crimson-and-gold walls greet me.

What color is the furniture? Kassandra asks.

My mind reels as her voice bites into my side.

I twitch. *What are you doing here?*

I'm stuck in you. Now—furniture?

My focus returns to the room. From my position on the floor, the red velvet drapes surround the four-poster bed, the chest of drawers and armoire stained black, the trim details more the color of brass than gold. It's as if someone designed the room to look regal without ever having been in the Pith before.

He could've used his own décor allowance, I think.

The chipped diamond bites into my rib playfully. Now that this space is known to the both of us—me for the first time, and Kass for the first time in decades, I can picture the path out of here, lacing directly down to the garden once I am done, avoiding the stupidity of the balcony.

My eyes fall on the servants' door, blending in if one did not know where to look. At the very least, I could escape that way, but then I will be seen, no doubt, by one of Dominik's attendants. After last night, we do not want to test anyone's loyalty—no one but each other's.

Has the tea been drunk? she asks.

A servants' stand is to the left of the bed. I crouch forward, slinking along the carpet, until I can see the two teacups.

Drunk dry.

Based on the snoring from the bed, the sleeping tonic has taken effect. Dominik will eventually wake and may even rise after I've made my move, but not before then. That is what matters the most.

So I crawl to the side of his bed. His slack expression faces me, his companion on the other side of him. I cannot reach him like this, and it would be too risky to loom over his bedfellow. I must wait until he rolls over.

I slide under the bed, heart pounding, hand slipping into my pocket. I take out the king's gold letter opener, perhaps the only real gold in this room, and clutch it tightly.

Then, I and a sliver of my lady wait like monsters under her brother's bed.

Time passes. Kassandra turns a page, her hand twitching with effort. The Illusion magic pulses behind her of an attendant who is not there. I strain for my mind to remain where I am—muscles stiff, under the bed, listening to the sleepers above.

How long has it been? I ask.

She turns another page. *Almost a half hour.*

The tonic may wear off soon.

Perhaps I can help.

Is that possible?

How is it possible that some of my essence has woven into yours?

I fight the urge to groan. *How do we know so little about magic?*

Because it's easier for them if we do not know.

I think on this. *What can you see?*

Nothing. I can only feel your emotions. Hear what you hear, what you think.

Can you move up my body?

What the planes are you saying?

I breathe. *It's as if you're stuck in my rib.*

Gross.

I roll my eyes. *If I can hear you in my mind, doesn't that imply some of your soul is already there?*

Philosophical little Avery.

Meld your magic with mine again.

How? We aren't touching—stop that!

I dig two fingers into the spot on my ribs, pain blooming through my side. I grit my teeth, pressing harder.

Ouch, what the—you're making it worse!

What worse? I demand.

I'm slipping away.

I notice it, too, my vision dampening, my heart still racing, but my body slick with clammy sweat. The black powder is wearing off, and we don't know yet if nature will allow us to keep our own magic or render us—or just me—a Molder. This was the risk we both took—it must pay off. And with my clearing and weary mind, anger rises, for this is what the males experience all the time. This power, this awareness, this unfair advantage. How often do they take it?

Move to my tongue, I think before I can get away from myself.

How the planes—
Find a way.

The mattress creaks above me. I pause, clutching the letter opener in my hand. As I drag myself out from under the bed, I feel it—a pinching in my throat, a scraping—as if I have swallowed a gemstone.

Kassandra has moved, and so must I.

Now, she says.

I spring to my feet, looming over Dominik, who sleeps on his back. My eyes flick to his lover—Rose Tunes—face slack in deep sleep, magenta hair slung over one shoulder.

He'll wake, I say.

Be quick, then.

I place the letter opener between my teeth. With trembling hands, I grab his shoulder and hip and heave. His body rolls onto his side, facing away from me. He startles, snores halting. His body twitches, a grunt escaping his lips.

This is the only warning she'll get. *He's waking.*

I rip the letter opener from my teeth and, with all my strength, plunge it into the base of his spine. Dominik's body spasms. He grunts, sluggish.

I push it in farther, his legs twitching, spine arching, body convulsing. Rose stirs. Her tonic may still be in deep effect, but his wears off as the injury registers. The lord inhales deeply, his back expanding, lungs filling—a throaty wail building.

Open your mouth! Kass screams, my tongue pinching with pain.

I have to trust her. I do not have a choice.

I open my mouth as a slippery, shimmering, ashen magic tumbles out—a voice so rich and full, so true in its nature, even I believe he's in the room. I believe it to be Maxian.

"Do not forget yourself, Dom," the king says—I speak—Kassandra spins.

Dominik shudders beneath the Illusion unlike any I've experienced before, the wail dying in his throat. I part my lips again, leaning just above his pointed ear, and let the king, let Kass, finish.

"You can clear the House, but never forget who owns the land."

I twist the opener, something snapping in the column of his back. He lets loose a high-pitched keening. Then I am backing away as his entire body convulses in pain, the golden crest blurring in the air.

I stumble into the shadows. My genius stretches outward, scrambling under the balcony doors, tumbling over the edge.

"Wha—" a muffled voice starts. Rose. She shifts in the bed, groaning.

Now, I shriek in my mind. *Now, Kass—*

My genius expands beyond me, almost out of me, stretching, reaching, screeching as I push it down down down to the maiden in the garden below. Her silvery magic shoots upward like a spout, and suddenly the two are crashing, smashing into each other, the remnants of the oily, unnatural power fading away.

Lace! Kass screams. *Lace!*

My mind cannot stretch any farther; I am in the lord's bedroom, I am on the bench below, I am in the air between. It is time to let go, like we practiced, and I do.

I trust Kassandra with my life, and dissolve into nothing.

As my body breaks down to the smallest form, I fly under the doors, my essence elongating like putty, over the balcony, and in a moment, it is snapping together like a rubber band and my body slams into the brick wall beside me, an emptiness in my ribs.

I collapse to the ground in a heap, gasping. Before me, Kassandra sits on her stone bench, back to me, air shimmering with an Illusion that flickers. She turns the page in her book.

"Stand," she rasps. "Please, stand up."

My legs feel clumsy, but I grip the wall for support.

"You can let go," I tell her when I'm up.

The Illusion drops. Kassandra slumps forward, dropping the

book. On weak legs, I circle the bench and kneel before her, picking it up. She keeps her face buried in her hands.

"Shall we retire?" I ask, throat dry.

My mistress nods. The comedown has begun, the colors of the world darker, the air damper. I reach out my hand, she takes it, and together we stand. We hobble around the perimeter of the Illusion courtyards until finally we reach her chambers.

Once the doors are locked, Kassandra rips off the gloves covering her debt rings and I kick off my boots. We collapse on the ground, bodies sweaty, hearts pounding. I glance over at my panting mistress. She grins back at me, face flushed.

"One day, we will get them both," she promises.

"For now, we can enjoy them turning on each other."

"As they have tried to do with us so many times." Kassandra stretches out a tattooed arm. I clutch her wrist, and we lie there, reeling in our advantage and debt and hope.

"What is this feeling?" she wonders. "I like it on you."

I let my emotions flood around us. "Victory."

"Victory," she repeats. "It smells like a garden."

A few minutes later, the vomiting starts, black bile surging up our throats. It does not stop for hours.

Chapter Fifty

Dappled sunlight filters through the office, the smell of ink and paper filling my nose. It has been a few days since what the Nest now calls the Silver Slaughter—Dominik's massacre and his crippling. At first, Kassandra and I spent each waking hour in silence, drinking to numb the itching before passing out in various places. Only once did I arise to find my arms around her before rolling off the settee, face hot and heart heavy. She didn't stir until her meetings began, and they have not stopped. After tending to Briar, I headed to House of Healing.

I approach the grand beveled desk as Eli leans back in his chair.

"Kassandra's note said it was urgent. How can I help?" he asks.

"First, we would like more pain tonic sent to Briar."

"Of course."

I pull out a letter stamped with a wax seal. "As you know, Lady Kassandra has been indisposed in meetings with members of Illusion. I have instructions from her to act as a valet and deliver your response to her directly. She has given permission for me to negotiate on her behalf."

Eli takes the letter from my hands and breaks the seal, reading.

"As you know, both her brother and father are unavailable, leaving her temporary head of House," I say, then add, "With the approval of the other Illusion families. Their responses came in today by raven."

"Go on."

"The Head of Illusion would like to know more about what this is and why she hasn't heard of it before." Digging into my pockets, I pull out a small leather pouch and toss it onto the desk. Eli unties the leather strap and peers inside. The black powder.

"I see." He takes off his spectacles, rubbing his face. "Do you know where your mistress acquired this?"

I stare at him pointedly.

"Right, of course you couldn't tell me even if you knew."

"If it's any consolation, my oaths to Illusion and Healing would ensure that the truth remains unknown."

"It's called Ashent. My father originally developed it as a cure for Molders."

"But only faeries are Molders."

He sighs again, looking away. "Because they do not know of the cure. And even if they did, they could not afford it."

I frown. So, being magically mute is not just a faerie disease. No, the High Fae simply jump-start their magic again with this drug. *How many High Fae advantages are just manufactured?*

To say this to the Head of Healing would be treasonous. "You said originally? What is Ashent used for now?"

"My cousin oversees its production at our base in Remiti. She's the Healing advisor and believes that it could be the key to a stronger kingdom. A way to help High Fae, faeries, and Molders alike."

"And what do you believe?"

"That it's addictive, especially this new formula. It leaves certain High Fae . . . not in control of themselves."

The two black lines on a table between Dominik and Maxian. The twitching that still crawls over my skin.

"How many High Fae know of it?" I ask.

"Just the Council of Keepers. There's a vote on regulating its distribution in a few months."

I study him. "You are nervous."

"I've advocated against Ashent from the beginning, but there are many voices at play."

"How do you imagine it will unfold?"

He eyes me. "Why would you like to know?"

"Lady Kassandra does."

"The advisors, heads, and heirs of each House typically vote the same. Until recently, House of Illusion and Reign were in favor of broad distribution. House of Death is against, and unfortunately, on this matter, House of Healing is divided between my cousin and me, as we have no Heir of Healing. The heir must be a legitimate successor, not temporarily named for the voting. The king's vote breaks the tie by counting as one vote if the number of council seats is even, or two votes if the council seats are odd."

"So the number of seats a House has on the council can change at any time," I say.

"Yes, to give each House a . . . chance."

"At what?"

"Dominance."

Another reason why marriages and children are so demanded, even if birthing another baby kills the mother.

I begin counting. "Before King Gregor passed—may he wander well—the vote would've been seven in favor of Ashent. Three each for Illusion and Reign, and your cousin. Four would've voted against it, including House of Death and you."

"Correct. But much has changed, as you know. The number of seats has shifted, and so have the Houses."

"What if the Illusion votes swing the other way?"

Eli scoffs. "It would be easier to secure an heir."

"That could take decades, it seems."

"Not if the female can prove her pregnancy. Then she can vote on behalf of the future heir."

I blink. "The fetus gets a vote . . . but not the female who carries it?"

"Yes, unfortunately."

"Why?" I ask, failing to keep the fury from my voice. Others have mentioned this before, but I want a male to say it to my face. "Explain it to me. Please."

Lord Eli does not meet my eye. "Because there is a chance the fetus could be male. The mother is not."

Disgusting, I think. This is so violent and volatile and depraved. This is a gambling den, but the stakes are thousands of lives and millions of coins.

"And the Hearts have no votes," I say.

"No, because they tend to switch Houses once married. They could sit on the council, though, if they fell pregnant with the next heir."

And what if the royal vote were female? I want to ask. *If the council numbers are odd, then could the royal vote count as three for that individual? Or will you change the rules once again?*

I do not voice any of this. Instead, I focus on the task at hand, on the bargaining chip Kassandra has given me—my price for paralyzing her brother.

"My mistress has a deal to offer," I state. "When the time comes, she will vote against Ashent, whether she is heir or head of House, or holds both votes because of pregnancy."

Eli sputters. "I—I know Kass is my friend, but why support my perspective?"

"Because she agrees with you. It makes the males more violent."

"What would she like in return?"

I dig out the paper with Benji's name on it. "For the House to absolve this faerie of his Healing debts. And if Dominik somehow makes a miraculous recovery, then she will personally pay back the balance."

I hand the paper to Eli, and he scans the name. "That's it?"

"And," I venture to say, "the legal protections of Healing for this faerie."

Once I knew that Benji's debts—all of ours—are only owed to three Houses because Death does not collect, the plan fell into place. Dominik needed to be stopped, Kassandra needed power, Benji protection, the king to be isolated. Kass absolved the remaining Illusion debts of Benji, Briar, herself, and me, and granted us legal protections. *When my power is secured,* she said this morning, *we can forgive all the debt.*

Whether she will doesn't matter because Benji's freedom doesn't rest solely on her or me now. Now Benji is forgiven by two of the three creditor Houses, and protected by them for the foreseeable future.

"Done," Eli says, scribbling.

My vision blurs. That is all it takes for the fae to free. Just the scribble of a quill on paper, and a legacy of suffering has ended. As he hands the message to his valet to take to the teller's office below, I smile because Benji's rings will only cover one arm now, like they did before Jae's death.

There is only one House left that owns him. And I will do anything to set him free of it, even if it means plunging a knife into another fae back.

BEFORE I LEAVE the House of Healing, I knock on my friend's door.

"Come in!" Lila calls.

Opening the door, I stop. She smiles at me from a reading chair, hair in fresh long braids woven with loose curly strands that fall toward the ends. She looks relaxed and refreshed, something I haven't seen since I've known her.

"Your hair!" I gasp. "You look celestial!"

She beams. "I met another black faerie who works in the Healing library, and we got to talking. She knows about my hand and so she offered to come over to help with my braids. Apparently, she does a lot of other girls' hair as well."

"The style is so whimsical," I say, kissing both her cheeks. "Oh, and when you're ready, I have something for you."

"I'm ready now."

Setting my small bag down, I take out the ring of skeleton keys that belonged to her father. Her eyes well. Then I take the letters out, one by one, from our friends in the Pith. Lila reads, tears rolling down her cheeks. Pouring myself some water, I watch my friend work through a myriad of emotions. Her lips move with each word, as if reciting prayer. When she's ready, she looks up, laughing.

"Thank you."

I wipe my face. "Kass is opening an artist-in-residence program for faeries, sponsored by Illusion. You should apply."

She gestures to the seat next to me.

We talk for hours. We divulge our feelings, our nerves, details about our fathers and mothers and new favorite herbs, what we had for breakfast that morning and what activities we want to do now that spring has fully formed. We talk until our throats are sore, until there is a knock.

"Oh!" Lila's eyes widen. "I forgot about my appointment. Hide in the armoire."

I wrinkle my nose. "I'm not hiding in the armoire—"

"It's with Hector Vandorne."

Why in the planes is Hector Vandorne here?

"Get in the closet, *now*."

I grab my bag and tread to the giant chest on the far side of the room, and Lila closes me into the armoire.

Lord Hector Vandorne enters, grunting a hello. The chair creaks under his weight.

"Tea?" Lila asks.

"Not today, thank you. Lila, is it?"

My jaw clenches. She has served him her entire life in the Reign Household and he does not know her name.

"Yes," she confirms. "How can I help?"

"I'm afraid I've come to you today out of great desperation," he says. "The king—he is not the same since the incident in the library."

"I am not the same, either, as you can tell."

Hector coughs. "Yes, well—"

"Seeing that he took my hand."

"Well, yes—of course, of course. And I hope you know that he has been *riddled* with guilt ever since. He . . . you see, he was not in a good place, as this is the week his mother died about a century ago. As you know, this time of year is extremely difficult for him, and I think he—and the kingdom as a whole—truly could use your kindness once more."

He can't be serious.

"The king has banned me from Reign," Lila murmurs.

"I can invite you back—"

"He does not want to see me. He made that very clear last time."

"Like I said, he has been struggling."

"So have I."

Hector clears his throat. "How much?"

"What?"

"How much do you need in your account to convince you to enter the Pith again?"

My nails dig into my palms.

"No amount. I am not for sale."

"I can't force you because Maxian will know it is Reign magic. I need for you to go willingly."

"I will never go willingly."

Hector lowers his voice. "The king has stabbed Lord Dominik."

Lila gasps, and this is a real, genuine reaction. I have not yet told her—and I never will. No one will ever know the truth but Kassandra and me.

"We cannot bring it up to him, of course," Hector continues. "It could've been a member of the Reign servants, but Lord Dominik heard Maxian's voice, and no one else has been in and out of those rooms. We believe it was retaliation for bedding Rose Tunes."

"Rose Tunes?"

"The king's—well, as of last week, the king's betrothed. I believe that arrangement has not yet been broken."

"Apologies, Lord Hector, I meant to clarify—this was over Lady Rose Tunes?"

"Yes," he says. "What else could've caused this?"

"I heard from Lord Eli how particularly brutal the Silver Slaughter was."

The hairs on the back of my neck stand. *No*, I think. *Lila, for once, please do not dig into this. Please let this go.*

A cough again from Hector. "Yes, it was a true shame. But what is to be done about it now?"

What is to be done about it now? His mistress was killed that night, potentially his child, and this is his response?

"What would you like me to do?" Lila asks.

"Just sit with him, talk with him. Name your cost."

My mind screams at Lila to decline, that no amount of money is worth it. Yet my friend hums, thinking.

"I'd like information," she says.

"Anything."

"Who is at the center of the Pith?"

I press my forehead against the armoire, forcing myself to unclench my jaw.

Hector laughs. "The Reign House, of course."

"No, sir. What resides at the very center of the palace?"

The plane around us halts, stumbling, as if Death has entered. Yet he has not. Hector, it seems, has gone mute.

"There is something there, then," Lila reiterates.

Still no response.

"Tell me, or I will not go to the king."

Then I hear the strangest noise, subtle at first, a sound I never expected from a High Fae, never mind the advisor to the king himself.

The sound of gurgling. The sound of a blood oath.

"You have sworn an oath of silence." My friend's tone picks up. "I will think on this and get you my response tomorrow."

Hector lets out a breath. "Thank you. Thank you, again."

Once the advisor leaves, I tumble from the closet, glaring at my friend. She sips her tea, smiling. I yank a pink scarf off my shoulders.

"Why?" I ask. "Why would you do that?"

"Because I wanted to know."

"*Why?*"

"Why would the second-highest-ranking High Fae in all of Amyria take a blood oath? You say that something is alive beneath the palace. I say it's something powerful, too."

I point to her arms. "Why'd you risk your safety? Your debt—"

"Has been paid off."

"What?"

"My debt has been fully paid off," she repeats.

My knees sink to the carpet, and I catch her wrist.

"May I?" I ask. She nods, and I roll up both her sleeves.

Deep umber, untouched skin. A miracle. It's a miracle. She's free, and with legal protections from Illusion, she could stay free. I brush a thumb across her wrist.

"Why didn't you say?" My voice cracks.

"You're skeptical of Eli, and I didn't want you thinking I was trapped here. He's a friend but nothing more. I don't think he'll ever be more. And it's not because of sex," she laughs. "It's just that, well, he's a High Fae."

"But—but you've—"

"I've been busy. Who do you think gave Kassandra the idea for the faerie artist-in-residence?"

I marvel at her, not for the first time.

"I still have one hand." She smiles. "I can write letters, you know."

"So you—"

"Lady Kassandra seemed the most logical fae to approach,

anyway. Illusion patronizes all the halfling and fae artists. Why can't they sponsor a philanthropic cause like that of elevating the faeries?" My friend grins. "I told her to tell the council that it can be Illusion's attempt at civilizing us. Those stupid fools loved that."

"But—why didn't she say anything?"

Lila shrugs. "It was our business to conduct."

"Why didn't you? I could've helped—"

"You would've meddled."

"What did you give her?" I ask, my heart racing. "What was the cost?"

"Besides that of the program?"

"Yes, why did she agree? Kass is . . . she's . . ."

But I don't have the words because I don't know what Kassandra is or who she's become. How did such change happen in only a season?

"I don't understand," I say, my hands clasping hers. "Where did this come from?"

Lila smiles. "From you."

"But I haven't done anything."

My friend leans forward, eyes glinting as she whispers: "You've folded her into your heart. Isn't that everything?"

"I—" I shake my head, voice cracking. "But I could only do that because you brought me into yours."

My friend's grin grows wider. "And I wanted to be your friend the moment I saw your and Briar's connection. I thought, *Now, that is someone admirable. That is someone I want in my life.* I'm just happy you felt the same way."

My chest swells. Little sparks of kindness, all beginning with a faerie who sought a family. Does she know that in her waiting and wanting and willingness, she has created one? I stand, blinking, wiping my eyes.

"Are you staying here?" I ask.

"No, I'm applying to the artist-in-residence program."

"Please don't go to the Pith," I beg.

"I don't think I will."

I pause, assessing her, seeing her glowing and happy. It has never been so clear to me as now that I must return to the king to fulfill this favor, whatever it may be. For if I don't go to him, he might come after my friends.

The question is: How much time do I have before he calls in his due?

Chapter Fifty-one

I HAND THE VIAL TO BRIAR. SHE DUMPS THE PAIN TONIC INTO her juice as I collect a plate of plain chicken from the Illusion kitchens.

"Want more tonic?" I ask when I return.

"How about a back rub?"

Sighing dramatically, I stand behind her. My hands massage at the tense muscles in her shoulders, careful to not move too deeply in fear of jostling her broken forearm.

Her otherwise unmarked arm. She is now free of debt, as with Kassandra's signature she deposited the rest of the silver coins. I run through the catalog of faeries I call family: Lila and Briar are completely free, Benji's Healing debts were paid off this morning, his Illusion debts erased yesterday.

"How long is your sick leave?" I wonder.

"Kassandra said until I feel better."

"Be sure to milk it."

Briar grins up at me. "It's fully paid."

I snort. "Spoiled faerie."

"Say that to my arm, again."

I keep massaging her shoulders, the older faerie leaning into the comfort that I feel honored to provide. It all began with the spry, unassuming faerie in front of me, the wisdom of her years and extension of her heart.

"Why were you kind to me when we first met?" I ask.

"It's scary, becoming a Night Crest."

"But you've seen so many of us, know we'll get replaced. Wouldn't it be easier to just not try, I guess?"

"That's when someone needs kindness the most."

"How?" I rest my hands on her shoulders. "How have you not let it all leave you bitter?"

She turns in her seat to look at me square on. "I am bitter, and that is exactly why I must try. Every time."

"I don't understand."

"Ask yourself, who benefits from your sadness? It's normal not to want to go on, to wake up and do it all over again. But we don't do it for them, never for them. We do it for ourselves. We do it because our despair is their success. It slows us, stops us. We can feel sad, but we cannot stop going on."

"To act like we don't hurt—is that not a betrayal to ourselves?"

Briar leans into me. "We do not need to be happy. We need to be joyful." She cups my face in her hand, her dry palm scraping against my cheek. "Joy in the face of such misery is its own rebellion." She lets me go, then calls, "Silas!"

Briar waves at the befuddled halfling, who strides across the Illusion dining hall to us, adjusting the stack of papers in his hands.

"How are the meetings going?" I ask him.

"The other Illusion families have approved me for the role of accountant."

Briar grins. "Do they know you're a halfling?"

"How can they, when they do not live at court?"

I laugh. "Congratulations."

He nods, then his attention falls to Briar. His cheeks flare with color.

"Briar." He bows. "I wanted to confirm . . ."

"Of course we're still on for lamb chops tomorrow," she says.

I glance between them. "What's this now?"

"I like to cook—"

"A date," Briar declares, laughing. "It's a date!"

Silas blushes harder, and he wipes the fog from his glasses. When he puts them on again, he looks to me. "Have you seen Benji yet today? He was just looking for you."

Perhaps to show off only his one arm of debt.

"I'll find him, thanks."

I leave the halfling and faerie together, Silas making small, quiet comments, and Briar cackling with an ease that fills my heart.

If joy is like a rebellion, then perhaps a rebellion is like joy: contagious.

I FIND BENJI playing jacks with a friend in a hallway off the common room. For a moment, I just watch, my heart brimming with an unspeakable emotion, as the children bounce a rubber ball on the ground between the jacks.

Benji's gangly limbs have grown, and it is the most beautiful sight in the world. His debt only goes up to one elbow. I kick off the wall.

"Hey, Bee," I say.

Benji looks up. "Hi, Avery!"

"So who's winning?"

"Me!" the friend shouts.

"No, he's not, he's lying."

I throw Benji a skeptical look.

He crosses his arms.

"Okay, so maybe he's winning, but just a little."

The other child beams up at me. "Benji says that you can light your arms on fire."

"Only sometimes." I laugh, then brush Benji's shoulder. "Is everything okay? Silas said you were looking for me."

"Yes!" He bounces on his heels, sticking out his arm. "The creditor said there was something in my account. All of my debt went away except for Reign. But there is an offer on my account that even that could be forgiven!"

Kassandra? My heart cracks in relief, and I scream, scooping Benji up in my arms.

"Put me down!" he giggles. "Put me down!"

I do, gasping, "This is incredible. How?"

"The creditor said the offer was conditional."

"Conditional?" I frown. "What do you mean?"

"The creditor said the condition is that you need to do something and then my Reign debt would be forgiven. I'll be protected by Reign under some special rule *and* I'll be unmarked!"

My brows furrow. "I have to do something?"

"I found this on my pillow earlier." Benji pulls paper from his back pocket. "It's addressed to you."

I take the paper from him and unfold it. Scrawled in elegant, familiar handwriting, is one word.

Soumeter.

My stomach plummets. "I . . ."

"We're not really sure what it means," the other boy says.

I stare down at the word.

Soumeter.

The babe is mine. So, in a way, mother and child are both mine, the king had said.

Benji's stable.

Benji's pillow.

The message is clear; he will not wait any longer.

I have run out of time.

"Let me see your arm," I say.

"What is it?" Benji asks, revealing the four remaining rings. "They're almost gone!"

So, this is all that remains—four debt tattoos on his right arm that all belong to House Reign. Submit, and the king will forgive

Benji's remaining debt and protect that freedom. The boy would be legally protected by all three of the crediting Houses. A privilege so few have, not even most High Fae.

Refuse, and tattoos could strangle all of his limbs once more. One stroke of the quill, and the wealthiest House will decimate a boy, as it has decimated countless children before. Would Healing and Illusion fight for Benji? Would they want to, potentially risking war? Not over a faerie, surely.

Soumeter.

"Avery?" Benji tugs on my sleeve. "Did I do something wrong?"

"No." I bend down to hug the child, my brother, the faerie who has already lost so much, too much. "Everything's okay. I love you."

"I love you, too." He hugs me back, planting a wet kiss on my cheek.

Reign begins with the body, and Maxian will not own Benji's anymore—not his labor, not his life. Even if I must pay for it with mine. I don't know what the king has in mind, but months ago I said I would do anything to free my family. And I will.

Pride, after all, is such a small sacrifice in the face of hope.

Chapter Fifty-two

If I go now, I could be back in time for dinner, and Kassandra will not suspect a thing. This is what I tell myself as I slip the golden moth onto my finger. Perhaps I can swing by the Mouth first, speak with Carter and Fern. But the sooner I go to the source, the sooner it'll be resolved. Whatever is coming my way, I have leverage: the scars on the king's back, the screaming voices, the blood bargains and blood oaths sworn to keep family secrets buried. And whatever remains, in the center of it all.

We may not be on equal footing, but that doesn't mean I hold no ground.

Taking a breath, I lace to the Pith.

I land on the wooden parquet floors, which rise to greet me. The fireplace to my right is cold and empty. The king's bed to my left is made, sheets tightly tucked into the corners. The apartments are empty. Did I misinterpret the message?

A floating bottle of sparkling wine appears before me, accompanied by two crystal goblets. A note attached to the bottle instructs me to pour. So I do.

Uncorking the bottle, I grasp it midair, then tip the liquid into a goblet. Before I can reach for the second crystal goblet, it drops to the floor, shattering at my feet. I stare, the bottle in one hand, the filled goblet in the other, shards all around my shoes.

"You always were clumsy."

I force myself not to jump, lest I step on the glass.

Maxian materializes before me in a loose white shirt and dark pants. Simple, clean, skin clear—he is the opposite image of a few days ago. His dark-honey hair falls in waves; his eyes spark with amusement. He does not look like a halfling, not at all, and suddenly I do not understand what a halfling is supposed to look like besides a tattoo on each wrist.

He extends a hand. I offer the goblet. He shakes his head, smiling.

So I offer him the bottle. Still he shakes his head.

"I want your hand, Avery."

"Yes, Your Magnificence."

I start to lower the bottle to the ground.

"Weren't you ever taught manners?" he says. "Never put an opened bottle on the ground. Someone might knock it over and spill it."

I watch him. *What does he want?* My gaze settles among the bottle, the goblet, and his outstretched hand. Bringing the goblet to my lips, I sip the wine. It's sickly sweet, bubbly. Maxian smiles, quirking a brow. I down the whole goblet, wipe my mouth with the back of my hand, the feeling acrid on my teeth.

"Again," he says.

So I pour a new glass and swallow that one down, too.

"Do you like it?" he asks.

"Yes."

"I thought you would. It's the wine from the coronation."

The bottle and goblet feel heavy in my hands, these strange weights leaving me vulnerable. Already, the two glasses of sparkling wine fizzle in my empty stomach. Perhaps coming here before dinner was a mistake.

"The wine from the coronation?" I ask.

"You had some, did you not? When Death arrived?"

There's a mischievous glint in his eye.

How could he know that? If I lie, will he perceive it as an affront? As a reason to wrap Benji in debt once more? Or will he find me rolling over and showing my belly to be boring? I go with the safe option: praising his intellect.

"I did not realize you knew," I answer. "How?"

"Well." He clasps hands behind his back. "I could smell it on your breath."

"I see."

"Shall you have another?"

"Do you want me to?"

He startles, blinking. "I want you to be relaxed. You're my guest, of course."

Scanning his face, I look for any signs of Ashent, the drug, the synthetic magic. The House of Reign may attribute his erratic behavior to him taking too much. In swapping the drug with fireplace ash, I fear the opposite: his withdrawal.

"Your thoughts, Avery."

"I'm trying to discern a second meaning in your words."

"What use do I have for many meanings?"

To prove you're clever.

"To detect if I am clever," I say.

He chuckles. The sound reverberates in the empty apartments.

"Do you enjoy my test?"

"I enjoyed the wine."

He laughs again. "Then have another."

But this is fae wine, and two glasses back-to-back have the room swaying.

"What's the matter?" he asks, circling.

"Nothing, I—"

"Then drink."

The situation is slipping sideways faster than I can grasp. I fill the goblet up to the top and force it down. Bile surges up my throat, and I swallow that, too. My belly bloats with alcohol and air. I don't think I could fit another glass into my body if I wanted.

"Again," he commands.

The goblet slips from my sweaty fingers, smashing at my feet, beads of glass nicking my ankles.

"It was an accident," I gasp, blood roaring in my ears.

"Again."

We watch each other.

Tipping the bottle back, I choke down the last of the effervescent liquid, my stomach roiling. I burp, wiping my mouth with my hand.

"Now put the bottle down."

I crouch, placing the item among the shards. I realize my mistake too late. I lose my balance and fall—

Something yanks me up, hauling me away. A shoe kicks off, and I yelp as the king swings me into his arms.

"You don't trust me?" he asks.

No, I don't, I almost say, before shutting my mouth. I close my eyes. This was a mistake. A terrible mistake. How, even after everything, did I think I could manage this? Was it pride, or was it something more dangerous like hope?

"I want to," I say, the half lie tasting just right.

He gives another laugh, moving away from the ring of broken glass. "I know," he coos. "I know."

The room whirls, and I will be sick if it doesn't stop; I need anchoring, and the only option is to cling to him.

You are already king . . . Why—

"I am."

Opening my eyes, I gaze up at his square jaw, those deadly lavender eyes.

"I said that out loud, didn't I?"

The corner of his mouth quirks up. "What did you mean by it?"

My fingers trace his full lips. "You enjoy being king?"

"Who wouldn't?"

"Then why is it not enough?"

His expression falters, brows knitting. A small voice in the back of my mind screams for me to stop, but my tongue feels loose, my thoughts spinning away.

Why must you be the center of my *world? You are already the center of everything else.*

My body sinks into a soft mattress. My eyes fly open—I had not known they had closed—and I take in Maxian's broad shoulders above me, blocking out the light. Beneath him in his bed, I understand now. He cannot forget what I did last time I was here, and so he must find a way to paper over it with other memories. Does it keep him up at night? If I weren't beneath the royal now, this thought would satisfy me. No, instead, anxiety ripples my body. This isn't a seduction for him, not even dominance. This is revenge. This is him reclaiming the control I stole.

I shudder. Maxian brushes a thumb along my temple, shifting hair from my eyes.

"Are you cold?" he asks, his weight descending across my stomach, but it's too much. It presses on the churning acid. Sweat breaks along my back, my vision blurring. No. No, I—

"I'm going to be—"

Maxian leaps back as I lurch over the mattress and vomit. He swears. My body pitches forward again, and a strong arm bands around my waist. More vomit and spittle drip from my mouth, my throat and nose burning.

"Fuck," he grunts, and then he's snapping his fingers. "Fuck."

A groan tumbles out of me as the king pulls back my hair. My breath is shaky, eyes welling.

"Don't worry about the floors," he says. "Someone else will clean it up; another faerie is on their way."

The last scrap of my control unravels.

I sob.

Great, heaving gasps, my face heating, twisting, wet with snot and tears and spit. It is not delicate. It is ugly and wretched and unstoppable.

The king swears again, lifting hair off my neck.

"It's okay," he whispers. "It's okay, you're not in trouble."

I sob harder.

Maxian gathers me into his arms once more, pressing me against his chest, and we are moving across the apartments. We enter the echoing ceramic bathing chamber. As I pull my head back, I catch sight of us in the looking glass: the golden hero holding his maiden. A faerie shattered only for the sake of his saving.

The king sets me down on a bench, a basin carved from stone to my left, and in front of me an empty inlaid pool, glinting sienna tiles. Lila was right; it is halved by a great jagged wall like the one in the Salon of Stars.

Maxian kneels before me and unties my shoe. I lean against the wall, breathing through the queasiness, as his warm, soft hands roll down my socks and clasp my bare heels.

"I always forget how strong fae wine is, especially for faeries." He looks up at me. "Why didn't you say anything?"

It hurts, how beautiful and monstrous he is.

"I wanted to impress you."

He huffs a laugh.

"Your naivety is endearing," he says.

Like a child is all I hear, and because I am feeling vicious and bitter, I ask: "Attractive?"

Thick fingers wrap around my ankle. "Perhaps."

I spit up on my tunic. Maxian reaches for me, hauling me to the basin. I clutch the stone counter and get sick again, my legs giving out. He holds me up as I vomit again and again, until there is only stomach acid, and even that I eject.

Footsteps.

"Your Magnificence, are you ill? I saw the—" The voice stops. Carter stands at the threshold with linens and a small vial. His attention lands on us, me hunched over the basin with the king behind me. "Oh planes. I—Avery? I—"

"It's all right," Maxian says. "Too much wine."

"Let me take her off your hands. I'm so sorry that you had to witness—"

"It's okay, like I said. Leave the towel and fresh shirt."

Carter doesn't move. "I . . . are you sure?"

"Yes, I'm happy to take care of her tonight." His grip on my hair tightens, my scalp tingling. "After you clean up the vomit in the bedroom, you're dismissed for the night."

The valet's eyes flare with concern, scrutinizing my face. The plane rumbles around us, unsteady territory. *Go*, I try to convey. *Please just go, you're making it worse.*

Carter blinks and the concern is gone, replaced with something else. He glances to his master. "Thank you, my king. This is truly kind. Please feel free to call for me anytime."

"Of course."

Fingernails dig into my hip. I hold back my grimace. Carter gives me one last wide-eyed stare before departing. The tension in the plane eases, like a bumpy path now smooth.

"Can you stand for a moment?" Maxian mutters, and I nod.

He crosses the chamber, gathering the items by the door. In the meantime, I splash water on my face, rinse out my mouth. He presses the tonic into my hand, and I uncork the ginger concoction and drink, and my stomach settles. Maxian grabs a small container to the right of the basin and opens it. Inside is a mint paste that I rub across my teeth and spit out. Although my reflection shows a sallow-faced faerie, I feel my strength gathering, head clearing. I just need to stall while I think of a plan.

Until the king stands behind me, his wide torso pressing into my back, and wraps his arms over my chest. His mouth grazes the tip of my ear.

"What did you think of my note?"

I shiver.

He smiles, interpreting it as something else, and then his mouth is descending, hot and wet, along my neck. I tense, my mind emptying. A hand wraps around my throat, tilting me to the side so that he has greater access. It was our position in the boxing ring, when he apologized for Dominik's bite, the press of his body against mine, his readjustments. Was he hard, even then?

Soumeter.

In the reflection of the looking glass, the bulky male falls on the female's throat, the crook of her shoulder. He nips at the skin and the female pales like a statue. The male lifts his head, eyes darkening, grip tightening on her neck, a rough mockery of my grasp on Rose's throat.

"Your thoughts, Avery."

Soumeter. Still, the female cannot school her expression this time, her body recoiling, every part closing up.

"Avery," he growls, his other hand cupping my chin, forcing me to look at him. My chin still aches from how he grabbed it in the library, despite the healed skin. Emotions flash across him like the purple and gray and blues of shadows on a mountain face. "Your thoughts on my note?"

"I want it in writing," I manage, mouth dry. "If you draw up the contract, I will—" I breathe, a piece of me breaking away like a clod from a riverbank. I can't think of an escape. No one is coming to help, even if they wanted to. The only plan is survival, and then I will reassess. I can survive this. So I let myself get sucked into the current. I will let myself drown in it, if it means that Benji can reach solid ground.

"You'll what?"

He has yet to use his Reign magic on me this evening. But that isn't the point of *soumeter,* is it? He is interested not in reflexive obedience, but rather in the slow and deliberate erosion of my will until it resembles his.

"Draw up the contract," I say. "And I will draw us a bath."

It seems I will not make it back in time for dinner.

Chapter Fifty-three

THE KING SHOWS ME THE PARCHMENT, THE TERMS, WITH BENji's name attached, and we stand, still clothed, before the streaming pool.

"Satisfied?" he asks as I read the words for the third time.

I cannot find a loophole. This note will ensure Benji's autonomy for now, at least, so that he can build wealth and a future. If the king revokes the boy's legal protections, and a complaint is leveled against him, then perhaps the other Houses will uphold their promises and defend the faerie. Perhaps not, but this letter grants time. Money. Savings.

So finally I nod, handing it back. Maxian snaps his fingers and the contract disappears.

"Your turn," he says.

Nausea sways me once more, but I push it down. I push everything down, then conjure images of another bathing chamber, a silver one, and the silver fae who swims in its water.

I pull my tunic over my head. Rolling down the undergarments, I step out of the pile of clothes, and my nipples peak in the cold. Before me, the king is fully dressed, his attention dropping to my waist, my thighs.

Let's play a game, let's play a game, let's play a game. I chant until my defiance and fear churn into something soft and acceptable: a coy challenge.

"Satisfied?" I ask.

"Get in the water."

I touch my toes to the steaming, simmering pool. The heat sears my skin. I suck in a breath.

"Keep going," he instructs from behind as his clothes smack against the floor. When I try to look back, he commands, "Forward."

So tonight, he will direct and I will have to play along.

The burning rises to my knees, my skin red, my body clenching in anticipation.

"One more step," he says.

I sink into the heat, the water singeing between my thighs. I gasp as it slaps against my sex, painful and pleasurable, and although I beg my body not to—it reacts. Shivers run up and over my skin, a betrayal my mind cannot comprehend. As the king moves farther into the pool, the water laps against me, then retreats, the chilly air rushing against my sensitive clit.

No.

I do not want this. I know I do not want this. But I want my friends to be free, I want to walk away with that contract in hand and leverage from his back and his lineage even if nothing else in me is intact.

Maxian maneuvers past me so I cannot see his scars, lowering himself onto one of the submerged benches. The water hits his chest, and he spreads his arms, leaning them against the ledge. The practiced movement of someone with something to hide. I try to relax my expression, keep out the twitching as something in me recoils in disgust. *Please stop this. I don't want to feel this.*

He cocks his head and observes every inch of me. *Does he know my true thoughts?* I wonder as I start to understand his. It is like that night in his bed, the fight in the library: He wants me to enjoy it, against my will, as he was aroused by me against his. The way he looked confused at his palm as I walked away. Well, he does not look confused now, and I cannot walk away.

He blows on the water, a strong, strange wind. The heat once again envelops my clit, then drops away, the dance of warm and cold like a lover's breath. My thighs press together.

"Avery," he chides.

I close my eyes, breathing. I do not want to let go. I must, I must give in, but still, a part of me claws against the rising tide of desire, the water kissing my sex over and over and over as he moves it with his mind. A low moan builds in the back of my throat. I fight it the entire way. The feeling of standing in a different bath, the vulnerable offer, the sting of rejection. My desire begins to ebb.

"Why are you denying what you want?" he drawls.

"I'm not," I breathe.

"Prove it, then."

Soumeter, soumeter, soumeter.

He will know if I fake it—I was his teacher in that lesson. I dip my hands into the water, then, dripping, palm each breast. I work each nipple, pinching, twisting. I am swaying, I am ascending, my breaths coming in ragged, the air thin and strange. I am only sensations: the lapping water, the biting pain, the cold air, the weight of his gaze dragging down my figure.

"I—I can't—"

"Yes, you can."

What I said to Rose, and she to me. Reign magic tumbles around me, a rocky grip, fortifying my thighs. He holds me in place as the water slaps harder against my clit over and over and over.

"No." But it's a weak protest, a playful, breathy one—to him.

Inside, I am screaming, begging my body to shut down, but it does anything but—not as solid arms wrap around my hips, hands knead my ass, pointed teeth graze across my stomach, and I cannot stop my own fingers from pinching my nipples harder as the Reign magic has taken over, as he has taken over. He is not betraying me; he is making me betray myself.

My hips buck, eyes burning with unfallen tears, as desire builds.

I thought it would be less painful this way.

"Are you almost there?"

"Yes."

His teeth are sinking into my hip, biting, and I cry out in shock. His hands are on my back, and he is lowering me, slipping a leg over one shoulder, then the other. The warm water embraces my spine as he lays me across the top step, my hips lifted in the air, my fingers twisting painfully, ceaselessly, at my nipples, the Reign magic locking them in. And what died, unspent, between Kassandra and me is once again resurrected against my will.

"Please," I beg.

Maxian descends, dragging his tongue up my center. I cry out again, bucking, but he holds me in place. He sucks on my clit, fingers gripping my thighs painfully, as I work—as he works—my sore breasts.

No, but it's too late, heat and humiliation warming my chest, my neck, my cheeks. He pulls back. "You're throbbing."

"Stop," I gasp, and finally our gazes lock. His cheeks are flush with desire, his hair damp and ruffled, between my legs. How many fae crave this sight, to have the king on his knees before them? How many would do anything for it?

"We can stop. We can stop anytime." His stubble grazes my thigh. "I'll just need to call Carter back in with the contract so I can void it."

"Wait—"

He cocks a brow, kissing my inner thigh, murmuring, "What will it be, then?"

My head falls back, and tears roll down my temples. I do not know the answer. I am too drunk on many things to be clever. His Reign magic drops away from my hands, but they move on their own volition now, my pussy pulsing, pelvis pushing closer. There is no answer, there is just the plan: survive.

"Please," I manage.

"Please, what?"

My voice echoes throughout the chamber, sounding small.

"Finish me."

"Good faerie."

He takes me into his mouth, tugging, working. But the body is hollow, mind severed from this moment. He notices and bites me hard, and I cry out, for maybe I cannot survive this, here with him. So I do not stay with him, or find Kassandra or any of the other beautiful High Fae.

I think of confessing this later to Jeremee, hiccupping and crying in his arms as I did after so many other losses, and him stroking my hair, kissing me because Death was right. I do not seek approval in males, only protection. They will touch us anyway, so we may as well find the gentlest ones. The one I would whisper to under the tables of the common room when we were kids, telling him all the things my father did. The one who worried, who refused me when I wanted him the most, my friend, my first and original friend, the only safe harbor in an unsafe world. Destroyed now. Jeremee a destination I can never return to even if I always long for it. Long for my home.

The king's grip is painful, grabbing my breasts, and my body floods again with feeling, that building, that swelling, that filling until I am bursting with it, until I can take it no more.

Then Maxian plunges two fingers into me and rips the orgasm out.

Chapter Fifty-four

MAXIAN BATHES ME. HE TUGS ME DOWN UNTIL THE WATER hugs my belly button, propping me up on his knee. I do not protest, do not even make a noise, as he washes away the moment, the soap bar scraping against skin. I wince as he cleans tender flesh, bruises developing across my chest, my hips. He must've grabbed me roughly, forced the Reign magic to do so, and I did not know until now, when pleasure has been washed out for pain.

He hums. He lathers my back, pulling wet hair onto one shoulder. Then he cradles my skull in one palm and looks down at me. His full lips part, his brow pinched in the smallest hint of concern.

"Do you trust me?" he asks.

"I want to."

He dips me backward. Seizing up, I scrabble for purchase, and he offers his other hand, which I grasp with both of mine.

"It's okay," he says. "I'm just washing your hair."

The panic abates, and he is not wrong. Maxian balances me with one arm behind my back, the other stroking my scalp. Still, I sink my nails into that forearm.

The king untangles my hair, and it floats around me, a weight off my neck. He massages my scalp in slow, gentle circles. The water is so warm, the air so thick, and Maxian is reduced to two tender hands, a strong arm keeping me from drowning.

A sigh heaves out of me. Is this what my mother felt like, puffy-eyed, exhausted but relieved, all those nights we returned to my father? Is this why she let him clean up the rooms, wash our clothes, hold her on their shared cot even after the worst of fights? He was the only comfort around.

Forgive me, Mama, I think. *I understand now.*

I was arrogant enough to criticize how she did the impossible, but she still did it. She left an abusive partner. But I cannot. Not yet. So, like a river flowing downhill, I concede. Maxian dries me and dresses me in the fresh shirt and a pair of his drawers.

In his bedroom, he waves a hand, and the fireplace roars to life. I dry my hair in front of it, kneeling on a lush carpet, using a comb he hands me.

Fern brings in a platter of fruits and vegetables and various cheeses and bread rolls. I keep my gaze on the fire, refusing to meet her eye. The king asks for more wine, and some water. No, just this platter is fine. When the king dismisses her, I feel the smallest graze of her hand on my back. Then she is gone, too.

Maxian finds his seat next to me on the floor, drawing down pillows, materializing a blanket. He sweeps my hair to one side, kissing my exposed shoulder.

I doubt he will allow me to touch him tonight, wind him undone again, as I did before. And yet receiving from him does not feel like taking or having or indulging. It feels hollow.

So there is nothing to lose. My hand trails up his back and lands on his scars.

The king freezes.

I trace the raised skin, the entire patchwork of wrecked flesh—knotted, deep, each scar as wide as my palm. These do not come from an ordinary torture tool. They come from the official weapon of Reign: the Golden Whip.

He swallows. The orange and crimson and gold of the flames dance before us. I turn my head, taking in the paling face of the king.

"I am sorry this happened to you," I say, and I mean it.

He lets out a shaky breath, gulping his wine, square jaw working. "It was . . . a lesson well learned."

Something in my chest cracks. I turn toward him, and we kneel before each other, knees touching like in the training halls and between our lover's legs and in the library.

"That does not mean it was well deserved," I say.

Maxian shrugs. "It taught me discipline, obedience."

"When did it happen?"

"A century ago."

A century ago. Where have I known that before?

His mother.

His brother.

Maxian glances at the fire, running a hand through his hair. I never got the full picture, could only draw conclusions from a tapestry.

"Do you want to speak of it?" I ask. "I still have the oath. I could never tell anyone."

"I should kill you for even asking."

"But you haven't. Why?"

He looks to me, then away. "Because I still haven't asked you something yet."

The world slides away from me. Have I not already given him what he's asked for? He wanted me to come against my will, to take me until it hurt—how is that not enough?

Still, I breathe until my pulse evens out.

"What . . . what do you want to ask me?" I rasp.

"It will only make sense once you know more about me." He pulls back, lying down on the ground. I decide I can do this—to know, to understand, I will do this. As he settles on the blanket, among the pillows, I crawl to him, rest my head in the crook of his shoulder. I let him tuck me into his side, allowing the illusion of our coupling to continue.

"It was over my mother," Maxian says. "And me."

I rub my palm over his chest in soothing circles.

"You see . . . my mother was the queen's faerie. Her attendant." He clears his throat, and I dare not move. "My grandfather had more bastards than you could count. They were all sent to the mines. I do not know if any have survived. They would be dead by now, anyway. My father was different. My father hadn't seeded any other bastards before me, and neither had the queen fallen pregnant. So it wasn't a problem that I was a halfling, because I was still strong enough to pass for fae. To continue the royal line. Strong like you."

"I am not strong," I say, bereft.

"There is something unyielding in you. Like those ancient trees in fae tales, with their deep roots and wide, tall trunks that can weather anything." He tilts his head so we are nose to nose. "You are the strongest faerie I have ever met. Save for one."

"Your . . . mother?"

He looks back up at the ceiling. "She and the queen both raised me, and I did not understand why the queen didn't hate her attendant until the end. But the beginning of the end was Phillip."

P.V.

Phillip Vandorne.

"A full-blooded, Reign fae child. A miracle. Except that Phillip, you see, was born without a genius."

The air in the room disappears. No, this isn't correct. No one is born without a genius.

"Did he become a Molder, your brother?" I ask, blood roaring in my ears. Is this why Eli's own father invented Ashent? To cure a royal of a faerie disease?

"You cannot lose magic you never had."

But a creature without a genius would be like a creature with no soul.

"I . . . I don't know what to say," I respond, numb.

"At first, House Healing believed that he was slow to develop, like my cousin Daisy. She did not develop a genius until six years old."

"What . . . what happened to her?"

"Born sick, like more and more of the Reign children seem to be. Eventually a fever did take her. Fewer and fewer make it to adulthood, and when they do, their geniuses are weak, but there. Until Phillip. They tested him for years. They could not find his genius. Could not develop it, even as they destroyed the boy in the process."

"Oh, Maxian" is all I can say, and this pain I do not falsify. What a terrible, brutal existence for a child, to lack the companionship of a genius, to be prodded and experimented on by Healers, to live in isolation of the plane, of plants and people.

"The medicine they developed for him did not work. The other Houses knew that the queen had birthed a sick child, and with this excuse, we kept him out of sight. But it was getting harder and harder to prove that his magic was only just delayed. By his tenth birthday, there was still no sign, not even a trace, of a genius."

I stare up at the thousands of candles that float above us, as if we are living on a star.

"What happened?" I whisper.

"My father."

Gregor the Great, Gregor the General, the fae who defeated House of Death during the Dark Rebellion and rebuilt the palace of Versara.

"My father did not want a child without a genius," Maxian mutters. "On Phillip's tenth birthday, when the Head of Healing—Eli's father—declared him magicless, my father took out the whip."

Goosebumps line my skin, despite the fire and heat of the body next to me. "The—"

"Yes, the Golden Whip." Maxian's voice is flat, distant. "At first, I refused to move, used all the power I had to protect Phillip. The queen did, too, and . . . and my mother as well. They stood side by side and we battled him, the three of us, with everything we had. I understood it too late: My father was a tragedy that had happened to them both. They fought like sisters. We fought like a family, but his genius was stronger. And he had the Golden Whip."

I gaze at the king. He squeezes his eyes shut, face taut with memory, tears rolling down his temples.

"I'm so sorry," I breathe. "How you survived is a miracle. Most faeries die after two lashes."

My heart pounds. This is the king's true testament, why Hector and the other nobles call him the Mountain, fear him. He survived the unsurvivable.

"I fainted after the fifth whip," Maxian says, voice breaking. "It was my first time with the lashings, you see. I wasn't used to them yet. And when I came to, they all were dead."

I cover my mouth.

"It took seven lashings to kill the fae queen. And my faerie mother? Eleven," he rasps. "*Eleven.* No one can endure that, but she did. My mother did. A mother defending a child that wasn't even her own."

"And . . . and your brother?"

"All my father had to do was kick him hard enough. Like killing a pup."

He shifts, covering his face with a hand, chest shuddering.

And then the king is crying.

Great, gasping wails like a child, the king is sobbing, and suddenly I am, too. We lie there, side by side like a couple in a crypt, and we weep. We weep for what we have done and who we've become, for the child who never was and the one I am trying to save. Most of all, I weep for this world we were born into, this kingdom of killers, and hope, one day, it will be kinder to those who will come after us.

Then Maxian rolls onto his side, drawing me close, turning me into his chest. Even the weight of his arms feels too heavy to squirm out of, and I am so tired of fighting. So I sink farther into the heat of his embrace, my tears across his chest, his weeping in my hair.

"I will never ever do that to my children," he rasps, a palm cupping the back of my head. "No matter who my fae wife will be, my children will have great, golden geniuses. No one will ever dare hurt them, for they will be powerful like me. But they will be strong like their mother. They will be strong like you."

My breath catches.

Large hands stroke my hair, upturn my face to him once more, cradle my skull in his grasp. A curl of bronze hair falls over his forehead, his thick brows, and my entire world becomes those strange violet eyes, that rough square jaw, the power washing us both away.

"Will you have and hold them, in secret and in silence, for the strength of the royal line and for the good of this kingdom?" he asks.

"Max..."

His thumbs brush under my jaw, pressing into my throat, and I inhale for air that doesn't come. He rests his forehead against mine, our bodies flush against each other. I finger the gold ring on my left hand, but to lace away now would undo what I've accomplished tonight. Would make what I gave him in the bath a meaningless sacrifice. That, I cannot bear. There has to be a reason for violence.

The plane presses down on us like a suffocating blanket and my time is no longer up—it has passed. I have made friends and choices and enemies. I have played the great game and lost. No one is coming to save me. So when his nails dig into my skull, I yield.

"Do you, Avery, accept your new position as mother of my children?" Maxian says.

My lips part. "I do."

Then the king of Amyria seals our vows with a crushing kiss.

Chapter Fifty-five

"Avery?" someone shakes me. Groaning, I roll over, swatting away their hand. They shake again, hissing: "Wake up!"

I blink in the sunlight. For a moment, I think I am outside, until I register the scratchy rug beneath my skin, the heavy male arm slung across my stomach. And the horrified expression of Lila, staring down at me.

"Lila?" I mumble.

"What—what happened?"

I struggle to prop myself up on my elbows, the weight of the king's arm, and his leg, lying over me. I wince at what I find: Maxian and me, half-dressed, tangled in each other in front of the dead fireplace in the king's bedroom. His shirt slides off my shoulder, and I catch a glimpse of my purple chest. My stomach drops, and Lila gasps.

"It's not what it looks like," I say, pushing the king's arm off me. He mutters in his sleep. Last night, we cried for hours, incoherent, raw, painful tears. We cried until we fell asleep. I squirm now, under my friend's scrutiny. "I swear—"

"You are *covered* in bruises!"

"I'm fine—"

"You don't look it."

I glance up at Lila again, fresh-faced and wearing a blue day dress. "What are you doing here?"

"Carter and Fern sent word of what was happening. I could only get to you by agreeing to Hector's terms. The executioner escorted me—"

"What's happening?" Maxian groans, eyes still closed.

Lila reaches down, hauling me to my feet. The room spins, my stomach bottoming out. Other than a few bites of cheese, I haven't eaten anything. My legs give out, little wounds from the glass reopening, and my friend struggles to catch me. Rivulets of blood curl around my ankle bones. Were the cuts this deep last night? It looks so violent now, in the light of day.

"What did he do?" she seethes.

"Nothing," I say. She's getting this all wrong.

"Avery, I—"

"Stop it." I yank his shirt to cover myself, wincing.

"Lila?"

I spin. The king stands in his rumpled nightshirt and pants, hair sticking up on one side, hand rubbing his neck. He looks boyish.

"It's okay," I say. "Everything's okay."

He gives a sheepish smile. "Hi, Lila."

My friend trembles. He is not a handsome stranger I could love in the dark corner of a tavern in another life. He is not the knife on which I can cut myself to feel something. He is the monster who mangled my friend, who tortured her. And I? I am the cunt who let him touch me.

"Lila," I start. "I am so, so sorry—"

"No." She shakes her head.

"Please, I—"

"Don't excuse him."

Him. Not the king, His Magnificence, our lord. Him.

The plane rumbles around us, Maxian's eyes flashing. "We are two consenting—"

"Don't start with that," Lila snaps, and my heart plummets, truly plummets, as I watch my friend who has always faked the brightest smiles in the shadow of a mountain finally give in to her fury. "I don't want to hear that."

He folds muscular arms over his chest. "It's the truth."

"But not the entire truth. You are the *king*."

"And you would do well to remember that."

"This is my fault," I say, stepping between them. "I got—I got—"

"What did he offer?"

"Nothing," I say, quickly. "Nothing, I—"

"Nothing she wasn't willing to give," Maxian says behind me. "A couple of coins, that's all. And it wasn't even for her debt."

He will not reveal what he has asked of me, and why should he? I am to be like his mother, unnamed and unknown, a scrap of faded fabric in an abandoned room. Never seen.

But Lila's gaze slides to me now. I do not find judgment, or disappointment. Just an unbridled rage in a faerie who has kept it in for so long.

"Benji?" Lila asks.

For a moment, I think—terribly—that she doesn't understand. She can't. It is something I can't explain to others. It is no different from what Kassandra and I are to each other. Except, perhaps, in that silver bathroom, when she rejected me.

I will never again take you, Kassandra said. *Not like this. Not when your only option is to give.*

I shake my head. "I wanted this."

"You wanted Benji's freedom!"

"Then why did she beg me for it?" Maxian says. "Why did her pussy shudder around my hand?"

Lila glares at the king with pure hatred. No, no, this is all wrong. Hector brought Lila here to smile at him, adore him, see good in him and reflect that back—not this. Not this seething, simmering faerie. I came to the Pith to offer myself to the king, hoping it was enough to deter his attention from my friends.

"This was my choice," I say.

"Choice?" she yells. "What choices do we truly have in this place?"

I flinch at the compassion Lila flings my way, a compassion I do not deserve.

"Come now, Lila. Don't be a prude." Maxian's presence grows behind me, the plane murmuring around us. "So your friend is a whore. Who cares? Most female faeries are. Avery accepted this about herself long ago. It's time you did as well."

The words die in my mouth. The temperature in the room drops. When I glance at Maxian, his expression is disturbingly tranquil. It is as if in Lila losing her calm, he has finally found his. He looks to her, lips quirking into a smile. She glowers, her skin starting to glow, herbal magic flooding the plane, and suddenly I know that I do not know how powerful she is. She has always held back, held her tongue. But not anymore.

"We should all take a breath," I say, tugging her arm so that she looks at me. "I think—"

"I think Lila is jealous she didn't get to watch." He looks to me. "Or is it that you got off more on betraying your friend in secret? Though maybe *friend* is the wrong word. For Lila to be yours, you'd have to act like one, too, I suppose."

Lila yanks me to her side, wrapping an arm around me. "You wouldn't know a friend if they stabbed you in the back! For that is what you do to yours," she snarls to the king.

The plane heaves, and I wince. "Lila, please, let's—"

"You still defend her, though she slept with your tormenter for some attention and coin?" Maxian steps toward us.

I shrink back, but Lila holds her ground.

"I *know* her. I love her. Not even a king can come between us."

The royal's eyes blaze, nostrils flaring, as if he craves what he cannot comprehend.

"What is it you really want, Lila?" he finally spits. "Why are you here, in my House?"

She squeezes my hand, and I know she means she's here for me. But there is something else, too.

"To see the center of the Pith."

I suck in a breath.

"We are in the center of the Pith," he says.

"The true heart of it."

A slow grin breaks across the king's face. "And why would I show you that?"

"Because I want to learn why you're so magnificent." Only a fool would perceive her tone as defeated and not calm, regrouping.

A vein throbs in his forehead as he scans her face, searching, almost desperately, for any emotion. "You want to see what makes me magnificent?"

Lila does not reply, does not move or look away. She just raises her chin, stares down the monarch and holds me.

"Fine," he says. A curl flops in front of his eyes, and he swipes it away, the plane grumbling. I take a shallow breath as the perspective of the king shifts in front of me again, for the last time, the true character under all that pomp. With caring or cruel eyes, above all, Maxian wants to be *seen*.

"So you'll take me?" Lila asks. "Unless someone else can?"

"We go now," he says. "All three of us."

Chapter Fifty-six

The king leads us to the bathing chambers, where the empty pool is still damp. He strides down the steps until he reaches the drain, then pulls it off. The plane shudders, almost roaring.

He looks up at us. "Are you coming?"

My friend steps forward. I grab her arm. "Wait, should we—"

"It's here. Can't you feel it?" She descends into the pool. My body pulses with energy, with fear, and I do not feel whatever magic she speaks of—only the roaring in my ears. It grows and grows until I realize it is the screams.

Lila and I reach Maxian in the center of the pool. He offers a hand to us both. I stare at his palm, uneasy. Lila reaches forward.

"We're not going down there, are we?" I say, pointing to the drain. "We can't fit."

"Not like this, we can't."

Then the king snags my arm.

And we lace.

We lace down down down, wind ripping up my condensing body, a rush of light, an elongation of limbs, and we smack into something hard, something wet, something that pulls us under. Water closes over my head, and my eyes fly open to a bleary vision, a shadow of land before me. Then Maxian is kicking upward, dragging us with him, and I reach, stretch, ache for air. We break the surface. Gasping, blinking, I cough, my body almost going limp with relief.

"Lila?" I call.

"I'm okay," she gasps from the other side of the king.

We have emerged in a large lake, the clear blue sky above us.

"Almost there," Maxian says, tugging toward the landmass at its center. An island.

We splash in that direction until my feet graze against bedrock. Maxian walks out of the water, up the bumpy bank, and onto the flat land above.

Lila and I drag ourselves onto the shore, tripping over the rocky sand. We collapse into the small bank that slopes upward. Ahead of us, Maxian strides to the very center of the flat island and throws out his arms.

"Welcome to the very heart of Versara," he says. "Welcome to Lucan's Tree."

He truly has gone mad. Pushing myself onto my hands and knees, I survey the barren island that plateaus out of the water.

"Where?" I ask. "Where is the Tree?"

Maxian gestures. "We're standing on it."

Lucan's Tree to the newer generation, the Tree of Life to the Unesse faeries—it doesn't matter. It's the same myth of existence. A Tree to explain to children why they are here, to comfort the old when they are leaving.

"Avery." Lila stands up on the level surface. "Avery, get up here."

With my last bit of strength, I heave myself over the rocky shelf and onto the soft, flat island center, roughly fifty feet in diameter. I brush away some of the sand that coats the surface, revealing rings beneath. Bands and bands and bands that meet in the center, several cracks running throughout. Words and thoughts spiral away as emotions swamp my every sense.

"No," I say. "No, this is not Lucan's Tree."

Maxian stands at its very center. "Did you think we'd build a palace around just any tree?"

Lila sways in horror. "You—you cut it down."

He shrugs. "Well, not me personally, but my grandfather took the branches. My father used the trunk."

"*For what?*"

"To build the throne."

"It's not Lucan's Tree," I repeat. "It can't be. Lucan's Tree is sacred."

"Oh?" He quirks a brow. "I mean, I guess it would be more accurate to call it Lucan's Stump."

Lila shakes. "You—"

But I am already dropping to my knees again, palms pressing into the soft wood. I send my genius out. My moth flutters down my arms, through my hands. It is like hitting a nerve, a network of nerves, all severed, all screaming.

Screaming, screaming.

Alive.

My ears flood with a thousand shrieks, my brain pulsing with a million synapses of pain.

This can't be. This cannot be.

"But . . ." Lila crouches beside me. "The wood isn't rotted. It isn't petrified, either."

Only for the sickly, oily, parasitic magic that latches into its pith and will not let go. Reign magic that keeps it alive, tortured, bent in a frozen state of submission. I try to distinguish a singular voice, a nature that I can speak to, that I can beg for forgiveness and ask: *What can I do? How can I help?*

"It's still alive," I gasp.

"Did you know this?" Lila demands of the king.

Maxian crouches down before us, his thumb scraping across a dark bubble that forms on the surface. He brushes the liquid against his lips, closes his eyes, and breathes. When he opens his eyes, they glow golden.

"It is the only way to get the sap," he says. "It's why we let it live."

"Let it live?" she cries.

But the voices keep screaming, screaming, and no matter how many times my moth signals, *Let me help, let me help,* there is no coherent reply.

"You call this living?" Lila cries. "You have mangled it, tortured it, used it. And still you keep it alive?"

He stands tall again. "Dead things don't serve us."

Pain and fury rip through me, singe my veins, like I am being sawed in half.

"This . . ." my friend gasps. "This is why it's called the Pith, isn't it? You . . . you severed the spine of our people! You destroyed the sacred for the convenient!"

Exhaling, I block out their conversation, to quiet the shrieking and the chaos and the thousands upon thousands of cleaved lives.

What is your story? I ask calmly, gently.

Finally, the voices respond, all at once, a thundering cry.

The same as yours.

My genius sinks into the Tree's, and it is all so much, a grasping and gasping and pushing of roots through rock and brick, spreading out from this mighty hill—no, it is the core of the hill itself. A system so ancient and deep, other plants have grown from the soil that collected in its divots, our tunnels like the trails of worms and—

A face so familiar, I cannot breathe, but this time, it is rounder, younger, brighter. A brunette faerie gripping the roots, groaning in the dark, in the quiet of a tunnel. Blood and water and wailing.

The shrieking of a babe expelled into this world, caught, held against her chest. The infant does not latch, will not, the mother sinking to the ground, blood streaking across brick.

Please, the faerie begs. *Please, or they will hear us.*

The child screams louder and a piece of us breaks off, willingly, an offering. The mother gapes down at the little root in her hand, palm sticky with sap, and gives it to the baby to suck. As the baby does, mouth gummy and happy, her skin glows brighter, irises flickering from brown to gold to brown again.

A feed before the rings. It is miraculous. It is a crime.

It is my mother, Olive. Olive, with her lilting voice and calm, calloused hands, her prayers to plants, and her lost, torn-up heart. Olive, young and hardy and life-giving.

And it is me, in her arms.

It is me, with a strange and strong genius.

It is me, with a magical marker unlike any other.

It is me, with power fueled by roots under the state gardens.

It is me, with a thousand voices saying *Hello again*.

It is me, with the trees trapped in doors.

It is me, with shifting, sap-colored eyes.

It is me, with screams in my ears, begging for aid.

It is me, with the power to help.

My eyes fly open, chest heaving. Maxian and Lila still debate. I reach for my golden moth ring and slip it off. In the very center of the stump, among the cracks and rings and sand, is a little crevasse, the smallest opening. And through it grows a singular green stem.

A sprout of hope.

I reach forward, fingers brushing the little creature.

Let me protect you, I plead. *Let me—*

"Great find, Avery," Maxian says, and then his boot slams down on the stem, crushing both it and my fingers.

The Tree shrieks in protest, a terrible howling—

"No matter how many times we weed it, it just keeps growing back."

He presses down harder, and I grunt, force my lips closed to not give him that satisfaction.

"Wait!" Lila drops to her knees, trying to pry his boot off my hand. "My king—"

"If you two are such good friends, maybe you should match."

He crunches down harder, and my nails begin to splinter. I cry out. Lila rips at his boot, but it's to no avail, his eyes glowing, magic roiling.

"Stop this, please," she says. "I understand."

"Do you? For even Lucan's Tree bends to my will. If you will not submit, I will make you."

"I do!"

His heel crunches the bones in my hand; I scream.

"Please—"

"Please, what?"

"Please, stop," Lila pleads.

"What will you do to make me stop?"

We both glance up at him. He will make her beg for it. He will make her give, as I have given, and she will do it willingly, even if just to make my pain stop. I cannot have that. Lila has the protection of House Illusion and House Healing now. She is a free faerie, all of her debts paid for, and she has friends.

"I vowed to you last night," I say. My friend sucks in a breath. "You have no need of her."

"Who are you to make demands of me?" The boot presses deeper into my fingers, the bones threatening to break. I catch his golden gaze with mine.

"The mother of monarchs."

Lila gasps, looking at me. "What are you saying?"

My free hand covers hers, prying it away from his boot.

"I love you, too," I whisper. "Not even in death will a king come between us."

"Avery?"

I shove the moth ring onto her finger. I think of safe harbor, of silver hair. I stretch my genius as far as it will go. I think of where I would've brought Lila if I had the power to do so in the library. I pray that Kassandra feels her coming.

Lila's mouth drops open. "Wait—"

Then she disappears, lacing into the plane.

The king roars, and I close my eyes, praying she will land safely.

Chapter Fifty-seven

"WHAT HAVE YOU DONE?" MAXIAN SCREAMS. HE GRABS ME BY the shirt collar and yanks me up, my legs flailing. "WHY WOULD YOU—"

"Because you would not!" I yell back.

He slaps me, hard, and I realize this is him being good. Greater violence lurks in that mind and body, and the threat of it is what trapped me like a tree as a door, used against my will. But even when I did not have the strength to call out for help, it didn't matter. My friends found me anyway.

"Why won't you do as you're told?" He shakes me, my head rattling.

Because I have taken down one High Fae, allied with another. Because I have loved their lovers and killed halfling guards. I will fight to the end, until Maxian bloodies his hands on the bones of my back, until I am nothing, and even then, I will not beg for forgiveness. I will not submit. Ever. The last thing the king will see from me is the hatred he could never buy, bargain, or beat from my eyes.

As he yanks me up, screaming in my face, I do not treat him like a king, not even like a halfling.

I fight Maxian like a faerie.

I spit in his eye. He rears back, recoiling. I swing my knee up between his legs. We go down. I scrabble away, kicking him in his nose. It crunches. The plane shakes with his power, tumbling around me like a rockslide. His Reign power will take me soon.

I press my palms into Lucan's Tree, my genius sparking once more as it connects to the veins of power, the root system that spreads under the entire palace of Versara. My mind splinters into a million beings, feeding into the Illusion courtyards, the Healing gardens, each plant and plot that has been meticulously sculpted, pruned back, forced into unnatural shapes and confined sizes, all screaming to be free.

Where should I go? I ask.

Where we are, the voices reply.

The connection snaps, my body picked up and thrown. I tumble across the stump. Maxian stands above me, twitching, sniffing, like that day in the boxing ring, only now nothing familiar remains behind those dilating eyes. *When was the last time he snorted Ashent?*

"Stupid faerie cunt!" he seethes.

"Isn't that what you want?" I snap back, scrambling to my feet. "Isn't that what you need?"

He lunges, tackling me to the ground once more, and we roll, biting, ripping flesh, and smacking jaws.

"Halfling bastard," I yell, raking bruised nails across his pretty face.

"I will—"

I bite his shoulder hard, incisors breaking flesh. Blood floods my mouth. He screams, rips me off him. Tumbling across the stump, grappling for a hold, I find a crevice, sticky with sap. My genius soars along the underground magic, finding a cluster in the outermost building of the palace. Maxian rises.

"You could've made a great king, halfling," I say. "You could've freed us all."

The vein in his forehead throbs. "Why would I—"

I lick the sap off my fingers, energy exploding through me like food, like sugar and nature and *life,* the opposite of Ashent. It is the purity of Lucan's Tree; it is the original state of faeries. It is a homecoming.

Hello again.

It is me, finally earning the title of my mother's daughter.

"What are you doing?" he screams.

"Leaving you," I reply.

My genius locks onto that bundle of nerves near the palace's perimeter.

I let the plane transport me there.

Chapter Fifty-eight

I SLAM INTO WOOD, HEART POUNDING, MOUTH DRY. BLINKING, I take in my surroundings, a grand, cavernous hall with gilded columns and a painting of Lucan's Tree across the ceiling. I have been here before, knelt here during the coronation.

My blood freezes as I realize what I am sitting on.

The throne.

Made from the trunk of Lucan's Tree.

I leap forward, jumping off the seat. A figure melts from the side of a column, and I jump.

"Death!"

"Faerie." The figure approaches, dark cloak trailing behind him. "What happened to you?"

I glance down at the sopping wet shirt, the cuts and bruises that mar my skin. The palace rumbles, deep and violent, as if the very earth it's built upon is splitting. I grip the back of the throne for support, then rip my hand away as if stung.

Because it hums.

The throne hums with power from Lucan's Tree, and I think of the hours Maxian spent lounging on it right before his testament during the coronation, when he made every attendant bow to him.

"The king," Death says. "What has happened?"

What has happened? I laugh, shivering. The palace shakes again. *What has happened?*

Everything. The fae king isn't a fae. The myth of Lucan's Tree is real, and it is severed, used for the chair on which I sat.

"They cut down Lucan's Tree and left it as a tortured stump in the middle of the Pith," I say.

The executioner startles. "Oh?"

"That's all you have to say?"

"I have felt the screams at night."

The building quakes, thunders, as if a mountain is coming down.

"The king is on his way to kill me."

"Will he change his mind like he did with Lila?"

"I'm afraid not."

"Then let's kill you first so that he cannot."

I lock gazes with the executioner, and his eyes flicker from amber to violet to amber beneath his hood. From my father's eyes to Maxian's to my father's once more.

"Your fear is shifting," he says. "Yet you hesitate."

"Any creature would."

"Three months ago, your soul ached to be taken. Now you sit on the throne with power pouring from your eyes. Golden, like the king."

Or perhaps he is golden like me. Like a faerie.

I redirect. "Why didn't you take my soul?"

"I do not believe in early deaths."

"Only late ones?"

"I do not believe in death at all."

The cloaked figure steps onto the dais. Only then do I realize I again grip the throne.

"You jest," I say, moving back.

"No," he says. "At least, not in the sense that the other Houses understand it."

The tapestry of the earthly plane thunders to the floor, slapping against the marble tiles.

"He grows closer," I say. "I do not have time for riddles."

"Then maybe a short, simple truth. Before the Dark Rebellion, the Houses went by different names. My House was known as the House of Cycles."

My brows raise. "What of the other Houses?"

"House of Reign was known for Control, House of Healing for Change, and House of Illusion for Creation. The four elements of magic."

How do we know so little about magic?

Because it's easier for them if we do not know, Kass had said.

"Well, I don't feel like being cycled into nothing tonight, but thanks for the offer," I say.

"You could always take the Desert Walk."

"So, either death by king or death by desert?" My gaze falls to the platform I stand on, pristine, untouched, as if my friend did not die by a halfling's hand a season ago. Only now I realize it was the wrong halfling who is to blame. It is the king.

"The Desert Walk does not necessarily mean you die."

"Whom does the king see when he looks at you?"

The executioner pauses, tilting his head. "I don't know. You would have to ask him."

The palace thunders again.

"What's the plan?" the executioner asks.

I grip the throne tighter, letting the energy pulse up and into my arm. It is strong and solid and lovely. Then I maneuver in front and take a seat. My body trembles, but I sink further into the magic as it emboldens my genius.

"I'm going to wait," I say. "What of you?"

"I will watch, and if I can, I will help."

The grand doors slam open, flying off their hinges. I grip the arms of the throne, one hand sore and bruised. The natural magic thrums behind me, a low, constant current. A silhouette stands at the threshold, light spilling around him. Maxian prowls into the space, dragging behind him something long and thin.

The Golden Whip.

I tense, clutching the throne. Even Death, from his column to the right side of the dais, sucks in a breath.

Maxian stops short, halfway down the aisle. "What the *fuck* are you doing?"

"Sitting," I say. "I'm on my break."

"Get. Up."

It's not just fury pulsing across his face—but fear. He knows I can feel the power beneath me. He fears what that could do to my magic. *Why?* Even as a halfling, he holds more power than most.

Maxian cracks the whip, its tail slamming into a column. A chunk of stone breaks off, smashes against the floor.

"Avery," he grits out, stalking closer.

"Yes?"

He pauses at the base of the altar, adjusting his grip on the handle. If he whips me now, he could destroy the throne, cut off the power boosts he gains in front of the public so that he may perform his tricks and testaments.

No, he will not do that. He is not willing to risk the façade just yet, afraid that the thing beneath it is weak and hollow. If he wants to whip me, he will have to remove me from the throne first.

"Get off," he growls.

"No, thank you, my king."

He takes a step forward.

The throne *shifts*.

Maxian stumbles back, mouth agape.

The throne unfurls.

Roots slither out from under the chair and wind around my ankles, my arms, securing me to the spot. My pulse flutters as panic threatens, but I force myself to keep calm.

Thank you, I tell it.

The only reply is a tightening of the plants around me.

"Call it back," the king snaps.

"I didn't do this."

Reign magic tumbles through my mind, encasing my own genius, trapping it. I shout in protest, and thorns protrude from the roots that surround me. I suck in a breath, but they do not come close to my skin. They point toward the king.

"I don't think they like the whip," I say.

"I don't care what it thinks," Maxian snaps, but his eyes fall on the thorns once more, the Reign magic tumbling away from my mind and body. Even if he forces me to remove myself, the throne will not allow it, not without damage.

The king takes another step forward.

"If you lace me away, I'll just lace back."

"You can't."

"I already did. And besides, if you harm the Tree, won't it stop producing sap?" I ask.

He meets my eyes. "It depends."

"On?"

"How much it can take."

Maxian advances. I press my back into the wood, the plant pulsing beneath me. It seems to cushion me, envelop me a little more. The roots tighten around my limbs, and although my heart pounds, although fear curls in my stomach, I keep breathing.

He discards the whip, kneels before me.

My breath catches. *He can't be conceding already, can he?*

The king's arm draws back, something silver flashing in the light. I realize it too late: the diamond dagger. I squirm.

The executioner steps forward. "Wait—"

Maxian plunges the dagger into the roots around my thigh.

A scream erupts, a thousand wailing voices, the howls filling the throne room. The Tree shrieks, and the executioner drops to his knees, covering his ears. My magic shudders, my throat raw, as the screeches rip from my tongue.

Maxian begins to saw.

The room wavers, the squealing and squawking higher and deeper than any sound I have ever heard. Blood drips from the king's ears.

Still, he hacks at the roots. Pain splinters through my entire leg and it is as if he is slicing me open and yanking out my entrails. He may as well be.

The roots around my thigh retreat.

He starts on the ones around my ankle. I reach for my genius, but it spasms in circles in my mind, the shrieking tearing holes in its wings.

The diamond dagger clatters to the ground, splattered in red and green liquid. He severed the roots from my leg. Now he reaches for my calf. I kick at him, but he grabs hold and yanks.

"Stop!" I say. "Stop that—"

Maxian jerks on my leg again. "Let go!"

"I can't, it's the Tree—"

Maxian wrenches with all his might.

Something pops in my hip. White-hot pain erupts in my socket, shooting down my leg. The world fades, darkness pulling me under. It would be a mercy, it truly would, I think, as the leg goes limp.

If I die, do not let my body go, I tell the Tree.

If the king is determined to rip me apart, to kill me, then I shall go down in the worst place possible. Let him try to explain why there is a faerie corpse on his throne. Let me stay here, decaying, rotting, staining his power. And if he chooses to keep the chair in the end, then he must brush aside my bones to sit on it and be reminded of who the throne chose. Just as how he lay awake at night in his bed, remembering who his lover preferred.

"Stay with us," Death says beside me then. "My king, you dislocated—"

"I don't care," he snaps.

"Sir, this is wrong—"

"Shut your mouth, and do not interfere."

The plane grumbles. The executioner stiffens. Then, in choppy movements, he steps down from the dais, his body under Reign magic.

Maxian grabs the dagger again. I take a breath. I am on my

own—and I will have to take more of this, much more, before my body gives out.

He stabs the roots around my other thigh. My body jerks as the Tree yowls again, the sound piercing and sharp and deep. The king grits his teeth and saws, blood dripping from his ears, from mine.

Something flickers over his shoulder, at the other end of the hall. Something shiny, silver—

The dagger flies from his grasp.

The king staggers back in shock, the Tree's tears abating. My forehead is slick with sweat. I am cold.

The dagger scrapes down the aisle, stopping halfway. At the end of the hall, in a blood-red gown, stands Kassandra. Her expression is frigid, and she lifts her chin, striding toward us.

"What is all this shrieking about?" She takes in the executioner, standing stiff at the bottom of the dais; Maxian, hands wet with blood, crouching before the throne; and then, lastly, me. Her eyes narrow slightly, and this is all that she gives away.

"Out, Kassandra," Maxian snaps.

"I think not."

He stands, the plane rumbling. "I said *out*."

"That too," she shouts over the quaking. "How can I get anything done when you keep breaking everything? I've gone through three quills today."

The king stalks down the steps. I squirm in my seat, but the pain in my leg sparks. Blackness tugs at the corner of my vision, and I try to breathe through it.

Maxian reaches for the dagger. It slides toward Kassandra.

He reaches again—and again, it slides to her feet.

"Stop that," he snarls. "You gifted it to me."

Kassandra flicks out her wrist. The dagger flies up from the floor, hilt landing in her palm.

"It was my hand that made it," she says. "It's my hand it'll always call home."

The king throws out his arm and the Golden Whip zings to him. They stare at each other, the plane crackling with potent tension. Finally, Kassandra sighs. "Not your best idea, Max."

"Don't call me that."

"Aren't we friends?"

"I am the *king*. You will obey me."

"And I am now heir to my House. If you whip me, then Reign will have declared war on Illusion. The council is already foaming at the mouth after what happened to Dominik."

"Dominik got what he deserved," Maxian spits. "And if you do not fall in line, if House Illusion does not fall in line, you will get a blade in your back as well."

Silence.

Kass tilts her head. "Interesting."

The executioner coughs.

"Speak." Maxian waves a hand. The executioner's shoulders drop and it's only then that I understand how much he is controlled by the king.

"My king, an open act of war on Illusion would trigger the Trium Treaty. Healing and Death would then have to declare war on Reign."

A war is fought with bodies, Dominik had said, and there was so much blood from that night.

"The one from House of Death is against war," Maxian scoffs.

"Apparently, they don't like that name," I mutter.

But the king's hearing pricks up. He pivots, gazing between Kassandra and me.

"How about a closed act of war, then?" he says. "Either I whip you, Kass, or I cut her out of that throne. If you do not choose, I will do both."

Silence falls over the coronation room. Kassandra uses the dagger to pick dirt from her nails. " 'Avery' does mean 'queen.' I think the exact translation was 'rulers of the eaves' in the old language. Or is it 'elves'? I can never remember. Eli wasn't the most exciting teacher."

"Kass!" the king snaps.

"Elves?" I start.

"Female fae," Kassandra replies. "At least, in the old Illusion tongue."

"It's more similar to the word 'nightmare' in the Death tongue," the executioner murmurs.

The plane rushes with stony energy. Kassandra and the executioner drop to their knees, foreheads against the ground. The dagger clatters from her grip.

"I've had enough of this," the king says. "I've made the decision."

He picks up the dagger and marches toward me once more.

"Wait," I say. "I—"

"I'm done waiting."

The king drops to his knees. There's muffled groaning behind us. Maxian waves a hand, and Kass and Death both gasp. He moves aside, and their heads lift in unison. Kassandra strains against the control, her face growing red.

She must watch him carve me up. No, I cannot pass the pain I hold for Jeremee on to her. Not after everything she's been through and all we've accomplished together.

Maxian grabs my leg, positioning the dagger over the roots.

"I'll take the Walk," I say.

The dagger hovers.

"Send me on the Desert Walk."

The king leans back on his heels, and a groan comes from Kass. Curiosity sparks in his expression, once again glancing between us. He tilts his head, and my mistress collapses out of his magical grasp.

"No," she rasps.

"Yes," I say. "Send me to the desert. It will get me out of this throne without sacrificing the power of the Tree, and I'll most likely die. Even if I survive the Walk, then banishment from Amyria will be my punishment, and you will never have to see me again. I will serve out my sentence at the House of Death, protecting the kingdom."

His eyes land on my hip. "Your leg is out of your socket. You cannot walk."

"Even more of a reason to do it, for I will most likely be dead in a day."

"No." Kassandra stands, emotion flickering in her eyes. "I will not allow this."

"Why not?" Maxian asks. "What use do you have for a servant who can't even listen?"

Kassandra opens her mouth, closes it, clears her throat.

"She's mine," she says.

"This kingdom is mine," he snaps. "And you are just a temporary heir."

She shakes her head. "Eli has declared that Dominik will never walk again. Even if he recovers, House Illusion has written that he will never hold a council position except for advisor, for he cannot have children. I am the Illusion heir. I will be the head of House."

Pride—this time, not for myself—floods through me.

The king watches her. "You wish for Avery to stay?"

"I do."

Maxian faces the executioner. "Send her on the Walk."

My body slumps, exhausted.

"Keep her hip out of its socket," the king instructs.

"A moment alone?" Kass asks.

"One moment, and then I'm ripping you away."

My lady nods, and Maxian even gives us the courtesy of stepping off, although he can still hear. Kassandra rushes to my side.

"You *fool*. What were you thinking?"

"I wasn't," I say.

"How did you even get into this?"

I glance down at her hands, which clasp me. On her finger glints my golden moth ring. I lean my head back.

"So they're safe."

Kass looks over her shoulder at Maxian. The air between us shimmers—an Illusion. "He will think we are arguing."

"Are we not?"

"Lila is safe and free. So are Benji and Briar. They are under Illusion's and Healing's protection."

I meet her eye. "Benji?"

"His debts are fully paid off," she says. "His balance hit zero last night."

I laugh, tears rolling down my cheeks. Oh, how I would have loved to see his last tattoo disappear. How I would've held him as we cried and giggled because the sensation *tickles*. I cup the sound of his laugh in my mind and memorize it. Yesterday was the last time I will ever hear it. It hurts to never see him without debt, but that is legacy. Jeremee gave Benji another chance at life, and my inheritance to him: hope. It is all and everything I can give.

Kassandra reads my expression, and her face knits with concern.

"Yes," she says. "Everyone is safe. Everyone but you."

We glance down at my arms, wrapped in vines and my remaining four tattoos. My Reign debt.

"You have to keep going," I say.

"How?" Her voice cracks. "You suggested the Desert Walk!"

"To buy you all more time to find proof."

"What is time without you?" She looks to me, her pretty blue eyes filling with tears.

"What is liberation, if not for all?"

"I am heir now. I could've protected you."

"So protect the others, for we are not done fighting. *I* am not done fighting for my life and my loved ones and my people."

My mistress looks away.

"Kass," I say again. "You are stronger than him. Whether it's because he's a halfling doesn't matter. What matters is that *you* can bend the hardest gem on this earth to your will—and no one else."

We stare at each other, at the roots holding me in place. Kassandra tilts her head.

"He's noticed the Illusion." She holds out her hand, the dagger flying into her palm. She lays the dagger along my wrist, tucking the handle into my grasp.

"What are you doing?" I ask. "You're not allowed to give me anything for the Walk."

"Come back to me," she says.

"Kassandra, I—"

"Like I said, you're hard to replace."

I stare into her face, pinched in pain, and I understand, with a striking clarity, that it is over me. She weeps for me, my mistress. She has maimed and killed—we have maimed and killed together, all to be free, and I am not done sacrificing and neither is she. But feeling her fingers grip mine, eyes pleading for me, for another way, I wonder if, in another life, we could have been something different, something more. Something like the soft shape of companionship.

"I await your return." She clutches my hands. "I will always wait for you, Avery. I promise."

It is a promise I know she will keep. But can I keep mine?

I swallow. "You . . . you are—"

Kassandra jerks backward, Reign magic depositing her onto the steps.

The king maneuvers around her form, gesturing for the executioner. The pair steps forward, blocking Kass from view. The executioner reaches out a gloved hand, the hand of Death that took my friend. My heart picks up. I am afraid. The cool leather of the glove rests on my forehead, and I feel what Jeremee felt.

"Good luck," the executioner says. I pay him no mind. Instead, I raise my chin and stare, unblinking, at the king.

Rotten thing, others have called me.

They were right.

I think of my friends, my family, the king who could change it all, who has known the pain of death and lashings of the Golden Whip, who knows the depravity the Houses dole out, the debt that strangles, the babies maimed, the lives that are lost, taken, ruined. All to feed their insatiable desire to hoard so that others cannot have. A king who refuses change for the sake of convenience, who heads this monstrous system, this kingdom of killers. I think of it all, and then I let my emotions fill in my eyes, let my hatred putrefy the plane around us. And it *reeks*.

The king's face falters before smoothing out once more.

"Your death does not change my plans," Maxian says. "I will just find another one."

A female attendant to incubate his children, for the fae have become weak with incest.

"You truly are your father's son," I reply. "Death hunted him down in the end, and now it's hunting you."

Then I become nothing.

PART FOUR

House of Death

With fear for their freedom, House of Cycles votes nay.

—HEARING ON [REDACTED]
BEFORE THE COUNCIL OF KEEPERS,
EVE OF THE DARK REBELLION

I FALL.

Wind rushes my clothes, my hair, tearing air from my lungs. It is short-lived.

My body slams into something soft. My hip cracks, pops, and then I am rolling. I scrabble for purchase, slicing my hands along sharp edges and soft spots. I am tumbling down a hill, but not sand. I slam into a long, thin object, and it catches me. The sky above me spins and spins until finally it stops.

The desert smells.

I did not expect it to smell like this.

Like trash.

Shaking my head, untwisting my body from the object behind me, I grasp a familiar feeling, the surface of a wooden table, turned on its side. I raise myself up and scan my surroundings.

Trash.

I am halfway down a mountain of garbage—from furniture to food to clothing. What is all this stuff? Where did it come from? Gingerly, carefully, I assess my injuries, the cuts and bruises, but my leg hurts less. I still wear only the king's tunic and a pair of drawers.

Grasping a table leg, I haul myself up. Something glints in the sand at my feet, blinding me.

I dig it up.

The diamond dagger.

My grip tightens around my only connection to my home. I will not let go.

The trash pile leads down far below, several items tumbling over a cliff. Beyond the cliff is mile after mile of tan sand. The Amyria Desert that I must cross. There is no other choice. I pick my way down.

After an hour, I reach the bottom, sweat and dirt and oil streaking across already burning skin. I could lie down right here, bake in the sun, shiver in the night until my body and brain have wasted away. Yet glancing down at the king's clothing I still wear, my cut and bleeding bare feet, my remaining debt, I think not.

I should like to don clothes meant just for me, not die in the tattered shirt of my torturer. I should like to watch my final four ringed tattoos disappear, and see once again those freckles and that birthmark. Hope feels hard to reach, so I clutch the dagger and summon my spite.

Picking through the trash, I salvage one boot too small, a sandal too big. I put them on. After some more digging, I manage a rucksack, a loaf of bread with only a little bit of mold on one end, so I tear that off. I search and search, but there's no water.

With the mud and oil and rotting food, climbing the mountain to the top to see what's on the other side proves impossible. Even if I could, I would still have my debt and wouldn't be welcomed in the borderlands. I need to go east, across the desert.

I yank on the bent handle of a parasol, its gray lace ripped in some places. It looks like Kassandra's.

"You're kidding me."

A half-ripped length of cloth also goes into the bag.

Still, no water. But there's a canteen, warmed by the sun, that swishes. From the vinegar scent after I untwist the top, I guess it to be fae wine. Reluctantly, I take it.

Returning to the cliff's edge, I watch the sunset in the far distance, the sand lighting up red, then orange and even purple, like the deepest flame. I move closer to the horizon.

The sands shift. I squint; must be a trick of the light.

The sands shift more, and then an animal, the largest I have ever seen, as large as Lucan's Tree, breaches out of the sand, as if it were water. I yelp, stumbling back.

It breaches again, a low tittering noise.

The cliff gives out.

I scrabble back, but the cliff dissolves, spilling down, taking me with it. Suddenly there is no bedrock beneath me; I am below the remaining cliff, the sand sucking up my legs. I scrabble and wave my arms but only sink deeper.

I am drowning in sand.

I scratch and claw, the desert swallowing up my waist, then my chest. Rumbling, and I wonder if I can feel Maxian's power from out here. A hard shelf rises from the sand, grains streaming off its edge, and I grab hold. The edge keeps rising, pulling my body out of the earth.

My feet land on something soft and I look down.

Scales.

I am standing on a carpet of scales. My heart almost gives out, but I clutch the surface above me. It is like a round, hard stump of some kind. A shell.

My gaze takes in the giant beast, my feet on one of its front legs, its shell offering shade and protection. I force myself not to panic, do not panic—for what do we do with a stinging insect? We swat it away. We kill it. And this might eat me. Don't they eat faeries?

A giant sand turtle.

The creature swings its neck, its enormous reptilian eye meeting mine. My heart picks up, but I don't dare move. The slitted pupil expands, encompassing the dark silhouette of a faerie.

Death said they only bother you if you bother them. Standing on the creature would count as bothering it, right?

I am mad, truly mad, for the only thing I can think to do is reach for my genius.

It is alive and full and flourishing, and it pushes my message along the plane.

Hello, I think. *How are you?*

The creature bellows, the scales vibrating beneath my soles. I cling on for life.

My foot grazes something rough, sharp.

So deeply embedded I thought it part of the animal's skin is a thick piece of twine tangled around its leg. I bend down, and the twine bites into my hands. Still, I work my fingers under the rope and lift it just enough to stick the knife under.

The creature bellows again, vibrating. But I cut, gently, slowly, until something snaps free. The twine springs away, leaving a deep indent behind.

The creature titters, then starts spinning around.

"Whoa, wait—"

I reach for the shell, hauling myself over its edge. Broad and domed, the turtle's shell is ringed in black. But it is not thick, heavy, disruptive like my tattoos. It has the ripples of age, and walking to its center, I gawk at the pattern—like a dozen tree stumps bound together.

It's beautiful. So beautiful to see traces of years conquered, a life being lived.

The creature slides toward the fading sun, the great expanse of desert I am supposed to walk.

"Oh!" As it begins its journey, I wonder if it will keep its shell above sand. I hope it does. Bracing on bare feet, I ask: "Is this all right?"

It doesn't reply.

Slowly, finally, I sit on the center of the shell, leaning against my rucksack. The sun slips away, and as the air cools, I take out that torn cloth. With little choice, I sip the wine, preserving it as much as possible. I nibble on the bread, but my throat is already scratchy.

When the sun comes up, I use the measly umbrella to avoid burning. It does little. Still, the turtle swims, and I wait, and the wind blows and the sun drops again. The turtle swims for days, I think, while I eat stale bread and drink fae wine. When the canteen is done, I collect and choke down my urine. I lose count of the moons and sun, and even figures seem to flit across my vision in the searing heat and deadly cold. Although it is not a Walk, I feel like I am dying.

I JOLT AWAKE, shivering, lips cracked, skin raw, eyes burning. The turtle grumbles. Before me is another soaring cliff.

"I can't climb that," I rasp, but the turtle is sinking, lowering, so I roll off the edge of its shell, down its leg, and tumble onto the dry clay of the cliff. Turning, I watch the turtle start to sink.

"Wait!" I call. The turtle titters one last time, then disappears into the dunes once again. I turn, surveying the cliff. Impossible.

Reaching forward, I touch the façade. It hums with energy. This is not just a cliff, this feels like life. Swiping my hand across the surface, I find a vine. I tug and it stays.

Just highly improbable, then. My head pounds and my vision swims and my bones ache and my organs pulse with pain. But there is nowhere else to go. Nowhere but up. If I can make it. So, after adjusting my rucksack, I hold the vines as ropes.

Painfully, slowly, carefully, I rise.

It is hard, so very hard. It feels pointless, but to look back is to fall. I am already here, on this cliff. I may as well keep going. And going. And going.

When I cannot climb anymore, I push out my genius to the plants, one last time. They cradle me, dragging me up and over the lip of the cliff. The sun is starting to set, the air cooling off. I collapse, gasping. The empty canteen skitters away from me.

Panting, chest heaving, I try to gather my strength.

It doesn't come. I have nothing left. Nothing left to give myself or anyone else. The Desert Walk will claim me, as it has done so many others. At least I can hold the knowledge that my family is free as my eyes droop closed. Death or debt, those have always been our choices, and today my body chooses for me.

I drift away.

"Congratulations on your Walk," a voice says. "You wandered well."

Death came so swiftly; I almost missed it.

"Thanks," I rasp, a shadow falling over me, blocking out the fading sun.

A figure before me, one I cannot discern. They crouch by my side, picking up a limp, burned arm, my tattoos barely noticeable under the dirt and filth.

"What are you . . ."

My sentence disintegrates as they pull out a black feather. A creditor's quill. I huff a laugh, for even in Death my mind will not let me escape this system. It has twisted my passing into some exchange with a teller.

The nib does not nick the skin, barely even touches it.

My mouth is so dry, my head so fuzzy, my body pulsing with pain. This will be a relief, a rest, even if it means my tattoos will go to my closest relative, no matter who that is. At least that relative and Benji and my friends can now benefit from that account. Then the strangest sensation happens along my arm. Not pain, no. Instead, I feel what a child once explained as *tickling*.

The two tattoos on my right arm tickle, then my left, as they thin and thin and thin.

They swallow themselves up and are no more.

I gaze at the familiar and unfamiliar body of scars and cuts and freckles and wasted muscles and bloodied feet and no debt. With time and care, the cuts could have sealed, the burns faded, the muscles grown anew, but that doesn't matter. It is perfect, all of it so painfully perfect, for it is mine.

And now it always will be.

"It's gone," I croak.

"Yes, Wanderer."

Dry lips crack into a smile. The celestial plane is so peaceful, and I am ready see my mother and Jeremee again. I can finally, *finally* rest.

Until hands slide under my back and knees, and someone hauls me up. The figure, pressing me to a flat chest, carries me away. We are moving, crunching over hard-packed dirt, and the distant sound of life wafts toward us.

"What's happening?" I gasp, squirming, but the figure holds me tighter. The voice rumbles in the chest, against my cheek.

"You made it, Wanderer. You're alive."

"Made it where?" I rasp.

"Why, the House of Death, of course."

I'm alive, I marvel, and it is not a question this time, but a statement.

And on the breeze that slips over my unmarked skin is the strangest sound and scent. A hushing of water, the caw of some unknown bird, the smell of salt.

"What is that?" I manage, words slurring again.

"You call it the Amyrian Desert, but here it goes by another name. The Great Beach."

"Beach? I don't know this."

Their chuckle rumbles my cheek. "Those of the valley know little, but it is no matter, for you will have plenty of time to learn."

Darkness tugs at me like a child on my arm. Exhausted, I turn to it as the figure speaks one last time: "Welcome to banishment, Avery."

I meet their green eyes and wonder if this is home.

Then inky freedom embraces me, and I embrace it.

Glossary of Terms, Places, and Phrases

Amyrian kingdom: The valley country founded by Wilhelm Cornelius Vandorne ("Wilhelm the Uniter") two thousand years ago, named after Wilhelm's beloved mother, Amyria, who envisioned a centralized valley and died before the task was complete.

Ashent: A black powdered substance that, when inhaled, bolsters the strength and abilities of an individual's genius.

blood bargain: A magical pact sworn between two individuals that is blood backed. If one or both parties break their promises, they will lose connection with their own geniuses and, therefore, magic.

blood oath: A magical, blood-backed vow an individual swears to an institution, often enforced with the aid of an enchanted object.

celestial plane: In the Three Planes religion, the transcendental realm from which the High Fae originated, and to which all souls return upon the death of the body.

Cont: The Reign city located at the base of the northern mountains, governed by the Tunes family. Known for its glacial lakes and dense surrounding forests.

creditor: One who is owed; a High Fae.

Dark Rebellion: The failed uprising by House of Death against the House of Reign, which resulted in the destruction of the original palace of Versara and the banishment of House Death from the royal court seven hundred years ago.

debtor: One who is owned; a faerie.

Desert Walk ("The Walk"): The process of bankruptcy that involves an individual crossing the Amyrian Desert to the House of Death and, if successful, being absolved of debt. Few succeed. The Walk can be voluntary or involuntary.

earthly plane: In the Three Planes religion, the physical world that contains nature and its creatures.

faerie: A creature of distant High Fae and human ancestry, possessing only root magic and subject to Moldhood. This class of creatures has been documented as stunted in lifespan, power, physique, emotions, and intelligence. NOTE: Faeries require governance.

five rings: The five rings tattooed on an infant upon being delivered by a Healer, one ring to each House for services provided to the living, and an additional ring to House of Healing for birth services.

four rings: The four rings tattooed on an infant upon being brought to the creditor right after an unassisted birth; rare.

Fraulus: The isolated Illusion stronghold in the southern mountains. Known for its dry, crisp white wines.

genius: The organ that allows individuals to connect with the plane of magic to perform supernatural tasks. Strength and ability of the genius are determined by class of creature (e.g., High Fae have the most powerful geniuses).

halfling: A creature with one High Fae parent and one faerie parent, and moderate magical abilities. NOTE: Halflings are only permitted to live when the paternal line is High Fae. POST-NOTE: Under certain conditions, halflings are allowed semi-autonomy.

High Fae: A creature of superior abilities, senses, physique, health, and intelligence. Descended from winged creatures in the celestial plane, High Fae now guide and govern halflings and faeries; bringers of magic in the Three Planes faith. NOTE: Male High Fae are naturally inclined toward leadership.

House of Death: The militant House that patrols the borderlands and protects the denizens of Amyria from giant sand turtles, scorpions, and other external threats. Its members excel in matters of the soul and include failed usurpers, desert repenters, and life-takers. Headed by UNKNOWN.

House of Healing: The academic House that oversees the medical industry in Amyria. Its members excel in manipulating blood and bones, and include record collectors, experimenters, and intellectuals. Headed by the Seccler family.

House of Illusion: The entertainment House that oversees public celebrations, arts, and palace ceremonies; it is famed for its silver stallions. Its members excel in manipulating the senses, and include distractors and tricksters. Headed by the Morella family.

House of Reign: The ruling House that owns the majority of land in the Amyrian kingdom; oversees all governance. Its members excel in controlling all areas of matter and mind, and include carvers and creators of the material world. Headed by the Vandorne family, the royal line.

human: A member of an extinct race of magicless creatures.

to lace/lacing: To break down one's (or another's) very matter into the smallest form so that the essence of said individual can transmit to another location using the plane of magic. NOTE: This advanced magical ability can only be performed by select Reign fae. POST-NOTE: A controversial paper recently published anonymously in the Healing archives titled "Whose Legacy Is Lacing?" argues that other individuals with strong abilities can transmute themselves along the plane of magic using other methods.

Lucan's Tree: (formal; High Fae term) The mythical tree of magic that grew from the celestial seeds planted in the earthly plane by Lucan the Wanderer; the source of all magical energy that individuals can leverage to perform tasks.

"May they wander well": Idiom used when one wants to wish a deceased individual an uninhibited afterlife in the celestial plane, including the ability to travel outside the geological barriers of the valley kingdom and the Amyrian Desert; references Lucan the Wanderer. NOTE: Some scholars argue the phrase has been co-opted by faeries to mean wishing a deceased faerie financial freedom in death, but this theory is not universally accepted among the House of Healing archives.

Molder: A faerie whose genius is rejected by nature and therefore atrophies with disuse, rendering the faerie magically mute.

GLOSSARY OF TERMS, PLACES, AND PHRASES

the Mouth: (informal; faerie slang) The private kitchen of the king, where all his meals are prepared.

the Nest: (informal; faerie slang) The common gathering space for faeries during time off to gather and eat.

the Peri: The faerie villages that surround and supply the palace of Versara, located at the base of the palace hill.

the Pith: (origin unknown) Term synonymous with the center of Versara; the residence of House of Reign.

plane of magic: The ever-present energy field in the air of the earthly plane that individuals leverage to perform transcendental acts; recognized under the Three Planes religion. It sprang into existence when Lucan the Wanderer descended from the celestial plane and planted celestial seeds that grew into Lucan's Tree, the origin of magic.

Remiti: The Healing capital in the western part of Amyria, governed by the Healing advisor, Thea Seccler. Known for medical advances, production, and sunny weather.

root magic: A magic that involves performing elemental tasks (moving dirt, water, air; sometimes conjuring flame); accessible to all but Molders; basic; sometimes known as faerie tricks, dirt magic, primitive.

teller: A halfling who collects debt from faeries on behalf of High Fae families and Houses.

Three Planes: The common religion accepted by the High Fae and faeries alike. It teaches that three planes (celestial, magical, and earthly) exist and that the magical plane sprang into existence after Lucan the Wanderer sacrificed his wings to plant celestial seeds into the earthly plane to save the beasts and humans. SEE Lucan's Tree.

Unesse: The ancient faerie faith whose members believe that there is only one plane of existence and that all things—living and dead—are connected as if in a network of nerves or roots. NOTE: This faith was banned from practice one hundred years post-rebellion (100 PR).

Unluckie: (informal; faerie slang) A faerie with four limbs of debt tattoos; sometimes without work or housing. Considered by the High Fae to be social leeches (SEE Unskilled). NOTE: Banned from receiving handouts of any kind by Amyrian law.

Unskilled: (formal; High Fae term) A faerie with four limbs of debt tattoos; lazy individuals of immoral disrepute; beggars. NOTE: Recent archival records indicate the usage of the term "Unluckie" by faeries for this class of creature. POST-NOTE: Official Amyrian legislation does not recognize nor support this term.

Versara palace: The center of the capital of Amyria where the heads, heirs, hearts, and, typically, advisors of the four Houses reside. Rebuilt once, it is the pinnacle of high society and includes kennels, stables, farms, state rooms, and the headquarters of Houses Reign, Healing, and Illusion. Admittance is by invitation only.

Acknowledgments

IT IS ABSOLUTELY THRILLING TO SEE MY NAME ON THE COVER OF a book as a debut novelist. However, *The Debtor's Game* did not come to fruition by my hand alone. The magic of this story and its distribution lies in hundreds of decisions made by many individuals.

First, to Haley Heidemann. My agent, my advocate; it all began with you. Thank you for believing in me, and for compelling others to believe in me, too. From the very first call, I was blown away by your intelligence, creativity, and insight. Thank you for answering all of my questions at every stage, and for transforming what could've been a stressful process into an exciting adventure. You said that *The Debtor's Game* is just the beginning, and with you by my side, it all feels possible. I cannot wait for our projects to come.

To Natalie Hallak, my brilliant editor. Thank you for making this book more itself—I didn't realize that could even happen. You encouraged my boldness, my whimsy, my heart, and this is reflected in the final work. Our three-hour mind melds would truly awe historians and scare scientists. I cannot wait to take these characters to new places, and this story to new heights, with you.

To Ivanka and Morgan, thank you for your supportive efforts and communications. And to the rest of the team at Ballantine

Books and Penguin Random House, a massive thank-you. Thank you to Saida Azizova, Francesca Ali, and the rest of the UK team for all your hard work across the pond.

To Kelly, my Kelly. There are not enough words in the universe, or skill to wield them, to properly capture what you mean to me. My best friend, my sister, my soulmate. When Avery came to me, jaded and sad, as I had once come to you, I knew what she needed. Lila, Briar, Fern, Olive: These faeries are just flickers of the woman you are. Thank you for loving me. Your care and kindness and compassion gave me back my life, gifted me a future. Your wit, humor, and curiosity are unmatched. Thank you, as always, for being my friend.

To Emily and Jacob. Emily, your unending enthusiasm and love have transformed my adult life. Thank you for reading many iterations of this story, for listening to my babbling, and for always celebrating the wins with me. Jacob, beyond thank you for biking over to my apartment and saving what was essentially the most important draft. Thank you for treating it seriously and carefully, even if finding the file was easy for you.

To Maddie, my moon! Without you, I would've never gone freelance, never taken the leap to craft this story. Thank you for bearing witness to draft zero (oh my planes, it was rough) and *every* draft since. Our creative sessions got this book written, as did your passion for my characters (they can never make me hate you, Rose Tunes).

To Yap Club: Sydney, Makiah, Lexi, and Symone. Thank you for bursting your way into my life and helping to pack up another's. We may not be the most studious book club, but we are certainly the loudest. Hopefully y'all get around to reading this one!

To Alex, for being one of my very first readers, and to Laney, for always understanding me even when my words fail. Thank you both so much.

To my hometown friends, can you believe it happened? Thank you for sticking with me through the many years of my underdeveloped prefrontal cortex and the havoc it wreaked.

To my parents, for creating and nurturing the reader in me, which allowed the writer in me to bloom. Thank you for allowing my creativity, even when it meant dealing with my dramatics. Especially to my mom, who read and loved my first story, "The Stone Horse," and who has never stopped bragging about it to this day. To my siblings, for always checking my ego. With this published book, you have your work cut out for you.

To you, reader, thank you!! Thank you for picking up this novel and for getting this far. I know I am unknown to you, but I hope you trust me with the next one. It's full of rot and ruin and friends being friends and lovers and enemies.

If you're interested in reading more on the topics and themes I've pulled for inspiration for this book, you can check out *Debt: The First 5,000 Years* by David Graeber, *Versailles: A Biography of a Palace* by Tony Spawforth, *An Immense World: How Animal Senses Reveal the Hidden Realms Around Us* by Ed Yong, *Braiding Sweetgrass: Indigenous Wisdom, Scientific Knowledge, and the Teachings of Plants* by Robin Wall Kimmerer, and *The Hidden Life of Trees: What They Feel, How They Communicate—Discoveries from a Secret World* by Peter Wohlleben.

Bringing a book from manuscript to what you are reading is a team effort.

Renegade Books would like to thank everyone who helped to publish *The Debtor's Game* in the UK.

Editorial
Saida Azizova

Contracts
Stephanie Evans
Sasha Duszynska Lewis
Isabel Camara

Sales
Megan Schaffer
Kyla Dean
Dominic Smith
Sinead White
Georgina Cutler-Ross
Ellie Walker
Jess Harvey
Natasha Weninger-Kong

Rights
Emma Thawley
Catherine de Mello
Alexis Alderton

Design
Fran Hambling

Tash Webber
Andrew Smith
Sara Mahon
Luke Applin

Production
Kelly Llewellyn

Publicity
Corinna Zifko
Isobel Williams

Marketing
Alex Haywood

Operations
Jairiza Rivera

Inventory
Victoria Stephenson
Dan Jones

Finance
Chris Vale
Jonathan Gant

About the Author

ISABELLE MONGEAU is a freelance writer and editor in Atlanta, Georgia. Her work has been nominated for the Pushcart Prize and published in *Bayou Magazine, Litbreak Magazine, The Merrimack Review, Cleaver,* and *Alloy,* and by Living Springs Publishers. She earned her MSt in creative writing from the University of Cambridge, and a BA in English/creative writing and film studies from Emory University.

TikTok: @izzysink1
Threads: @isabellemwriter
Bluesky: @isabellemwriter.bsky.social
Instagram: @isabellemwriter

RAISING READERS
Books Build Bright Futures

Dear Reader,

We'd love your attention for one more page to tell you about the crisis in children's reading, and what we can all do.

Studies have shown that reading for fun is the **single biggest predictor of a child's future life chances** – more than family circumstance, parents' educational background or income. It improves academic results, mental health, wealth, communication skills, ambition and happiness.[1]

The number of children reading for fun is in rapid decline. Young people have a lot of competition for their time. In 2024, 1 in 10 children and young people in the UK aged 5 to 18 did not own a single book at home.[2]

Hachette works extensively with schools, libraries and literacy charities, but here are some ways we can all raise more readers:

- Reading to children for just 10 minutes a day makes a difference
- Don't give up if children aren't regular readers – there will be books for them!
- Visit bookshops and libraries to get recommendations
- Encourage them to listen to audiobooks
- Support school libraries
- Give books as gifts

There's a lot more information about how to encourage children to read on our website: **www.RaisingReaders.co.uk**

Thank you for reading.

---

[1] OECD, '21st-Century Readers: Developing Literacy Skills in a Digital World', 2021, https://www.oecd.org/en/publications/21st-century-readers_a83d84cb-en.html

[2] National Literacy Trust, 'Book Ownership in 2024', November 2024, https://literacytrust.org.uk/research-services/research-reports/book-ownership-in-2024